RANDOM
HOUSE

LARGE
PRINT

THE FINAL TWIST

Also by Jeffery Deaver
Available from Random House Large Print

The Goodbye Man
The Never Game

THE FINAL TWIST

JEFFERY DEAVER

RANDOM HOUSE
LARGE PRINT

Copyright © 2021 by Gunner Publications, LLC

Published in the United States of America by Random House Large Print in association with G. P. Putnam's Sons, an imprint of Penguin Random House LLC.

Cover design: Tal Goretsky
Cover image: Jonathan Arias / iStock / Getty Images Plus

The Library of Congress has established a Cataloging-in-Publication record for this title.

ISBN: 978-0-593-41038-7

www.penguinrandomhouse.com/large-print-format-books

FIRST LARGE PRINT EDITION

Printed in the United States of America

10 9 8 7 6 5 4 3 2 1

This Large Print edition published in accord with the standards of the N.A.V.H.

To the Sunday Afternoon Crew:
Joan, Cleve, Kay, Ralph, Gail

For the powerful, crimes are those
that others commit.

—Noam Chomsky

THE STEELWORKS

Colter Shaw draws his gun. He starts silently down the stairs, descending into the old building's massive, pungent basement, redolent of mold and heating oil.

Basement, he reflects. Recalling the last time he was in one. And what happened to him there.

Above him, music pounds, feet dance. The bass is a runner's heartbeat. But up there and down here are separate universes.

At the foot of the stairs he studies where he is. Orientation . . . Always, orientation. The basement is half built out. To the right of the stairs is a large empty space. To the left are rooms off a long corridor—fifty feet or so in length.

Scanning the empty space to the right, he sees no threat nor anything that would help him. He turns left and navigates toward the corridor past the boilers and stores of supplies: large packs of toilet paper, cans of Hormel chili, plastic water bottles, paper towels, Dixie paper plates, plastic utensils. A brick of nine-millimeter ammunition.

Shaw moves slowly into the corridor. The first room on the right, the door open, is illuminated by cold overhead light and warmer flickering light. Remaining in shadows, he peers in quickly. An office. File cabinets, computers, a printer.

Two bulky men sit at a table, watching a baseball game on a monitor. One leans back and takes the last beer from the six-pack sitting on a third chair. Shaw knows they're armed because he knows their profession, and such men are always armed.

Shaw is not invisible but the basement is dark, no overheads, and he's in a black jacket, jeans and—since he's been motorcycling—boots. They're not as quiet as the Eccos he usually wears but the beat bleeding from the dance floor overhead dampens his footsteps. He supposes it would even drown out gunshots.

The men watch the game and talk and joke. There are five empty bottles. This might be helpful: the alcohol consumed. The reaction-time issue. The accuracy issue.

If it comes to that.

He thinks: Disarm them now?

No. It could go bad. Seventy-five percent chance of success, at best.

He hears his father's voice: Never be blunt when subtle will do.

Besides, he isn't sure what he'll find here. If nothing, he'll slip out the way he came, with them none the wiser.

He eases past the doorway, unseen, then pauses to give his eyes, momentarily dulled by the office lights, a chance to acclimate to the darkness.

Then he moves on, checking each room. Most of the doors are open; most of the rooms are dark.

The music, the pounding of the dancing feet are a two-edged sword. No one can hear him approach, but he's just as deaf. Someone could be in an empty room, having spotted him, waiting with a weapon.

Thirty feet, forty.

Empty room, empty room. He's approaching the end, where a second hallway jogs right. There'll be other rooms to search. How many more?

The last room. This door is closed. Locked.

He withdraws his locking-blade knife and uses the edge near the tip to ease the deadbolt back into the tumbler. He pulls on the door to keep the bolt from snapping back into place as he gets a new grip with the blade. After repeating a dozen times, the door is free. Knife away, gun drawn and raised, finger off the trigger.

Inside.

The woman is Black, in her early twenties, hair in a complicated braid. She wears jeans and a dusty gray sweatshirt. She sees the gun and inhales to scream. He holds up a hand and instantly holsters the weapon. "It's okay. You're going to be okay. I'm getting you out of here. What's your name?"

She doesn't speak for a moment. Then: "Nita."

"I'm Colter. You'll be all right."

The place is filthy. Uneaten chili sits in a flat pool on a paper plate. A bottle of water is half drunk. There's a bucket for a toilet. She's not bound but she is restrained: a bicycle cable is looped around a water or sewage pipe and her ankle is zip-tied to the cable. Shaw shuts the light off. There's enough illumination to see by.

Shaw looks back into the corridor. The flicker from the screen continues as the ball game continues. What inning is it? Would be important to know.

"Are you hurt?"

She shakes her head.

He takes his knife out and opens it with a click. He saws through the plastic tie and helps her to her feet. She's unsteady.

"Can you walk?"

A nod. She's shivering and crying. "I want to go home."

Shaw recalls thinking of the game Rock,

Paper, Scissors just ten minutes ago. He wishes he'd played harder, much harder.

They step into the corridor. And just then, Shaw thinks:

The third chair.

Oh, hell.

The six-pack didn't need its own seat. Someone else was in the office watching the game.

And at that moment the third man comes down the stairs with another pack of Budweiser. Just as he sets foot on the concrete floor he glances up the corridor and sees Shaw and Nita. The six-pack drops to the ground. At least one bottle shatters. He calls, "Hey!" And reaches for his hip.

In the baseball room, the flickering stops.

PART ONE

JUNE 24

THE MISSION

Time until the family dies: fifty-two hours.

1

The safe house.

At last.

Colter Shaw's journey to this cornflower-blue Victorian on scruffy Alvarez Street in the Mission District of San Francisco had taken him weeks. From Silicon Valley to the Sierra Nevadas in eastern California to Washington State. Or, as he sat on his Yamaha motorcycle, looking up at the structure, he reflected: in a way, it had taken him most of his life.

As often is the case when one arrives at a long-anticipated destination, the structure seemed modest, ordinary, unimposing. Though if it contained what Shaw hoped, it would prove to be just the opposite: a mine of information that could save hundreds, perhaps thousands, of lives.

But as the son of a survivalist, Shaw had a

preliminary question: Just how safe a safe house was it?

From this angle, it appeared deserted, dark. He dropped the transmission in gear and drove to the alley that ran behind the house, where he paused again, in front of an overgrown garden, encircled by a gothic wrought-iron fence. From here, still no lights, no signs of habitation, no motion. He gunned the engine and returned to the front. He skidded to a stop and low-gear muscled the bike onto the sidewalk.

He snagged his heavy backpack, chained up the bike and helmet, then pushed through the three-foot-deep planting bed that bordered the front. Behind a boxwood he found the circuit breakers for the main line. If there were an unlikely bomb inside it would probably be hardwired; whether it was phones or computers or improvised explosive devices, it was always tricky to depend on batteries.

Using the keys he'd been bequeathed, he unlocked and pushed open the door, hand near his weapon. He was greeted only with white noise and the scent of lavender air freshener.

Before he searched for the documents he hoped his father had left, he needed to clear the place.

No evidence of threat isn't synonymous with **no threat**.

He scanned the ground floor. Beyond the living room was a parlor, from which a stairway led upstairs. Past that room was a dining room and, in the back, a kitchen, whose door, reinforced and windowless, led onto the alleyway. Another door in the kitchen led to the cellar, an unusual feature in much of California. The few pieces of furniture were functional and mismatched. The walls were the color of old bone, curtains sun-bleached to inadvertent tie-dye patterns.

He took his time examining every room on this floor and on the second and third stories. No sign of current residents, but he did find bed linens neatly folded on a mattress on the second floor.

Last, the basement.

He clicked on his tactical halogen flashlight, with its piercing beam, and descended to see that the room was largely empty. A few old cans of paint, a broken table. At the far end was a coal bin, in which a small pile of glistening black lumps sat. Shaw smiled to himself.

Ever the survivalist, weren't you, Ashton?

As he stared into the murk, he noted three wires dangling from the rafters. One, near the stairs, ended in a fixture and a small bulb. The wires in the middle and far end had been cut and the ends were wrapped with electrician's tape.

Shaw knew why the two had been operated on: to keep someone from getting a good view of the end of the cellar.

Shining the beam over the back wall, he stepped close.

Got it, Ash.

As with the rest of the basement, this wall was constructed of four-by-eight plywood sheets nailed to studs, floor to ceiling, painted flat black. But an examination of the seams of one panel revealed a difference. It was a hidden door, opening onto a secure room. He took the locking-blade knife from his pocket and flicked it open. After scanning the surface a moment longer, he located a slit near the bottom. He pushed the blade inside and heard a click. The door sprung outward an inch. Replacing the knife and drawing his gun, he crouched, shining the beam inside, holding the flashlight high and to the left to draw fire, if an enemy were present and armed.

He reached inside and felt for tripwires. None.

He slowly drew the door toward him with his foot.

It had moved no more than eighteen inches when the bomb exploded with a searing flash and a stunning roar and a piece of shrapnel took him in the chest.

2

The risk in detonations is usually not death.

Most victims of an IED are blinded, deafened and/or mutilated. Modern bomb materials move at more than thirty thousand feet per second; the shock wave could travel from sea level to the top of Mount Everest in the time it takes to clear your throat.

Shaw lay on the floor, unable to see, unable to hear, coughing, in pain. He touched the spot where the shrapnel had slammed into him. Sore. But no broken-skin wound. For some reason the skin hadn't broken. He did a fast inventory of the rest of his body. His arms, hands and legs still functioned.

Now: find his weapon. A bomb is often a prelude to an attack.

He could see nothing but, on his knees, he patted

the damp concrete in a circular pattern until he located the gun.

Squinting, but still seeing nothing. You can't **will** your vision to work.

No time for panic, no time for thinking of the consequences to his lifestyle if he'd been permanently blinded or deafened. Rock climbing, motorbiking, traveling the country—all endangered, but not something to worry about right now.

But how could he tell where the assault was coming from? In a crouch he moved to where he thought the coal bin was. It would at least provide some cover. He tried to listen but all he could hear was a tinnitus-like ringing in his ears.

After five desperate minutes he was aware of a faint glow coalescing at the far end of the cellar. Light from the kitchen above.

So his vision wasn't gone completely. He'd been temporarily blinded by the brilliance of the explosion. Finally he could make out the beam of his tac light. It was ten feet away. He collected it and shone the bright light throughout the basement and into the room on the other side of the hidden door.

No attackers.

He holstered his weapon and snapped his fingers beside each ear. His hearing was returning too.

Then he assessed.

What had just happened?

If the bomber had wanted an intruder dead, that could've easily been arranged. Shaw shone his light on the frame of the hidden door and found the smoking device, gray metal. It was a large flash-bang—designed with combustible materials that, when detonated, emitted blinding light and a stunning sound but didn't fling deadly projectiles; its purpose was to serve as a warning.

He looked carefully to see why he'd missed it. Well, interesting. The device was a projectile. It had been launched from a shelf near the hidden door, rigged to explode after a half second or so. This is what had hit him in the chest. The trigger would be a motion or proximity detector. Shaw had never heard of a mechanism like this.

He carefully scanned the room for more traps. He found none.

Who had set it? His father and his colleagues had likely made the secret room, but they probably would not have left the grenade. Ashton Shaw never worked with explosives. Possessing them without a license was illegal, and, for all his father's serious devotion to survivalism and distrust of authority, he didn't break the law.

Never give the authorities that kind of control over you.

Then Shaw confirmed his father could not have created the trap. When he examined the device more closely under the searing white beam, he noted that it was military-issue and bore a date stamp of last year.

Shaw flicked on an overhead light and tucked his

flashlight away. He saw a battered utility table in the center of the twenty-by-twenty space, an old wooden chair, shelves that were largely bare but held some papers and clothes. Other stacks of documents sat against the wall. A large olive-drab duffel bag was in the corner.

On the table were scores of papers.

Was this it? The hidden treasure that others—his father among them—had died for?

He walked around the table, so he was facing the doorway to the secret room, and bent forward to find out.

3

Colter Shaw was here because of a discovery he'd made on his family's Compound in the soaring peaks of eastern California.

There, on high and austere Echo Ridge, where his father had died, Shaw had found a letter the man had written and hidden years ago.

A letter that would change Shaw's life.

Ashton began the missive by saying that over his years as a professor and amateur historian and political scientist, he'd come to distrust the power of large corporations, institutions, politicians and wealthy individuals "who thrive in the netherworld between legality and illegality, democracy and dictatorship." He formed a circle of friends and fellow professors to take on and expose their corruption.

The company that they first set their sights on was

BlackBridge Corporate Solutions, a firm known for its work in the shadowy field of corporate espionage. The outfit was behind many questionable practices, but the one that Ashton and his colleagues found the most reprehensible was their "Urban Improvement Plan," or "UIP." On the surface it appeared to help developers locate real estate. But BlackBridge took the brokerage role one step further. Working with local gangs, BlackBridge operatives flooded targeted neighborhoods with free and cheap opioids, fentanyl and meth. Addiction soared. As the neighborhoods became unlivable, developers swooped in to buy them up for next to nothing.

This same tactic won results for political clients: PACs, lobbyists and candidates themselves. The infestation of illegal drugs would cause a shift in population as residents moved out, affecting congressional districting. The UIP was, in effect, gerrymandering by narcotics.

BlackBridge's schemes became personal for Ashton Shaw when a friend and former student of his—then a San Francisco city councilman—began looking into the UIP operation. Todd Zaleski and his wife were found murdered, a close-range gunshot for each of them. It appeared to be a robbery gone bad, but Ashton knew better.

He and his colleagues looked for evidence against the company, hoping to build a case for authorities. Nearly all BlackBridge workers refused to talk to them but he managed to learn of an employee who felt the UIP had crossed a line. A researcher for BlackBridge, Amos Gahl, found some evidence and smuggled it out of the company. The man hid what he'd stolen somewhere in the San Francisco area. But before he could contact Ashton or the authorities, he too was dead—the victim of a suspicious car crash.

Ashton had written in his letter: **It became my obsession to find what Gahl had hidden.**

Then BlackBridge learned of Ashton and those who shared his obsession. Several died in mysterious accidents, and the others dropped out of the mission, fearful for their lives. Soon, Ashton was alone in his quest to bring down the company that had killed his student and so many others in the City by the Bay—and, likely, untold other cities.

Then on a cold October night, Colter Shaw, sixteen years old, discovered his father's body in desolate Echo Ridge.

Since then, he'd become well aware of the shady figures he was up against:

Ian Helms, founder and CEO of BlackBridge. Now in his mid-fifties and movie-star handsome, he had had some national defense or intelligence jobs in the past and had worked in politics and lobbying.

Ebbitt Droon, a "facilitator" for the company, which is to say a hitman, was wiry with rat-like features. After several personal run-ins with the man, including one that featured a Molotov cocktail hurled in Shaw's direction, he was sure that Droon was a certifiable sadist.

Crema Braxton, BlackBridge operative in charge of stopping Ashton—and now stopping his son. Of her Ashton had written:

> **She may look like somebody's grand-mother but oh, my, no. She's the picture of ruthlessness and will do what needs to be done.**

She was an external relations supervisor, a euphemistic job description if ever there was one. Ashton had concluded his letter with this:

> **Now, we get around to you.**
>
> **You've clearly followed the breadcrumbs I've left leading you to Echo Ridge and now know the whole story.**
>
> **I can hardly in good conscience ask you to take on this perilous job. No reasonable person would. But if you are so inclined, I will say that in picking up where my search has ended, you'll be fighting to secure justice for those who have perished or had their lives upended by BlackBridge and its clients, and you'll be guaranteeing**

that thousands in the future will not suffer
similar fates.

The map included here indicates
the locations in the city that might
contain—or lead to—the evidence
Gahl hid. After leaving this letter and
accompanying documents, I will be
returning to San Francisco and I hope
I will have found more leads. They can
be found at 618 Alvarez Street in San
Francisco.

Finally, let me say this:

Never assume you're safe.

A.S.

4

This was Colter Shaw's mission. To check out each of the locations on his father's map—there were eighteen of them—and find the evidence Amos Gahl had hidden.

As he now looked over the documents in the secret room of the safe house's basement, he realized they had nothing to do with BlackBridge. They had to do with engineering projects and shipping. Some in English, some in Russian or perhaps another language using Cyrillic characters. Other printouts were in Spanish, a language that he could speak, and they related to shipping and transportation too. There were a number in Chinese as well.

Someone was using the secret room as a base of operations. One of the original members of his father's circle? Or, like Shaw, second generation? A man or a woman? Young? Middle-aged? Some of these materials were dated recently. He turned to the duffel bag on the floor and—after an examination for a tripwire—unzipped it.

Inside was the answer to the question of gender. The clothing was a man's, of larger-than-average physique. T-shirts, work shirts, cargo pants, jeans, sweaters, wool socks, baseball caps, gloves, casual jackets. Everything was black, charcoal gray or dark green.

Then he saw in the shadows against the back wall another stack of papers. Ah, here was his father's material. It was Ashton from whom Shaw had learned the art of calligraphy, and the man wrote in a script even more elegant—and smaller—than Shaw's.

His heart beat just a bit faster, seeing these.

Shaw carried the stack upstairs and set the papers on the rickety kitchen table. He sat down in an equally uncertain chair and began to read. There were more details about the UIP, and references to other schemes the company engaged in: dodgy earthquake inspections of high-rises (some located **on** the San Andreas Fault, no less), government contract kickbacks, land-use and zoning ploys, stock market manipulations, money laundering.

There was a clipping about the death of a California state assemblyman, with two question marks beside the victim's picture. The man had died in a car crash on the way to meet with a state attorney general. The resulting fire had destroyed his auto and boxes of records he had with him. The crash was curious but no criminal investigation was begun.

He found as well articles about Todd Zaleski, his father's former student turned city councilman whom Ashton believed was murdered by BlackBridge.

Everything he found hinted at the company's guilt. But this wasn't evidence—at least not enough for a prosecutor. Shaw had some experience on the topic of criminal law. After college he'd worked in a law firm, while deciding whether to take the LSATs and apply to law school. He'd been particularly inspired to study the subject by one Professor Sharphorn at the University of Michigan and thought he might take up the profession. In the end, his restless nature put the kibosh on a desk job, but an interest in the law stayed with him and he often read up on the subject; it was also helpful in his reward-seeking job.

No, nothing his father had found would interest the D.A.'s office.

Shaw then found a note, presumably from a colleague of Amos Gahl, intended for Ashton. It was a small sheet of paper folded many times. This no doubt meant it would have been left in a dead-drop, a spy technique of hiding communiqués under park benches or cracks in walls, avoiding the risk of electronic intercepts.

Amos is dead. It's in a BlackBridge courier bag. Don't know where he hid

**it. This is my last note. Too danger-
ous. Good luck.**

So "it"—the evidence—was in a company bag
hidden in one of the eighteen locations Ashton had
identified as a likely spot. An arduous task, but
there was no way around it. He'd have to start with
the first and keep going until he found the courier
bag—or give up after none of them panned out.

But he soon learned he wouldn't have to investigate eighteen locations. In fact, he didn't need to
check out any.

He discovered in the stack a map identical to the
one he'd found in Echo Ridge—well, identical except for one difference. All eighteen of the locations
were crossed off with bold red **X**s.

After leaving the map at the Compound, Ashton,
as he'd written, had returned here and searched the
sites himself, eliminating them all.

Shaw sighed. This meant that the evidence that
would destroy BlackBridge could be squirreled away
anywhere within the entire San Francisco Bay Area,
which had to embrace thousands of square miles.

Maybe Ashton had discovered other possible sites.
Shaw returned to the material to look for more clues,
but his search was interrupted at that moment.

From Alvarez Street, out in front of the safe house,
a woman called out. "Please!" she cried. "Somebody!
Help me!"

5

Shaw looked out the bay window to see two people struggling in front of the chain-link gate that opened onto a scruffy lot containing the remnants of a building that had been partly burned years ago.

The dark-haired woman was in her thirties, he guessed. Dressed in faded jeans, a T-shirt, a scuffed dark blue leather jacket, running shoes. A white earbud cord dangled. She was looking around frantically as a squat man, dressed in a dusty, tattered combat jacket and baggy pants, gripped her forearm. The man was white and had a grimy look about him. Homeless, Shaw guessed, and, like many, possibly schizophrenic or a borderline personality. The man held a box cutter and was pulling the woman toward the gate. He seemed strong, which wasn't unusual;

life on the street was physically arduous; to get by you needed to practice a version of survivalism. Even from this distance, Shaw could see veins rising high on the man's hands and forehead.

Through the front door and down the concrete steps fast, then approaching the two of them. Her face desperate, eyes wide, the woman looked toward him. "Please! He's hurting me!"

The attacker's eyes cut to Shaw. At first there was a mad defiance on the man's face, which struck Shaw as impish. With his short height and broad chest, he might be cast as a creature in a fantasy or mythological movie. His hands indeed looked strong.

"Oh, yeah, skinny boy, you want some of this? Fuck off."

Shaw kept coming.

The man waved the weapon dramatically. "You think I'm kidding?"

Shaw kept coming.

You'd think the guy wouldn't be in a carnal mood any longer, given the third-party presence. But he gripped the woman just as insistently as a moment ago, as if she were a home-run ball he'd caught in the stadium and wasn't going to give up to another fan. Without loosening his hold he stepped closer toward Shaw.

Who kept coming.

"Jesus! You deaf, asshole?"

In the Shaw family's Sierra Nevada enclave, where he had taught his children survival skills, Ashton had spent much time on firearms, those confounding inventions that are both blessings and curses. One of his father's rules was borrowed—straight from Shooting Practices 101.

Never draw a gun unless you intend to use it.

Shaw drew the Glock and pointed it at the attacker's head.

The man froze.

Shaw was taking his father's rule to heart, as he usually did with the man's lengthy list of don'ts. He believed, however, that the definition of **use** was open to interpretation. His was somewhat broader than Ashton's. In this case it meant not pulling the trigger but instead scaring the shit out of someone.

It was working.

"Oh . . . No, man . . . no, don't! Please! I didn't mean anything. I was just standing here. Asked her for some money. I ain't ate in a week. Then she starts coming on to me."

Shaw didn't say anything. He wasn't someone who negotiated or bantered. He kept the gun steady as he gazed coolly at the puckish face, which was encircled with damp, swept-back hair in a style that, Shaw believed, mercifully ceased to exist around 1975.

After a brief moment, the attacker released the woman. She stepped away, leaning against a segment of chain-link fence, breathing hard. Eyes were wide in her stricken face.

The building must have burned five years ago

but, with the weighty moisture in the air, you could still detect burnt wood.

The man retracted the blade on the box cutter and started to put it away.

"No. Drop it."

"I—"

"Drop. It."

The gray tool clattered onto the gravelly sidewalk.

"Out of here now."

The man held up both his hands and backed away. Then he paused. He cocked his head and, with narrowed eyes and a hint of hope in his face, he asked, "Any chance you can spare a twenty?"

Shaw grimaced. The man ambled up the street.

Shaw holstered the gun and scanned the area. Only one other person was on the street—a bearded man in a thigh-length black coat and dark slacks, a stocking cap and an Oakland A's backpack. He wasn't nearby and was facing away. If he'd seen the incident, he had no interest in the participants or what had happened. The man stepped into an independent coffee shop. San Francisco, with its Italian roots, had many of these.

"My God," the woman whispered. "Thank you!" She was a little shorter than Shaw's six feet even, but not much, with an athletic build, toned legs and thighs under her tight-fitting distressed jeans. She had slim hips and lengthy arms. The veins were prominent in the backs of her hands too, just like her attacker's. Her brown hair was loose. She wore no makeup on her face, which seemed weather-toughened. A scar started near her temple and disappeared into her hairline.

"I don't know what to say. Are you, umm, police?" She glanced toward the weapon on his right hip and then perused him. She was wary.

With his short blond hair, muscular build and taciturn manner, Colter Shaw could easily be mistaken for law enforcement, a fed or a detective running complex homicides—the stuff of anti-terror cases. Today, she'd think, he was undercover, as he'd ridden here on the Yamaha in his biker gear: the jacket, navy-blue shirt under a black sweater to conceal his weapon, blue jeans and black Nocona boots.

"Kind of a private eye."

"I'm Tricia," she said.

He didn't give his, either real or a cover.

She shook her head, apparently at her own behavior. "Stupid, stupid . . ."

Shaw said, "Find a better quality of dealer. Or don't use at all." But he shrugged. "Easy for me to say."

Her lips tightened; she looked down. "I know. I try. This program, that program. Maybe this's a wake-up call." She offered him a wan smile. "Thank you, really."

And, in the opposite direction of the creature from Middle-earth, she walked off.

6

Shaw returned to the safe house, headed for the kitchen and the documents, but he got no farther than the living room.

He stopped, staring at a shelf on which sat a six-inch statuette, a bronze bald eagle. Wings spread, talons out, predator's eyes focused downward.

Shaw picked it up and turned it over in his hand, righted it once more.

To the casual observer, what he was holding looked to be a competently sculpted souvenir from a wildlife preserve gift shop, one of the more expensive behind-the-counter items.

But it was significantly more than that to Colter Shaw.

He had last seen it on a shelf in his bedroom in the Compound many years ago. Before it went missing. He had from time to time wondered where it had ended up. Had he stored it away himself when he'd cleaned his room to make space for gear or weapons he'd made or discoveries from his endless hikes through the mountains surrounding the Compound: rocks, pinecones, arrowheads, bones?

Finding it here gave him considerable pleasure, at last understanding the artwork's fate. His father must have brought it with him here as a reminder of his middle child. Shaw was thankful too it was not lost forever; how he'd come into possession of the sculpture was an important aspect of his childhood, a memento of an incident that had undoubtedly launched him into his present career and lifestyle.

The Restless Man . . .

But this icon of a bird in muscular flight brought sorrow too. It resurrected other memories of his childhood: specifically of his older brother, Russell.

Years ago, during a bad spell, Ashton Shaw had insisted that Dorion, then thirteen, make a one-hundred-foot free-climb up a sheer rock face in the middle of the night. This was a test. All of his children had to make the ascent when they became teenagers.

Russell and Colter already had done so. But had come to believe that the rite of passage was pointless, especially for their sister. Dorie was as talented athletically as her brothers with chalk and rope, and more so than Ashton himself. She'd already proved her ascent skills, including night climbs.

With a mind of her own even then, Dorion had simply decided she didn't need to . . . or want to. "Ash. No." The girl never shied.

But her father wouldn't let it go. He grew more and more riled and persistent.

The older brother intervened. Russell also said no.

The confrontation turned ugly. A knife was involved—on Ashton's part. And Russell, using skills his father himself had taught, prepared to defend his sister and take the weapon away from the wild-eyed man.

Mary Dove, her husband's psychiatrist and med-dispenser in chief—had been away on a family emergency, so there was no adult present to defuse the situation.

After a boilingly tense moment their father backed down and retreated to his bedroom, muttering to himself.

Not long after, Ashton had died in a fall from Echo Ridge.

The circumstances were suspicious, and more troubling, Shaw learned that his brother had lied about his whereabouts at the time of Ashton's death. He was, in fact, not far from Echo Ridge. Shaw believed that Russell had murdered the man. He was sure it had been agonizing, an impossible decision on his brother's part. But he guessed that at some point Russell had come to believe it was Dorie's life or Ashton's, and Russell made his choice. By then Ashton Shaw had become someone very different from the kind and witty man and teacher the children had known growing up.

Shaw had made his own impossible decision: accepting that his brother was guilty of patricide. The thought tore at him for years, and tore him and Russell apart.

Then, just weeks ago, the truth: Russell had had nothing to do with Ashton's death. It was a BlackBridge operative responsible, trailing their father to Echo Ridge on that cold, cold night in October.

Ebbitt Droon himself had told Shaw the story. "Your father . . . Braxton wanted him dead—but not yet, not till she had what she wanted. She sent somebody to, well, talk to him about the documents."

"Talk" meant torturing Ashton into giving up what he knew about Amos Gahl's theft of company secrets and evidence.

Droon had explained, "Near as we can piece it together, your father knew Braxton's man was on his way to your Compound. Ashton tipped to him and led him off, was going to kill him somewhere in the woods. The ambush didn't work. They fought. Your father fell."

But until that revelation, Shaw had indeed believed in his heart that Russell was their father's murderer. Devastated by false accusation, even if unspoken, Russell had vanished from the family's

life. No one had heard from him since Ashton's funeral, more than a decade ago.

Colter Shaw made his living finding people—
good ones and bad, those lost because of fate and
circumstance and those lost because they chose to be
lost. He had devoted considerable time and money
and effort to tracking down his brother. What he
would say when he found him, Shaw had no idea.
He'd practiced a script of one brother talking to the
other, explaining, seeking forgiveness, trying to find
a path out of estrangement.

But all his efforts had come to nothing. Russell
Shaw had vanished, and he'd vanished very, very well.

Shaw recalled discussing this very subject with
someone just last week, describing the impact.

The man had asked, "What would you say was
the greatest minus regarding your brother? What
hurts the most?"

Shaw had answered, "He'd been my friend. I was
his. And I ruined it."

Seeing this eagle now made him feel Russell's absence all the more.

He set the statue on the kitchen table and returned to the stack of his father's materials. For an
hour he pored over the documents. He found two
notes in his father's fine hand. They didn't relate to
the eighteen locations, which meant he'd discovered these spots after completing the scavenger hunt
of the map.

One note was about a commercial building in the Embarcadero, the district along the eastern waterfront of San Francisco: the Hayward Brothers Warehouse.

The other was an address in Burlingame, a suburb south of the city, 3884 Camino.

Shaw now texted his private eye, requesting information. Mack McKenzie soon replied that she could find little more about the warehouse beyond that it was a historic building dating to the late 1800s, was not open for business to the public, and was presently for sale. The Burlingame address was a private home, owned by a man named Morton T. Nadler.

Shaw also found a business card, which represented a third possible location as well, the Stanford Library of Business and Commerce.

The library was located not in Palo Alto, where the university was situated, but in a part of town known as South of Market. Maybe it had nothing to do with Gahl's stolen evidence; it would be an odd place to hide a courier bag. Possibly Ashton Shaw had used it for research. He had never owned a computer, and certainly had never allowed one in any residence of his, so maybe he'd gone to the library to use one of its public workstations.

Shaw decided the library would be his first stop. It was the closest to the safe house. If that didn't pan out he would try the house in Burlingame and then the warehouse.

First, though, some security measures.

San Francisco was BlackBridge's turf. Odds were ninety percent that they didn't know he was here. But that dark ten percent required some due diligence.

He called up an app on his phone.

It happened to be tracing the whereabouts of Irena Braxton and Ebbitt Droon at that very moment.

Just the other day—under a fake identity—Braxton had talked her way into Shaw's camper and stolen what she thought was Ashton's map marking the places were Gahl's evidence was hidden and other materials.

Shaw had tipped to who she really was. What he'd intentionally left for her to steal was a map with eighteen phony locations marked and a copy of Henry David Thoreau's **Walden**, filled with code-like gibberish in the margins. A GPS tracker was hidden in the book's spine.

In the past two days the tracker had meandered over various locations he'd marked on the map and spent time in a commercial skyscraper in downtown San Francisco, on Sutter Street, probably BlackBridge's satellite office. This was its present location.

He now shifted to Google Maps and examined the neighborhood in which the Stanford library was located. He hardly expected trouble but it was a procedure he followed with every reward job. Information was the best weapon a survivalist could have.

Which didn't mean hardware should be neglected.

Shaw checked his gun once more.

Never assume your weapon is loaded and hasn't been damaged or sabotaged since the last time you used it.

The .380 was indeed loaded, one in the bedroom and six in the mag. It was a good dependable pistol—as long as you held it firmly while firing. The model had a reputation for limp wrist failure to eject: spent brass hanging in the receiver. Colter Shaw had never had this problem.

He seated the gun in his gray plastic inside-the-waistband holster and made sure it was hidden. The rule was that if you're carrying concealed, you should keep it concealed, lest a concerned citizen spot the weapon, panic and call the cops.

There was another reason too.

Never let the enemy know the strength of your defenses . . .

7

A new threat.

As he stood beside his bike Shaw was aware that someone was watching him.

Slight build, leather jacket, baseball cap.

The giveaway was the sunglasses. Hardly necessary this morning. The day was typically foggy—sometimes the cloak burned off, sometimes it remained, sluggish and dull, like an irritating houseguest. Now the haze hung thickly in air redolent of damp pavement, exhaust, a hint of trash and the sea. In San Francisco, you were never far from water.

Shaw had examined the street subtly after leaving and locking the safe house. At first he saw no one other than the bearded man he'd spotted earlier, in the thigh-length black coat and stocking cap, Oakland A's backpack at his feet. He was at a table outside the coffee shop, sipping from a cup and text-ing. Then Shaw glanced into the Yamaha motor-bike's rearview mirror and spotted the spy, a block and a half away.

Odds he was mistaken? Fifty percent.

He casually turned, checking out the rear tire of the Yamaha and looking back while not exactly looking.

The man disappeared behind the corner of the building where he'd been standing.

Bringing the answer to the surveillance question to nearly one hundred percent.

Who could it have been?

He was built like Droon—but if it were anyone from BlackBridge, how could they have learned about the safe house? Besides, in that case, they would have been on him the instant he stepped out-side. A team would have forced him back into the safe house to have a "discussion" about what he was doing here in the city and where he believed Gahl's evidence was hidden.

Instead, he suspected it was the Russian- and Chinese-speaking inhabitant of the safe house, the man who was so adept at loud and blinding booby traps. Make that sixty percent.

And the odds that the man wasn't happy Shaw was now in residence and had likely examined charts and graphs he'd gone to great lengths to keep secret? An easy ninety-nine percent on that one.

Was it one of his father's colleagues? Or a successor in interest, like Shaw himself?

Possibly. No way to estimate the odds without any more information.

Dalton Crowe? The lug of a bounty hunter had crossed paths and traded blows with Shaw over the years. He was presently under the erroneous impression that Shaw had cheated him out of tens of thousands of dollars of reward money. Crowe didn't live anywhere near here but the man was a bully bordering on psychopathy. A drive of a thousand miles or so to collect a debt, even mistakenly, was well within his wheelhouse.

True, Crowe sported a refrigerator's physique, twice the size of the spy. But that didn't mean he hadn't recruited an underling. When you believe in your heart a man owes you $50K, you'll spend some capital to get it back.

Someone from a past job out for revenge? Absolutely a possibility. Just a few weeks ago, Shaw had made some enemies in Silicon Valley when a simple reward job turned into something considerably darker. The foes he'd made in the tech world of video gaming were particularly resourceful and, he had to assume, vindictive.

He thought of the squat, broad-chested man he'd confronted earlier, Tricia's attacker. Unlikely he'd return but people bested in a fight had been known to come back with superior firepower for a touch of revenge. It would be stupid and pointless, but those two words described more than a little slice of decisions made by the general population. He dismissed this, though, on the basis of the difference in physique.

He turned back to the front of the bike and unhooked it from the lamppost, stowing the impressive chain and lock. As he did, he took another glance in the rearview mirror and noted that his shadow had eased back into observing position.

Shaw tugged on his helmet and black leather gloves.

He unzipped his jacket and lifted the sweater for easy access to his weapon. Then, in an instant, the engine clattered to life and Shaw's boot tip tapped into first gear. He twisted the throttle hard. The rear tire swirled and smoked and he spun the bike one hundred and eighty degrees, launching into the street.

The figure vanished.

Shaw hit forty. As he neared the intersection where he'd turn to the right to confront the spy, he downshifted and eased off the gas, skidding to a fast stop. Shaw had to assume that the watcher was armed and targeting where he would spin around the corner, so without presenting himself as a target, he leaned the bike to the right and used the rearview mirror to view the cross street.

There was no threat but, damn it, he could see a car speeding away.

He gunned the engine again and pursued.

For about thirty feet.

Oh hell . . .

He slammed the rear brake hard, then gripped the front, the trickier of the two, the one that could send you over the handlebars. He managed to control the skid and bring the bike to stop just in time, before he ran through the bed of nails that the spy apparently had tossed onto the cobblestones before climbing into his car and speeding away. It was a clever trick, an improvised version of the nail strip that the police use to end high-speed chases. If the watcher had more in mind than just spying, he'd return with a weapon the minute Shaw set the bike down.

He caught a glimpse of the vehicle—a dark green Honda Accord with California plates. He couldn't make out the number. It vanished to the left, speeding toward the entrance ramp to the freeway.

Now that the spy had been made, would that be the end of him?

Shaw thought: ninety-nine-point-five percent no. But he had no facts for this number, just intuition.

He dismounted, found a piece of cardboard and swept the nails into a storm drain—concerned for fellow bikers' safety, of course, but also because, if there was an accident, he wouldn't want emergency vehicles in the area, their lights and sirens attracting attention and the police might go door by door to ask for witnesses.

He couldn't go on to the library just yet.

Somebody—clearly a hostile—now knew about the safe house. He climbed onto the bike and sped back to the safe house. There he photographed every one of his father's documents and encrypted and uploaded them to his secure cloud storage system, copying Mack.

Returning then to the Yamaha, he fired the bike up once more and sped into the street, accelerating hard, as he headed for the main road that would take him to the Stanford library.

Suddenly, thoughts about the spy's identity and purpose were gone. It took only a few yards for the exhilaration to wrap its arms around him. Rock climbing was a complex, intellectual joy. Low-gear, high-throttle racing around corners on slidey tires, powering up and over hills . . . well, that was a pure, raw high.

Shaw had seen the police thriller **Bullitt**, from the '60s, in which the actor Steve McQueen—to whom, Shaw was regularly reminded, bore more than a passing resemblance—had muscled his Ford Mustang through the winding and hilly streets of San Francisco in pursuit of two hitmen in a Dodge Charger—the best car-chase scene ever filmed. When in town here, on his bike, Shaw never missed the chance to exploit the tricky and exhilarat-ing geography of the city just like Detective Frank Bullitt, occasionally going airborne and enjoying lavish skids.

He now plowed through the neighborhood the safe house was located in: the Mission.

Shaw had some affection for the area, where he'd spent weeks on a reward job a few years back. The district had been sparsely populated until the infamous 1906 earthquake, which destroyed much of San Francisco. Because there was more open land and therefore less quake and fire damage in the Mission, residents began to move here to start life anew. These newcomers were Anglo—largely Polish and German—as well as Chicano and Latino. In the early to mid-twentieth century, the neighborhood was tawdry and rough-and-tumble and more than a little lawless. So it remained until the '70s, when counterculture hit.

The Mission was the epicenter of the punk music scene in the city, and of the gay, lesbian and trans communities as well.

Shaw had learned too, in his search for the Benson twins, that one of the more interesting aspects of the district was the number of inhabitants whose families came from the Yucatan. In the portion of the Mission he was driving through now, the Mayan language—expressive and complex—was the main tongue of many residents. He sped past grassy In Chan Kaajal Park, which in Mayan means "My Little Town."

As he traveled north he left the Mission behind and cruised into SoMa, the silly urbanized abbreviation of "South of Market." It was also known—mostly among the old-timers—by the more interesting nic "South of the Slots," after a now-defunct cable car that had run along Market. Like the Mission, SoMa had a colorful history but now that color was giving way to enterprise. This was home to scores of corporate headquarters, museums, galleries and traditional performing venues. What would the punksters have said?

Shaw soon arrived at the library, which was located on the north border of SoMa, the more affluent portion of the neighborhood. This portion of SoMa was close to the financial district and the legal firms and corporations that would use the services of a university business library.

Shaw pulled to the curb and idled his bike across the street from the library, which was a functional two-story structure constructed of glass and aluminum framing. Architecturally, the place didn't approach interesting. But Shaw observed it closely. He saw people were coming and going, dressed in conservative business attire for the most part. Some messengers, a few delivery people.

He pretended to make a phone call as he observed the entry procedures.

There was one entrance into a large lobby and inside were two doorways. One, to the left facing the guard station, was for visitors. The other, to the right, was members only. Visitors to the public side had to walk through a metal detector and dump pocket litter into a basket for examination. You also needed to display an ID, and your name was jotted down on a clipboard sheet, but there was no confirmation of your identity.

He dropped the bike into gear and drove up the block to a space reserved for cycles and scooters. He locked the Yamaha to a post with a snaky cable. He affixed his helmet too. Looking around, he slipped the holstered gun and blade into a locked compartment, under the seat, he'd built for this purpose. He'd made sure the hidden GPS transmit system, like a LoJack, was active—even a double-chained motorcycle can be stolen by a determined thief.

Colter Shaw didn't like leaving the weapons but there was no option. Then he reminded himself not to let his father's paranoia enwrap him entirely. After all, how much trouble could he possibly get himself into in a library?

8

He had his story ready.

Legal associate Carter Skye, of the law firm Dorion & Dove, had been sent by his firm to look up an insurance law issue. This cover was not made up entirely out of whole cloth. When he was a legal assistant years ago, he'd had to do some research on the topic for one of the partners. It was a tricky question of subrogation—when an insurance company pays off a claim and then earns the right to sue in the insured's name.

The pleasant Latino guard, however, had no interest in what Skye/Shaw's purpose might be, and Shaw had been undercover enough times to know never to make an otherwise innocent story seem suspicious by volunteering information.

"There a charge?" he asked.

The man explained that if you weren't affili-
ated with a school, entrance was ten dollars, which
Shaw handed over in cash. Then, on request, he displayed his ID, which happened to feature his picture, height, weight and eye color, but the name,
Skye, was his cover from his most recent undercover
role. Mack was an expert at ginning up new identities. (This was completely legal as long as you didn't
try to trick the law or scam someone.)

A machine hummed and out eased a sticky-
backed badge with his picture on it. He plastered it
onto his chest.

Shaw debated about showing the picture of
Amos Gahl—he'd taken a shot with his phone from
the article about the man's death—and asking if the
guard remembered his being in here. The man,
though, was young and if Gahl had used the library
it would have been years ago.

"What's over there?" Shaw pointed to the double
doors to the right.

MEMBERS ONLY

"Historical documents mostly."
"Legal?"
"Some. And planning and zoning, real estate,
government filings."
"That right? My partners're handling a case with

some issues going back thirty, forty years. I'm look-ing for some old housing rulings that city hall doesn't have. Is there any way I can get in?"

He hoped a senior librarian wouldn't pop out and ask what, specifically, he wanted.

"You gotta make an appointment. Call this num-ber." The man handed Shaw a card, which vanished into his jeans pocket. It was more likely that his father or Gahl had used the public side of the place. If he found nothing there, maybe he'd bone up on old California real estate law and try to get inside the private portion.

Shaw thanked the man and then walked through the unresponsive metal detector into the spa-cious and well-lit open-to-the-public portion of the library.

Now, where to go from here?

It was an upscale facility, as you might expect, being attached to one of the best endowed univer-sities in the country. In the center was a librarian's station, circular. A Black man of about thirty-five in a beige suit sat there, focused on his computer monitor.

Radiating outward from the center were rows of tables and spacious computer workstations with large monitors. The screen saver—a moving block of the name of the library—ricocheted in a leisurely fashion around each monitor. The desks and cubicles offered office supplies: pens, pads of paper, Post-it notes and paper clips. Ringing this open space were the stacks, containing books and periodicals. There were floor-to-ceiling windows in the front and on the side. Against the back wall were what seemed to be a dozen offices or conference rooms. Circling the second-floor balcony was a series of stacks and rooms, just as down here.

There weren't many patrons in this portion of the first floor. Two older businessmen who'd doffed their suit jackets pored over old books. A young woman in a plaid dress and a slim man in a dark suit and white shirt—both looked to be mid-thirties—were on computers.

Instinctively Shaw examined the library for escape routes. He sensed no threat, of course, but scanning for exits was a survival thing. He did it everywhere he went, automatically.

Never lose your orientation . . .

There was the front door, of course, and a stairway that led to the second floor. An elevator. A glass door in the back of the stacks led to the members-only side of the library. It opened onto a conference room, which might lead to other exits in the back of the structure, though it was presently occupied; a middle-aged businesswoman in a suit and a lean man in dark casual jacket sat with their backs to the glass door. A somber-faced man with bright blond hair sat across the table from them. The door had a latch but Shaw had no way of knowing whether or not it was now locked.

The left-side floor-to-ceiling windows featured a

fire door, fitted with an alarm. It exited onto a side street. There were men's and women's restrooms, and a door on which was a sign: SUPPLIES.

He tucked this information away and got to work. Assuming that his father had identified the library as a place where Gahl might have hidden the evidence, where would the man have concealed it?

Shaw guessed that he probably had not stashed the entire courier bag, which he guessed from the name was not a slim piece of luggage; it would be conspicuous. He would probably have emptied it and put the contents—copies of incriminating emails, correspondence, spreadsheets, computer drives or disks, whatever it might be—in an out-of-the-way place. Maybe in the pages of a book or journal, maybe in the shadowy areas behind the volumes in the stacks or on top of the racks, maybe in the spaces beneath drawers in a workstation.

He strolled through the stacks, filled with such titles as **Liability in Maritime Collision Claims: Bays and Harbors**; **Piercing the Corporate Veil**; **Incorporation Guide for Nonprofits**. Easily four or five thousand books. He noted that many were outdated, like **Who's Who of San Francisco Commerce: 1948.** What better hiding place for documents or a CD or thumb drive than a book of that sort? In plain sight, yet inside a volume that no one would possibly need to refer to.

Yet Shaw calculated it would take a month to go

through all the volumes. And it would be impossible to do that without arousing suspicion . . . No, Gahl was not a stupid man. He hid the evidence because he knew there was a chance he would be killed. It would be hidden in a place that somebody, a colleague, the police, could deduce.

Shaw noticed the librarian was looking his way.

He nodded a friendly greeting to the man, walked to one of the workstations and sat down. A swipe of the mouse revealed the main screen to be an internal database of the library's contents. Just what he wanted. He typed in **Gahl, Amos.** Nothing. Then **Shaw, Ashton.** Negative on that too.

But with **BlackBridge**, he had a hit.

The reference was to a book titled **California Corporate Licenses, Volume I.**

Had Gahl reasoned that Ashton Shaw or someone would do this very thing, run a computer search for the company, and accordingly hidden the evidence in the book?

An elegant and simple clue.

The listing sent Shaw to a stack near the librarian station. Yes, there was the book: thick and bound in dark red faux leather. He lifted the tome off the shelf and set it on the floor. Then he removed the adjoining volumes and examined the space behind them. Seeing nothing, he reached in and felt along the cool metal. Nothing. He returned the other books and took **Corporate Licenses** back to the workstation.

He began his examination, first opening up the book to see if Gahl had hollowed out a portion and slipped a thumb drive or chip inside. No, he hadn't. Nor were there any folded documents or notes between pages. The book was simply a listing of corporations with licenses to do business in the state. Shaw turned next to the BlackBridge entry, thinking that would be a logical place to hide something or to leave a message about where the material was. Nothing. Shaw read the listing. The company was merely mentioned by name, without any other information. The headquarters was given as being in Los Angeles, which Shaw already knew, with offices in San Francisco and other cities.

He examined the hefty volume page by page. No evidence, no notes, no margin jottings. He probed into the spine too.

Nothing.

Hell. He re-shelved it and returned once more to the computer.

More searches. The councilman who'd been killed by BlackBridge: **Zaleski, Todd**. No hits there. Had Gahl been clever with anagrams or other subtle clues? He typed in variations on the search terms.

He tried **UIP** and **Urban Improvement Plan.**

Without success.

He deleted his search history then swiped the computer to sleep, deciding that it was likely the library **wasn't** a possible hiding space for Gahl's materials after all. Maybe Shaw's other theory was correct.

His father simply had used the library's computers to do online searches.

So, a waste of time.

Colter Shaw, however, corrected himself. No, that wasn't true; **eliminating** a possible lead is never a waste; the visit had gotten him one step closer to his goal. He'd learned to embrace this attitude in the reward-seeking business. Step by step by step.

It was time to get to the warehouse in the Embarcadero and the home in Burlingame, the last best chances for finding the evidence.

Before he left, though, he pulled out his phone and called up the tracking app, receiving data from the device he'd hidden in the copy of **Walden**, which Braxton and Droon presumably still had with them.

He was disappointed to see that the tracker was malfunctioning. The map that popped up showed Shaw's, not the book's, location. Well, he hadn't believed the device would last forever. He then frowned and noticed that the pinging circle indicating the whereabouts of the tracker was coming not exactly from where Shaw sat but about thirty or so feet away.

A refresh of the system. The ping remained in the exact position it had been a moment ago.

No, impossible . . .

His breathing coming quickly, pulse tapping hard, he sent a text to Mack, including the code they used for immediate attention, asking her about the library.

In sixty seconds—the woman seemed always to be on duty—her response was:

Library has no affiliation with Stanford or any other university. Owned by an offshore corporation. CEO is Ian Helms, head of BlackBridge. R U there now?

He texted:

Yes.

Two seconds later his phone hummed with her reply.

GTFO.

This was a variation on the emergency plan all survivalists have, to escape when an enemy is coming for you. The more common, and less coarse, version is: Get the Hell Out.

9

The library was a cover.

It was the members-only portion of the building and not the high-rise on Sutter Street downtown that was BlackBridge's base of operation in San Francisco.

Shaw gazed in the direction where the tracker indicated the book was, and he realized that Irena Braxton and Ebbitt Droon were the very people whose backs he'd noted through the glass door that opened onto the other side of the building.

He glanced once more that way and saw a fourth man in the conference room. He was pacing, arms crossed, as he appeared to be debating something. He posed a question, it seemed—his hands were raised and his face appeared irritated. Then, when someone must have answered, he nodded and he paced some more, gazing absently into the public side of the library.

It was the CEO, Ian Helms. The athletic, handsome man wore a well-tailored suit and a Rolex on one wrist, a bracelet on the other, both gold.

This was the first time Colter Shaw had glimpsed the man responsible for his father's death.

Helms would probably have no idea what Shaw looked like but it was not the time to take any chances. He slipped from the workstation and disappeared into the far reaches of the stacks.

GTFO . . .

He started to circle around the perimeter of the library to the front door. He kept his head down, moving steadily but not too fast through the stacks.

Only twenty feet later he stopped.

He'd been busted.

From the shadows of the rows of books, Shaw saw a large security guard in a dark suit enter the public side of the building from the lobby. The well-tanned man's head was cocked and he appeared to be listening to the Secret Service–type earpiece with a curly wire that disappeared into his jacket. He walked to the librarian at the central station. They shared some words, both of them looking around. The guard's jacket parted and the grip of a pistol showed. A second guard joined them. He was slimmer and more pale than the first, but tall too. Also armed. Shaw noted his hand was near his own pistol.

How would they have learned about him?

Then he got his answer:

The taller guard, more a bouncer than your average rent-a-cop, strode forward to the terminal where Shaw had sat and gazed about. The slimmer one joined him.

Shaw had just typed in a smorgasbord of words that would turn the bots within the system into frenzied hounds.

Shaw . . . Gahl . . . BlackBridge.

Some software had been programmed to report in when keywords were searched. The computer had dimed him out.

And it got even better, Shaw thought sardonically. Peering through the stacks, he noted that right above the volume in which he'd found BlackBridge's name was a security camera. The book might've been placed there for that very reason: to get a picture of anyone with an interest in the company. The bigger guard was now looking at a monitor at the librarian's station. Both security people turned to the spot where the volume had been shelved.

Okay, escape plans.

Toss a book in the opposite direction and when the guards moved toward it, just sprint out the front?

No, that wouldn't work. Droon, Braxton and the BlackBridge op with the bleached blond hair had now joined in. They were in the lobby and headed for the public section of the library. Alarm showed in Braxton's face. Droon and Blond were as focused as hunters closing in on an elk. They were accompanied by Ian Helms.

Shaw slipped toward the back wall, hidden by the rows upon rows of books. As he moved to the rear of the facility he noted that many of the titles were duplicated. Two, three, a dozen times. This added to the supposition that while one might do some legitimate research in this portion of the library it was also a trap.

BlackBridge security people would have come up with the tactic. Anyone with an interest in the company—investigators, competitors, those with a grudge or out for revenge—might find clues that led to the library. There would be minimal security to get inside. Then the interloper would ask some questions of the librarian or, like Shaw, type in a computer search, and he'd get tagged as a threat.

They would then use sophisticated facial recognition and other techniques to identify the person and decide what kind of risk they were, or—depending on what they browsed—that they were no threat at all. He wouldn't have been surprised to find that BlackBridge had some DNA scanner on doorknobs and computer keypads. Certainly devices would be capturing fingerprints and retinal patterns.

The offenders would then leave, having conveniently deposited their names in the database that BlackBridge was sure to maintain.

Or, perhaps, the inquisitive customers would not leave at all.

Maybe Ashton had suspected this was a BlackBridge facility and was going to check it out but was killed before he had a chance. That might have been how his father came by the business card Shaw had found in the secret room on Alvarez Street.

The bigger guard was glancing back at Irena Braxton and pointing his finger directly at the chair in front of the computer where Shaw had been sitting a few minutes ago.

Shaw evaluated the enemy. Ian Helms appeared fit enough, but Shaw assessed that there was less than a twenty percent chance he'd want to get his hands dirty, especially with armed minders present. Braxton was a stocky, middle-aged woman. She might be ruthless but she wasn't much of a physical threat unless she had a weapon in her many-hued shoulder bag.

In addition to the security guards, the other two threats were Ebbitt Droon and the bright-haired, sullen-faced minder, Blond. Droon, though of small stature, was wiry and strong and was likely carrying the same .40 pistol he'd threatened Shaw with previously. It was probably silenced so that the cries resulting from the bone-shattering impact would be louder than the report of the weapon itself.

Blond looked to be pure muscle and would likely also be armed.

On the other hand, Shaw had the benefit of witnesses: the four patrons, the three men and the woman. He doubted they were involved. This meant BlackBridge probably couldn't take Shaw down the easy way—with a gunshot.

If he could dodge the hostiles and work his way to the front, as they sought him in the stacks, maybe he could make the sprint after all.

But then Shaw's safety net vanished. The librarian approached the four potential witnesses and apparently asked them to leave, and to leave quickly. Which they did, concern on their faces. They had probably been told that there was some security issue. In this day and age, a brief warning was all the information people needed to evacuate. Thinking: terrorists, a crazy man with a gun, a bomb.

Eyes still on the front door, Shaw noted Ian Helms walk quickly outside; he wouldn't want to be connected to whatever was going to happen.

Braxton stationed herself at the front door, while rodent-faced Droon spoke urgently to the two security men, who towered over him. They hurried to the central station where the librarian pointed to a large monitor, which was probably now in security camera mode. They'd be scanning the vids recorded in the past half hour and would soon know that he was still on the main floor.

Shaw noted that the elevator light went out. It had been shut down.

And what about a run to the stairs and then out the upper floor windows?

Shaw dismissed it as having only a twenty percent chance of success, at best. A leap from a second story isn't impossible, given a landing zone of grass or trash, but Shaw had observed that the surfaces on all four sides of the building were sidewalk, asphalt or cobblestones. That would have meant a likely sprained ankle. The resulting pain wasn't the problem—he'd suffered worse—but that injury would have limited his ability to flee and left him a sitting target for Droon and the others. And you had to land perfectly to avoid a broken bone, and **that** pain was debilitating. Besides, the windows were probably sealed, as they were on this floor.

A jump from the roof was not an option at all.

Keeping in the shadows against the back wall, he considered the front door once more. Five to ten percent. To reach it he'd have to go past Droon, Blond and the two armed guards. Maybe the librarian was armed too. And he supposed that that exit was now locked down.

The windows? He gave that escape route ten percent tops. The glass was thick, intruder-proof. A chair would take multiple blows and Droon and the others would be on him well before the pane shattered.

A 911 call?

Ashton certainly was unreasonably paranoid

about many things, but Shaw recalled the note the man had left in the safe house:

Don't trust anyone. Some local authorities—SFPD, others—on Black-Bridge payroll. Evidence should go to D.C. or Sacramento.

Besides, even if the police officers who showed up were legit, Shaw would have to explain what his suspicions about the company were, and at this point he wasn't able to expose BlackBridge—not without Gahl's hard evidence.

He'd also have to answer for making an emergency call when there was no apparent threat of violence, and Braxton would deny everything. She'd report him as a dangerous trespasser.

He'd put a call to police/fire down as a last resort and try some other way to get out.

He decided that he would get to the fire exit. He put this at a seventy percent chance of success. Since the door opened onto that side street, he couldn't run directly to his cycle; that would mean crossing in front of the library. The hostiles would see and simply hurry from the front door to intercept him.

No, once on the side street he would turn right, away from his Yamaha. A half block away he'd turn right again onto another narrow street he recalled from the map he'd studied earlier. He'd continue on this for three or four blocks, where he'd come to a park surrounded by businesses and restaurants. There he could vanish into crowds and continue north, then cut east and finally south and get to the motorbike without approaching the library.

Shaw was a good runner. Ashton had trained the children in the art of both sprinting and long-distance running, using as models the famed tribal runners, the Tarahumara in Mexico and the Sierra Madres.

He was sure he could out-sprint scrawny Droon and the musclebound Blond.

The other guards? The tall one couldn't be a runner; he was too stocky. The slighter one? Maybe he was fast.

Shaw couldn't dodge their bullets of course, and the big unknown factor was: Would they risk drawing and using their weapons in public? Probably.

Which is why the fire door escape offered only a seventy percent chance of success.

He looked through a gap in a row of insurance industry books. Braxton stood at the door to the lobby, scanning the first floor, arms crossed. Droon and Blond started walking toward the stacks on Shaw's left, as he faced them. The security guards remained together and began the right-side flanking movement.

Shaw slipped to the fire door.

PUSH BAR. ALARM WILL SOUND.

Shaw hoped it wasn't like the emergency exits at airports; with those, pushing the bar resulted in a blaring alarm, but the lock didn't unlatch for fifteen seconds—to give security a chance to approach and see who wanted to get out onto the tarmac.

He took a deep breath, readying himself for the sprint.

A firm push on the bar of the fire door.

The bar traveled all the way to the base of the device, without resistance. Nothing happened. There was no alarm, and the lock didn't disengage.

The mechanism had been disabled.

Shaw fished the safe house keys from his pocket and tried to jimmy the lock. It didn't work. He tried the slimmer motorcycle key. Nothing.

He slipped into a workstation and looked out from underneath. The net was closing. He could see legs and shoes. The four hunters would converge on him in minutes.

Time for the last resort. He glanced at a nearby wall and, in a crouch, hurried to it and knelt, directly underneath the fire alarm box.

His right hand snaked upward aiming for the alarm.

"Now, lookee here." The voice behind him was singsongy, eerie because of its phony cheer. Ebbitt Droon continued, "We shut that little old alarm thing down too, don'tcha know? All in honor of you, Mr. Colter Shaw."

10

Droon and Blond were now joined by the two security men.

Rising, Shaw looked over Blond, whose cold eyes were the shade of ebony, suggesting that the shocking yellow of his hair came not from genes but a bottle. Shaw had seen eyes like that before: he'd earned a reward of twenty thousand dollars by tracking down an escaped serial killer near Tulsa. Once in handcuffs the man had stared at Shaw with a look that said: If I ever escape again, you're next on my list. Blond's gaze was of the same species.

Droon said, "So here you are, Mr. Didn't Listen to What I Told Him. And not more than a couple of weeks ago, wasn't it? Heavens. You are something else."

Shaw fired a focused gaze at Droon. The scrawny

man—the gangs would describe him as a **skel**—
wasn't the one who had grappled with his father on
Echo Ridge, combat that resulted in Ashton's death,
but he worked for the organization that was responsible and this made him as guilty as the killer, in
Shaw's mind.

Droon squinted back and his haughty impishness
vanished. He looked away.

Shaw surveyed the area, checking left then right.
His eyes made a leisurely circuit. Sizing up the
guards and Blond.

Droon's confidence returned. He repeated, "Coupla weeks. During which you had plentya time to
muse over what I said, about you keeping out of
our matters here. But didn't take, looks like. How
come?"

The upper Midwest patois was pronounced and
what he brought to the sound was the tone of the
unstable.

"Who's getting into whose space, Droon? Answer
me this. You **were** in Tacoma just a few days ago,
setting fire to somebody's perfectly nice SUV, just so
your boss could rob me."

The fire, which had engulfed a Nissan Pathfinder,
had been initiated to distract Shaw, so that Irena
Braxton could steal the phony map and the GPS-
rigged copy of **Walden.** Shaw now feigned irritation. He needed to keep on life support the façade
that the map and book weren't a setup.

Droon said, "Oh, think I'll plead my Fifth

Amendment right on that one, son, don'tcha know?"
He looked Shaw up and down. "Do say I'm sorry we
didn't get to go one-on-one. That would be a most
enjoyable five minutes." He glanced at Blond with a
wink. The big man beside him said nothing, those
dark marbles of eyes peering at Shaw. His arms, and
they were substantial, dangled.

The two security guards remained back five or
six feet.

Droon said to Blond, "The one I was telling you
about. Doesn't look so balls-out, does he? Told you."
A laugh. His bravado was fully recovered. Another
sweep over Shaw. "Now. Listen here. I see what
you're up to, the way you're calculating, looking
'round. Well, no cavalry's riding out of the hills to
save you. You're solo, and there it is.

"Now, without givin' too much away—always a
good rule in this life, don'tcha know? Without givin'
too much away, we're looking for a certain . . . **thing**,
let's call it. A thing that your daddy was looking for
too. And before he went to meet his sweet Maker I
think he found out where it was. Since you're here,
we're suspecting you've got some sound thoughts on
where it is."

Irena Braxton approached them, slipping away
her phone. He wondered whom she'd rung up so
urgently—and triumphantly—about his capture.

Droon nodded to her and continued, "We've
been visiting all sorts of fun and exciting places on
Daddy's map but we're not finding a single pearl in

the oyster. So we need some help-out, you know what I'm saying?"

Shaw frowned. "What exactly is it you're looking for, Droon? Tell me and maybe I can help."

Droon clicked his tongue. "For me to know and you to find out. Just fill in the details. Is there another map? Did Daddy find something else?"

"How can I tell you anything about the map since you stole it?"

"You made a copy, didn't you? Sure you did, a buttoned-up boy like you. You're on the treasure hunt too!"

He looked around the library. "You really think people don't know I'm here?"

Irena Braxton joined in. "No," she said. "Nobody knows you're here. Now, Colter." She was condescending in both tone of voice and her use of his given name, assuming the role of a mother or schoolteacher none too pleased with a youngster's behavior. "Stop the nonsense. Of **course** you made a copy. And we have your history." A nod at the computer terminal. "You searched **Amos Gahl**. So, no more games. We both know what's going on here. You've got some other leads. A man like you, a professional tracker after all. What do you people say? 'Hot on the scent.' So, tell me about those notes in your father's book. They're codes. We know they are."

Actually they were gibberish. But Shaw said, "The book you stole." Summoning faux indignity.

She offered a perplexed frown. "We can't make

heads or tails of it. We need you to decipher them. Your father writes in riddles."

"He's not writing anything now," Shaw said evenly.

Irritated, Braxton said, "As you've been informed, his death wasn't our intent. And the person responsible is no longer of this earth." She crossed her arms over her broad chest.

"That doesn't bring him back."

"This won't do, Colter. We've still got a half-dozen locations on the map to check out and you're going to help us. Amos Gahl stole something, and we have a right to it. He was our employee. You're aiding and abetting that crime."

"You got me. I confess."

Her eyes narrowed.

"Let's call nine-one-one. I'll give myself up."

The headmistress smiled kindly. "Once we have it, all the rough stuff goes away. And we're out of your life forever."

Shaw was eyeing his opponents even more closely than the matronly Braxton was studying him.

Droon displayed the want-to-smack-it-off grin. Blond was expressionless. He had a habit of flexing his fists. He'd been a boxer. But then, noting scars, Shaw decided that since boxing wasn't chic anymore, he'd probably be into bare-knuckle boxing or mixed martial arts. And when he killed—there was no doubt in Shaw's mind that he was a murderer—he did so without conversation. It was a job to complete; he'd kill, collect his check and get home, turning the pits of his eyes to TV or computer porn.

The other two, the guards in the suits, were uneasy. They didn't smack of military and had probably never seen combat. They were a threat, certainly, given their weapons, but they would be second-tier risks.

Braxton, as he'd decided before, was probably not a danger—unless that colorful purse of hers, macramé, of all things, held a Glock or Smith & Wesson.

The woman said to Droon, "We have that meeting tomorrow. I want to tell him something. Something concrete." She nodded to Shaw.

The petite, wiry man said, "Oh, I'll get something. He may not be in a talkative mood now. But that's gonna change. I guarantee it."

Braxton looked over Shaw. "Here's what's going to happen. We're going down to the basement and . . ."

Her voice faded as Shaw rubbed his eyes, shook his head slowly. He winced.

She gazed at him with curiosity, frowning.

"Not feeling all that great."

Droon muttered, "Why's that our concern, son, what you're feeling, what you aren't?"

Shaw closed his eyes and leaned against the wall.

"What's he doing?" one of the security men asked, the bigger one.

"Watch him," Braxton said.

"Let's get him downstairs," Droon said. He looked around. "This's gone on for too long." A glance at Blond. "You want a piece of him?"

The man with the bleached hair and the inky eyes said nothing but gave a brief nod.

Droon said to Braxton, "My man here gets good results."

She said to the security guards, "We'll be down there for an hour or two. No disturbances. Open the library back up. If anyone asks what happened, tell them it was a medical emergency. Nothing more than that."

"Yes, ma'am," said the bigger one. "We'll make sure."

Staring at Shaw, Droon asked no one, "The hell is he about?"

Shaw said, "Just . . . light . . . headed. Not feeling too well." He sagged and rubbed his eyes again.

"Jesus," Braxton said, angry. "Is he sick?"

"What're you doing?" Droon snapped. "What's he doing?"

"I'm dizzy."

Which wasn't an answer to the question. The true response was that Colter Shaw was engaging in the art of misdirection: keeping everyone's attention focused on his eyes, shoulders, torso, arms.

Not on his left foot.

Which was presently easing up the wall to the electrical outlet near the floor.

A paper clip protruded from one slot in the outlet,

another from the second slot, millimeters apart. He had taken them from the cubicle where he'd been just before he'd run to the wall. He had no intention of pulling the alarm, which he'd figured had been disabled too. What he wanted was to get to the wall and stick the paper clips, which he'd unfolded to triple their length, into the outlet.

Droon started toward him.

Still leaning against the wall, Shaw held up his hand. "Just give me a minute . . ."

Frowning, Droon paused.

Shaw pressed one paper clip into the other with the upper part of his left shoe.

The resulting spark and staccato bang, impressive, were like a firecracker detonating. Instantly the library went dark.

11

Droon and the security guards dropped into a crouch, looking around, not understanding what had happened.

"Shots!" the skinny man cried and ducked.

Shaw, protected from the current by his rubber soles, sprinted to the fire door.

"Wasn't a shot, you idiot," Braxton raged.

Shaw had taken a gamble—that the system overriding the latching mechanism of the emergency door would deactivate when power was lost.

Before Droon and the others could recover and pursue, Shaw grabbed a chair and then slammed into the exit bar with his hip. The door crashed open. He shoved it closed and wedged the chair back against the door handle, bracing it.

A shout. Shaw believed it was "Stop him!" He knew for sure it was Braxton's voice.

Shaw was tempted to run straight to his cycle but he kept to his original plan, turning to the right, away from the Yamaha, and sprinted full-out for the cross street. He heard a crash. It would be the fire exit door being muscled open and the chair that barred it flying into the street.

"Shaw!" Droon was shouting.

Shaw sprinted harder. At the side street, Morrison Lane, he turned to the right again.

And learned he'd made a mistake. Morrison did end at a park, but it was filled with people, who'd be in the direct path of any shots.

Then Shaw noted ahead of him an alley, on his left. He knew from the map that it would lead him to several parking garages, which he could weave through, giving him the chance to shake Droon and Blond. Shaw could then emerge and circle around to his bike—and his weapon.

Thirty yards until the alley.

Twenty, fifteen . . .

A glance back. No pursuers in sight yet.

Ten.

Five.

Before he got to the alley, he stopped and ducked behind a dumpster. He looked back at Droon and Blond moving in his direction. They were alone. The black-suited security people would have continued along the street on which the library was located.

Okay, into the alley . . .

He sprinted around the corner.

And stopped fast.

A dead end.

The alley was completely blocked by a construction site wall, ten feet high, plywood. The paint job—dark blue—was relatively new; only a few graffitied obscenities and gang tags marred the surface. This explained why the barricade had not been depicted on the map he'd examined in the safe house.

Shaw didn't bother to look for alternative forms of escape. The alley was doorless and windowless and though his father had taught him how to ascend walls of various heights and configurations, the technique for surmounting a ten-foot sheer surface was not part of the repertoire, not without rope or timber.

He'd no more than turned around when Droon and Blond stepped into the mouth of the alleyway.

Both were breathing hard and Blond winced with an apparent stitch in his side. He wasn't happy for the exercise.

Droon might have had a pain somewhere but he was also smiling broadly, as if Shaw's irritating attempt to escape had given the crazy man license to be particularly hearty—and creative—when it came to the torture that would follow.

12

Noting the absence of doors and windows opening onto the alley, Droon returned to the mouth and peered out. He looked up and down the street. His face revealed a hint of satisfaction, which meant no traffic, no pedestrians.

No witnesses.

He joined Blond once more. The two stood about twenty feet from Shaw. Neither was holding a weapon. They knew Shaw wasn't armed; he'd been through the metal detector. Blond now drew a silenced pistol. The SIG Sauer—a big, expensive and accurate gun—was pointed at the ground.

Blond: "We need a car."

Droon: "I'll text the Men in Black. They'll get one."

"Soon. Out in the open here. Don't like it."

Droon sent the message. He was grinning. "But maybe he'll cooperate 'fore they get here. And we'll just leave him be." He gestured toward Blond. They rolled the dumpster into the mouth of the alley, largely protecting them from view. Blond used only his left hand and kept the gun trained near Shaw. The safety was off, the finger outside the trigger guard. He knew what he was doing.

Shaw's impression was that neither man reported to the other. Blond, a facilitator like Droon, would also work for Braxton.

"Now, son, let's have ourselves a confab, don'tcha know?" He reached under his jacket and withdrew a knife from a camo scabbard. Shaw recognized it. Long, serrated. It was a SOG SEAL Team Elite fixed blade.

Looking around, Shaw judged angles and distances.

No good defensive solution presented itself, let alone an offensive one.

"Number one, that manuscript of your daddy's you so kindly let me have down in Silicon Valley coupla weeks ago, that was just a waste of good tree, wasn't it?"

Not for Colter Shaw, it wasn't. The four-hundred-some-odd-page stack of notes, maps, drawings and articles that Ashton had assembled was ninety-nine percent misdirection. But it contained the code that had directed Shaw to Echo Ridge, where he found the map and the letter that led to the Alvarez Street safe house and started Shaw on his mission here.

"I wouldn't know. You stole that from me too, didn't you? I never had a chance to read it. Did it have anything interesting in it?"

Shaw wondered if a passerby, someone in a window or on a rooftop, seeing a man with a gun, would call the police.

Droon was pointing the wicked blade Shaw's way. "How'd you find our library? Your daddy knew about it, did he?"

"Think he mentioned it."

"And you remembered that? From all those years ago?"

Blond said nothing. He was a block of wood, if wood could be attentive, suspicious and deadly.

Shaw told Droon, "I have a good memory. I'm lucky that way."

"Naw, naw. There's someplace here. Your daddy'd have a buddy in town you're staying with." He looked him over closely. "Or maybe a safe house all his own. Yep, betcha."

Somebody **must** have seen the pursuit and called 911.

But not a siren to be heard.

Not a ripple of flashing light to be seen.

Shaw was watching Blond. The big man's face was completely placid, as if were he to have any emotion that might distract him, that would lower his defenses. The eyes scanned constantly, the coal-black dots complementing the swarthy face, jarring with the sunburst of yellow hair.

Droon was a wild card. Blond was a pro.

Blond asked, "Where should we take him? The basement?"

"Library's compromised. I'd say the Tannery."

Not, of course, a place where you morphed into a beach bum under UV rays.

Droon sent another text and read the reply. He told Blond: "Irena'll meet us."

Shaw leaned toward the scrawny man. "Will Helms be there too? I hope so."

Droon was silent for a moment, unmoving, as if trying to process Shaw's interest and intent. "He went back to the hotel."

Not getting his hands dirty in sports like torture.

"But Irena's lookin' forward to our chat. As much as I am. Probably more. I do assure you, friend, that you will not like what's going to happen." He mimicked stabbing and twisting motions with the blade.

Shaw shrugged.

Droon thumbed the steel. "Everybody breaks, don'tcha know? Tell us what you've found out about Gahl and what he stole from us. You do that, and you're free to go. Get yourself a gelato."

"I don't like it," Blond said.

The rattish man glanced not toward his companion but toward Shaw.

"His eyes. He's working something. Doesn't look that bothered."

Droon said, "Checking stuff out, is all. He does that. The first time we met . . . Remember that, Shaw? I was having a laugh with a harmless little firebomb and you were sizing me up—and down and sideways. Every whichaway."

Blond muttered: "He's planning a move." He removed something from his inside jacket pocket. It appeared to be a thick rod of black metal, about a foot long. He said, "I cover him. You break something. Take him out of commission." He offered the bludgeon to Droon.

The man took it and slipped the knife back in its sheath. He nodded to the gun that Blond was holding. "Why not?"

"You need him alive. Don't want to risk a bleeder."

A pro's pro . . .

Droon seemed to agree. He hefted the rod and his expression reported that he liked the idea of breaking bones.

"Shaw, sorry t'have to do this. But, fact is, you just don't look desperate. You know what I'm saying? My word, you are the **least** desperate-looking person I have ever seen on this earth. You're not wasting time on worry; you're running through a big list. What can I do with this, what can I do with that?"

Pretty much.

There's not a lot an unarmed man can do in

combat against two opponents when one of them is holding a gun and the other a bone-breaking rod with a knife on his belt.

With some cheer, Droon said, "Man up. Hold your hand out and let's do this fast . . ." He cocked his head and gave an odd grin, which pinched his face. "Or, better idea, you can tell us what you know. And waltz around an icky bout of pain now followed by the main course—a trip to the Tannery with my knife."

"I don't know what you're talking about."

"Okay, hand out."

Shaw held his right arm out.

"Nup. Other one. You may need to write down your ABCs for us, draw a pretty map, or some such."

Shaw did as instructed.

He now incrementally shifted his balance, so that most of his weight was on his right leg. When Droon swung the bar, Shaw's right hand would move in an arc and clamp down on the man's wrist. The mass of the heavy rod meant the slim man's arm would be driven toward the ground and he'd be off-kilter. Shaw would then spin him sideways, turning him into a shield against Blond's weapon and executing a choke hold, rendering Droon largely nonresponsive.

Shaw's right hand would dip into the jacket for the pistol he hoped the man still had on him and draw. He wouldn't threaten Blond, tell him to drop the SIG. He'd just fire away. He'd aim for the gun arm and hand. He recalled where the safety was located on Droon's Beretta.

If Droon didn't have the gun, or if Shaw couldn't get to it instantly, he'd rip the bar from Droon's hand and fling it toward Blond's face, then break a wrist and pull the knife.

He and his siblings had been taught the art of knife throwing by Ashton. It was hard to hit your target with the point, but you could count on your enemy to be distracted by a spiraling razor-sharp blade. Shaw would charge Blond when he ducked and try to wrestle the SIG from his hand.

If not, as a last resort, he'd vault the dumpster. The other men didn't look like they could follow him in a leap. It would take some seconds to push the unit out of the way. He would turn back toward the library—the direction they would least expect him to run, and the one with the fewest innocents on the street.

Shaw plastered an expression of dread on his face as Droon stepped forward, hefting the metal. The facilitator's gaze was one of pleasant anticipation.

Four feet away, three feet . . .

Playacting again, Shaw said, "Look, let's work this out, can't we? Money. You want money?"

Droon was drawing back with the bar.

"Wait."

Droon was beaming. "Don't you go whining, there, boy."

Shaw was perfectly balanced, ready to move,

awash with the exhilaration that comes just before combat. Irrational, mad, intoxicating.

Which is when Blond said, "Stop."

Pausing, Droon turned.

"Get back. He's going to move on you. We'll do it this way." He looked down at his pistol.

13

Droon frowned. He clearly didn't see what Blond
saw. "He'd take you," the big man offered.

"I wouldn't be so sure about that, my friend."
But Droon stepped away from Shaw.

Blond said, "I'd risk a bullet. Top of the foot
shouldn't be much bleeding."

Shaw sighed.

Droon walked back to Blond, who lifted the gun
and pointed it at Shaw's foot. Now, he really meant
it when he said, "We can work something out. You
want information. I'll get you information."

Blond aimed carefully.

Even if he survived the Tannery, what would a
bullet wound do to his foot? Shattering the complex
bones of the appendage would render the Restless
Man disabled for a very long time.

Silencers do not, in fact, make a weapon completely mute. There's a distinctive **phhhht**, followed by the click of the gun's slide snapping back and then returning into position. Often you can hear the ring of the spent shell jittering on the floor or concrete or cobblestone, like what the men were standing on now.

Colter Shaw heard the first two of these, the muted gunshot and the click of the pistol as the gun reloaded for a second shot. He did not hear the dancing of the spent brass.

He did, however, hear another sound. The wet, smacking snap of a bullet hitting Blond's forehead. The big man gave no facial reaction to the impact. He simply dropped.

Shaw crouched. The gunshot had come from above and behind him—the shooter was in the air, maybe on some scaffolding on the other side of the wooden construction fence.

Droon's sense of survival kicked in. Not waiting to parse the situation he tore back to the street—and proving Shaw wrong—easily vaulted the dumpster. He landed and rolled, then righted himself and sprinted back toward the library.

Shaw immediately thought of the green Honda Accord, his shadow. Had the driver followed him here and been aiming at Shaw, but hit Blond by mistake? He leapt forward and rolled through the grimy alley, snatching up Blond's SIG Sauer pistol.

Rising, in a crouch, Shaw glanced at Blond—he

was dead—and drew back the slide of the SIG a quarter inch to make sure a round was chambered, something you always did with a weapon not your own.

He went prone behind the man's body—the only cover in the alley—and trained the weapon on the plywood construction site wall.

A man's voice called, "I'm not a hostile." Then to Shaw's surprise, the caller added, "Colter, I'm coming over the fence. Don't shoot."

He knows my name?

Something fell to the ground with a thud. It was a backpack, Oakland A's.

This would have to be the man he'd seen at the coffee shop up the street from the safe house on Alvarez—the bearded man in the thigh-length black coat and stocking cap. He climbed over the fence and landed lithely on the cobblestones, his low combat boots dampening the force.

Colter Shaw gasped. Which was something he had not done for years—since a piton gave way and he dropped twenty feet on a half-mile-high rock face before the safety rope arrested the fall.

He was not sure which shocked him the most at the moment: That he'd been saved from the fate of being shot with only seconds to spare.

Or that the man who'd done the saving was his long-lost brother, Russell.

14

Russell said, "I understand. You have questions. I do too. Later. First, this."

He was then on his phone, speaking in modulated yet commanding tones.

His brother was nearly identical in appearance to the man Shaw had last seen years ago at their father's funeral. He'd had a beard then, though it was shorter than this, as was his hair. These were two reasons Shaw hadn't recognized him near the safe house. Also, who the hell would expect the Reclusive One to be in San Francisco at the same time Shaw was?

The skin around the eyes was more weathered and ruddier. The beard was a uniform brown, without a touch of white or gray. The same was true for the tufts of straight hair protruding from the stocking cap.

One other difference between then and now: his eyes were presently cold, utterly inexpressive about the fact he'd just killed someone. Remorse, or even concern, let alone guilt, did not register.

"Help me here," Russell said, nodding toward the dumpster. Shaw noted his brother's voice was reminiscent of their father's. He was startled by the near mimicry, though he supposed he shouldn't be.

Shaw kept the muzzle of the SIG pointed away as he clicked the safety on and slipped the gun into his waistband—Russell glancing at him as he did so, apparently taking note that his younger brother had not forgotten their father's endless lessons and drills about weapons.

They pushed the dumpster out of the mouth of the alley.

Shaw was wondering why his brother had wanted to move the big contraption; doing so would expose Blond's body for any passerby to see. But the minute the dumpster was pushed aside and the alley was clear, a white van skidded to a stop in front of them and the side door slid open quickly.

Growing cautious, Shaw lifted the gun.

"They're mine," Russell said.

Three people climbed out.

Had the moment been less fraught—and confusing—Shaw might've smiled. He'd seen two of the trio earlier. One was Tricia, the woman in the street in front of the Alvarez Street safe house, and the man who'd attacked her—a verb Shaw put into mental quotation marks, since there'd been no assault at all, he now understood. Her screams for help had been merely a strategy to force Shaw outside and learn if he were a threat or not.

The broad-chested man had cleaned up considerably from his role as Homeless Man One. Russell introduced him as Ty. He glanced at Shaw without comment or other acknowledgment.

The third, whose name was Matt, was a slim, somber man of mixed race, with dark hair. His eyes scanned the alley and the street where the van was parked.

All three wore dark green jogging outfits and blue latex gloves.

A driver, whom Shaw could see only in silhouette, remained behind the wheel.

As Russell and Matt kept an eye on the side street, hands near their hips, Ty and Tricia—introduced now as Karin—stepped quickly to Blond's corpse.

Shaw said, "There're two other security people from the library. White. One heavy, one thin. Both armed. In dark suits, and—"

Karin said, "We know. They're in the parking garage on Harrison, picking up wheels. We have two minutes before they're here."

The phony attacker unfurled a body bag and he and Karin got to work with Blond. Soon the body was inside, zipped up tight.

"One, two . . . lift," the man said. The pair grunted simultaneously and hefted the weighty bag by the handles and began shuffling back to the van. Shaw thought about asking if they needed help but they didn't seem to. They were both quite strong, and—it appeared—had done this before. They got the bag to the van and muscled it inside.

Matt reached into the van and removed a broom and a spray bottle. He returned to the site of the shooting and spritzed liquid onto the bloodstain. The bullet would have been a hollow point, designed to expand in the brain, causing instantaneous lethal damage but remaining within the skull. Exit wounds created the biggest leaks.

He slipped the bottle into his slacks pocket and swept dirt and gravel over where the body had lain. This had some sort of procedural precision to it and was done to confound a crime scene crew, though Shaw doubted any police would ever investigate. Certainly Droon and Braxton would not be calling 911 to report that the BlackBridge employee had met his end.

"Give her the SIG."

Shaw withdrew the weapon and handed it to Karin grip first. She removed the magazine and the round in the chamber. She locked the slide back and then deposited the gun, the mag and the solo slug in a thick plastic bag. She put what seemed to be a damp cloth inside and sealed it up.

"My prints are on it," Shaw told her.

A faint, amused squint. Meaning: They won't be for long. Shaw wondered what the magic material was.

Broad Ty said, "Behind us. Hostiles."

An SUV was speeding toward them. Shaw could not see through the glary windshield but he supposed that Droon had been picked up by the two black-suited security guards earlier than he'd originally anticipated. The vehicle skidded to a stop and all three got out. They were trotting forward, cautiously, hands inside their jackets.

Russell nodded to Matt, who replaced the broom with an H&K submachine gun, mounted with a silencer. The man pulled the slide to chamber a round. He aimed toward Droon, who, with the others, fanned out, seeking cover behind trashcans.

Russell said, "No personnel. Vehicle only."

A muted chain saw of firing, and the slugs shredded the vehicle's grill. He'd been careful to group the rounds so that they didn't spill past the car and endanger anyone in the park.

Matt then joined the others, who were already in the van. Shaw slid the side door shut. He noted that it was particularly heavy and wondered if the panel was bulletproof. The vehicle's tires squealed loudly as the male driver, lean and dark-complected, steered, skidding, into the side street, away from the alley and the smoking SUV, and accelerated fast. Shaw held on tight. Russell made his way to the front passenger seat. Shaw and those in the back were

benched against the wall. Matt was looking over a
tablet. "No activity. We're good."

Russell said, "First his bike. Then the safe house
on Alvarez."

I understand. You have questions . . .

An understatement, if ever there was one.

15

"How'd you place me at the library? From the air?"
There were so many questions to ask. Shaw
wondered why he led with one of the least significant.

The two of them were alone in the safe house's
dining room, illuminated with an ethereal glow
from the windows, as the sunlight knuckled away
the pale pastel fog. They sat at a maple table, dinged
and scraped, a wedge under one leg for stability.

Reading a text or email on his phone, Russell said
absently, "Use drones some. Not in cities usually.
FAA and Homeland Security're problems."

"That right?"

His older brother seemed to be debating what to
say and what he shouldn't. "Mostly, we had you on
traffic and security cams. Algorithms. Handoffs."

A shrug. Meaning he didn't want to—or legally couldn't—be more specific.

Russell finished sending a message and rose and looked out the bay window in the front of the living room. Then he moved to the side windows and examined the view from there. It was limited. They admitted light only, as they faced a solid brick wall about ten feet away. Russell made a circuit to the back, where another bay overlooked the small garden, the alley and, beyond, an apartment that resembled Soviet-era housing. Shaw realized that there were no windows in any adjoining buildings—front, side or back—that faced the safe house. This would be one of the reasons why their father had selected it.

Shaw walked to the front window and peered outside. He could see quiet Alvarez Street and the burnt-down building across the way, the site of Tricia's, well, Karin's, supposed attack. He reflected that it was surprising no one had bought the lot and constructed residential property. The Mission was vastly popular and developers could make a killing. Then again, **could** was the operative word; San Francisco was a pressure cooker of a real estate market. You could go bust as fast as you could make ten-figure profits.

Shaw's eyes moved from the building to the streets nearby. He was scanning both for BlackBridge ops, despite Russell's associate's reassurance they were clear, and for the Honda, his tail.

His brother returned to the table. The stocking

cap was off and his dark hair wasn't **longish**; it was long, period.

"Does one of your people drive a dark green Honda Accord?" Shaw asked.

"No. Why?"

"Somebody was tailing me. They placed me here."

"No, not us, not part of my operation. You get the tag?"

"No."

Silence descended and now it was time for explanations.

Russell said, "Back there. Why were you targeted?"

"They weren't trying to kill me. They needed me alive. For the time being."

"Could see that. Angle of his aim. Still."

"They wanted information. I'll show you."

Shaw rose and from the kitchen gathered the material Ashton had left in the basement.

"This was in the secure room."

"Did you know about it before?"

"The room? No. All I had was the address."A glance around the living room. "But I knew what to look for. Remember, Ash taught us how to build one, make it blend in and dim the outside lights. He called it 'the camo of murk.'"

Russell's eyes narrowed, as a recollection arose— probably of the time Ashton had taught the three Shaw children how to build a disguised door for a hiding spot in the shed behind the cabin. He had told them, "Anybody can hide hinges and latches. The most important thing in fooling intruders is the **dust.** Dusty walls don't move." He taught them how to use rubber cement spray on the disguised door and surrounding panels and then shake a feather duster over the adhesive. Six-year-old Dorion had done the best job.

Russell said, "You missed the flash-bang. I got an alert."

"Careless. But at that point I didn't know anybody else had been here, and Ashton wasn't the IED sort."

"No. He wasn't."

"You know, some people use Ring or Nest for home security—not explosives."

Unsmiling, Russell shrugged, then nodded to the material on the table. "Saw that when I was here back a couple of years. Didn't mean anything to me. Assumed it was Ash's but you know . . . his rambling, the paranoia."

"Wouldn't mean anything without this." Shaw dug into his backpack and retrieved the letter their father had written about BlackBridge.

Russell read. "So BlackBridge's a dirty-tricks outfit. Never come across them before." Spoken in a tone that suggested he was more than familiar with such operations. "Where did this come from?" A nod at the letter.

Shaw hesitated. "He hid it on Echo Ridge."

The location where Shaw had convinced himself Russell had murdered their father.

His brother gave no reaction. "In the alley, they were all BlackBridge?"

"Right. The library was a front."

"I know that. When you went inside, I checked. Found out it wasn't connected to the university. And offshores don't own libraries. Not legitimate ones."

His resources were probably as good as Mack's. Most likely considerably better.

Russell looked over the letter once more. "Half of Ashton's worries were smoke."

"At least."

"Not this."

"No."

Shaw handed him the dead-drop note, written to their father by a sympathetic employee of BlackBridge.

> **Amos is dead. It's in a BlackBridge courier bag. Don't know where he hid it. This is my last note. Too dangerous. Good luck.**

"'It'? The evidence Ashton was talking about."

"That's right." Shaw waved at the rest of the material he'd brought up from the basement. "Not like this, not supposition and suggestion. Whatever Gahl found is enough to get indictments."

"Ash told us 'Never go to Echo Ridge. Terrain's not so kind.' But it wasn't any worse than anywhere else in the high country. Maybe he didn't want us going there because it was a dead-drop for him and his circle." Russell glanced at Shaw, who nodded his understanding of the spy term. His brother continued, "The letter was meant for one of his colleagues. How'd you find it?"

"Long story. Came across some clues that led me there."

"Any of the friends still around?"

"Maybe, but most are dead or in hiding. BlackBridge is good at arranging accidents."

Shaw didn't tell his brother that he believed the letter had been left not for a colleague but for him. It was he who had been given, and who deciphered, the clues that led to Echo Ridge—and ultimately to the safe house. It wouldn't have been impossible for a colleague of Ashton's to deduce where the letter and map had been hidden. But why situate a dead-drop three hundred miles from San Francisco, where most of their father's associates were?

"And BlackBridge, they're behind Ash's death?" Russell eyed Shaw closely. "At the funeral, the word was 'accident.' But back then I got the feeling you didn't think so."

Was there something in his brother's tone? Did he or did he not know Shaw had silently accused him of murdering their father?

A chill flowed through him. "No, I didn't." He hesitated. "Some things didn't add up. His shotgun, the Benelli, was nowhere near where he fell. And did you ever know him to lose his footing on rock, ice, snow, sand, gravel?" He was speaking quickly. Did he sound defensive as he threw out some of the reasons why he'd formulated the theory of patricide?

He felt Russell's eyes on him still, and he chose to meet the man's gaze. Shaw said, "A couple of weeks ago I learned for sure it was BlackBridge." He explained what Ebbitt Droon had told him about the company's operative coming to the Compound to "talk" with their father. "That is, **torture** him and get him to tell them where the evidence was hidden. Ashton tipped to the op and ambushed him. But he was no match for the BlackBridge man."

"Hmm."

Shaw wanted so badly to grab his brother by the shoulders and shout: I was young, **you** were secretive. I saw the fight you and Ash had. And you were evasive about where you were on the night he was killed. I was wrong. But was what I did reason enough for you to vanish from the family altogether? Do you know what that did to our mother, our sister?

To me . . .

But of course, Colter Shaw couldn't ask that question because the answer might very well be what he feared: Because I can't forgive you.

Before he could stop himself he said, "The Reclusive One." Was it a subconscious jab at his brother's disappearance?

"What?"

"Looks like your profession, whatever it is, it's kept you true to your name."

Russell squinted. "The nicknames. When we were kids. Reclusive. You were restless. Dorie was clever."

"You're using the house for some kind of operation. How did you know about it?"

"I was in San Francisco for some training, long time ago, and Ash said there was a house he used when he was in town. We met here. He gave me a key. My group has operations here from time to time, so I use it as a command post."

"Group?"

Russell said nothing.

It would handle government security of some kind, he guessed. But out of the mainstream. The FBI, CIA, DoD, NSA and most of the rest of the alphabet soup of government entities couldn't get away with shooting someone with a silenced pistol and making the body and accessories go away as if you were cleaning up a broken jar of pickles dropped on a kitchen tile floor.

Shaw said, "I looked at the paperwork in the secure room. It's classified?"

"Not anymore, I guess."

"That a problem?"

A pause. "Not really."

"You speak Chinese, Russian?"

He didn't answer, but obviously he did. Russell had had years to learn quite a few skills since Shaw had seen him last.

"We have a full security setup when we're active but we closed the file on that op early this morning. All the cameras and mics were packed up and gone."

Shaw could only laugh. "That was smooth. The assault outside. Karin and Ty."

"When the device went off I got a message. The secure room was compromised. And we had to find out who."

"You, Karin and Ty, you put the whole set together in minutes? The costumes, makeup."

Russell lifted an eyebrow. "What we do. We train for things like that. Improvise. And they were nearby. She was wearing a body cam. She started to run your picture through our facial recognition database, but . . ." He shrugged. "I saw the image. After, I put together a surveillance package on you."

Why? Shaw wondered.

A moment later, Russell asked, "So you're here because of Ashton and BlackBridge? There's no reward?"

Shaw must've reacted.

"You're in the news some."

So he was curious about me. But not curious enough to pick up the phone and give me or our mother a call.

"No reward. It's all about BlackBridge."

Russell's look conveyed a question: But why?

Shaw: "I know what Ashton said. 'Never pursue revenge. It goes against the grain of survivalism.'"

"Was thinking that, yes."

"Well, this isn't revenge. It's finishing what he started. His mission."

There was really nothing more to add.

16

Russell sent a text on his elaborate phone. It was a brand that Shaw had never seen before.

He regarded his brother's luxurious beard. You'd think it would be a problem in clandestine work, if that's what Russell engaged in. He'd be instantly recognizable. Maybe he was famous in his field, though, and he sported the facial hair as a trademark.

His brother's phone hummed.

"Nothing in our system about Urban Improvement Plan or Amos Gahl," said Russell. He put the phone away. "Basic information about BlackBridge but they're not flagged with any red notices."

Shaw imagined his brother had access to a database that was exceedingly robust.

"Appreciate you checking. This group of yours . . . can you tell me?"

"No."

"Just 'group' with a lowercase 'g.'"

"What we go by." After a pause Russell asked, "You always use the Yamaha in your work?"

Shaw explained about living in the Winnebago but renting cars on his jobs to stay unobtrusive. Much of the rewards business is surveillance and questioning witnesses, and nothing blended better than a black Avis or Hertz (he picked that color because it gave the impression he was law enforcement, though he never said he was). "Still might rent a car here. Depends on the weather."

Russell took a call. He listened for a moment. He said, "That's right. Tell them it's closed permanently." He disconnected.

Silence drifted between them.

Shaw asked, "You have a family? Anyone in your life?"

"No. You?"

He thought of Victoria. "No."

"I heard you were married."

He thought of Margot. "No."

Roiling silence. Russell checked his phone once more.

"Dorion's good," Shaw told him.

"I know. I saw her and the girls last month."

"**Saw** them?" Shaw couldn't keep the surprise from his voice.

"I saw **them**. They didn't see me."

"Last I heard, at the funeral, you were in L.A."

"Based there. Near there."

The chitchat depressed Shaw and appeared to bore Russell.

All these years they hadn't seen each other, and this was the best they could do?

"Another question," Shaw asked.

Russell lifted his eyebrow.

"Why the hell the Oakland A's?" Shaw glanced at his brother's backpack.

No response to the levity.

The children had laughed a lot growing up. With very few other friends their age, they relied on one another for amusement and diversion.

Another blister of silence, then Russell said, "Need to get my team out of here."

"So you're leaving." Shaw had tried to keep his expression neutral. He wasn't sure he was successful.

"Assignments we're scheduled for. It's a busy time."

Spoken like a department store buyer planning for Christmas shopping season.

"Sure."

Russell walked down to the cellar and returned a moment later with the duffel bag. The sun had burned away the last tatters of fog by now and the water bottles bent the light, pasting fracturing shapes of brilliant white on the plaster walls.

His silent message resonated like a siren

through the pleasant, yellow room: Your fight with BlackBridge isn't my fight, even if the company killed our father.

Shaw tipped his head. "Don't need to say I appreciate you showing up when you did."

Russell reciprocated the nod.

Shaw tried: "You want to give me a phone number?"

"We get randomly generated ones once a month."

Shaw wrote down his number in one of his notebooks. He didn't tear off the page and hand it to his brother. He held it up.

Russell looked for about ten seconds. He nodded.

Was it memorized, or discarded?

Shaw thought once more: Confess now. Tell him that I was wrong to accuse him of murder . . .

But no. This connection with his sibling might grow into something in the future—maybe Russell had indeed tucked the phone number away. But right here, right now, it was so very fragile. Gram for gram, the strands of a spider's web are stronger than steel. But it takes no more than a gust of wind, not even one so fierce, or the transit of a broom in the hands of a busy housekeeper to bring the creature's home, world and perhaps life to an abrupt end.

Shaw said, "It's good to see you're okay. I'll tell Mary Dove."

"Do that." His brother walked to the door and let himself out.

17

Shaw fished in his backpack. He left his personal iPhone there and pulled out a burner. If he was concerned that his calls might be monitored, he used this one—an Android with some Linux kernel modifications for added encryption and security.

The call he was making now had nothing to do with BlackBridge or the UIP or Amos Gahl. Still, under the circumstances he wanted all the security he could get.

"Hello?"

"It's me."

"Colt." The woman's voice was, as always, low, steady. "You're at the house?"

"That's right. It's a safe house. Ash had a hidey-hole in the basement. I found more relevant material. Haven't made too much headway yet."

There was a pause. His mother was in effect saying: What else? Because there was obviously something else.

"I wanted to let you know. I saw him today.
Russell."

"My God . . ." Mary Dove's whisper tapered to
silence. She was a woman to whom the word **surprised** could rarely be applied. "He's all right?"

"Yes." Shaw was sipping coffee, tamed with milk,
slowly. It was very hot.

"That answers the big question. He's alive."

All these years the family had not known whether
Russell was still of this earth.

"How'd that come about?"

He explained that his older brother too had
known about the house on Alvarez and used it occasionally.

"Yes, that's right. Ash mentioned he'd seen Russell
in San Francisco once or twice."

"He's with the government, it looks like. CIA sort
of operation, though not them."

"What does he do for them?"

"Intelligence of some sort."

He did not tell his mother about Blond's fate.

Her lack of response might have been a hum of
skepticism about his answer.

"It's called the group. Not a formal name." Silence
again. Then: "He seemed . . . okay. Good at his job."

"And he's—"

"Gone. An assignment. Couldn't tell me what."

A very rare sigh. "That boy . . . I never knew exactly what was going on in his mind. Remember? He'd spend days in the woods? And not part of Ash's training. I'd wake up, get the coffee and biscuits going and find that he'd left before first light, with rations and his weapon."

Her resonant voice was painted with discontent and for a moment Shaw regretted telling her about crossing paths with his brother. Maybe her hopes had been up momentarily that he'd return for a visit. "Well. He's who he is. But . . . did he say **why** he vanished, all these years?"

In honesty Colter Shaw could tell his mother, "No, he didn't." Because Russell had not spoken of his profound disappointment that the younger brother had silently accused the older of murder.

"It's going well, the search?"

"Good."

"A mother's got to say, 'Be careful.'"

Shaw chuckled.

Then Mary Dove said, "Glad you told me about your brother. Imagine you were debating letting me know. But it was the right thing." Then her tone changed and she said, "Anybody else you want to say hey to?"

"Matter of fact . . ."

"Hold on."

18

"Hi." Victoria Lesston's voice was also low, and there was a particular tone about it. Shaw tried to think of what the analogy to describe it might be. Then it occurred to him: a musical instrument. In particular, he refined: a cello, rich and resonant. In the middle strings range only.

"Tacoma was interesting. Got robbed and I'm responsible for a Nissan Pathfinder burning down to the rims. No injuries."

"Never dull with you, is it, Colt? What'd they get?"

"I'll go into it later. In person."

She laughed airily. "Sooner, not later, I hope."

Shaw pictured her deep-gray eyes and her ringlets of hair, which morphed from pale brunette to dark blond according to the whim of the sun or moon.

"The big news: my brother surfaced."

"Really? You said you weren't even sure he was alive."

"He's doing some kind of clandestine work. Think he needed to stay undercover."

"Like those KGB agents."

"Maybe something like that."

"When you're finished, will he come down here with you to see your mother?"

Thinking no, he said, "Maybe."

Her voice lowered. "How are you dealing with it?"

Not a question he was prepared to respond to. "Still surprised." He asked how she was feeling.

The beat told him she recognized, and respected, the deflection. "All good here. Your mother is pretty much amazing."

He had met Victoria a week ago, on a mission he'd had to the wilds of Washington State. The incident had started as a reward assignment but had soon turned into an undercover operation, which he'd undertaken, in part, to save Victoria from an enigmatic organization that might or might not have been a dangerous cult.

She'd been injured in a fall from a cliff's edge into a lake. A former Delta Force officer, Victoria was in fit shape and while the fall might have killed another person, she survived with only minor harm. Shaw had suggested she might want to return to the Compound where his mother, a general practitioner MD, as well as a psychiatrist, could help her with physical therapy.

Shaw had another reason to ask her to the homestead, and she apparently had a similar motive in accepting his invitation; he remembered their lengthy kiss outside her bedroom the night before he left on the drive that ultimately led him here to the safe house.

"Where are you?"

"The Western Hemisphere. Maybe."

Even with the encryption, he was reluctant to be too specific.

Never assume your conversations are private . . .

"You're a stitch, Colter. Your mother sometimes calls you 'Colt.' Which do you like?"

Their courtship, if you could call it that, had been intense (a knife fight—between them—had figured) but they really hadn't known each other all that long.

"Either's good."

"Any excitement yet?"

"Not so much."

"Keep me posted on that."

"Most definitely."

"How do you like your pheasant?" Victoria asked.

"Never been asked that before." This was true. He considered. "Probably rarer than weller."

"I agree. Mary Dove and I're cooking tonight. A bird she got last season."

"You hunt?"

"I have but the last time I got pheasant was a couple years ago."

"What's your scattergun?" He was thinking of his father's wonderful Benelli Pacific Flyway, with a chrome receiver. An elegant weapon.

"I don't have one."

"What'd you borrow?"

"I didn't use a shotgun," she said.

"I don't think you can legally use a rifle on birds. Not in California."

"It wasn't in California and I didn't use a rifle."

"You didn't use a rifle?"

"Colter, how many times are you going to keep asking me questions I've already answered."

"Well, what did you use?"

"My Glock. The seventeen."

"In the air?"

"Of course, you can't shoot a bird on the ground. And it wasn't quick-draw Annie Oakley or anything like that. I was already holding the weapon."

"How many . . ." His voice faded.

"Rounds did I use, you were going to ask?"

He'd stifled the insulting question, but yes, that was what he was going to ask. Her Glock would hold seventeen rounds and you could probably get off three a second, aiming carefully.

Then he noticed she was silent once again.

Finally Victoria said, "It was one."

He reminded himself not to ask: A single shot?

Shaw was talented with sidearms but he didn't think he could hit a flying bird with either of his pistols and never with one shot.

"I mean, I aimed. I wasn't firing from the hip. Anyway, I agree: rare is best. Pheasant's lean. Dries out when you cook it too long. When are you back?"

"Hope it's not more than a couple of days."

"You need any help, I'm feeling better."

Victoria ran her own security consulting firm, based out of Southern California.

"I'll keep that in mind."

"You know, Colt, there are two kinds of people in the world."

Living/dead. Blond/brunette. Short/tall. Liberal/Conservative. Sexy/not so much. He did not, of course, say this, but replied with: "Okay?"

"Those who keep something in mind when they say they're going to keep something in mind. And those who have no intention of keeping something in mind when they say they're keeping something in mind."

"I'm the first type."

"I had a feeling you were. But I liked hearing you say so."

They made conversation for ten minutes or so, then he was eager to get on the trail of the BlackBridge evidence. He told her he'd better go. "I'll call you soon."

"You know, Colt, there are two types of people in the world . . ."

He laughed and said goodbye and they disconnected.

The two of them were similar in many ways. She was nearly as itinerant as he was, and as much of a calculated risk-taker. They shared a wry humor and an intolerance for bullying and stupidity. They'd certainly developed a rapport in Washington State and it didn't hurt that not only had he saved her life, but that she'd saved his.

And that kiss . . .

The relationship had a way to progress on that slippery, serpentine road on which matters of the heart pace before certain things could be said and asked.

This was fine with him. He was in no hurry. Velocity in love, like velocity on the motocross course, had in the past occasionally gotten Colter Shaw into trouble.

Best for restless men to take things slowly.

19

S haw told himself: assess.

He was in the kitchen of the safe house. He'd supplemented Mack's research on the two leads as to where Amos Gahl might have hidden the BlackBridge evidence. Morton Nadler, who owned the house in Burlingame that his father had been interested in, was retired. He had spent most of his working life as a management-level employee at San Francisco airport. What was his connection to Gahl? Would he have left Nadler the evidence to keep safe? Or was Nadler the **source** for incriminating information about BlackBridge, maybe because of his connection to the airlines and private aircraft?

The other spot, the Haywood Brothers Warehouse in the Embarcadero, had survived the Great San Francisco Earthquake of 1906. It had not been a functioning warehouse for some years, which did not bode well for Shaw's mission. Probably the building had been emptied out and if Gahl had hidden anything there the evidence would likely be in some other facility or, more likely, a landfill. Because the building was for sale, there was a representative on-site, from whom Shaw might learn something.

His Android hummed. He pressed ANSWER and before he could say a word there came: "You into coincidences, Colt?"

The voice was a grumbling baritone. Caller ID told Shaw who the person on the other end was but even if it hadn't he would've known with the first syllable. Teddy Bruin was a former Marine who—along with his wife, former soldier Velma—ran the business side of Shaw's reward operation. They lived beside Shaw's property in Florida, though he'd seen them just the other day; they were on a road trip out West and had spent a few days at the Compound with Shaw, Victoria and Mary Dove.

A call from the Bruins meant one of two things: He had failed to collect a reward check, which usually happened because the offeror turned out to be on hard times.

Or they'd just learned of an offer.

"Coincidences?" Shaw queried.

"Three weeks ago, give or take, that offer in Silicon Valley, that girl? Father worried about her?"

"Right."

The reward that sent him deep into the world of

the video gaming industry. A missing student had been kidnapped, it appeared, by a perp who was acting out a violent video game in real life.

"Well, we got a replay." Teddy chuckled. A joke on the game motif, Shaw noted. Teddy looked and sounded scary but he had quite the sense of humor.

"Hi, Colter." A woman's voice, as melodious as her husband's was raw.

"Velma. Where are you two?"

"Reno. I have a roll of quarters and I'm not coming home until I win back all the gas we spent on the drive here."

The couple owned a Winnebago that was the size of Shaw's—a thirty-footer. It would take a string of jackpots to make that miracle happen.

"She's convinced that the odds're better with the slots in Reno than Vegas. You know, to attract tourists. Second-city kinda thing."

Shaw wouldn't know. He didn't gamble.

His eyes on his father's documents, he said, "Replay?"

Teddy: "Single **mom** this time, not dad. But another missing daughter. Mother's a widow. And the girl's older than the one a couple weeks ago. Twenty-two or -three."

Not only did the Bruins themselves scan social media and law enforcement posts for announcements of rewards, but they supervised a software program that sniffed out offers too. Velma had named it Algo after **algorithm**. "Where?"

"Why we're a-calling. San Francisco."

"Got a lot on the platter here."

"I know, Colt," Teddy said. "But a couple things. I'll just throw 'em out there. The reward? It's for seventeen fifty."

"You mean seventeen thousand, five hundred."

"No, I mean seventeen **hundred** and fifty buckaroos."

Very low for a missing child. And the low sum meant the mother had scraped together every penny she could.

"The other thing?"

"The offer," Velma told him. "Listen to what she posted online. I'm quoting: 'Please, please, please help!!!' A bunch of exclamations here. 'Tessy, love of my life, has gone missing in San Francisco. I'm sick with worry over her. I'm offering a Reward. I've started a GoFundMe page to raise more. Please.' More exclamation points. Then a picture of her. Sweet kid."

Shaw's experience was that parents rarely posted a shot of demonic-looking children. "That kind of money, nobody'll go to the trouble to look for her."

"Exactly."

Shaw looked at his father's map with the eighteen red **X**s on it.

"When was it posted?"

"Couple days ago."

Before BlackBridge knew he was in town, so it wouldn't be a trap.

He looked at the notes in such delicate and perfect script:

**Haywood Brothers Warehouse, the
Embarcadero
3884 Camino, Burlingame**

After a moment he said, "Send me the offer."

They said goodbyes and a few seconds later his
phone dinged with Maria Vasquez's reward notice.
He read through it once. Shaw started to read it once
more and put the mobile down. He thought: Why
bother? Either you're going to do it or you're not.

Please, please, please help

Followed by a bunch of exclamation points.

20

One question was answered.

Maria Vasquez, mother of the missing woman, lived in the heart of the TL.

This explained the low sum she was offering for information about her daughter. Very few residents of San Francisco's Tenderloin would be able to come up with a big enough reward to snag anyone's attention.

The neighborhood, in the central part of the city, was infamous. Seedy, dilapidated, graffitied, marred by trash-filled streets and sidewalks, the TL was home to street people, those working in the sex trade—traffickers among them—gangs and those involved in all phases of drug enterprises: manufacturers, transporters, sellers and, of course, consumers. The SFPD has defined more than six hundred "plots," small geographic areas of the city, for the purpose of analyzing crime stats. Seven of the ten most dangerous plots in San Francisco were in the TL.

Shaw hadn't been here for years. Back then the place was filled with single-room occupancy hotels and small shabby apartments, adult bookshops, massage parlors, bodegas, Asian and Filipino grocery stores, tobacco/vaping places, cell phone card and wig shops and nail salons.

Much of that atmosphere persisted to this day but Shaw now saw a few nods toward improvement. Outreach programs operated out of storefronts, helping runaways, trafficking victims, addicts. There was even some gentrification, albeit modest. Across the street from Maria Vasquez's walk-up was a ten-story apartment building that offered studio and one-bedroom units, which the poster described, with an inexplicable hyphen, as DE-LUXE. There was a Starbucks wannabe on the ground floor, along with an art gallery and a wine bar. Changing . . . but not changed: the windows on the first two floors of most buildings along this block were covered with thick iron security bars.

He chained his bike and helmet to a lamppost then walked to the door of the apartment building. He pressed the intercom and, when a woman answered, he said, "I called earlier. About the reward you posted."

"You're—"

"Colter."

The door buzzer sounded and he stepped inside and climbed to the third floor, smelling fresh paint, garlic and pot. He knocked on the door of 3C. He heard the creak of footsteps and she answered.

Maria Vasquez looked him over cautiously, eyeing the leather jacket and jeans and boots.

In most assignments, when meeting with offerors he wanted them to see him as a professional—part lawyer, part detective, part psychologist. His garb would be sport coat, laundered jeans, polished shoes, dress shirt in dark shades. Not an option now, not with the Yamaha.

She'd have to deal with the reward-seeker as biker.

Something about his face, perhaps, put her at ease, though. "Come in. Please, come in."

Vasquez, in her forties, was about five eight or nine, a pretty face and trim figure. Her dark features suggested blood from Mexico.

The one-bedroom apartment was nicer than he'd expected. The furniture was cheap but the walls had been painted recently—and were hung with bold floral posters and a half-dozen fine-arts photographs, reminiscent of the work of the famous West Coast photographers of the mid-twentieth century: Ansel Adams, Edward Weston, Imogen Cunningham.

She asked if he wanted anything to drink and he declined. They sat and the woman held her hands to her face. "Oh, it has been a terrible year. Such a terrible year. My husband, he died without insurance, and I lost my job. I was a receptionist at a tech company." A cynical grimace. "Big start-up! Oh, we were going to all be millionaires. They promised everything. Stock bonuses. All that. It went under. I've been doing **that** since then." She waved toward a pink waitress's uniform. "We lost our house. And the bank owns it and still they're suing us! I never wanted a big house in the first place. But Eduardo . . ." She shook her head, as if exhausted at replaying the car crash of her last twelve months. "And now this."

Tears formed, and she found a tissue in a battered, cracked beige purse with an old-style clasp on top. She blotted her eyes.

From a pocket in his leather jacket, Shaw extracted one of the 5-by-7-inch notebooks in which he jotted information during interviews like this. His handwriting, like his father's, was extremely small and precise. The notebooks were not ruled but each line of his script was perfectly horizontal.

He used a Delta Titanio Galassia fountain pen. The barrel was black and it featured three orange rings toward the nib. Occasionally an offeror or a witness might glance at the pen, which was not inexpensive, as if using it were pretentious or showy. But this wasn't the case. The pen was largely practical; filling page after page of notes in Shaw's minuscule script was tough on the hand and the gold-tipped fountain pen eased words onto the paper smoothly and with less effort than the best ballpoint. It was also a pleasure to use the fine device.

Someone once asked him why he didn't just use a tape recorder or at least type answers into a computer or tablet. His response: Speaking or typing creates just a glancing relationship with the words. Only when you write by hand do you truly possess them.

Shaw said, "Let me tell you who I am and what I do. You can look at me like a private investigator that you don't pay until I'm successful. I'll try to find your daughter. If I do that, you pay me your reward. You don't have to pay for any expenses."

A reward is, under the law, a unilateral contract. The offer is made but there is no enforceable bargain until one party—the reward-seeker—successfully completes the job. Then an enforceable contract comes into existence.

Vasquez nodded. "Yes, sir."

"Tell me what happened."

"Two days ago Tessy was gone when I got home from my shift. She was supposed to be at work at six but she didn't show up. Her phone doesn't ring. It just goes to voice mail. She didn't show up for work that night. I called her friends . . . Nobody's heard from her."

"Was she going someplace before work?"

"I don't know. She played guitar with friends some."

He asked if she'd talked to the police.

At this she grew silent for a moment. "Not yet. I heard with someone who's older, the police won't be interested for a few days."

They **might** be interested. But what she was really saying was: mother and daughter were undocumented and the cops might report them to Immigration and Customs Enforcement. That was a big concern he'd found in the immigrant community; while some police departments might not report them, by federal law they were required to.

"Did you have a fight? Did she run off?" The most common cause of missing youngsters.

"Oh, no, no. We are very close. We never fight. She's the love of my life!"

Parental kidnappings were the most common form of abduction. Even with children above the age of majority, like Tessy, a mother or father might coerce the youngster to come live with him or her. More and more were living at home until later in life nowadays. Vasquez was a widow but the general principle could apply.

"Have you had a partner or someone you're seeing who might've had an interest in her?"

She gave a laugh. "I work twelve-hour days, two shifts. That is the **last** thing on my mind."

"So you think someone forced her to come with them."

She sat forward, her hands shredding the tissue. "Here's what I'm worried about, sir. Tessy had some drug problems a few years ago. She fought it and won. She goes to meetings. She's a good girl. But there was this man, older. They dated. Mostly she went out with him because he supplied her. After she got sober, her sponsor told her she couldn't see him anymore. She broke up with him. He got furious. He stalked her."

"When?"

"Six months ago."

"What's his name?"

"All I know is Roman. I think it's a nickname."

"Address?"

Vasquez shook her head.

"Arrests?"

"Probably. I think so."

"Describe him."

"He's about thirty, no, probably more. Not tall, slim. Has a shaved head. Or he did. He's white but has a darker skin. There's a tattoo of a cross on his neck. An old-fashioned cross. Like the ancient times."

Shaw took a few moments to jot these notes. Then he asked, "Where does she work?"

"In a folk music club, in North Beach."

Shaw got the name.

"Every time I look at those, I want to cry." She waved at the photographs on the wall.

"She took those? She's talented."

A nod. "She studied, art school. And she can sing too. She has a nice voice."

She looked out the window. Her jaw was tight. "I wasn't there for her like I should have been. So expensive here . . . Working two jobs, both Eduardo and me. We weren't there . . . She got into trouble."

She touched a finger to a lower lid and examined it—for running mascara. Of which there were some streaks. She grimaced and, taking a compact mirror from her purse, examined the damage and blotted some of the stain away.

Her hands were delicate, her skin smooth. She must have been in her early twenties when the girl was born.

Shaw asked questions he'd developed over the years in cases involving missing young people and jotted down her answers in his distinctive hand-writing.

Friends' names and numbers. There was no find-my-phone app on her mobile. The phone was in her name, so her mother couldn't have the phone company ping it; only the police could and even then only with a warrant. Tessy had one of her mother's credit cards, but she hadn't used it.

"When was your last contact?"

"A phone call. She left a message. I couldn't pick up." Her lip trembled. She'd be thinking that maybe it was the last chance she would have had to speak to her daughter.

"Play it."

She did. They heard a light, cheerful voice chatting briefly and saying she'd call later. She was outdoors, on a noisy street.

Shaw asked, "Can you send it to me?"

She didn't understand. "Send . . . ?"

He explained, "You can save a voice mail as a WAV file."

"A wave?"

"**W-A-V**. It's a sound-recording format. You can save it on your phone. Google it. It's easy to do. Then email the recording to me." He gave her his address: ColterShawReward@gmail.com.

She said she would.

"I'd like to see her room."

"She doesn't have one. She sleeps here—on the pullout."

"Any personal effects? Papers, computer?"

She waved around the sparsely furnished place. "Most everything of ours is in storage in Mountain View. Where we had the house that was foreclosed."

"I think I have enough to get started. I'll need a photo. A better one than you posted online."

She didn't have any hard copies but she uploaded one to his phone.

The young woman, with long dark hair, was striking. High cheekbones, broad lips and big eyes, deep brown.

"Has anyone else called about the reward?"

"A couple of people." Her voice lowered. "They were just assholes. They didn't know anything. Just making stuff up about her being here or there so they could get the money."

"That happens. All right. I have other projects going on. But I'll do what I can."

She shook his hand warmly. "Thank you, Mr. Shaw."

"Colter."

"Thank you. Bless you." She touched the silver crucifix at her throat. Then said brightly, "It's more now."

"More?"

"What I can offer. I looked at the GoFundMe page an hour ago. People've contributed another $234. And I'm praying that there'll be more."

Shaw said, "Let's find her first. We'll worry about that later."

21

Never be blunt when subtle will do . . .

Colter Shaw was adept at guile. He liked outthinking the criminals he was pursuing, liked strategizing against the geography, the elements, the forces that conspired to keep him from finding a missing person.

But sometimes you just had to throw clever to the wind and go for it.

Blunt . . .

When he stepped out onto the pungent street in front of Maria Vasquez's apartment he caught a glimpse of the green Honda.

In one sense, there **was** some subtlety involved, in spotting the car. The driver had not parked directly on Vasquez's street, but around the corner.

As he scanned around him he saw the Honda in a reflection—a newly washed plate-glass window was at the apex of a triangle, which also included Shaw and the green car.

Since there was no direct view of Shaw's bike from the car, that meant that the driver wasn't now in the vehicle but was one of dozens of people on the street, lying low and surveilling him. That population included shoppers, folks delivering packages and envelopes and restaurant provisions, shopkeepers hard at work in the never-ending job of scrubbing the sidewalks, some women and men who were probably sex workers, a few pushers hawking their wares, and their consumers, those just standing around, talking to others in person or on cell phones and a few talking exclusively, and with animation, to themselves.

Only one way to find out who.

Shaw made sure his holster was snug and turned in the direction of the cross street walking quickly toward the side street where the green Honda was parked.

He flushed the spy in one second.

Dressed in black jeans and a gray windbreaker, head covered with a black baseball cap, the spy— about two hundred feet from Shaw—turned instantly and ran back toward the car. It began as a fast gait, then a sprint, though he paused briefly to speak to two large workers, in T-shirts, one with a shock of curly red hair, the other with a black, unwashed ponytail. Colleagues? Shaw didn't see how.

They were unloading supplies from a battered cab truck, double-parked at the intersection around the corner of which sat the green Honda.

The driver continued sprinting, Shaw was closing in. He'd catch up before the man could leap into the car and speed off.

Or that **would** have happened, if not for one problem.

As he approached the delivery truck, the two men stepped directly into his path and held out hands. Curly growled, "Not so fucking fast, asshole."

Shaw tried to dodge but Ponytail jogged in front and grabbed him by the arm.

"Out of my way." Shaw lowered his center of gravity and got ready to grapple him to the ground.

Curly took the other arm and they pushed Shaw up against the truck. He was pinned.

"Going to break more bones? Lemme ask. That make you feel like a man?"

Ponytail, who bathed as infrequently as he shampooed, growled, "Me and him oughta break a few of yours. See how **you** like it."

"Okay. Take it easy." Since Shaw had no idea what was going on, he only offered those generic words. He relaxed a bit and when Ponytail did too, Shaw yanked his right arm free and got the man's meaty wrist in a come-along grip, dropping him to his knees.

"Fuck no." Curly casually slugged Shaw in the belly, and he too went down.

Shaw caught his breath, slowly rose and backed away.

He heard, from around the corner, a car start and tires cry.

Hell . . .

The men started toward him. Shaw backed up farther and lifted his left hand toward them, palm up, and with his right, pulled his jacket open and sweater up, revealing the gun.

"Fuck, you a cop?"

"Look, man . . . We didn't know."

The nausea faded. He snapped, "What'd he say to you?"

"Who?"

"The man I was chasing."

The workers regarded each other.

"You got it wrong, mister," Curly said.

"Wasn't no man. Was a girl."

"And hot, you ask me."

He spent several hours in his search for Tessy Vasquez.

The music club where she worked didn't serve lunch but Shaw was able to talk to the manager, a skinny young man in clothes two sizes too big and with a droopy Vietnam War–era mustache. He wore a stocking cap not unlike Russell's, but in green. He couldn't provide any helpful information and had never seen anyone fitting Roman's description interacting with Tessy, who was a waitress and occasional performer at the club.

"I've asked the staff if they know anything about where she is," the guy said, "and nobody does. She just didn't show up for work. That's when I called her mother."

Outside the place, Shaw called the friends whose names Maria Vasquez had given him—at least those whose numbers he could find. Three answered but no one had any knowledge of where Tessy might be. One young woman, though, did tell him that Tessy was really into busking—street singing—lately. She'd mentioned she'd worried about some of the "pervs" in the parks and the squares she sang in, but she could provide nothing specific.

Shaw biked back to the safe house.

The place, which had seemed alive thanks to Russell's presence, was now stark. A newly formed fog didn't help much.

June gloom . . .

Shaw hung his leather jacket on a rack near the front door and tugged off his sweater, draping it on the rack too. The house was warm. He walked into the kitchen and pulled out a bag of ground Honduran coffee from the cupboard. He brewed a pot through a filter and poured a cup for himself. He hadn't brought the milk from the Winnebago, but he found some powdered Carnation in the refrigerator. Apparently his brother liked coffee the same way he did.

And where was the man now?

On a private jet to Singapore?

In a bunker in Utah?

Tracking down a terrorist in Houston?

The survivalist skills that Ashton had taught the family were a double-edged weapon. They could keep you safe from intrusion. But they could also be used to get close to your enemies, eliminate them and then evade detection as you escaped.

He recalled the matter-of-fact expression in his brother's eyes after he'd killed Blond in the alley. The only concerns were practical—getting his team there efficiently and quickly for the cleanup and getting away.

He sat on the couch and stretched back, boots out in front of him.

Thinking of the driver of the green Honda.

A girl . . .

And hot . . .

But who the hell was she? What was **her** mission?

One thing about her was clear. She was smart about keeping him from catching her: pitching the nails into his path. Smart too in using the two Neanderthals on the street in the TL. They'd said she'd been panicked and begged them to help; the man chasing her was an abusive ex, who'd put her in the hospital a dozen times. He'd broken her arm twice.

"You believed her?" Shaw had muttered.

Curly had shrugged. "'Course. She was like, yeah, you know, beautiful."

Ah, beauty. A lie detector that Shaw had heard of before.

They knew nothing else and had not seen the Honda's tag, so he'd left them to their labors. He'd made a brief canvass of the street where she'd parked the Honda. No one had noticed the woman or the car—at least that was everyone's story.

He wondered how her presence here would play out.

In the absence of fact, any theories were speculation, and trying to formulate any deductions was a waste of time.

His eyes strayed to something on the shelf nearby: the dark statuette of the eagle he'd seen earlier.

Colt, no. Don't! It's not our job . . .

22

Are they crazy? They're going to die."

Russell is peering up the side of a steep snow-covered mountain, as he speaks these words to his younger brother. Colter is fourteen, his brother twenty. Russell is visiting his family in the Compound over semester break.

They are in snowshoes and dressed for the January cold, which is cold indeed at this elevation. They've been looking, unsuccessfully, for bighorn sheep, whose season is the latest of any game in the state. You can hunt them well into February.

Colter follows his brother's gaze to watch two people snowshoeing across a steep slope. One is in navy-blue overalls and stocking cap, the other wears lavender with a white head covering. The build of the latter tells Colter it is a woman. They are hiking from one side of the angular hillside to the other, about a hundred yards below the crest.

The land here is Shaw property but this particular location is about three miles from a public preserve. Ashton posted much of the land but generally doesn't make an issue out of trespassing unless there are firearms involved, which might include hunters or—as Colter learned just last year in an armed standoff—an ominous intruder, overly interested in Ashton Shaw and his property.

His concern at the moment is not their legal right to be here, though. It's that the couple—apparently on a photographic safari—are at serious risk.

The pair is trudging through the heart of an avalanche field. They've come from Fresno or Bakersfield or Sacramento to record in pixels the soaring whitewashed mountains after several days of impressive blizzarding.

"City slickers," Russell mutters, using a term Colter understands though he's never heard it. Russell has spent two years away from the monastery of the Compound and has been exposed to many, many things that Colter cannot even imagine, new words and expressions among them.

"Don't know what the hell they're doing. Got to warn them."

A hissing wind lifts powder from the crest and continues down the slope. Upwind, the couple couldn't hear them from where they stood.

"We have to go up, get closer."

Russell nods. "But stay out of that field. It's a land mine."

In his survivalist training sessions, Ashton spent hours lecturing the children about avalanches. And Colter sees instantly how dangerous these conditions are. Snow is at its least stable immediately after a storm, as now. And it's particularly erratic on north faces, like this. The south sides of mountains get more sun, which melts and packs the fall. North side snow is **hoar**, as in hoarfrost, unpacked, loose and slippery as grains of sugar. Another factor: any incline above thirty degrees makes a mountain avalanche prone, and this slope is easily that.

Colter and Russell trek as quickly as one can on snowshoes and burdened by their rifles and backpacks.

The couple pauses, balancing on the tricky angle, and shoots some pictures that are surely magnificent and that also might represent their last view of this planet.

Of fatalities in avalanches, seventy percent are due to suffocation, thirty to blunt trauma. Few snowslides are exclusively of fine powder; most torrents are filled with sharp slabs of gray dirty pack and crushing ice like blocks of concrete.

The boys are about a hundred yards below and twenty behind the couple. They are breathless from the altitude and from the effort of climbing quickly uphill.

Finally Russell gestures his younger brother back

and continues forward about ten feet, stopping on a high drift. He's right on the edge of the field, though how safe he and Colter truly are is unknown. Snow travels in any direction snow wants to travel. It can even go uphill.

Cupping his hands to his mouth, Russell shouts, "Hikers! It's dangerous! Avalanche!"

The wind—which happens to be another risk factor—whips his words back behind him; they didn't hear.

Both boys are now shouting.

No response. The man points into the distance and they take more pictures.

Russell starts uphill once more and edges into the field, telling his younger brother, "Stay back."

He stops and calls again, "It's dangerous! Get back! The way you came!"

A high rocky path led the couple to the mountainside. Once on it again they'd be safe.

Colter notices tiny white rivulets rolling down the hill from where the trespassers stand. Like white-furred animals scurrying from danger. The bundles travel fast and they travel far.

He wonders about using his rifle to fire into a tree and get their attention. Ashton lectured that most experts don't believe that sounds, even a big-caliber rifle shot, will start an avalanche, but he isn't going to take the chance. Also, indicating your location by firing a weapon is usually useless, thanks to echoing.

Russell moves closer yet to the couple. "It's dangerous!"

"Avalanche!" Colter shouts and waves his arms.

Finally the two look down and wave. "What?" The man's shout carries easily on the wind.

"Avalanche. You're in an avalanche field!"

The man and woman look at each other. He lifts his arms and shakes his head broadly. Meaning he doesn't hear. They plod along the difficult slope in the ungainly shoes.

Russell hurries back to his brother and they climb onto a rocky ledge on the border of the field. "We'll go up through the trees."

Just as the brothers start uphill, Colter hears a faint scream. The woman has lost her balance. Her legs go out from under her and she begins sliding on her back, arms splaying to stop the descent. There's a technique to slow yourself using snowshoes but she doesn't know it or, in panic, has forgotten.

Here it comes, Colter thinks.

But there is no avalanche.

The woman slides downward amid a cloud of powder and comes to a stop about even with the brothers, thirty, forty feet away from them. She struggles upright in the thigh-high powder, anchored by her wide mesh shoes. She checks her camera and other gear. She touches her pocket, shouting uphill. "Phone's okay!" She actually laughs.

Her friend gives a thumbs-up.

The woman is now in hearing range and Russell

explains the danger. "You have to get out of there now! Both of you! It's an avalanche field. Dangerous!"

"Avalanche?"

"Now!" Colter calls. He thought her tumble would start one. People are the number-one cause of avalanches: skiers, snowmobilers and snowshoers, who go carelessly where they should not. But so far the massive ledge holds.

Russell says, "Get over here, off the slope! Unhook the snowshoes and pull them out. And your friend, he needs to go back to the trees, the path you were on. He needs to turn around!"

She looks up and waves to him and then points to his left, meaning to return to the path. He gives yet another raised arm of incomprehension.

She pulls her gloves off and digs out her phone. She makes a call. Colter sees him answer.

"Brad, honey, these boys say it's an avalanche area. Go back to the trees. That path we were on before we started across the hill."

Russell says, "Tell him to move very slowly. Really."

She relays this information, puts the phone away and bends down to unhook her shoes. She gets one undone and, after a struggle, yanks it out.

Can't she go any faster?

Uphill, Colter sees, the man starts toward the safety of the path.

He glances down and sees the trickles of snow accelerating away from beneath his feet.

More and more of them.

He panics and charges forward, slamming the oval snowshoes hard on the surface.

"No!" Colter and his brother shout simultaneously.

Just as the man scrambles out of the field, literally diving to safety, a shelf of snow breaks away and cascades downward. It is only ten feet wide or so and shallow but avalanches are a chain reaction. Colter knows this will trigger a much bigger fall.

The woman evidently hears the **whoosh** too and looks up at the wall sliding toward her. A brief scream. She is still forty feet from the safety of the high ground where the boys are. She's trapped in place by the remaining snowshoe. She bends down into the froth and frantically tries to undo the strap.

Colter assesses:

Odds that the whole field will give way? Eighty percent.

Survival of somebody who has no deep-snow training? Five percent.

Somebody who had **some** training? Unknown but better than that.

He drops his backpack and discards his weapons.

Russell is staring at his younger brother.

"Colt, no. Don't! It's not our job."

No time for discussion. Colter leaps off the ridge and runs quickly across the field, in the ungainly lope of a snowshoe jogger.

Just as he reaches her, the rest of the mountain

cuts loose, a vast swath of snow, fifty or sixty yards wide, dropping, tumbling, picking up speed. Tides like this can easily exceed a hundred miles an hour.

As he pops the quick release of his shoes and steps out of them he sees her panicked face, tears streaming. She has large dark eyes, an upturned nose and lipstick, or sunscreen, that matches her violet snowsuit.

"Your other shoe?"

"What's going to happen?" she cries.

"Shoe?" he snaps.

"Undone." She straightens up and tries to pull it out. She blinks as she looks him over, maybe realizing for the first time how young he is.

"Leave the shoe!" Colter orders.

He lifts her camera off and tosses it away. In the turbulence of an avalanche, solid objects, even small ones, can maim and kill.

A glance crestward. They have thirty seconds.

"Listen to me. When it hits, don't fight it. Pretend you're swimming, kick with your arms and legs. Swim **with** it, like you're in the surf. Got that?"

No answer.

"Have you **got** it?" he insists.

"Yes, swimming."

Twenty seconds till the tide slams into them.

"When you feel yourself slowing, curl up and take a deep breath, as deep as you can. And with one hand clear a space around your mouth for air. Lift the other arm up as high as you can, so the searchers know where you are. Make a big space around your mouth. There'll be enough air for a half hour."

"I'm scared!"

Ten seconds. The wave is six feet high, now seven, now eight and accelerating. It's trailed by dust swirling and thick as forest fire smoke.

"You'll do fine. Swim, hand to mouth, arm up."

It's a slough avalanche—more loose snow than slabs. If they died it would be by suffocation, not a blow to the head. Colter doesn't know which is worse. Suffocation probably.

She stares at the wave. Colter turns her around so that she's facing downhill.

Five seconds.

Colter shuffles away so their bodies don't become bludgeons.

"Swim!"

She does. He does too and takes a deep breath.

In the time it takes to fill his lungs, the world turns black.

23

Mary Dove finishes tending to the wounds on her fourteen-year-old son's neck and cheek.

While **most** of the avalanche was slough—granular hoar snow—Colter didn't escape a chunk of sharp ice. Or possibly a rock.

The damage isn't severe.

They are in her office, which is a typical physician's, except for the walls, which are—as everything in the cabin—made of hand-hewn logs.

"Anywhere else?" she asks.

"No," Colter says. "Just a little sore."

"How far did it sweep you?"

"Football field," Colter says, though he doesn't have much frame of reference, only pictures in newspapers or magazines. He's never seen a game. In a home with no TV and no internet, one doesn't have a chance to view broadcast spectator sports, and the nearest teams are those of the colleges and high schools around Fresno. When the family went there, they always had errands to run or acquaintances and family to see. None of the children had much inclination anyway. If parents aren't excited about sports, their youngsters probably won't be either.

Mary Dove executes some range-of-motion tests, arms and legs, which her son seems to pass. More or less.

He goes into his bathroom and takes a very hot shower, minding the rule to keep the bandages dry. He towels off, dresses and lies down on his blanket, which is brown and woven in a Native American design.

He closes his eyes briefly, picturing the torrent of snow enwrapping him.

He followed the same advice he'd given the woman.

When he slowed, though, he realized that extending his arm to signal his whereabouts would do no good. He was too far under the surface, so he'd pulled his arm back, and taken another deep breath and, using both hands, cleared a large air reservoir in front of his face.

Finally he stopped sliding and he wasted no time in attempting to free himself, kneeing and punching and elbowing. The space he opened up before him was completely black, and he was disoriented as to where the surface might be. He recalled his father's lesson and made small snowballs and dropped them near his face and hands to see where they landed, so he could tell which way was down.

Never question gravity . . .

Then came the digging—scooping the snow down, packing it and then pushing upward with his feet and arms. Inches at a time.

Finally there was slight illumination over his head and he broke through, sucking in the air, which as in all snowfields gave off a sweet electrical scent.

He climbed out and rolled onto the snow surface, catching his breath. He called to his brother, who was probing the field nearby with a long branch. He dropped it and ran to Colter to help him up.

"The woman?" Colter asked. "She all right?"

His brother pointed.

The man who'd been with her, Brad, was digging her out of a deep pile of snow near the avalanche's toe—the end. She'd been swept much farther than he'd been. Colter saw that she had survived and was helping to dig herself out. She was unhurt.

Colter struggled to his feet, with Russell helping. His brother looked up the mountain and said, "The whole pack didn't come down. There's more that's unstable, a lot more. We should get them out and into the trees."

They walked to the couple.

"We spotted her arm," Russell said. "That's how we found where she was. You told her that."

Shaw nodded, and the foursome made their way to safety.

Now, in the Compound's rustic cabin, Colter is finally warm once more, inner core warm, and in only slight pain. He rises from his bed and walks into the living room where Russell and Dorion are sitting near a soothing dance of flames in the stacked-stone fireplace. They are both reading. When Colter enters the room, Dorion, eleven, leaps up and hugs him. He tells himself to give no reaction to the pain and he doesn't. She regards the bandage with still eyes, which means she's troubled.

"It's all right. A scratch."

"Okay," she says.

"Hey," Russell says and goes back to his book.

"Hey."

Dorion sits once more. "You know what the biggest one in the world was?"

She'd be talking about old-time locomotives, which, for some reason, she is passionate about.

"No clue."

"Union Pacific's Big Boy. Come on, Colter, look!" She shows him the book. According to the caption, the engine depicted was Locomotive Number 4014, and was an impressive piece of machinery. It had a 4-8-8-4 wheel arrangement, which, she explained to him a few years ago, was the number of locomotive wheels from front to back; it's how the machines are classified.

"Biggest expansion engine there ever was. It

weighed more than a million pounds. It's in a museum in Los Angeles. I want to see it someday."

"We'll make sure that happens."

"You'll come too, Russell?" she asks.

"Sure." The older brother doesn't look up from his book. Colter wonders what he's reading. Russell has been into spy thrillers lately.

Mary Dove is in the kitchen, preparing dinner, while Ashton is in his study, the door closed, where he disappeared an hour ago after learning that his sons were all right.

Colter stretches and happens to glance to the mantel, where he sees a trio of framed pictures—two artist renderings and one photograph. The picture to the left is a sketch of a woman who has some Native American features. A handsome face, black hair parted severely in the middle, the sides dangling to her shoulders. She is Marie Aioe Dorion, the nation's first mountain woman. She was of Métis heritage, indigenous people in the central part of the United States and southern Canada. Widowed early, Dorion survived in the wilderness for months with two small children, in hostile territory.

The center picture is a reproduction of a painting of a handsome, rugged man wearing leather and a raccoon hat that encompasses much of his head. He is John Colter, an explorer with the Lewis and Clark Expedition.

The photograph on the right is of Osborne Russell, the explorer, politician and judge, who was in part responsible for founding the Oregon Territory. He is the most recent of the three, surviving into the late 1800s; hence the photographic image.

These three individuals were the sources for the Shaw children's names.

The study door opens and Ashton walks into the living room. He has changed a lot, Colter thinks, in the years since the family left the Bay Area for the Compound—to escape some threats that troubled him greatly but that he hasn't discussed much with the children, other than to warn them to be on the lookout for strangers on the Compound. His hair has gone mostly white and is often, like now, mussed. He wears jeans, a white shirt with pearl buttons—Mary Dove made it—and a leather vest. On his feet, tactical boots, the sort a soldier might wear.

He is carrying a cardboard box.

"Everyone," he says.

The three children look up. Mary Dove remains in the kitchen. The word was uttered in his speaking-to-the-children tone.

When they settle he looks at them one by one. Finally he says, "Never deny the power of ritual. Do you know what I mean?"

"Like in Harry Potter? The ceremonies at Hogwarts?" Dorie is a fan, to put it mildly.

"Exactly, Button."

Colter is thinking of the Lord of the Rings trilogy but he doesn't say anything.

Russell seems to be thinking of nothing in response. He just watches his father and the box he is holding.

"A general rule of survivalism is: 'Never risk yourself for a stranger.' But that's not what I believe. What's the good of learning our skills if we can't put them to use and help somebody else?"

The three of them—his children, his students—sit motionless on couch or chair, looking up at the intense eyes of their father.

"Colter saved somebody's life today. And I thought we should have a ritual."

The boy's face burns and he's sure it turns red. Dorion's, on the other hand, blossoms with happiness as she looks Colter's way. He gives her a smile. Russell now gazes at the fireplace, where the flames had turned from energetic blue to subdued orange.

Ashton reaches into the box and extracts a small statuette of an eagle in flight. He hands it to Colter, who takes it. It's heavy, metal. He's worried that his father will expect him to make a speech. At fourteen he has rappelled down hundred-foot cliffs and borrowed a motorcycle from a friend in White Sulfur Springs, the nearest town, and hit ninety miles an hour on a road of imperfect asphalt. He has also pulled a pistol on an intruder in the Compound—that incident last year—and sent him on his way.

He would do any of those again rather than make a speech, even to this small audience.

"But he couldn't have done that without the love and support of his brother and sister. So our ritual includes both of you too." Ashton reaches into the box once more and takes out a statuette of a fox and hands it to Dorion. Her eyes ignite with pleasure. The only thing she likes more than locomotives is animals.

"And here's yours." He hands Russell a bear statuette. His brother says nothing but stares at the bronze, weighs it in his hand.

Shaw suddenly has a snap of understanding. The statues echo the nicknames of the children. Dorie is the clever one. Russell the reclusive one. And Colter the restless one.

Then the ritual is over—no speeches required—and Mary Dove announces that it's time to eat.

After dinner—which would have been bighorn sheep but is now elk—Colter takes the statuette into his bedroom and sets it on a shelf beside his copies of the Lord of the Rings trilogy, Ray Bradbury's short stories and a half-dozen law books, which for some reason he enjoys reading.

Now, years later, in the kitchen of the Alvarez Street safe house, Colter Shaw was looking at the same statue as intently as he was the night of the avalanche.

He recalled that when he left home to attend the University of Michigan and was packing his duffel bag for the trip he had noticed that the eagle statue was nowhere in his room.

Yet here it was now.

There was only one possible explanation for its appearance. His father had taken it with him when he'd come to the safe house. It was, maybe, a sentimental reminder of his son, something that Ash wanted to have with him. To make him feel close to home.

A perfectly reasonable, heartwarming explanation.

But Shaw believed there was another reason, a more important one, that Ashton had brought the eagle to San Francisco. It was the clearest message yet that Father wanted Colter, of all his children, to carry on his mission.

24

Shaw's phone pinged with the sound of an incoming text. It was from his private investigator, in Washington, D.C., to whom he'd sent an encrypted email before his bike ride from the Tenderloin back here.

Charlotte "Mack" McKenzie might have been a model. With steely gray eyes, she was an even six feet tall, her complexion pale and her brown hair long. This was a problem for her in street work. Like a spy, PIs benefit from being inconspicuous. And no one could ever say that of Mack McKenzie. Her days of tailing people, though, were long past. She had put together a security and investigative operation that hummed, and she had a talented crew of staff and contractors to do the sweat labor.

Maria and Tessy Vasquez.
Largely under the radar—likely
undocumented—but social media and
level-one governmental data confirm
their identities. No criminal records.
Probably legit. No AKA "Roman" in CA
or U.S. criminal databases in SF area.

Mack was a woman after Shaw's own heart. In keeping with Shaw's approach to life, little was ever zero percent or one hundred percent with her, even if she wasn't quite as quick to assign a precise number as he was.

Probably legit . . .

She finished with:

Your requested analysis presently
underway.

He replied, thanking her, and looked over the notes he'd taken at Maria Vasquez's apartment, a decent place in a modest building surrounded by the complex 'hood of the TL. He was concerned about the young woman, the talented singer and photographer.

For-profit kidnapping? Near zero percent.

The odds she'd been murdered and the body

disposed of? Not great. Ten percent. That wasn't as common as cable TV would have us believe.

And what about her being in a meth house somewhere, strung out, after having relapsed? Thirty percent. She seemed to be making good on a fresh start. But add Roman into this equation and that boosted the number to sixty percent.

He suddenly saw his BlackBridge mission as a distraction from the reward job, which was, after all, his main profession. But he'd make it work. He'd do whatever was necessary to find the girl, or at least get some answer for her mother.

It just then happened that his phone hummed, and he took a call from one of Tessy's friends. The young woman couldn't provide any information about the missing girl. But in response to his question about Roman said, "Is he involved? Shit."

"I don't know. Her mother thinks it's possible."

"He's trouble. I think he's crazy. I mean, really, like a psychopath."

Shaw asked if she had any specific information on him.

"No, I never really knew him. He didn't want Tessy hanging with us. He wanted her all to himself. He's dangerous, mister. He hangs with some really bad people. You know, gangs, that kind of thing. I heard he killed somebody. Jesus, I hope she didn't go back to him."

He tried the people he'd called earlier and, when none of them answered, left new messages. This was all he could do on the reward assignment for the time being, until Mack got back to him with his earlier request.

Back to the scavenger hunt of Amos Gahl's stolen evidence.

Glancing at his phone, he checked the tracker app. The chipped copy of **Walden** was still at the library.

He wondered what Helms, Braxton and Droon would be thinking about Blond's death. Was the mysterious bearded shooter a friend of Shaw's or was the incident merely a coincidence? Had Blond, who reeked of hired killer, been gunned down in retaliation for some earlier offense?

Shaw sat back, stared at the ceiling and silently asked Amos Gahl: What did you find?

And where is your courier bag hidden?

It was time to look at the two leads that might hold the answers to those questions: the house on Camino in Burlingame and the warehouse in the Embarcadero.

The coffee cup froze halfway to Shaw's mouth when he heard the doorbell ring.

He turned fast, hand near his pistol. He stood.

A voice called, "Me. I'm coming in."

The front door opened and Russell stepped inside. Still in the black hat, still in the dark, thigh-length coat, the tactical boots.

He walked into the kitchen.

"There's an issue." He took off his coat, revealing

a green T-shirt. The muscles of his arms were pronounced. His jeans were held up by dark red suspenders. He sat. "Man in the alley?"

"Droon or the other one?"

"The dead one. Karin was handling disposal. She
found a note, handwritten. In his pocket."

His brother displayed a photo on his phone.

**Confirmation from Hunters Point crew.
6/26, 7:00 p.m. SP and family. All ↓**

Russell remained stone-faced as his brother
looked over the screen, then sat back.

Shaw said, "Does the 'All' and the arrow mean
what I think it does?"

A nod. "It's a kill order. A hit on someone with
the initials SP and his family. Or **her** family."

Shaw noticed that it had been folded many times,
like the notes Amos Gahl's colleague had left for
their father.

"Dead-drop," Shaw said.

"Some messages you don't send electronically no
matter how good the encryption. We do it too."

Used dead-drops?

Or issued kill orders?

"Did Karin find his ID? Anything else?"

"Not yet. Running prints and DNA and facial
recognition. May get it right away, may take a while.
May never find out. People in this line of work do a
lot of track covering."

Shaw asked, "With Blond gone, will they still go ahead with the hit?"

"Who?"

"The guy in the alley. My nic for him."

"Have to assume it's still a go. Handwritten KO, dead-drop, the arrow on the whole family. They'll assume that Blond got disappeared for some reason unrelated to this. That woman Braxton'll just find another triggerman."

"Thanks for telling me. But I can't go to the police. Ashton didn't trust them."

"Wouldn't want them anyway."

Of course. The note would be accompanied by a question: How did Shaw come by it? And the disquieting answer to that inquiry was: because his brother had shot someone in the head.

Russell looked at his watch; it was an analog model, brushed steel or titanium. "Two days until they die. We need to figure out a plan."

Had Shaw heard right? "'We'? You don't want to get involved in this, Russell."

His older brother clearly wasn't happy. "I do not, that's true. But what this's become, it isn't your thing. It's not a reward job, Colt. You can't do it on your own." He stalked up the stairs. "I've got reports to file. We'll talk strategy in the morning."

THE STEELWORKS

After the third guard draws his weapon and fires, Shaw returns one shot, missing, and he and Nita step into one of the empty storerooms. Shaw looks out occasionally, Glock ready. One or two of the men near the office will fire his way, but casually without aiming. It's covering fire only, to keep them down, to keep them back.

And it's working.

Shaw called 911 and reported the shots.

Why, though, are the three not charging him? Moving forward, shooting . . . They could overwhelm Shaw and the young woman. She's crying, shivering.

Rock, Paper, Scissors . . .

Still not charging them. Shaw then looks around the corner and sees why.

A man walks down the stairs, listing under the weight of a five-gallon gasoline can. He takes it into the TV room.

Because he's armed, they must assume that Shaw is an undercover cop, or at the least he's called the police. So the order has come from the owner of the place to destroy the physical evidence, the computer files.

Everything has to disappear.

Including the witnesses.

And in the process, they can avoid getting shot by charging Shaw.

With a crisp whoosh, the massive fireball fills the office and rolls into the corridor. Orange, black, yellow. Uncontrolled boiling, mesmerizing if it weren't so deadly. The men vanish.

Down here, Shaw notes, there are no sprinklers.

Shaw calls 911 again and reports there's now a fire.

For what good it will do. The entire building will be a pile of cinders in twenty minutes.

The stampede above them is a roar and is accompanied by muted screams. He believes he hears, "We have to get out. Help us!" The smoke will be rising to the dance floor.

The flames illuminate the basement. Shaw hopes he'll be able to see another exit. There is one but it's chained, and his lock-picking skills only go so far.

There's one way out.

"Come on." He takes Nita by the arm and leads her straight toward the conflagration.

"No!" she screams.

He tugs her more firmly. "Our only chance." She comes along.

They approach the turbulent flames, the heat scraping their skin. Just before it becomes unbearable, Shaw turns to the right, into the storeroom across from the office. The flames are lapping at the outer wall but have not yet eaten through.

He moves to the side facing the stairs and begins to kick the Sheetrock. This wouldn't work if he were in his rubber-soled Eccos but his boots' leather soles, the heels in particular, make indentations in the wall. Again, again. Finally he breaks through. It's a small hole. He ducks and looks through it. Yes, the area at the foot of the stairs—only ten feet away—is empty of hostiles. But soon it will be engulfed in flame.

More kicking. The hole grows slowly larger.

Nita helps. She's strong. When Shaw cracks a piece, she pulls it free. The hole is now about eighteen inches around. Almost big enough to fit through.

Kick, pull.

Both are coughing. His eyes sting and stream.

The fire is stealing the oxygen. He feels light-headed.

Kick, pull . . .

Now, finally, it's big enough for them to fit through.

"Go on."

She wriggles through and collapses on the other side.

The pounding feet on the dance floor above them have stopped. Everyone has evacuated. The roar of the flames is the only sound.

Shaw turns to the hole they broke open in the Sheetrock and says to Nita, "Up the stairs now, fast. There'll be police."

"But . . . what about you?"

He smiles to her. "Not yet."

And turns back, jogging to the far end of the corridor.

PART TWO

JUNE 25

THE GREAT EARTHQUAKE

Time until the family dies: thirty-two hours.

25

The Shaw brothers had two missions, interwoven like ropes in a Gordian knot.

One, saving the SP family from the hitman who would replace Blond; the other, bringing down BlackBridge. In saving the family, they might find hard evidence linking the hit back to Braxton, Droon and maybe even Ian Helms himself. Or, finding that evidence in the first place might allow them to identify and save the family.

Their initial task was to try to identify Blond, and so after leaving the safe house they drove to Hunters Point, a neighborhood on the eastern edge of the city, jutting into the Bay.

Hunters Point and neighboring Bayview were among the toughest parts of the city, and the most densely populated with gangs.

Confirmation from Hunters Point crew. 6/26, 7:00 p.m. SP and family. All ↓

Which gang could the hit order mean?

Shaw had enlisted some help and this morning had sent a text to his friend and rock-climbing buddy, Tom Pepper, who, at the FBI, had worked terrorism and organized crime.

As Russell's SUV—a Lincoln Navigator—idled in a parking lot, Shaw's phone hummed. He answered, "Tom."

"Colt."

"You're on speaker here with my brother, Russell."

A pause. Shaw wondered what the man would be thinking. He knew of the estrangement, though not its basis. "Hello, Russell."

"Tom."

"Here's what I've got. Two main crews in Hunters Point—Bayview. One's Anglo. The Bayneck Locals. You know the Peckerwood Movement?"

Shaw replied, "Vaguely. White supremacists, prison culture, drugs. Started in the South, right?"

"In the thirties. Then spread, lot of the members ended up in California. Skinheads, yeah, but they have some alliances with Latinx gangs. The Baynecks aren't technically Peckerwoods—there was some falling-out—but they're cut from the same cloth.

"The second main gang in that area is Black. The

Hudson Kings. It's rap based, like the old West-mob and the rival Big Block. Okay, listen. They're all businessmen first—drugs and guns mostly—but that doesn't mean they're not violent and territorial and will take out a threat in an instant. I'm saying: They won't be inclined to cooperate."

Shaw said, "I'm going to appeal to their better nature."

Pepper chuckled. "Whatever you're doing, make sure it's during the daylight hours."

"We're here now," Russell said. "They have a social club, hang someplace?"

"The Kings had an HQ in a storefront on North-ridge. I think near Harbor. The Baynecks used to operate out of a biker bar on Ingalls. Bayview and Hunters Point have complicated boundaries, so I'm not sure which 'hood they're in. I don't know anybody in the Baynecks but there's an O.G. high up in the Kings. Kevin Miller. He was a stand-up guy. Didn't exactly cooperate, but he kept things calm. Nobody got shot. And that's saying something."

Russell was on his phone, checking GPS.

Pepper said, "I hope it's a damn big reward you're after."

"No reward."

"So. Last week you nearly got killed in a cult and there was no reward. And now you're tap-dancing with the crews in Hunters Point, and there's no reward."

Shaw said, "Sums it up."

"Good luck. Nice meeting you, Russell."

"Same."

Shaw disconnected. "Which first?"

"Hmm. Bikers're closer."

26

As they drove through the streets, both residential and commercial, Shaw looked around him. Hunters Point had always borne the brunt of commerce unwelcome in other parts of the city. At one time it was acres upon acres of slaughterhouses, power plants, tanneries and ship-yards, all of which dumped waste into the land, the air and the water of the western Bay.

A hard place, battered and grubby, the Point was only somewhat improved over its nineteenth-century incarnation. Part workaday industrial, part slowly emerging residential and retail redevelopment, part weedy fields and labyrinthine foundations cleared of superstructure. Quite the mix: they drove by a series of vacant lots and a burned-out building right next to which was a small, Victorian-style opera house, painted bright green. Just past that was a construction site on which a sign announced this would be the future home of a division of a well-known internet company, whose headquarters was about fifteen miles south, on the eastern edge of Silicon Valley.

They soon spotted their destination. Lou's was the name of the bar and it was right out of central set design for a 1960s chopped-cycle movie. Peeling paint, grimy windows, a few unsteady tables and less steady chairs out in front, presently unoccupied. Two Harleys and a Moto Guzzi cycle leaned at the curb.

Russell parked and the two men got out, adjusting jacket and coat to make sure their pistols were invisible.

The interior of the bar was dim and smelled of Lysol and cigarette smoke. The only décor, aside from the ignored NO SMOKING sign, was old and fly-specked posters of surfers—more women than men—along with a wooden Nazi iron cross and a picture of Berch-tesgaden, Hitler's mountain retreat.

There were a half-dozen Bayneck crew sitting at three tables. They'd been talking, before they turned en masse to gape at the newcomers. Breakfast beers, in bottles, and coffee mugs clustered on the scarred table. Four of them were classic bikers: huge and inked, with long frizzy beards and hair to the shoulders or in ponytails. Their cloth of choice was denim. The remaining two—slimmer—had shaved heads. One wore a Pendleton flannel shirt, the other a T-shirt under a bomber jacket. Both were in Doc Martens boots. One had a skateboard at his feet. Shaw knew that in this gang culture, extreme sports like boarding and, his own, motocross, were popular.

The smallest of the bearded men—marginally the oldest, Shaw estimated—looked them over and said in a gravelly voice, "Well, you're here for some reason. They don't letcha wear face hair like that in the Bureau or SFPD so this's about something else. Maybe you're with an organization"—he rolled the word out, adding an extra syllable or two—"that might have a contrary interest to ours."

Shaw noticed the bartender, a stocky man, balding, drop his hands below the level of the bar. And one of the shaved-headed men casually put his hand on his thigh. "This's a private club. Why don't you get the fuck out?"

Russell unbuttoned his jacket.

Shaw said, "Who's got the MGX-21?"

It was a top-of-the-line Moto Guzzi, and a beautiful cycle. The body was black and the cylinder head and front brake pad bright red.

The leader of the gang cut a glance to the bartender, whose hands became visible once more.

"Mine," said the biggest of the bikers.

"Hundred horses?" Shaw asked.

"Close enough. You ride?"

"I do."

"Bike?"

Shaw said, "Yamaha."

"XV1900?"

This was the largest Yamaha in production.

"Smaller."

"Figured," the leader said, both grunting and snickering simultaneously.

The leader said, "Now that we're done comparing dicks, why don't you take my young associate's advice." He nodded to the door.

Russell said, "We're looking for somebody. If you can help us it'll be worth something for you."

"Explain yourself."

Russell said, "I'm reaching for my phone." He did this very slowly. He held out the picture of Blond.

The man wouldn't know he was looking at a dead man. Karin had yet another talent apparently: Photoshop. She'd removed the bullet hole and adjusted the eyes a bit. Apparently there was a filter called "Liquify," Russell had explained, which gave the deceased man a bit of a smile. The image was grotesque only if you knew the truth.

"He scammed our mother out of twenty K," Russell added.

The brothers had prepared what they thought was a credible story, Russell providing most of the material. After all, he was the one who had been the director of the "mugging" theater outside of the safe house yesterday morning.

The leader frowned. Whatever this gang did for a living, robbing mothers was apparently off the table.

Shaw said, "We know he's some connection

with a crew here. You get us his real name and who he runs with, there's a thousand in it for you. So, he wear your colors?"

The six men looked at the picture again, then regarded one another.

The leader said, "Not one of us. Never seen him."

The others agreed. Shaw believed they were telling the truth. There had not been a single flash of recognition in any eye.

Russell put his phone away.

The Bayneck in the flannel shirt—a twitchy man—said, "I think our looking was worth something." It was he who'd placed his hand on his thigh earlier, and the fingers now moved closer to where his weapon would rest.

For a very long moment not a soul moved.

Then the biggest of the bikers said, "Naw, forget it. Too early for that kind of shit. And I ain't finished but one beer yet. So I'm not in any mood."

The leader said, "All I'll say is why weren't you looking after your mother? Two grown men like you. Sad. Now, get on out."

27

Now the SUV was cruising through a different part of the district.

They were on their way to the Hudson Kings' headquarters.

They were near the waterfront and Shaw looked out on the dark water at the decommissioned Hunters Point Naval Shipyard, dominated by the massive gantry crane that bore a skeletal resemblance to the battleships whose turrets it lifted off so that the cannon could be replaced fast. A huge civilian and naval shipbuilding and repair facility for more than a hundred years, the yard was now closed and parcels were being sold off for condominiums and commercial buildings—that is, if and when the land was decontaminated. The place was a Superfund toxic waste site and much of it was still tainted, including by radioactive materials. It was from this shipyard that the USS **Indianapolis** sailed to the Mariana Islands, its cargo parts for Little Boy and Fat Man, the atomic bombs that were dropped on Hiroshima and Nagasaki in August of 1945.

Cleanup was a big business here. Many small craft operated by a company called BayPoint Enviro-Sure Solutions were collecting drums with hazard warnings stenciled on the sides. The workers were wearing so much protective gear, they looked like astronauts laboring on the moon.

Russell turned and steered away from the water. A moment later he pointed to a storefront. "That's it."

There was nowhere to park nearby so he drove a block and a half farther, and pulled to the curb. The brothers climbed out and started to walk toward the storefront.

A trio of rats slipped from an abandoned warehouse nearby and nonchalantly vanished into a drain.

"Yo, you buying, man?"

The voice belonged to a skinny young man sitting on an unsteady chair in front of a dubious shop selling prepaid phones and minutes cards, along with vaping paraphernalia. Two figures inside were speaking into flip cells.

The brothers moved on without responding.

Some kids, from teens to mid-twenties, were clustered together on the corner between the brothers and the social club. They were smoking joints, a few cigarettes. The clothing was hoodies and T-shirts and baggy slacks. Their running shoes were nice, and the hairstyles ranged from shaved to elaborate works of art. A few wore medallions, chains and other bling. They looked over the white men walking slowly past and grew energized, whispering and snickering. They were assessing the men as easy targets: beard on one, slim build on another.

Three of the crew broke from the clutch and strode up the sidewalk, stepping in front of and stopping Shaw and his brother.

"You need directions? I give you directions. You know what I'm saying? C-note, and I give you directions."

"You lost? They lost."

"What you about, man?" A young man got right in Shaw's face.

The brothers had no time for a fight.

Never resort to violence unless you have no alternative.

Ashton might have added: especially with foolish teenagers.

Two others joined the trio. The newcomers postured, gesturing broadly with bony hands. The grins were cold.

Courage in numbers isn't courage.

"I'm talking to you an' you ignoring me. That rude."

"Is Kevin Miller around?" Russell asked.

They fell silent.

Shaw said, "It's all good. We've got money for him."

The skinniest of them—a boy of about fifteen or sixteen—said, "I'll take it to him. Save you the trouble, you know what I'm saying?"

It was then someone else joined the clutch. A tall, lanky man in his mid-thirties. His face was wrinkled and he bore tats in the shape of teardrops near his eyes. They could signify either a long prison term or that he'd committed murder.

The boys glanced at him with a measure of respect.

"Yo, Kevin!"

"What up, Kevin?"

Signs were flashed, fists bumped.

So this was Tom Pepper's O.G.—original gangster—one who had earned his colors years ago and managed to survive life on the street.

"My man."

"Dog."

Both Shaw and Russell looked at him, holding his gaze steadily. Neither of the brothers said anything. Eyes still on the interlopers, Kevin said to the crew, "Right. Everybody, move off."

"But . . ." one protested.

A brief glance was all it took. The kids cast murderous looks toward Shaw and Russell but headed down the sidewalk.

"You wanted me, you got me." Kevin swiveled back, smooth, looking them over. "You L.E.?"

"We're not law."

A squinting assessment. "No. You don't smell law. How'd you get my name?"

"Tom Pepper vouched."

Kevin nodded. The teardrop beneath his eye was inked well. A bit of skin showed through the black and gave the image three dimensions.

Russell displayed Blond's doctored picture. "We're trying to find this man. He's got a connection with a crew here, Hunters Point, Bayview."

"That hair, it ain't normal."

Blond's complexion had grown lighter in death but the hairdo remained as brightly jaundiced as ever.

"I've got a thousand, if you help us out."

"Why here? He's white."

Shaw asked, "Don't you do business with everybody—regardless of race, creed, et cetera."

Kevin chuckled. "Talk to the rednecks."

"We did. They don't know him."

"Lemme see that picture again."

Russell displayed it.

The O.G. nodded with a thoughtful frown. "Sorry, brother. No idea. And I'm as connected as they come."

"Any other crews here?" Russell asked.

"Nothing righteous. Some franchises from Salinas keep flirting with the shorefront, north. They show up, we discourage them. They go away. They come back. You know what it is. All right. I got business." He looked at Shaw. "Tom Pepper. He was okay. Fair man. Good thing he still with us."

Kevin returned to the social club, and the men to the SUV. "We could canvass here a week and that's the only answer we're ever going to get. There's got to be a better way," Shaw said.

"Yeah. Find the courier bag. Use it as leverage to stop BlackBridge." Russell started the big engine.

Shaw looked out the passenger window. He saw one of the young men who'd confronted them on the street—one of the skinnier, with a shaved head. The kid stood on a pile of rubble about thirty feet away. He reached up under his burgundy hoodie as he stared toward the vehicle with a demeaning smile.

Shaw tensed and his hand went toward his hip.

Russell glanced his brother's way.

Suddenly, the kid's hand zipped from under the sweatshirt and, with his fingers formed like a pistol, pointed at Shaw and mimicked firing, the hand jerking back in recoil. The smile vanished. His hand tightened into a fist and the next gesture involved a single finger. He clambered down the rubble heap and vanished.

Shaw said, "Let's pick up on Ashton's leads. Burlingame first."

"Put it in GPS."

Shaw pulled out his phone, then paused as he looked over the screen. "Not yet. Braxton and Droon are on the move."

28

The GPS tracker hidden in the spine of Henry David Thoreau's meditation on self-sufficiency had led them back to the Tenderloin.

They were not far from where Shaw's unexpected reward job—to locate Tessy Vasquez—had begun.

Russell parked the SUV in a spot in front of a dilapidated retail storefront, closed now. The window bills pleaded for lessees. A homeless man, wrapped in a gray blanket, slept in the doorway. A few dollar bills peeked from under the corner of his covering. Russell knelt and pushed them out of sight. Shaw had been about to do the same.

Orienting himself, glancing around the neighborhood, then at the GPS app, Shaw pointed to an alley.

The brothers declined an offer from a pale young

woman in her early twenties and they stepped over another man, about the same age, unconscious and lying in the mouth of the alley. He too was presumably homeless, though his clothes were more or less clean and he didn't have any of the accoutrements that most street people possess: bags, shopping cart, blankets, extra clothing. Was he dead?

Russell apparently caught his brother's thought. He nudged the man's arm with his shoe and got a reaction. Three doors away was a storefront of a community outreach service. Shaw walked to it and stepped inside. A thin man of about fifty in a clerical collar looked up and offered a pleasant smile. "Help you?"

"There're two men, up the street, passed out. Maybe you've got somebody who could help. One's drunk, I think, but the other one might've OD'd. Out the door to the right."

He rose and called into the back room, "Rosie, come on and bring your bag." He said to Shaw, "Terrible. Overdoses're up fifty percent in the past couple months, and we've got a gang injunction here. I don't know what's going on."

The Urban Improvement Plan is what's going on.

Shaw returned to his brother and they proceeded down the alley, with Russell behind, checking for threats from that direction, just as Shaw did in the front. This was instinctive.

Never believe your enemies aren't pursuing you.

At the far end of the moist, soiled passage, they found themselves on the edge of a large area—taking up several blocks—that was in the process of being cleared. Bulldozers and backhoes, their yellow and black paint jobs spattered with mud, sat unoccupied, parked in the north section of the space. The site was a mix of partially demolished buildings and vacant ground. Pits of oily standing water shimmered and modest mountains of scrap materials from the destroyed buildings dotted the landscape. The terrain was light in color, almost beige. The soil would be clay.

In the center of the flattened area sat a black SUV, a Cadillac Escalade. The GPS indicated that it was the source of the pings. Braxton probably had with her a briefcase or backpack containing the material she'd stolen from Shaw's camper the other day, including the bugged book.

The Escalade's doors opened and Droon, who was the driver, and Braxton climbed out. They looked around—Russell and Shaw crouched behind a pile of scrap wood and plasterboard. When they rose and looked again, the pair from BlackBridge was in a heads-down conversation. Droon was nodding.

Another car pulled in and the two BlackBridge employees looked up. It was a Rolls-Royce, dark red. The sleek vehicle eased slowly over the uneven ground and parked, side by side with the Caddie.

No doors opened.

Braxton took a phone call.

Droon stretched and lit a cigarette.

Russell took out his phone, snapped some pictures, then put it back. "Look at the tags."

On the Rolls there was a sheet of white cardboard or plastic over the license plate. The illegal obfuscation would be only temporary; as soon as they hit the street, the driver would pause and pull off the rectangle.

Who was the visitor?

Braxton disconnected and the driver of the Rolls, a huge Asian man in a black suit, got out. He looked around, necessitating another dodge by the brothers. Then he opened the back passenger side door. The man who climbed out was of fair complexion, short, balding and round. He wore a pinstripe suit, navy blue, a pink shirt and a wide burgundy tie. A white handkerchief exploded from the breast pocket. His white-rimmed glasses were oversize and the lenses square—maybe stylish, maybe necessary for a serious vision malady. His expression suggested irritation or impatience.

Russell's phone appeared again and he took pictures of the newcomer.

Braxton and Droon joined him, rather than he them, which meant he was a BlackBridge client and, given the wheels, a valued one.

Shaw recalled what the woman had told her lieutenant earlier, in the Stanford library.

We have that meeting tomorrow. I want to tell him something. Something concrete . . .

That something would have been what they'd tortured out of Colter Shaw—the location of Gahl's evidence. Shaw guessed that where they now were was an example of the UIP. He thought of the unfortunate addicts on the street they'd just walked around, and all the clearing going on before them. The man in the Rolls was probably a developer who'd bought the land for a song.

Braxton and Droon would now have to share that Shaw had not, in fact, led them to the evidence, which would implicate Mr. Rolls too.

How chilly would the meeting be?

The body language suggested that the BlackBridge duo felt something other than respect for a wealthy client. Shaw was looking at two very intimidated people, and to see Irena Braxton this way—an ice queen, if ever there was one—was oddly unsettling. As the chubby man spoke with them, unsmiling and gesticulating with his stubby hands often and broadly, she nodded and gave a polite, attentive frown, like a schoolgirl who'd flubbed a homework assignment. This attitude was, Shaw had no doubt, wholly alien to the woman.

But after what seemed to be her breathless reassurance, the client calmed. He gave them a smile of the sort you might affect when you hand a dollar to a homeless man, and his hands began to fidget less.

They were moving on to other business. Droon unfolded a map and held it up against the side of their SUV. Why not the hood? Shaw wondered. Oh, because the client was too short to see the map there. Everyone consulted the fluttering sheet.

"Who uses a paper map instead of a computer or tablet?" Russell asked.

Shaw nodded at the rhetorical question. Someone who doesn't want electronic evidence, that's who. You can set fire to paper and it's gone forever, unlike digital data, which will last as long as bones from the Jurassic era. Russell produced a range-finder telescope. He looked, then handed it to Shaw.

After five minutes of discussion, the fat man pointed to several locations on the map and Droon marked them with a Sharpie. Then heads nodded and hands were shaken. Braxton and Droon remained where they were while the client stepped to the door of his Rolls. The driver swung the back passenger door open once more. Shaw got a look at two tanned legs, protruding from a short red skirt. Also: impressively high heels, which he thought odd for a woman to wear in the company of a short man like this, who, given the vehicle and his clothing had a surplus of ego. But, of course, there was no accounting for taste . . . or desire.

Before he got into the Rolls he turned and, no longer smiling, fired off more words, accentuated by the curious, jittery hand gestures. Braxton and Droon responded with scolded-dog nods. The man climbed into his sumptuous vehicle. The driver too, and the car sagged under his weight. The car rocked away over the packed construction site dirt.

29

Standing beside their SUV, Irena Braxton lifted a phone from her purse and made another call.

The vibrant handbag was similar to one of Margot's, Shaw recalled from their time together. Hers had been made by indigenous people in South America. It wasn't inexpensive but much of the purchase price went to a nonprofit organization that opposed the burning of the Amazon rain forest. Had Braxton, a known killer, bought hers from the same seller and for the same purpose? In his rewards business, Shaw had learned that the values and priorities people embraced were infinitely contradictory and enigmatic.

She replaced the phone and she and Droon fell silent. Less than a minute later a white van, with no markings on the side, pulled up. Out climbed two men, both white, both in good shape. Their outfits were similar: dark gray slacks and jackets, zippered up. One was tall and bareheaded, with a crew cut, the other short and crowned with a black baseball cap. They were unsmiling and cautious, but didn't scan the surroundings, perhaps assuming if Braxton and Droon were here, the place was safe. Their right hands, though, stayed gyroscopically close to their right hips, where their guns would reside.

They joined Braxton and Droon, who opened the map he'd had moments before and spread it out on the hood of the Escalade. The discussion among them was brief and ended with a nod from the two newcomers, one of whom kept the map. Then Braxton and Droon climbed back into the SUV. The vehicle left.

The brothers, however, remained. The BlackBridge ops were waiting for something and Shaw and Russell wanted to see what it might be.

The answer arrived about five minutes later: two slim men, in shorts and T-shirts, one of them loud red, the other white. The shirts were untucked— a likely indication of concealed weapons. They had light blue vinyl shoulder bags slung over their shoulders. Their heads were shaved and their complexions dark. The TL was the home to several pan-Asian gangs, most notably the notorious Filipino

Bahala Na Gang, more ruthless than the Mafia or the Mexican cartels, Shaw had heard. The BNG's heyday was the end of the last century but many of the murderous crew still were active up and down the West Coast. San Francisco was their primary turf.

"Cutouts," Russell said. "The white-van men. They're insulating the man in the Rolls and Braxton and Droon. The actors never know who they're ultimately acting for. This is pro."

Among the men on the ground a discussion ensued. One of the van men pulled open the side door and took out two clear plastic bags, appearing to weigh two pounds each—maybe a kilo. Russell looked through the telescope again. He then gave it to Shaw, who scanned the clearing. He could see that the bags contained small packets of pills. These they handed over to the gangsters. The van man who'd kept the map now unfurled it.

"UIP," Shaw said. "Ashton's letter I showed you?"

His brother nodded, understanding blossoming in his face. He'd be recalling the Urban Improvement Plan, the cruelly ironic name for the BlackBridge operation that dumped hundreds of pounds of drugs on the streets of neighborhoods to destroy them.

Shaw said, "Monkey wrench." He dialed 911.

The woman's calm voice: "What's the nature of your emergency?"

"There's a drug deal in the construction site

behind Turk at Simpson. I think they might have guns . . . wait, yes, they do!" He put some urgent dismay into his voice, a rattled citizen. He described the men and then disconnected without giving the requested identifying information about himself. Dispatchers were often skeptical about anonymous calls, but with a big drug deal, they'd definitely send a patrol cruiser.

And indeed they did. Almost immediately Shaw heard a vehicle approaching over the gravel. It was an SFPD car with two officers inside.

"That was fast," Russell said, frowning.

The squad car drove right up to the van and the cops climbed out. The driver was a Latino patrol uniform. The other, a tall Anglo, was a detective, wearing a light gray suit, a badge on his belt. They looked over the van men and the two Filipinos. Shaw found himself tensing in anticipation of a firefight. He and Russell would not want to get involved, but he dropped his hand near his gun, in case any of the crew charged their way to escape up the alley, with their own weapons drawn.

The foursome turned toward the cops. One of the men from the van nodded a greeting. The detective smiled back.

"Hell." A whisper from Shaw.

The gold shield had a discussion with the van men. Then all six in the construction zone turned and gazed around them, as Shaw and his brother ducked once more.

"Why they were here so fast," Russell said. "The cops were up the street standing guard."

"They going to come looking?"

But no. The men in the center of the cleared land stopped scanning; they'd apparently decided that whoever had dimed them out via the 911 call had, like most concerned citizens, hightailed it away. The two officers gave some words of farewell, maybe including the advice: pick a less visible place to meet next time. The taller of the van men gestured to one of the BNGs who fished some packets of Oxy or fent out of his bag and handed them to the officers, who nodded thanks then drove away.

The bangers and the BlackBridge duo pored over the map once more, so the distributors knew what neighborhood they were to poison today.

"How much?" Shaw asked.

"Value? At the group we don't get into that much. Guess a hundred K."

Scattering it on the street for free or at a bargain price. But, of course, Mr. Rolls would be making a thousand times that in the real estate deal.

The business was concluded—thick envelopes were handed out to the BNG men, who placed them, along with the drugs, into the shoulder bags. The van men returned to their vehicle, which was soon speeding away, leaving a trail of dust.

It was only then that Shaw realized it was a workday, and construction equipment and supplies were present, yet the site was completely devoid

of workers. The owner—presumably Mr. Rolls—
would have ordered the place closed down for the
meeting.

And who are you? Shaw wondered of the man
in the Rolls. Did you ever hear the name Ashton
Shaw? Did your hands twitch and your mouth smile
as Irena Braxton told you that one of her men was
on the way to the Shaw Compound to have a "conversation" about what he'd discovered?

They didn't have license tags for an ID, but maybe
Karin could get a facial recognition hit.

The BNGs donned flashy wraparound
sunglasses—the lenses orange—and started out of
the site.

The brothers rose.

As Shaw started after the gangbangers Russell
turned the other way—back to the alley where
they'd parked their SUV.

Both men realized they were on opposite courses
and looked back to regard the other.

Shaw whispered, "We've got to stop them. This
way." Nodding toward the BNGs.

Russell said, "No."

Shaw flashed back immediately to the avalanche
field of their youth so many years ago, when he had
sped out to save the life of the woman photographer
on the steep and dangerous slope—and Russell had
held back.

It's not our job . . .

He was about to lay out the urgent case for

stopping the BNGs when his brother said tersely, "You thought I was leaving?"

Shaw didn't reply.

"Hawker's Pass," his brother muttered, seemingly irritated, and continued on his way.

Shaw said, "Oh."

30

In the shadows, close to the brick walls in the alley, Shaw followed the slim men who stalked up the cobblestones out of the demolition zone. He stepped over several dead rats and two more men, sprawled on their sides. They were breathing.

Where were the two Filipinos going to scatter their goods like farmers sowing corn seeds in the spring? What property did Mr. Rolls have his eye on?

He picked up his pace; the men ahead of him were walking quickly.

When they were nearly to the end of the alley, one glanced down and touched his partner on the arm. They stopped, removed the gaudy sunglasses and glanced at the wallet, lying on the cobblestones. They looked up and down the alley and spotted Shaw. He was strolling along in the same direction as they, paying the two no mind, pretending to talk on his cell phone as if in the middle of a pleasant conversation, perhaps a romantic one. Their looks revealed they didn't consider him a threat.

Red Shirt took a packet of drugs from his bag. While they were being paid to scatter the product on sidewalks and in alleys, what harm could there be in selling a bit? A little double-dipping never hurt anyone. As White Shirt bent and lifted the wallet and started to go through it, Red Shirt offered the packet toward Shaw.

He said, "I'll call you back." And slipped the phone away.

Shaw gave an intrigued smile as he stared at the drugs. He approached to within six feet and stopped. BNG crew were often skilled at the devastating forms of martial arts known as Suntukan and Sikaran, punching and kicking. The Philippines were also home to several grappling styles of combat.

The banger could be thinking to lure Shaw close and mug him. After all, why sell your product when you can make off with both the cash and the drugs?

"What is it?" Shaw asked.

"Oxy."

"How much?" He squinted at the bag.

"Twenty."

"How many pills? I can't see."

The BNG held the packet higher.

Which is when Russell stepped into the mouth of the alley and came up behind White Shirt and

Tased him in the kidney. He groaned, shivered and dropped.

Red Shirt spun and reached for his weapon, which Shaw, lunging forward, snagged with his left hand, while seating the muzzle of his Glock against the man's ear.

"**Mapanganib ito** . . . Dangerous what you do!"

Shaw pulled Red Shirt's silver revolver from his hand. His confrere had a Glock and a switchblade knife, both of which Russell pocketed. They took the men's phones too.

Rising unsteadily and wincing against the pain in his back, White Shirt said in a thick accent, "You fucker, you die. You aren't know."

Russell picked up his wallet—emptied of ID and containing only cash—and slipped it back into his hip pocket. While Shaw covered both men, his brother plucked the barbs from White Shirt's skin. Then he collected the man's shoulder bag. Shaw gripped the strap of Red Shirt's tote but the man held on to it hard and turned, looking up at Shaw with furious eyes. "You stupid. This danger shit. It get you cut."

Russell had reloaded the Taser and was aiming. The man slumped and Shaw pulled the bag away.

"Run," Shaw whispered.

The man glared once more and, after White Shirt picked up his sunglasses—as enraged at the scratches on the lenses as at the theft of the drugs and money—they strode off, looking back. For the second time that day the brothers received a single-finger salute.

"They'll be stealing burners in five minutes and calling it in. We've got to go." Russell nodded up the alley. They walked to the SUV and climbed in. Russell pulled into traffic and the heavy vehicle sped out of the TL.

Hawker's Pass . . .

A battle between a settlement and a group of claim jumpers in Northern California during the Silver Rush days. The settlers planted a half-buried strongbox on the back road into the camp, and when the outlaws found it and started to dig it up, one group of settlers came in from the north side of the road, the other from the south and easily took the distracted jumpers. Shaw remembered sitting beside his father and brother and watching Ashton draw a map of the battle, as he lectured the boys about tactics.

Never attack an enemy directly when you can distract and flank . . .

So, no, Russell had not intended to leave. He had made stopping the BNGs his fight, as well as Shaw's, and had come up with a good strategy to do it with no bloodshed.

They left the TL and Russell drove back to the waterfront at Hunters Point, where they pitched the drugs and the BNGs' guns and phones and the knife into the Bay.

They returned to the safe house on Alvarez.

Russell ran the plate of the van—it was not obscured, like the Caddy's and the Rolls's—and the
information came back that it was registered to a
corporation that was undoubtedly owned by an offshore entity. Russell sent the picture he'd taken of
Mr. Rolls to someone—presumably Karin. Soon he
received a text in return.

"Too far away for facial recognition."

"Burlingame now. Nadler's house." The town was
south of San Francisco, a working-class and com-
muter community, the home of San Francisco airport. Shaw had seen a picture of the house, which
Mack had sent. It was a tidy one-story dwelling,
painted yellow and set amid a small but well-tended
garden.

Shaw was calling up the address when his phone
dinged with an incoming email.

It was from Mack McKenzie. He read the
message.

He said, "We have to make a stop on the way."

31

Ghirardelli Square—part of the tourist magnet Fisherman's Wharf—wasn't busy on this cloudy day. Rain threatened.

Shaw and Russell were in the SUV, parked near the corner on which a man strummed a guitar. His case was open and people would occasionally toss coins or bills in. He was tall and lean and long blond hair flowed from beneath a cowboy hat with a tightly curled brim.

You could smell chocolate, exuding by chance or design from the Ghirardelli building. He explained to Russell how he'd come to take on the reward job to find Tessy Vasquez.

He then told him that his private investigator had, among her contractors, an audio analyst, to whom she'd sent Tessy's message. The expert had filtered out the young woman's voice and analyzed every sound on it.

The email Shaw had just received in the Tenderloin contained the results of that analysis. He called it up and the men read.

> Music: Ambient music from outdoor café, recorded.
>
> Music: Performers, including live guitar, drums, rap music and applause, possibly accompanying hip-hop dancers. Occasional breaks in vocal performances to say "Thanks" or "Thank you," presumably in response to tips. Hence, street performers.
>
> Sounds of children laughing and occasionally breathless: Playground.
>
> Foghorns, decibel level suggesting distance of three to four miles. Echoing off tall structure nearby. Possibly Avnet Tower on California Street.
>
> Ship horn 1: This matches the tone of the Marin Express, ferry with

service from Pier 41 in the Embarcadero to Sausalito, approximately one mile away.

Ship horn 2: This matches the Alcatraz Cruiser, a ship operated by Bay Cruise Tours, approximately one mile away.

Ship horn 3. This matches the tone of the Sea Maid III, operated by Cruise Tours Unlimited, docked at Eureka Promenade, approximately 300+ feet away.

Cable car bells, from opposite directions, probably the north terminus of the Powell/Mason line to the east, and Powell/Hyde line to the west. Powell/Mason is closer.

Correlating these data, I think the location is the southwest Fisherman's Wharf area, likely Ghirardelli Square.

"Whoever did it is good," Russell said.

Shaw was looking around. "I'll be back in a minute." He climbed out of the vehicle and approached the guitarist. He pulled a twenty from his pocket and dropped it into the guitar case.

"Hey, man, thanks." His eyes were wide.

"Got a question."

"Sure." Maybe hoping: Was he free to sign a multimillion-dollar recording contract?

"Do you know this girl? She's gone missing. I'm helping her mother try to find her."

"Oh, yeah. Tessy. Jesus. Missing?"

"When did you see her last?"

"I just got back from Portland. Before that. A week maybe."

"You know her well?"

"No. Talked about music some. Mostly just to divide up the corners, you know. So we didn't sing over each other. This sucks. I hope she's okay."

"You ever know if she had trouble with anyone?"

"Never saw it. Guys'd flirt. You know. She could handle it."

"Was she ever with a man named Roman?" Shaw described him.

"Doesn't sound familiar."

Shaw thanked him. He studied the block, turning in a slow circle. His eyes came to rest on a gift shop, specializing in saltwater taffy and objets d'art based on cable cars, the Golden Gate Bridge and Alcatraz.

He caught his brother's eye and nodded at the store. Russell joined him.

"Video?" his brother asked.

"It's right in the line of sight. Hope so."

The two men greeted the manager of the store, dressed for some reason like a clerk in an Old West general store. Straw hat, candy-striped shirt, suspenders and a sleeve garter. When they explained why they were here, he said, "Oh, no. Terrible." He added that he knew Tessy. She occasionally would come into the store and exchange the tip coins she'd received from performing for bills.

He handed over the counter to another worker, and the men followed him into the back room.

He logged on to a cloud server and typed in the date and time from the call Tessy had made to her mother. Scrubbing back and forth . . . Finally, in fast motion, Tessy walked into view, removed her guitar from the case, which she opened for the tips, and then slung the instrument over her neck. She was in a red blouse and a black gypsy skirt. Her dark hair was loose.

She began to sing, smiling to passersby. The chord changes seemed efficient. No fancy jazz riffs. He'd heard that a guitar had never been intended as a lead instrument, but a rhythm one. That came from his distant past, from Margot, who'd been a source of much of his popular cultural knowledge. The woman had then added, "But tell that to Jimi Hendrix."

Shaw's own personal favorite guitarist was the Australian Tommy Emmanuel, who seemed to pry an entire orchestra from his git-fiddle.

Shaw was amused that her guitar was a Yamaha, the same brand as his motorbike. He supposed they were the same company—though that was about as diversified a manufacturing operation as you would find.

"Can you scrub to where she leaves?"

The man did. They saw her put her guitar away and pull a phone from her pocket. She made a brief call—probably the one to her mother. She then picked up the guitar case, slung a purse over her shoulder and started up the street away from the store. She walked to the corner and turned right.

"You catch that?" Shaw asked.

"The van," Russell said.

A gray minivan, which had been parked on the same side of the street as Tessy was on, pulled into traffic as she walked by and proceeded slowly, as if following her. It made the same turn she did.

"Christ, you think they did . . . I mean, did something to her?" The manager's face radiated concern.

"Scrub back to where it arrives."

That was about twenty minutes before she left.

"Let it play in normal time."

Yes, it was suspicious. After the van parked, no one got out. And no one got in; it wasn't there to pick someone up. Then the passenger side doors opened and two men got out. They were Anglo, pale with thick black hair—one's was slicked back, the other's was a disorderly mop. They were in dress shirts and slacks. The one from the front seat removed a phone from his pocket and took a picture of the square, then fiddled with the screen.

"He's sending the picture."

A moment later, after what seemed to be a text exchange, Slick put the phone away. He lit a cigarette and the two climbed back into the van.

"We should call the police."

Russell said, "We will. Any way we can get a copy of that vid?"

"Sure." He rummaged in the desk and found an SD card. "From the time she arrived?"

"If you would, yes."

He typed some commands and within a minute the video, in the form of an MP4 file, was on the card.

Shaw said, "We'll pay you for it."

"No, no. Just get it to the police right away. God, I hope she's okay."

Shaw described Tessy's ex, Roman. "Was she ever in here with somebody who looked like him?"

"Not that I remember."

They thanked him. He handed them a business card. "Please let me know what happens."

Russell said they would and the men returned to the SUV.

As his brother fired up the big vehicle, Shaw sent a text to Mack, with the priority code, requesting information on a vehicle. He'd memorized the van's California license tag.

"Let's look at the cross street." Russell pulled into

traffic and, following the same route as the gray van, turned the corner. The street was not much more than an alley—it was lined by the backs of buildings and loading docks, no storefronts or residences.

"Couldn't've picked a better place for a snatch," Russell said, "if we'd planned it out ahead of time."

32

Shaw's phone hummed with a text.

Gray van is registered to a California corporation, Specialty Services, LLC. No physical address. P.O. box. Specialty Services is owned by an offshore. Have lawyers in St. Kitts and Sacramento looking into ultimate ownership.

Shaw read this to his brother, as he piloted the SUV to Burlingame.

"Doesn't look good. Police? This isn't a BlackBridge thing."

"They're undocumented. Tessy and her mother.

They'll be deported. Or Maria will be, by herself, if I can't find Tessy. Anyway, the police won't get on board with what we have."

He couldn't tell his brother's reaction.

After fifteen minutes of silence, Russell asked, "It's like PI work then?"

"The rewards? Pretty much. Looking for escapees, suspects. Some private. Like Tessy."

"You do BEA?"

"No." Bond enforcement agents pursued bail skippers and FTAs—"failures to appear" at hearings or trials. The criminals whom bond agents pursued were invariably punks and drunks and could usually be located with minimal mental effort—in places like their girlfriends' or parents' basements or in the same bar where they got wasted the night they committed the crime they'd been hauled to jail for in the first place. He explained this.

"You want a better quality perp."

"A more **challenging** perp."

More silence.

"What're the rewards like?"

"You mean, amounts?"

Russell nodded.

"From a couple of thousand. To twenty million or so."

"Million?"

"Not my kind of work, generally. It's a State Department reward. The way those work is somebody in the bad guy's organization gets location information to the CIA. Then it's time for SEAL Team Six."

"Who's the twenty million?"

"Guy named Idrees Ayubi . . . He's a . . ." Shaw's voice faded as he saw his brother nodding knowingly. Given his profession, it wasn't surprising that he'd know the name of the terrorist with the highest bounty offered by the U.S. government.

After some silence Shaw said, "But it's not about the money. What I like about a reward is it's a flag. It means there's a problem that nobody's been able to solve. Never be bored."

"Was that one of Ash's? I don't remember it."

"No."

The boys had once asked their father—whom Russell dubbed the King of Never—why he phrased his rules beginning with the negative. The man's answer: "Gets your attention better."

Russell fell silent once again. Shaw wondered if he was still angry at the suggestion that he was running away from confronting the BNGs.

"A cult? Tom Pepper was saying?"

"Last week. Washington State."

"Somebody posted a reward to get a follower out of the place?"

Shaw explained that, no, he had learned about the cult on a reward job and he'd been troubled by the cult leaders' sadistic and predatory behavior. "I went in undercover, found a lot of vulnerable people—there were a hundred members altogether. I did what I could to save some of them. Made some enemies."

Shaw now realized two things: One, he was rambling, and he was doing it for the purpose of encouraging his brother to engage, to dive beneath the surface of their cocktail-party small talk.

And, two, Russell was simply filling the thorny pits of silence; he evidently had little interest in Shaw's narrative.

Finally Shaw said, "Something on your mind?" He didn't think he'd ever asked his brother this question.

Russell hesitated then said, "An assignment I have to get to."

"Here?"

"No. Can't say where."

"You don't want to be doing this, do you?" Shaw asked. He gestured toward the pleasant street they were coursing along in Burlingame but meant the pursuit of BlackBridge.

"Just, we should get it done."

Another voice ended the conversation: the woman within the GPS announced that their destination was on the left.

M a'am, I wonder if you'd be willing to help us out," Shaw said.

The woman in the doorway was early seventies,

he estimated. She looked at them with a smile but with still eyes, as one will do with doorbell ringers who seem polite but are wholly unexpected. She'd be wondering about this pair in particular, who bore a very slight resemblance to each other. She wore an apron, not the sort serious chefs donned like body armor, but light blue, with frills and lace, insubstantial. A garment from a bygone era.

"My husband will be back soon."

Offered as a reason that she might be less helpful to them now, being only half the complement. And spoken too as a shield. Reinforcements would arrive momentarily.

Her name, they'd learned thanks to Mack's research, was Eleanor.

Shaw introduced himself and Russell and then said, "My brother and I are looking into some family history."

This was indisputable. Not the whole truth, but how often is **that** really necessary?

"We were going through some old family papers and found out our father had some interest in this house or whoever lived here."

Russell qualified, "A long time ago."

"Well, this's my husband's family's house. He's lived here thirty years. Who's your father? Oh, you said 'had.' Does that mean he's not with us any longer?"

"No, he's not," Shaw told her.

"I'm sorry." Her face exuded genuine sorrow. This was a woman who had experienced loss herself.

"What was your father's name?"

"Ashton Shaw."

A squint, and faint lines appeared in the powdery face. "I don't think I know the name. Maybe Mort does. You have a picture? Maybe it'll jog my memory?" She was more comfortable now, since the men weren't trying to talk their way inside and sell her insurance or aluminum siding.

Shaw was irritated with himself for not thinking to bring a picture of their father. He was surprised when Russell produced a small photo—and not on his camera but from the location where family pictures used to be kept: his wallet. Shaw was stung even deeper at the thought that he had accused his older brother—even if silently—of killing a man whose picture he carried around with him after all these years.

Glancing down at the faded rectangle, he was more surprised yet to find that the shot was not of Ashton alone, but of the three Shaw men: father and sons. Ashton was behind, the boys in front. Shaw was about twelve. They were rigged for rappelling in the high country.

He turned back to Eleanor, expecting her to say, **My, I can see the resemblance**, or something similar.

Instead she was frozen, gaping at the picture.

"Ma'am?" Russell asked.

"I **do** know him."

Shaw's pulse picked up. "How?"

"Years ago, ages. He was older than in your picture and his hair was wilder. And whiter. But I remember him clearly. It was at the funeral. He was looking very distraught. Well, we all were, of course. But he seemed especially troubled. We thought that was odd since no one in the family had a clue who he was."

Shaw: "Whose funeral was it?"

"My son. Amos."

"Amos Gahl?"

"That's right. I'm Eleanor Nadler now. I remarried after my first husband passed."

She tilted her head and looked each of them over, and it was a coy, conspiratorial gaze. "Why don't you come in? I'll make some coffee. And you boys can tell me why you're really here."

33

The house smelled of mothballs, which, Shaw supposed, most people associate with grand-parents' homes and old clothing in odd cuts and colors stored away forever.

Shaw's thought, though, was of snakes: during one particularly dry, infestive year, Ashton and the children had ringed the cabin and gardens with pungent spheres of naphthalene to ward off persistent rattlers searching for water and mice.

Eleanor nodded to a floral couch, and the Shaw brothers sat. She disappeared into the kitchen. Given his childhood, Shaw had no reference point for television sitcoms but he and Margot had occasionally lain on inflatable mattresses during one of her archeological digs and, on a tablet or computer, watched the shows her parents and grandparents had loved. Surreal to have just made love to a sultry woman, in the wilderness of Arizona, your pistol handy in case of coyotes, and be watching **The Andy Griffith Show** (funny) or **Bewitched** (not his style).

This home was immaculate, well dusted, pastel. There were many objects sitting on many surfaces. China figurines were outnumbered only by family photographs.

Five minutes later the woman returned with a silver tray on which sat three delicate porcelain cups, filled with black coffee, on saucers. A sugar bowl and pitcher filled with viscous cream, not milk, sat beside them. Also, three spoons and three napkins folded into triangles. She passed out one cup each to Shaw and Russell and took one for herself. The brothers doctored with cream. The coffee was rich. African. Kenyan, Shaw was pretty sure.

In her soft voice she said, "I have a feeling that this isn't about 23andMe genealogy, is it?"

"No, Ms. Nadler—?" Russell began.

"Eleanor," she corrected. "I have a feeling we have something important in common. First names seem appropriate."

"Eleanor," Shaw said, sipping again and putting the cup down. The clink seemed loud. "We're here looking into how our father died." He had to say the next part. "We think he was killed under circumstances similar to your son's death."

"It was no accident," she muttered. "I know that."

Russell said, "Not long before he died, our father was in touch with some coworkers who knew Amos."

"At BlackBridge." Her lips tightened.

A nod. "They think Amos smuggled some evidence out of the company. Evidence of crimes they'd committed."

Shaw went on to explain about the Urban Improvement Plan and other illegal activities that the company was involved in: the stock manipulation, the kickbacks, the phony earthquake inspections.

She didn't know UIP or other specifics—Shaw supposed her son intentionally didn't tell her too much, to protect her—but she said, "There was always something wrong about that place. He was never comfortable there." Her eyes strayed to a picture on the wall. It depicted Gahl in his early twenties. He was in a soccer kit. Curly dark hair, a lean face. "He was such a good boy. Smart. Good-looking . . . Oh, he was a catch. I'd thought he'd bring home the most beautiful girl in college." A laugh. "He brought home some beautiful **boys** . . . That was the way he went. Fine with me." A sigh. "My son was happy. He loved academia."

"Where did he teach?" Russell asked.

"San Francisco State. He was happy there." Her face tightened. "Then he joined that company. It wasn't a good place. It was dark. But he got tempted. Where else could somebody with a history degree make the kind of money they paid him?"

Shaw: "Are you comfortable telling us more about his death?"

She was silent for a long moment, her eyes fixed on a ceramic statue of a bird, a mourning dove on the coffee table.

"Officially it was a car crash. He went off Highway One. You know how bad that can be south of the city?"

Both men nodded, and Shaw thought of the article in Ashton's secret room about the state assemblyman's crash and the ensuing fire that destroyed some records he had with him.

"It was near Maverick. The beach." The extreme surfing capital of the state.

"Only he had no reason to be driving that way. He'd left BlackBridge and was spending all his time in the city on some project of his. That was odd—why he was fifty miles south of the city. And then . . ." She took a moment to compose herself. "And then there was the mortician."

Shaw encouraged her with a nod.

"He asked me if the police found who attacked him. I was dumbfounded. Attacked him? What did he mean? Oh, the poor man was beside himself. He thought I knew. You see, the body was badly burned but in getting it ready for the crematorium, he noticed stab wounds, deep ones. Someone had . . ." She steadied herself. A few breaths. "Someone had stabbed him and then twisted the knife. To cause more pain."

Shaw pictured the SOG knife, recalled Droon's gesturing with the blade yesterday morning.

Insert, twist . . .

His torture method of choice.

With her jaw tightly set, she whispered, "He said it looked like he was stabbed in the leg and the blade hit the femoral artery. **That** would be an accident. They wanted to keep him alive—I guess to find out where the evidence you mentioned was."

Had they caught him at the library yesterday Shaw too would have been strapped down and the SOG knife plunged into his arm or leg.

And with each question would have come another twist of the blade.

"Did Amos leave anything here? Records, files, computers, hard drives? Maybe a briefcase? He called it a courier bag."

She sipped from the cup and thought for a moment. "No. And near the end he didn't come by very often. He seemed paranoid. He believed he was being watched. But he would meet a friend here. At first, I thought it was sweet. Bringing a boyfriend home to meet Mom and Stepdad. They were . . . well, it was easy to see they were close. He was a coworker at BlackBridge, though I think he'd quit by the time he came here. But they weren't completely social get-togethers. We'd have a meal and then they'd go down to the cellar to talk. I think they wanted a place that was completely private and secure." Her eyes darkened.

"Maybe Amos and his friend thought their own houses were bugged."

"Do you remember his friend's name?"

"I do. Because it was one you don't hear very much. A pretty name. La Fleur. Last name. It means 'flower' in French. I don't remember his first."

"Do you know where he lives?"

"Marin, I think he said at dinner. Nothing more than the county. Maybe he was paranoid too. Even here."

"And you think La Fleur had quit BlackBridge?"

"I'm pretty sure so." A scornful laugh. "He probably had a conscience."

"Anyone else Amos met with from the company?"

"La Fleur's the only one I remember." She chuckled. "If I thought Amos was paranoid, you should have seen the friend. During dinner, he asked what kind of encryption our phones used. Mort and I laughed. Heavens! We thought it was a joke. But he was serious. When we said we didn't have an idea Amos made us shut our phones off. We thought he was humoring his friend. I suppose not. Sometimes it's not really paranoia at all, is it?"

Again, the brothers shared a glance.

They rose and thanked her for her time. Shaw said he'd be in touch if they learned anything else.

She walked them to the door. She looked out into the front yard, a pleasant setting. A Japanese maple dominated. Some bright flowers, purple and blue, lorded over recently mulched beds. Shaw, like all

THE FINAL TWIST   225

survivalists, knew some plants well—those that are edible, that are toxic, that can be used as medicines and antiseptics. Of flowers that were merely decorative he was largely ignorant.

Eleanor said, "Amos wasn't a fool. He'd know there was a chance that he'd get found out. And that means he wouldn't hide the evidence, this bag, so far out of sight that it couldn't be found by somebody else after he was gone."

Which echoed Shaw's very thought when he was searching for the bag in the Stanford library yesterday morning.

The woman continued, "You two are that somebody else."

She looked from one brother to the other, then tugged tight the drawstring of her frilly apron, not a stain upon it. Her placid, sitcom-grandmother face grew hard. Her eyes locked onto Shaw's. "Find it. And take those motherfuckers down."

34

Sausalito is a quaint bay- and cliffside suburb north of the Golden Gate Bridge.

The demographics are artists and crafts-people and, given the views, the fine scone and muffin bakeries, and the high-speed ferries to downtown, well-heeled professionals.

In Russell's SUV the brothers were presently rocking through the winding and hilly streets, which were lined with dense foliage.

The inimitable Karin had tracked down La Fleur—first name Earnest, spelled the nontraditional way—and gotten his address but, interestingly, the group's databases offered little other information about him.

The man was off the grid. No phone, no social media. Amos Gahl's mother had said that La Fleur had been an employee of BlackBridge but even that assertion, which Shaw had every reason to believe, was not available for confirmation. Shaw suspected his identity had been scrubbed to vapor.

Learning this about La Fleur, Shaw reflected how his father had come up with perhaps the best form of scrubbing in existence—never entrusting a single fact about himself, his work, his family, to the digital world.

"That's it," Russell said, nodding ahead of them to a cul-de-sac.

The narrow street, on which there were no sidewalks, was bounded by old-growth trees and interwoven tangles of foliage. In this part of town were few houses and the ones they'd passed were fronted with short picket fences through which grew thick greenery. La Fleur's property was different. It was protected by a solid pressure-treated stockade fence, eight feet tall, aged to gray. The slats topped with strands of barbed wire.

Russell parked and they walked to the gate, which was locked.

"No intercom," he said.

Shaw knelt and looked through a foot-round hole that had been cut in the wood for mail. All he could see was more foliage.

Russell took a small flat object from his pocket—like a black metal fingernail file—and, after examining the crack between gate and fence, slipped the latch in with a swift move and pushed the gate open.

They stepped inside and looked over La Fleur's house. The rambling residence, an architectural mess in Cape Cod gray, was on a steep hillside, with stilts holding it aloft, forty feet above the rocks below. This entire area was subject to tremors of varying magnitude and Shaw would not have lived in a stilt house here for any money, whatever the view.

On the other hand, the building was at least three-quarters of a century old and had clearly survived various past shakings, perhaps damaged but suffering no mortal injury.

The men started toward the structure down a serpentine path, which was, curiously, interrupted every ten feet or so with oil drums filled with concrete. They were a version of what you saw in front of embassies and government security agencies overseas, to prevent suicide bombers from plowing their explosive-filled Toyota pickups straight into the front door.

"Hmm," Russell said.

As they approached the last drum, Shaw suddenly tilted his head. Russell too.

Both men dropped fast, taking cover behind one barricade.

Nothing is more distinctive than the creaking sound of a homemade bow being drawn.

The arrow hissed over their heads and lodged in a tree to the left, fired by a figure standing just inside the front door of the house. They couldn't see clearly but his garment appeared to be a variation on nighttime camo—various shades of blue and black. He wore dark brown leather gloves.

The arrow was a crude projectile, also homemade, but it still traveled at typical arrow velocity—around two hundred feet per second—and embedded itself neatly in a eucalyptus, which is not a soft wood.

"'That's a warning shot. Get the hell out of here!" The voice was raspy and manic.

"Mr. La Fleur," Shaw called. "We just want to talk!"

"You're trespassing!"

Russell: "You don't have an intercom."

Shaw said, "And you don't have a phone either."

"How the fuck did you know that?"

Another arrow banged into the steel drum to their right.

The men surveyed the field of fire. Shaw estimated: fifteen feet to the bottom step, then three up to the narrow porch, three more to the door.

Shaw tried to calculate the odds. A crossbow, which takes some effort and time to cock and fit with a bolt, would have been no problem. They could easily cover the ground in the time it took to reload. But a recursive bow like this? One could fire about eight arrows a minute, if the archer were aiming carefully.

A **skilled** archer, that is. It didn't seem that La Fleur was. He dropped another arrow as he tried to notch it. Then he got it ready to launch. Shaw noted that his hands were trembling.

"Sir, we're not a threat!" Russell called. "We'd just like to talk to you about—"

Clunk . . .

This arrow hit the drum they were behind.

Shaw was getting irritated. "Hey, cut it out! You could hurt bystanders doing that!"

"No, I could fucking hurt **you**!"

The brothers regarded each other again and nodded.

Another arrow hissed in their direction. As it flew by, Shaw and Russell were instantly on their feet, sprinting to the door. Shaw slammed into the heavy panel with his shoulder. The door in turn bowled the man to the floor.

La Fleur howled, dropped the weapon and held his hands up.

Russell pushed into the foyer just after Shaw, his pistol drawn, in case La Fleur chose to attack with a knife or, who knew, a broadsword or battle-axe.

But the skirmish was over as fast as it had begun.

He skittered over the oak to a corner, huddling and crying out, "Bastards!"

The man had wild white hair, not unlike Ashton's toward the end, though La Fleur's was pulled into a sloppy ponytail. He had lengthy blanched eyebrows. He was gaunt. Beneath the camo, he wore a red floral shirt and on his feet were sandals with tie-dye straps. Bronze earrings dangled. The man was a combat-ready hippie.

"Nazis! Fascists! I have rights!"

"Calm down," Shaw said, pulling the man's gloves off and zip-tying his hands behind him. He noted he hadn't trimmed his nails in ages. They were yellow.

"No!"

Shaw: "I'm just doing this so everybody's safe. We're not going to hurt you."

"You already did. My butt aches."

"Calm. Down."

The volume of the muttering diminished some and La Fleur nodded, as if he were afraid of the consequences of even speaking to the two home invaders.

Shaw re-latched the many locks.

"Anybody else in the house?"

A negative twisting of neck and head.

Guns drawn, the brothers went about clearing the place anyway. Though they hadn't seen—let alone trained with—each other since they were children, they fell instantly into the procedure that Ashton Shaw had taught. "Door closed, left . . . Bathroom, half-open right . . . Clear. Breeze from second bedroom, window open. Barred . . . No hostiles. Clear! . . . No cellar . . . Attic sealed . . ."

They returned to the living room. Shaw looked over the place, which was perfumed with three distinctive smells: damp fireplace ash, rich pot and ocean. Two windows faced east, the direction of San Francisco Bay. These would have offered stunning views had they not been covered with thick metal shutters. Shaw knew their make and model. They were bulletproof, expensive and a favorite of cartel bosses. He knew of these qualities from a reward job a few years ago. He could also attest to the fact that when hit by automatic gunfire, the resulting bang was as loud as the muzzle burst itself.

The house could have been outfitted by a survivalist. There were stacks upon stacks of sandbags, piled halfway up the walls, enough to stop a fusillade of bullets. Ports had been cut into the wall through which he could pepper attacking hordes with his caveman arrows. La Fleur also had medical supplies aplenty, including a satchel labeled SELF-SURGERY KIT.

Also fifty-gallon drums of drinking water and hundreds of pounds of MRE. Meals ready to eat were a staple for the armed services . . . and for gullible pseudo-survivalists who listened to paranoia-dishing talk radio hosts.

Ashton Shaw had taught the children that true survivalism means learning how to grow, gather and hunt for your own food.

One difference between this cliffside dwelling and the Compound: La Fleur had a computer and a TV. In the Compound there'd been no electronics whatsoever, except an emergency cell phone. It was kept charged but shut off. The only time Shaw remembered its being used was the cold October morning when he went off to look for his father on Echo Ridge, after the man had gone missing.

35

The brothers helped La Fleur into an indented armchair of faded green fabric and Shaw cut the restraint off. Now the grizzled man was trying a different tack; he was contrite. "It's all a mistake. Me shooting at you? I thought you were burglars. Really. There's been a string of robberies in the neighborhood. I have clippings. Do you want to see them? I would never have shot you if I'd known you weren't burglars. Don't hurt me!"

Russell frowned. "Burglars? Hmm."

"Who'd you really think we were?" Shaw asked.

"From BlackBridge?" Russell asked.

The man froze and then looked down. It was as if the very word paralyzed him. He gave the faintest of nods.

"We're not," Shaw said.

Russell tapped the grip of his SIG Sauer. "If we were BlackBridge, you'd be dead. Right?"

La Fleur rubbed his wrists. He reached for a bong and a lighter on the chair-side table.

"No," Russell said.

"You want some?" he offered the stained glass tube. Both men ignored him. He put it down.

"Amos Gahl's mother told us about you."

His face softened "Eleanor! How is she?"

"She's fine."

"And her husband? Mort."

"Apparently okay," Shaw said. "He was out. Now, Earnest. We need your help. Amos found some evidence against BlackBridge. We think it's proof about the Urban Improvement Plan. You know about it?"

He frowned, taking this in. He remained cautious. "Who are you?"

"Our father," Shaw said, "was killed by Irena Braxton and Eb-bitt Droon. Ian Helms too."

"Your father?"

"Ashton Shaw. Did you know him?"

"I don't remember the name. But there was somebody . . . wild-eyed, like a cowboy."

Russell displayed the picture.

"That's him. He stopped me outside where I was living. He told me he was a professor and one of his students had been killed by BlackBridge."

"Todd Zaleski, a city councilman."

La Fleur squinted. "That was it, yes! Supposedly a robbery but your dad didn't believe it. Like you guys—he was looking for what Ame had taken from BlackBridge. I told him I couldn't help him. He left and I never heard from him again."

"You were close to Amos, his mother told us."

A nod and his weathered lips drew taut.

"Will you help us? Whatever Amos found is in a courier bag. He hid it somewhere in the Bay Area."

Eyes again on the floor, La Fleur mumbled, "I don't know anything. I swear to God."

In the rewards business, Shaw had done a fair amount of kinesics analysis—using body language to spot deception. Included in that fine art was noting verbal tics. Anyone who ends a sentence with the assurance that they're not lying probably is, and it's a double hit if a deity is invoked.

Shaw stared at him until La Fleur added, in a whisper, "BlackBridge is the devil—the whole company. Everybody. Not just Helms and Braxton. It's like the buildings are evil, the walls are evil . . . It's so dangerous. Why do you think I'm living like this?"

"Don't you want Helms to go to prison for what they did to your friend?" Shaw asked.

The man looked away.

Shaw felt frustration. This man knew something. He said, "There's a family that Droon and Braxton are going to kill tomorrow."

La Fleur's face revealed some concern at this. "Why?"

Russell: "We don't know."

"We find Amos's evidence and go to the FBI.

They arrest Ian Helms and Braxton and Droon. We stop the killing. Help us save them."

Russell stirred impatiently. Shaw had refined his interviewing and interrogation skills over the years in seeking rewards. Though he could be firm, he generally used logic, empathy and humor to win over the subjects. He suspected his brother took a somewhat different approach.

Shaw persisted. "You and Amos met at Eleanor's house a few times. You met there because she hadn't been 'Gahl' for years. She'd remarried and changed her name. So Braxton and Droon wouldn't know about her."

Shaw studied La Fleur patiently until he decided, it seemed, it wasn't too incriminating to answer. "That's right."

"What did Amos tell you when you were over at his mother's, the last time you met?"

He fidgeted, played with the bong. "Nothing. Really! We just chatted. Chewed the fat." His evasive face gave a smile. "My grandmother used to say that. When I was a kid I never knew what it meant. I still—"

Russell snapped, "What did Amos tell you?"

Shaw said patiently, yet in a firm voice, "They're going to murder a **family**. There was a note we found, a kill order. It didn't say 'target' singular or 'couple.' Husband and wife. It said 'family.' That means children. We have no idea who they are and we've only got twenty-four hours to find out and save them."

Russell said nothing more. With dark, threatening eyes he stared at the man.

Good cop, bad cop.

"The evidence," Shaw said. "Amos was going to hide it. I think you know where."

La Fleur shook his head vehemently. "No, no, no! We didn't talk about anything like that. We talked about plants, fertilizer."

"At midnight?"

"How did you know that's when we met?" The man's eyes grew alarmed.

Shaw hadn't, but it was logical.

"I'm a gardener. Look outside!" He uttered a forced laugh. "My last name, you know. 'Flower' in French. Amos was into plants too. We had some wine and talked about gardening." The sadness returned.

Russell shot a glance to his younger brother, who handed off the interview to him, easing back and falling silent.

As Russell leaned close, La Fleur shied, kneading his hands into fists then opening his fingers. Over and over. "I'll send an anonymous text to BlackBridge, attention Braxton and Droon. It'll have two items in it. One, your name. Two, your address."

"What?" A horrified whisper.

"When they come at you with their M4 assault rifles, your arrows aren't going to do anything but piss them off."

Bad cop had become worse cop.

His shoulders slumped. He sighed. "I'm probably screwed anyway. They tracked you on your phones."

"We have shielded and encrypted burners," Shaw said.

He didn't seem to believe them. "Oh yeah? What's your algorithm?"

"AES, Twofish and Scorpion."

With a glance toward Shaw, Russell said, "That's mine too." Curiously the brothers had, on their own, picked the same encryption package.

La Fleur snapped, "Let me see."

Russell offered his phone. La Fleur grabbed and studied it, then for some reason shook the mobile as if to see what kind of data would rattle out. He examined the screen once more. He handed it back. He seemed marginally relieved and didn't bother with Shaw's unit.

The man's zipping eyes settled on the knotty-pine floor. He rose and walked to a shuttered window. He opened the metal slat a few inches, ducking—as if to slip out of a sniper's crosshairs. After a moment he stood, crouching, and looked out.

Apparently satisfied there were no surveillance devices, or rifles, trained his way, he closed and re-latched the shutter. Walking to a far corner of the room, he turned on an elaborate LP record player and, pulling on latex gloves, removed an old-time album from its sleeve. He set the black disk gingerly on the turntable and, with infinite care, set the needle in the groove of the first track.

Music pounded into the room, some rock group. Anyone trying to listen in would hear only raging guitar and fierce drums.

La Fleur removed the gloves and replaced them in the box. He looked his intruders over. "You two really have no clue what's going on."

And with a defiant look at Russell, he grabbed the bong, lit up and inhaled long.

36

The smoke spiraled upward, dissolving at its leisure.

Never into recreational drugs, Shaw nonetheless found the rich smell of pot pleasant. He waited until La Fleur exhaled and sat back. A twitching tilt of his head like a squirrel assessing a tree. The man put the blue tube down.

"Oh, yes, Amos found something, and he hid it. But it had nothing to do with the Urban Improvement Plan. I have no idea why you're harping on that. Your father was wrong: there **is** no evidence against the company. If there were, Ame would have found it. He searched and searched. But there wasn't and there'll **never** be any evidence. Helms and his people're too smart to leave anything incriminating. They used cutout after cutout, encoding, anonymous servers, shell companies, encryption. The CIA should be as good as BlackBridge."

"Facts," Russell said. "Not drama."

La Fleur shot him a look that managed to be simultaneously hurt and defiant.

"My poor Ame . . . He got himself in over his head, didn't he? He took it upon himself to end the UIP. Helms had something his main client wanted desperately. It was code-named the Endgame Sanction. Braxton and some thug had found it in the Embarcadero. Maybe Droon. Looks like a rat, doesn't he?"

Shaw said, "The Hayward Brothers Warehouse?"

"I don't know. But she found it and it was like . . . the ring of power. The client had wanted it forever, was paying a retainer of millions to track it down." A faint chuckle. "And you'll never guess what Ame did. He heard Helms talking about it, about how it was the end-all and be-all . . . and when the big boss stepped out of his office, my Ame simply waltzed in and nicked it! Dropped it in his courier bag and walked out the front door with a nighty-night to the guards."

"Why?"

"He was going to use it as leverage, get the company to shut down the UIP program. Or maybe stealing it, he thought the client would fire Helms, and then BlackBridge'd go out of business. I don't think he had a plan. He was just sick of working for such a vile bunch of men and women."

"What was this thing?"

"He never had a chance to tell me." His voice went soft. "He stole it about five p.m. He hid it about an hour later. Then at ten that night he called me. I'd never heard him so panicked. He said he'd done some research and found out what the Sanction was, and it needed to be destroyed. It was devastating. The client could never get it, no one could. He was going to destroy it himself but he couldn't get back to where he'd hidden it. He knew BlackBridge ops were searching for him. If anything happened to him, I was supposed to find it and get rid of it."

Shaw looked toward his brother, who frowned. What on earth was it?

"And he died while they were torturing him to find out where it was?" Shaw asked.

"That's right, I'm sure."

A new track came on, louder. The men had to huddle close to hear and be heard.

Russell asked, "Where did he hide it?"

"He was afraid of the phone lines, so he gave me two clues. One was the 'dog park.' He meant Quigley Square. A friend of ours lived there and we'd walk her dog if she was traveling."

Shaw knew the place, a transitional neighborhood in the city.

"The other clue was 'It's hidden underground, someplace you'd be expecting.'"

Great, thought Shaw. More scavenger hunt.

Another hit of the weed. "Then I heard a shout. It sounded like he dropped the phone. Then it seemed like there was a scuffle." He grew silent for a moment. "That was the last time I heard his voice."

"Any guesses where he meant?"

"No."

Russell: "You ever think about going to Quigley Square and doing what he wanted to? Destroying it?"

His eyes, more tearful, looked down at the dimpled wood floor. "I thought, yes, but I didn't. I'm a coward! Helms and Irena and Droon . . . they didn't know I existed anymore. I erased myself. I thought about it, finding whatever it was, doing what Amos wanted. But in the end, I balked. They're so powerful, so dangerous. They've got all the power of the police and the CIA!" His eyes grew wild—the way their father's occasionally had. "You just don't know . . . Besides, he died before he told them, so hidden it was and hidden it would remain. Forever. It was **like** being destroyed."

"Except," Shaw said, "they're still after it. And we have to get to it first."

"To save that family." La Fleur's voice was low.

"That's right." Russell called up a map of San Francisco on his phone. He focused in on Quigley Square. There were dozens of buildings bordering the park. Presumably they'd all have undergrounds— cellars or maybe tunnels.

Shaw asked, "Would it be in the friend's house? The dog friend?"

"Amos would never endanger anyone. In any case, she moved years ago."

Shaw wondered aloud: "Sewers? Transit system?"

"No BART station there," Russell noted. "Where would we **expect** it to be hidden, when we don't know what it is?" he muttered.

Shaw offered, "Maybe he hides it in a book and puts it in a cellar of a library or bookstore. He's got a CD or tape, he hides it in a music store basement. It's a computer disk, so it's in the basement of a school with a computer science lab." He shook his head. "We can't keep throwing out ideas. 'Never speculate.'"

Russell finished their father's rule: "'Make decisions from facts.'"

Shaw asked, "Who's the client that wanted the Sanction?"

La Fleur said, "Banyan Tree Inc. It's a big conglomerate. International. Into healthcare, medical equipment, transportation, communications, environmental work, real estate—"

"Real estate," Shaw said. "UIP."

Russell nodded.

Shaw asked where Banyan's headquarters was.

"In the city here. It's a skyscraper downtown."

"Four hundred block of Sutter?"

"Could be, yeah. That sounds right."

He said to Russell, "The tracker I tagged Braxton with placed her there."

Shaw had a thought. "Who's the head of Banyan Tree?"

"Jonathan Stuart Devereux."

Russell fished out his phone and displayed the picture he'd shot of the round bald man with the busy hands and the fancy British car at the site of the drug handover in the Tenderloin.

La Fleur examined the screen. "That's Devereux, yeah. Oh, he's a son of a bitch. Ruthless. He just drove a competitor into bankruptcy. Devereux's industrial spies—BlackBridge probably—found out they were breaking some laws or regulations and turned them in to the feds. It broke them. The CEO committed suicide."

La Fleur angrily exhaled a wad of smoke. "You know what a banyan tree is?"

Shaw said, "It's a fig. It strangles any tree competing with it for light."

La Fleur nodded. "And it's got the longest root spread of any tree on earth. Any doubt why Devereux picked the name?"

Russell said, "Endgame Sanction . . . Wonder in what sense."

Sanction was one of those odd words that had contradictory meanings: it could be either permission—as in you're sanctioned to attack—or punishment, as in imposing sanctions.

La Fleur said, "Or it might mean nothing. BlackBridge uses code names a lot." He grew thoughtful. And tugged at his ponytail, then picked up the bong and lighter once again.

Shaw wanted to get to Quigley Square and get started on the search. He rose. Russell too.

La Fleur inhaled deep, let the smoke amble from his mouth. Then he rose, shut the music off, and walked to the door with the brothers. He began to unhitch the various latches and locks. "I gave Amos some advice. It's one of those old clichés, but it's true. When you aim for an emperor, you better not miss. He aimed and he missed. I guess the same happened to your father. You two? You can still walk away."

He cracked the door, looked out and then pulled it fully open.

Russell eyed him sternly. "La Fleur, let me give **you** some advice." The man eased back, his face revealing alarm at the brother's fierce, dark eyes.

"First, never provide your enemy with cover." He nodded at the drums sitting staggered along the path to the street. "Get rid of them or move them. Second, never use inferior materials in your weapons. Make a new bow. Use locust, lemonwood or yew. It should be a foot longer. And fletch your arrows with short, parabolic feathers. You don't need accuracy at distance on a shooting zone this short. You need velocity. And order some parachute cord for the string. You got that?"

"Yessir," La Fleur whispered. "I'll get right on it."

37

Endgame Sanction. The hell you think it is?" Russell was piloting the SUV through the roller-coaster streets of San Francisco, on their way to Quigley Square.

Shaw only shook his head. He received an email from Mack McKenzie. He'd requested a profile of Devereux and Banyan Tree.

Shaw read her response aloud to his brother:

"Jonathan Stuart Devereux. Estimated worth, $1.4 billion. CEO and majority shareholder of Banyan Tree Inc. BT is solely a holding company. Devereux is known in the business world as the king of subsidiaries, which run all of the company's business. This is done to protect Banyan Tree and Devereux from liability. One reporter said, 'Nobody hides behind the corporate veil better than Jonathan Devereux.'"

Shaw looked at his brother. "She gives a list of everything he's into, which La Fleur told us. But there are some others. Data collection, information processing, media."

He returned to the email. "Recent incidents that have made the news: A subsidiary in the UK, Southampton Analytics, is being investigated by MI5, the domestic criminal investigation division, for hacking and interference with elections in the UK, France, Germany and the U.S. One of the board members is a Russian national who had been a military intelligence officer. There was no evidence that Banyan Tree was directly involved. Devereux either.

"Another one: Police in New Delhi arrested the managers of a huge call center after a fire killed twenty-four workers, on the grounds of failing to maintain a safe workplace. The company was owned by layers of shell corporations, set up by Banyan Tree. But, again, Devereux and the company weren't implicated.

"I found at least six similar incidents. Let me know if you want details.

"Banyan Tree has been in the news in California. The **Pacific Business Review** reported that over the past few years it's acquired one hundred and forty-seven small companies in the state. He's fired all the employees and's keeping them as shells. In the filings the stated purpose of them is to quote 'engage in various services for the public.'"

The king of subsidiaries . . .

"Mack has some things on Devereux's personal life. Born in England, U.S. citizen now. He's fifty-one. Married. His wife's fifty-six. I have a feeling she was not the miniskirted one in the Rolls at the UIP drop."

"Hmm."

Shaw summarized: Devereux had two teenage sons. His homes were in San Francisco, L.A., Miami Beach, London, Nice and Singapore. He was described as tireless, obsessed, always in motion.

Shaw remembered the constantly moving hands when the brothers had spied on him at the drug exchange.

Russell asked, "Anything about a relationship with BlackBridge?"

"No."

Shaw continued to read. "It's disputed by genealogists, but Devereux claims he's descended from Robert Devereux, Second Earl of Essex. It was during Elizabeth the First's reign, the fifteen hundreds. He was a favorite. And then he led a coup against the throne."

"Assume that was a bad idea."

"Beheaded in the Tower of London. The executioner wasn't exactly a pro. Took him three swings to get the job done."

38

Underground, where you'd be expecting.

Not much in the clue department.

"Think," Russell said. He brushed his beard absently.

The brothers looked around modest Quigley Square, at the center of which was a pleasant urban park—half concrete walks and benches and half trim lawns, bushes and trees. The surrounding streets echoed the San Francisco of the 1960s and '70s. Head shops and stores offering LP albums, souvenir tie-dye shirts and windup cable cars. You could even buy cassettes of classic thirty-five-millimeter adult films from that era.

Shaw looked over his phone. "The tracker's dead."

"In the **Walden** book?"

He nodded. "To fit in the spine, it was a small

battery. Lasted longer than I thought. Or they might've found it."

Russell said, "So, we're black on hostiles. Act accordingly."

Shaw slipped the unit away and turned his attention back to the neighborhood.

Trying to guess Amos Gahl's clue—"underground, where you'd be expecting"—the brothers noted the retail shops, as well as an old red-brick hospital, a classic diner, bodegas, a sushi restaurant that Shaw would avoid at all costs, dilapidated industrial buildings, car repair shops.

"Where would we **expect** something to be hidden?"

"And underground." Shaw pointed to a small regional bank. "Safe deposit box? A downstairs vault?"

"Need a key and ID."

They walked half a block to a warehouse. The building was huge and, they could see through the barred doors and windows, filled with construction equipment. If Amos Gahl had hidden the Endgame Sanction in the basement, it would take eons to find it.

Besides, why would they **expect** it to be hidden there?

"Underground," Shaw repeated absently, eyes on a sign in the concrete at his feet.

NO DUMPING

FLOWS TO BAY

The words were stenciled beside a storm drain grate. There were dozens of them. But nothing could have survived after all these years down there. You heard much about California's droughts and Shaw recalled the lessons his father gave the children in distilling salt water to make it drinkable. But the winter season here could still be counted on to dump a billion gallons on the city. Anything in the drains would have disintegrated and slushed into the Bay years ago. How did one get into a storm drain anyway?

"Where you'd be expecting . . ."

Shaw and Russell walked around the square, side by side. Homeless, always the homeless in San Francisco. Shaw could hardly blame them. Why live on the street in Minnesota or Anchorage? He would have come to San Francisco, the home of a warmer clime and wealthy executives, ready to toss a coin or bill into an inverted baseball cap.

He observed that none of these street people seemed strung out, unlike those he and Russell had seen that morning in the TL. Apparently, BlackBridge hadn't targeted Quigley Square for the Urban Improvement Plan. At least, not yet. But he could see it coming: two blocks away was a long expanse of glittery, glass-fronted high-rises. A developer standing on the soaring roof might look down at Quigley Square and think, "That's my next conquest. Get the BNG to work."

More scanning.

Then Shaw stopped fast, looking up.

No, couldn't be.

A glance to his right. He wasn't surprised to see that Russell was looking at exactly the same thing he was.

"It possible?" Russell said.

Where you'd be expecting . . .

They were looking at the hospital.

BETH ISRAEL OBSTETRICS AND MATERNITY CENTER

There was no doubt a good portion of the patients inside would certainly be **expecting**.

"Hmm." Again Russell almost smiled. He pulled out his phone and sent a text as they walked to the looming structure.

At the receptionist's station in the lobby, Russell slipped his phone away and stepped in front of Shaw and said, "We're here to visit a patient. Abigail Hanson. She had a C-section."

A computer screen was consulted. "Room seven-forty-two," she told them.

"Thanks," Shaw said.

So that was the text Russell had sent. As they walked to the elevators, Shaw asked, "Karin?"

"Hmm."

She was good.

In the basement Shaw had expected locked doors or gates. But no. The cellar was an easily accessed storage area. Lights were, however, a problem. Only two of the twenty overhead bulbs were functional. Shaw had not brought his tac flashlight. After a search for more switches, Russell cocked his head, looking up, and gripped one of the darkened spheres in his substantial fingers and twisted. It came to life. Maintenance staff had apparently been ordered to partly unscrew the bulbs to keep utility costs down.

The men executed the same maneuver a dozen or so times and the place was soon awash in glare.

Shaw noted that the diminutive size of the room did not mean their task would be an easy one. It was packed with cabinets, cartons, wooden boxes, cases of what seemed to be antiquated medical instruments—even, he was amused to see, the same fifty-gallon drums of civil defense water they'd found at La Fleur's sanctuary. Shelves were filled to overflowing with books, files and—eerily—organ and tissue samples in jars of what was probably formalin. Hearts and kidneys were especially popular.

The brothers paused. Footsteps sounded not too far away. A creak too, like a janitor's cart whose wheels needed oiling. It faded.

They resumed their search.

Where would Amos Gahl have hidden his courier bag?

While Russell began with filing cabinets—easily

picking the simple locks—Shaw stepped back against the wall and gazed over the room.

The trick to finding something that's been hidden in plain sight is to look for what's just a bit out of order. Like those puzzles in the magazines he and his siblings would read when they were children: Spotting what was the difference between two adjacent cartoons or drawings. What's wrong with this picture?

What was out of place in this chamber of outmoded instruments, cold soggy organs and dusty faded treatises on medical practices and procedures that had most likely become outmoded a year after they were published?

He circled slowly.

What's wrong with this picture?

Shaw stopped.

"Russell."

His brother looked toward him and then at what Shaw was gesturing toward.

High on a sturdy gray shelf containing scores of medical treatises, one object stood out. It appeared to be the spine of a book, though wider and taller than the others. Yet the brown leather did not bear any title, author or other information.

Russell, the taller of the two, slipped it from the shelf.

Was this the pot of gold?

It turned out to be a large briefcase that opened from the top.

"Courier bag?" Shaw asked.

"Hmm."

He started to open the bag, but his brother touched his arm. "No." The creaking had resumed. "Not here."

39

As soon as the brothers had left the hospital, they walked to the Quigley Square Diner, not far away. It was a please-seat-yourself establishment and soon they were sitting across from each other in a booth. They'd bought sandwiches neither was interested in—rent for the booth.

In the deserted back portion of the place, Russell ran a nitrate detector over the case to sense for explosives.

Never assume an object that's been in your enemy's possession is harmless.

No unstable substances were present.

Then he scanned it for transmitters. This too was negative.

Russell picked the lock securing the top flap of the case in five seconds and popped it open.

A laminated card was inside.

Property of BlackBridge Corporate Solutions, Inc.

And there was a number below with the request to please return if found.

The brothers shared a look.

Then they began to unearth the contents.

The top layers consisted of folded copies of **San Francisco Chronicle**s and **People**s and **Time**s from years ago.

Then, like the archeological sites Margot Keller was so adept at excavating, things got more interesting the farther down you went.

Beneath the innocuous periodicals were hundreds of documents—both photocopies and originals. Most were corporate or financial in nature: spreadsheets, balance sheets, contracts for services and goods, maps, memos about cash transfers, real estate plots, shipping schedules, accounts receivable, along with various contracts.

They found a series of draft bills for some bodies of legislature, something that Gahl, the historian, had discovered in his job as a researcher for BlackBridge, Shaw guessed. Probably they'd been drafted for a governmental client of the company, one who—they gathered as they read through the papers—favored eliminating regulations on the environment, manufacturing and banking. Shaw read one that proposed redefining **probable cause** in criminal matters to make it far easier for the police to get warrants and detain suspects. Another proposed bill eased the burden of getting permission for surveillance. The authoritarian nature of the documents was troubling.

They continued to dig, briefly examining each piece of paper: more spreadsheets, some documents that were quite old, one more than a hundred years.

Shaw finally came to the bottom of the courier bag.

Nothing referred to the "Endgame Sanction."

He did note, though, a bulge on the inside of the case—there was what seemed to be a hidden compartment, sealed at the top with Velcro. Shaw looked at Russell, who nodded.

Shaw pulled the flap open with a tearing sound, and looked into the space.

Bingo . . .

He extracted an old-style cassette player. Inside was a tape of the sort that could be played in a Walkman or similar device from the 1980s. There were no batteries, which was fortunate. After all these years, they would have corroded and chemical leakage might have destroyed the tape itself.

Russell left Shaw and walked across the street to a bodega. He returned with a package of AA batteries. Shaw loaded them in and, glancing once at his brother, hit REWIND. The unit worked.

So. This was the moment.

What was on the tape? Was it the Endgame Sanction itself? A recording of a secret meeting about it? The contents might put all the other documentation in the bag in context, answer clues, tie everything together.

Devastating . . .

When the tape was at the beginning and the REWIND button popped up, Russell hesitated a moment and pushed the PLAY button.

40

Suddenly rock music poured out, loud. And tinny, given the small speaker.

A few customers glanced their way.

Russell turned the volume down. "Black Eyed Peas," he said.

"That's a group?"

A nod.

Fast-forward.

"Beyoncé."

Fast-forward.

"Ludacris."

"What's ludicrous?" Shaw asked.

Russell eyed his brother. "You don't get out much, do you?"

Fast-forward.

"Mariah Carey."

Shaw: "I know her. Some Christmas song, right?"

On and on. Pausing at the end of each tune to listen for a voice explaining what the Sanction was, why it would be disastrous if it were to come into Jonathan Devereux's possession.

But no, there was just a gap of static and then the next song would begin.

Russell's still eyes gazed at the player.

They listened to the entire tape, both sides. Russell let it run all the way to the end and snap loudly off.

"Hmm."

Shaw said, "What's that technique called for hiding information in pictures and music?"

"Steganography." He was stroking his beard. "But that only works with digital media. Bytes of data. Analog?" A nod at the tape player. "No."

Shaw asked, "What about tracking? Something recorded over or under the music? Something we can't hear, like a dog whistle. Can that be done?"

Russell considered this. "Don't know. I'll see." He looked up a number on his phone and called.

A moment later he was saying, "It's me . . . You free? . . . I'm going to play some music clips. Tell me if there's anything out of detectable audio range." He listened for a moment. Then: "No project number . . . I know. I'll work it out later."

Perhaps a reference to the fact he was using the group's resources for a very non-group operation.

He set the phone beside the speaker and pressed PLAY. It was a country western song. After a minute he stopped and fast-forwarded the tape. He played another sixty seconds or so of a different song. He did this a half-dozen more times.

"You got that?" Russell said into his phone. Then he was listening to the person on the other end of the line. "'K." He disconnected. "She'll get back to us."

Five minutes later, after the brothers had gone through the contents of the courier bag once more and found nothing that even suggested the words **endgame** or **sanction**, Russell's phone hummed. He took the call. As usual, his face gave nothing away. When he disconnected he told his brother, "Nothing she could pick up. She's going to try a deeper analysis. But it doesn't look likely. High frequency on analog is not a known technique."

Shaw suspected Russell's group was quite well versed in **all** the known techniques.

"Karin?"

"No."

Shaw asked, "Could the names of the music groups spell out something? Or the songs."

The suggestion even **sounded** lame. But they tried. Russell knew most of the groups, though only about half of the songs. After five minutes of playing the anagram game, they gave up.

"The lining?"

A nod.

Shaw set the bag in his lap and, after making sure no one was near, opened his razor-sharp locking-blade knife. He cut into the cloth linings. He put the knife away and reached inside. The search was in vain.

"Microchip?" Shaw asked his brother.

"Hmm. I can order a scan. Doubt it."

The men found themselves looking at the please-call-if-found tag.

They shared a glance.

"Maybe," Russell said. His own knife appeared. It seemed the brothers both owned Benchmade folding knives, among the best on the market. Shaw's was a Bugout. Russell's was the Anthem model, costing about three hundred dollars more.

Russell used the blade to slit the tag and slowly pulled the lamination away from the cardboard.

He found nothing.

He dropped the tag and wire inside the courier bag and folded up the knife, put it away.

Shaw suggested, "The newspapers and magazines?" He explained: maybe there was something marked in an article, or several of them, that could point them in some direction.

"Possible."

"But back at the safe house," Shaw said, looking around. "We've been here too long."

"Agree."

The men gathered up their booty and left the diner.

On the way to Russell's SUV, Shaw voiced what had been in the back of his mind from the moment the first arrows hissed their way from Earnest

La Fleur's bow: "Percentage chance that Gahl was unstable and paranoid? He never had the Sanction at all. Ash—and Braxton and Droon—just **thought** he did."

Russell didn't put a number on it but he said the exact word that Shaw was thinking: "High. Too high."

Which meant that what their father had perished for was not evidence to bring down one of the most ruthless corporations on earth, or this mysterious Endgame Sanction.

Ashton Shaw had died for a greatest-hits mixtape.

41

Was that the car? The green Honda?

"Turn left. Fast."

Russell, behind the wheel of the big SUV, apparently trusted his brother's instincts. He spun the wheel hard, braking a little. Shaw would have gone faster.

Ahead, two blocks away he saw a green car reverse fast into an alley.

"There. I think that's her. Catch her."

"Her?" Russell asked.

Shaw hadn't told him that the driver following him was a blond woman. He mentioned this now, leaving out the "hot" part.

The SUV picked up speed and approached the alley the Honda had zipped into.

"When you get to the mouth, turn but don't drive in."

"Why?"

"She may have left a booby trap."

"These windows are bulletproof."

"What about the tires?" Shaw explained about the nails the woman had scattered earlier.

Russell lifted an eyebrow then skidded the vehicle to a stop.

Yes, a blanket of nails littered the front of the alley. Ahead of them, several blocks away, the car vanished into traffic.

"They have big heads," Russell said.

Shaw looked at his brother.

"The nails. They're roofing nails. You run over average nails, they stay flat. These, when the tire hits them, the points turn up, and into the tread." He knocked the Navigator into reverse. "You have no idea who she is?"

"Might be related to a job I did in Silicon Valley a couple of weeks ago. Made some enemies in the high-tech world."

Russell backed up and turned toward Alvarez.

"Keep an eye out when you're on your bike. She throws some in front of you, at speed, you'll set it down. Won't be good."

"I'll keep that in mind."

He parked two blocks away, not far from the coffee shop where Shaw had first seen Russell, though he hadn't known it at the time. Shaw was keeping his cycle locked here too, away from the safe house—in case someone had made one of the vehicles and traced it.

Inside, Shaw lifted Amos Gahl's courier bag onto the kitchen table and divided its contents into two piles.

He pushed one toward Russell and kept the other. The two men began reading through each sheet of paper carefully once more. Were there helpful notes in the margin? Were passages circled? Was a magazine opened to a certain article, a newspaper folded in a particular way?

Had Amos Gahl, who apparently loved his puzzles, been cautious and coy once again, using these publications and other documents to send a message about what the Sanction was?

Shaw thought again about the word **sanction**.

Permission. Punishment.

Or just a meaningless code name?

But poring over the contents uncovered no clues, no codes, no secrets subtle or obvious.

After an hour, both men sat back. "Maybe he just liked to read the news," Shaw said.

They sat in silence for a moment. Shaw gazed at the cassette recorder and, after collecting his tool kit from his backpack, unscrewed the back. Nothing inside but solid state electronics. He used a magnifier on the cassette itself but could see no writing or code. The labels on each side, which were blank, were glued tightly to the plastic; they couldn't be pried up to reveal a message hidden beneath them without tearing the paper.

Nodding at the stack of papers, Shaw said, "I'm not accepting it."

Russell glanced his way.

"That this is just somebody's imagination. It's real, the Sanction. And it's here." Pointing at the material on the table.

"You making that assumption?"

"Call it that."

After a pause Russell said, "I agree."

"So. We'll have to go through everything—"

Just then a persistent beep came from Russell's phone.

Instantly he was on his feet. His hand was near his weapon. "Have a sensor, front door. Somebody's picking the lock."

Shaw drew his Glock and crept to the closest window. "Droon, plus an entry team, five, six. Long guns too. How'd they make us?"

His brother shook his head.

Shaw saw one of the attackers standing at the open tailgate of an SUV. The men looked up and down the street. He then pulled something from the vehicle, turned and eyed the front of the safe house. He squinted directly toward Shaw. Then raised to his shoulder what looked like a large shotgun with a blunt object protruding from the muzzle. He pulled the trigger.

"Grenade!" Shaw shouted.

The brothers dove to the floor.

42

Irena Braxton, wearing a staid gray suit, stood with her arms crossed over her chest, surveying the interior of the safe house, as if she were waiting for her grown son and daughter-in-law and the brood of grandchildren to arrive for Sunday supper.

Other BlackBridge workers—a lean, unsmiling blond woman in a black tac outfit and a solidly built Latino—were tossing the living and dining rooms. **Tossing**. That was the technical term for searching a home or office, though there was in fact nothing sloppy about the process. They were meticulous and careful and breaking or destroying nothing. Drawers were opened, cabinets, the refrigerator and freezer, the microwave, the closets, the spaces under cushions, under couches, under chairs.

Another man from the team was examining

the empty BlackBridge courier bag. He was the one who'd fired the grenade launcher. He had set down the weapon but like the others—aside from Braxton—he wore a sidearm, another expensive SIG Sauer.

One of the ops, a tall brunette woman, was in the living room. Hands on hips, she called, "Nothing. The Sanction's not here."

"What?" Braxton snapped, turning on her. "Is your search **finished**? How can you say it's not here if you're not finished?"

"Yes, ma'am. The case was empty, I assumed they took it with them."

"Oh, they didn't hide it here maybe? Do you think that's a possibility?"

The woman scurried back to work.

The others kept quiet and continued their tasks.

Ebbitt Droon came down from upstairs. "Didn't get out that way. Windows locked from the inside. Clothes, ammunition. Nothing helpful."

This scene was unfolding on Russell's laptop, four split screens. And remotely. The brothers were a block away—in the coffee shop where Shaw had first seen the man with the thigh-length coat, stocking cap and the A's backpack, the texting customer who had turned out to be his brother.

The grenade had not been a deadly fragmentation model, just a large flash-bang to stun and deafen, similar to the one Russell had used as an alarm on the door to the secure room in the cellar. The projectile had been fired accurately. But what the BlackBridge assault team didn't know—nor did Russell or Colter Shaw—was that in fitting out the safe house years ago Ashton had installed bullet-deflecting windows. The grenade would have hit the plexiglass at about four hundred feet per second, slow enough so that the device merely bounced off. This bought the brothers a little time, since the tables were turned and the device flashed and banged outside.

Upon learning they were under attack, the Shaw brothers knew they weren't in any position to engage four heavily armed tac ops. They chose to escape. Shaw shoveled the contents of the courier bag into his backpack, as Russell grabbed their computers.

"Basement," Russell said, at the same time as Shaw said, "Cellar."

So his brother had seen the coal bin too. Shaw had recognized right away that it was fake; the house wasn't more than fifty years old. No urban dwelling of that age had ever used coal for heat.

Ever the survivalist, weren't you, Ashton?

As they heard footsteps above them, they'd pulled the bin away and slipped into the four-foot-wide tunnel, then pulled the bin back in place behind them.

Never use a safe house that doesn't have a trapdoor . . .

A moment later they'd heard: "Cellar clear" and the thud of footsteps up the stairs.

The brothers had continued through the tunnel

for about thirty feet and come to another wooden panel. They'd muscled it aside and, guns ready, stepped into the basement of the Soviet-bloc apartment building across the alley from the safe house. The large, mold-scented room was empty. They left via the service entrance and five minutes later were in the coffee shop, more unwanted food and drink at hand, just any other customers, watching Braxton, Droon and the others.

When Russell had returned to the safe house with the news about the text ordering the hit on the SP family, he'd brought with him surveillance equipment. The four cameras, fitted with sensitive microphones, were in household objects—lamps, a clock, a picture frame. They were wireless but transmitted on the same frequency as Russell's internet router in the closet in the front hall—so anyone scanning the house for surveillance, as Droon had done, would see only the server transmissions, not the spy cams.

Shaw said he was impressed, and Russell said his group had some people who came up with "clever ideas."

On the computer screen it was easy to see that Braxton was growing angrier. "We had eyes on them. They were here. How'd they get out?"

"Back window?" one of the male operatives said.

"And then why weren't any of you in the back?"

No one had an answer for that, and the searching continued.

"Look," Shaw said.

He was referring to Droon, who was only marginally interested in the cassette player. He punched a button, listened to a few seconds of a tune, then fast-forwarded and did the same several more times. He shut the unit off, shrugged toward Braxton and continued searching the room, leaving the device on the table.

Shaw continued, "They'd have to have audio engineers too, like your group. It means the Sanction's not electronic."

"Hmm."

Droon then took over examining the courier bag. He did so as closely as Shaw and Russell had done. He could see that the lining was cut but he was taking no chances. Maybe he was searching this carefully because it was his nature. Maybe it was self-preservation, so desperate were the minions to please Devereux.

Russell said, "Be helpful if they said what they're looking for. Help us narrow it down."

If anyone from BlackBridge mentioned a keyword, it might be possible for the brothers to identify the Endgame Sanction in the stack of material sitting in Shaw's backpack.

Russell typed. A camera scanned to the left, taking in the blond woman operative. Then to the right.

Shaw then said, "Notice a pattern?"

Russell nodded. "All they want is paperwork. That's why they don't care about the cassette. It's definitely paper, and probably—the way they're fanning pages—a single sheet."

After five minutes Droon muttered, "Bastards took it with 'em, don'tcha know?"

Braxton now seemed to accept this possibility. She nodded. "We found it once. We'll find it again. Devereux brings in ten million a year. And you know what the bonus'll be when we get it."

Braxton's attention turned to the window. The doorbell buzzed and one of the ops walked into the front alcove.

Then, just barely audible through the microphone, came the sounds of a creaking floor as a large man in a black suit stepped into sight. Shaw recognized him. He was Devereux's Asian American bodyguard and driver. Shaw recalled him from the construction site in the Tenderloin, where the BNG gangbangers had gotten their Johnny Appleseed bags of drugs to plant around the community as part of the UIP program.

The man looked around and, apparently after verifying that it was safe, he eased back into the alcove.

Jonathan Stuart Devereux stepped into the living room.

"You all right?" he asked in his cheery prime minister accent.

Braxton nodded in return.

Devereux sighed. "Your look, I can see your look. Your face. Don't faces tell us everything? We don't need words. Words lie, people lie. Faces don't. It's not here, is it?"

"We're on course. We're moving in." Braxton added, "We found the courier bag Gahl stole."

"All those many years ago."

"It had that tape recorder inside." She nodded toward the unit.

"But I'm not so very interested in a tape recorder, am I?"

Devereux examined the courier bag, peering inside, pulling it open wide. He paced through the house, gazing around him. Not looking for the Sanction, it seemed, just assessing what kind of lair his enemies had. In the kitchen he opened the refrigerator, plucked out a bottle of water and drank down half of it. He strolled back to the living room, picked up some of the items that the ops had searched. He studied magazines that had been here since Ashton's time. "My. Look, a cover story about that young, fresh unknown Taylor Swift." He dropped it. "And Prince Charles." Then he said, a hint of mocking in his voice, "But you're on course, you're moving in."

Braxton cast a taut glance to Droon.

A red-haired woman, twenty years younger and six inches taller than Devereux, stepped into the front hallway. Was it the same one as in the Rolls earlier? Her skirt and shoes were different. She was in a clinging white dress, hem high, top low. It clearly wasn't his fifty-six-year-old wife.

Braxton's glance toward her gave away nothing, but she couldn't be happy that he'd brought the woman to a professional endeavor. Devereux looked back at her with a grimace and he shooed her off with a wave of his hardworking fingers. She vanished.

The CEO of Banyan Tree walked in a slow circle. At a shelf he picked up some figures and examined them one by one. "This is cute, isn't it? A cat. Is it a cat? Bit dodgy. Maybe a dog with unfortunate ears. Yes, I think that's it."

He set it down and his hands went back to being energetic.

The grenade shooter continued his search, looking up under the furniture, until Braxton waved at him to stop.

"Was there anything else in the bag?"

"It was empty when we got inside."

"And they were here when you came knock, knock, knocking on the door?"

"We saw them, yes."

"And the sentence that would accompany that one is: But we don't know how they got out."

"That's right."

"With my prize, my prize . . . What's on the recorder? My, it's quite the old one, isn't it? Don't see those outside of movies."

"Just music."

"Was Gahl a music lover?"

"Apparently so," Braxton said.

"And you've explored every place that he had a connection with, **everywhere** he could have hidden it?"

"Yes."

His expression perplexed, Devereux said in a snide voice, "Oh, but wait. Wait. That can't be right."

She looked at him, lips tight.

"It appears you **didn't** explore one place. The one where Mr. Colter **Shaw** found it and you did not." He looked at the woman, eye to eye. They were the same height. "Do you suppose he gamed you, Irena? That map you stole? Do you think it was fake?"

Her face went still. She didn't answer.

"What is our only priority? Mine and yours and Ian's?"

"The Endgame Sanction."

"Ex-actly," purred the man.

"We'll find it, Mr. Devereux."

He could see it pained her to use his last name. He'd probably done some whip-cracking about protocols when he signed on as a client of BlackBridge. He'd want to be worshipped. He was the heir to sloppily beheaded royalty. His company was in better economic shape than Spain. And as his minions had not delivered the precious Sanction, he could snap a vicious whip whenever he wanted.

She offered, "It's a minor setback. Shaw did most of the work for us. He found the courier bag. Now we just have to get the Sanction from him."

A hurry-up gesture of Devereux's hands. "But he got away from you here."

"He did. But I'm sure he doesn't even know what it is. He'd never recognize it."

Shaw shook his head. He'd hoped they would say something more about it, so they could identify it in the contents of the courier bag—or know for certain that it wasn't there and begin a new search.

Devereux glanced back toward the street, where the woman in the white dress would be waiting for him. Then his eyes took in the blond BlackBridge op, looking her up and down. The gaze was the same as that in the faces of Shaw's nieces when they were about to devour ice cream sundaes.

"Who's the other one? The one with the beard?"

"We don't know. Maybe the son of another one of Ashton's colleagues."

Devereux examined another ceramic figurine. "How do you propose to find him?"

"Oh. He'll come to us."

His flitty British accent seemed more exaggerated than earlier as he asked, "And that will happen how?"

The woman pulled a piece of lint off her sweater and let it spiral to the floor. She didn't answer Devereux but said to Droon, "Get some people to Bethesda. And find somebody in Fresno. Somebody good."

"I'll do it now."

His heart pounding, Shaw looked at Russell, whose face had gone cold.

Their sister, Dorion, lived in Bethesda, Maryland.

And Fresno was the closest large city to the Compound, where their mother, Mary Dove Shaw, was at that very moment.

43

Hello?" the woman on the other end of the phone line asked. Her voice was melodious.

Colter Shaw said, "The roses arrived. They look good."

There was silence, as he knew there would be. Dorion Shaw was processing the words.

"Anything I should know about them?"

"No details at this time."

"Thanks. Good talking to you." Dorion hung up.

Those words put in motion Escape Plan B. This involved the recipient's dropping everything and leaving the premises instantly—along with other family members. In Dorion's case that would include her husband and the ice-cream-loving daughters.

Before Dorion married, she'd told her fiancé about certain irregularities of her life growing up, and that there might be the occasional threat, some worse than others. Plan B meant that they were in imminent danger. It was one of Ashton Shaw's two most serious alerts, and one that nobody in the family ever questioned.

The sturdy woman in her late twenties would by now already be marshalling children and spouse and grabbing GTFO bags from the cellar and heading, via a circuitous route and a cutout car or two to a "vacation house," which is what the girls would think of it as. They were out of school and they might feel some pique that they had to miss photo camp or soccer practice. But they too would have received some lessons in what life might be like if you were a Shaw.

His next call was to his mother. His message to Mary Dove was different. He said, "Dinner will be late tonight."

"I'm sorry to hear that."

"But the guests'll be arriving soon."

"I'll look forward to seeing them."

Both hung up simultaneously.

This message invoked Plan A. It did not signal escape, but defense. Dorion lived in a vulnerable suburban setting, while Mary Dove was on the Compound, a place she would never be forced from—especially in the case of invaders responsible for her husband's death. The whole point of Ashton's survivalism was to prepare for threats like this. His mother was the best shot in the family, and she had

a go bag ready in case she needed a temporary retreat into the wilderness—and pity any BlackBridge
op who followed her there.

But against this crew it would be wise for her to
have allies. Hence, the soon-to-arrive "guests." Of
course, she had one ally in Victoria Lesston, the dec-
orated former Delta Force officer who could bring
down a game bird with a single shot from a handgun.
But Shaw wanted more, so he called Tom Pepper
and told the former FBI agent specifically what the
concern was. He said he'd have two armed former
special services ops at the Compound in a half hour.

"Would Mary Dove mind a helicopter landing in
her backyard?" Pepper asked.

Shaw considered this. "Just tell them not to use
the garden as a landing zone if they can avoid it. She
just planted the root vegetables and she's especially
partial to them."

44

The Embarcadero.

This was the name of both a lengthy road that runs along the northeast waterfront of San Francisco and the district for which that highway is a spine.

The two-mile-long strip was for years associated with transportation: the roadway itself, of course; a Belt Railroad, lugging products and produce north and south; an impressive pedestrian footbridge; and a second subterranean road.

It was, however, vessels that defined the Embarcadero. Liners, cargo, ferries. The ships operating out of Piers 1, 1½, 3 and 5, in the central Embarcadero, would transport thousands of passengers and untold tons of freight daily to ports foreign and domestic, including the picturesque waterway up to Sacramento. During the Second World War, the Bayfront became a de facto naval base.

Then came the Bay Bridge, connecting San Francisco to Oakland.

And almost immediately the Embarcadero began to die. Not helping the vitality of the neighborhood was the transition from the old-style break-bulk vessels to enormous container ships, which needed massive piers and cranes and warehouses for which only Oakland had the space—and aesthetic tolerance.

The dilapidation of the Embarcadero lasted only so long, however. Given that much of the neighborhood was flanked by upscale Telegraph Hill to the north and the spreading financial district to the west, it was only a matter of time until the neighborhood began to recuperate. It was now largely gentrified and farmers-marketed, though its original blunt scruffiness could still be found in the southern regions.

It was in one of these neighborhoods that Russell parked his SUV, near Rincon Park, in which Shaw could see the Cupid's Span sculpture, a huge bow facing downward with an arrow buried in the ground. Supposedly this was a nod toward San Francisco's reputation as the City of Eros, or something like that. Shaw wasn't sure he got it, and the sculpture now brought to mind not art but Earnest La Fleur's sharp-tipped greeting in Sausalito.

The brothers climbed from the vehicle and walked half a block to an ancient three-story red-brick building. Above the arched doorway was etched in sandstone: HAYWOOD BROTHERS WAREHOUSING & STORAGE.

"Optimistic," Shaw said.

Russell looked at him with a frown of curiosity. Shaw nodded at the lintel over the door.

"Warehousing and storage. Their business plan was set in stone. Literally. Never thought they might have to diversify."

"Hmm."

Russell was simply not going to fall victim to humor.

They walked into the scuffed lobby with checkerboard tile for flooring. The walls were yellow stucco and the crown molding featured grizzly bears, the state animal of California.

Which, of course, put Shaw in mind of the statuette his father had given his brother, following the incident on the avalanche field so many years ago.

The Reclusive One . . .

A double door at the back of the lobby was chained and padlocked. To the right was a glass door on which a stenciled sign read: MANAGER.

Inside, a round man in a white short-sleeved shirt sat hunched over a computer. Shaw noted that when he and Russell entered, the man's right hand had strayed toward a drawer before assessing there wasn't much threat these two presented. The Embarcadero was not completely tamed.

"Help you?"

They had a cover story, which was similar to the fiction they'd spun upon first meeting Eleanor Nadler, Amos Gahl's mother. They were brothers researching their late aunt's life—she was a well-known professor at Cal—for a self-published book. It would be a Christmas present for their mother—the woman's sister.

"Mom'll love it," Shaw said.

The manager said, "Women do seem to like that family stuff, don't they? More'n us guys, I'd say."

Russell said with a faint, utterly uncharacteristic laugh. "You got that right." He really was quite the actor.

"We found a reference to the warehouse here in one of her diaries," Shaw told him. "We're curious what the connection was. Has this always been a working warehouse?"

"Not a working anything now. We're closed up." He nodded at the computer. "I'm making appointments for prospective buyers. The partnership owns it is putting it up on the block. This neighborhood is changing, you can see. Going to be condos and retail, probably."

The air was close, the temperature hot in the office—a renegade boiler, it seemed—and the man mopped his brow with a Kleenex, which he'd taken from his pocket, unfolded, used and then replaced.

"Only thing is, unless your aunt was connected with the government somehow, I doubt she would've had much to do with the place."

Shaw said, "Yessir, she did some government work."

"On occasion," Russell said, looking toward the door that seemed to lead to the warehouse proper. "What was stored here?"

The manager continued, "You know the earthquake, nineteen oh-six?"

The brothers nodded. The estimated 7.8- or 7.9-level event had destroyed about eighty percent of the city, killing three thousand.

"The quake was bad enough but it was the fires that did the most damage. Stop me if I'm telling you something you already know."

"Please." Shaw gestured with his hand for the man to continue. He seemed happy for the visitors. Shaw noted it was not an appointment calendar but a game of solitaire that was on his computer.

"The fire chief was killed in the initial quake and no one knew back then how to fight blazes that big, you know, ruptured gas lines and all. They dynamited buildings to make firebreaks but didn't do it right. That just started more fires. Worst part was that insurance companies wouldn't write earthquake policies but they would for fire damage. So people started setting fire to their own houses for the coverage—and most of them were wood. You can imagine.

"Anyway, there was fire in the Embarcadero, a lot of buildings went, but not these blocks, so the government workers loaded up all the official documents and records and drove them down here for safekeeping. Drove hell for leather, with the blaze right on their heels. The city and state removed a lot of the crap over the next decade. Went to the new city hall and the state and federal buildings. But they still left the warehouse half full. Millions of documents."

Shaw regarded Russell. "So, that's what she was doing, I'll bet. Researching something in the archives."

Shaw assessed that their acting was acceptable. Not Broadway, but superior community theater. To the manager: "She was a history prof."

"Was she now?"

"Can we show you a picture of her?" Russell asked.

He frowned. "Would this've been in the last two years? That's as long as I've been here."

"Lot longer than that."

"Well, I took over from a guy'd been at this desk for twenty years. Jimmy Spilt. I know, the name's a burden."

"You in touch with him?" Shaw asked.

"On and off."

"What's your name?"

"Barney Mellon."

Russell shook his hand. "I'm Peter and this's Joe."

Shaw gripped Barney's palm too.

"Say, Barney, any chance we could send Mr. Spilt a picture? See if he recognizes her?"

Russell added, "Tall order, but we'd appreciate it."

"You boys sure must love your mom."

"That's the truth," Shaw said.

Russell asked for Barney's phone number and sent the picture, which was of Irena Braxton.

Colter Shaw didn't have enough information to assess the odds of success. The best he could come up with was: Long shot, but let's hope.

Barney sent the photo off to the oddly surnamed former manager and it was no more than thirty seconds later that his mobile hummed. He regarded the screen and answered. "Heya, Jimmy, how's it hanging? . . . You still getting out to the mountains? Uh-huh . . . Heard it was bad, lost twenty thousand acres . . . Now, about that picture . . . These two fellows are here, doing something up nice for their mother." He listened for some moments, nodding broadly. "Sure, I'll let 'em know. So, what're you doing on Wednesday? . . . Good, good . . ." A fierce grin was on his face. He sat back, made the used Kleenex reappear and mopped his brow.

Russell and Shaw shared a glance. Russell's eyes dipped to the drawer, then the phone in the man's hand. Shaw gave a slight nod.

Russell stepped forward fast and clamped a hand on the drawer, an instant before the manager got to it. Simultaneously Shaw plucked the phone from his hand and disconnected.

Barney's chair rolled four feet and hit the wall. "Please, don't hurt me!"

Russell opened the drawer and removed the little

.25 semiauto, ejected the round in the chamber and pushed out the bullets from the mag one by one. He pocketed them.

"What'd he tell you?" Russell asked bluntly.

When Barney didn't answer, Russell drew his own weapon.

Barney eyed the SIG and, vacillating between fear and rage, said breathlessly, "You didn't goddamn tell me your aunt was a psychopath. Now, what the hell do you really want?"

45

So," Shaw said, "Spilt recognized the picture."

"Of course he did. Wouldn't **you** remember somebody who handcuffs you, drags you through the archives and threatens to shoot you if you don't cooperate?"

"What was she looking for?" Russell said.

"I don't know. How would I know?"

Shaw said, "Call him back."

"What?"

"Call Spilt back." Shaw nodded impatiently, and Barney did as told.

Shaw took the phone from him.

"Barney," came the urgent voice on the other end. "Are you okay? What's going on?"

"Jimmy," Shaw snapped. "Listen to me. Barney's okay. So far."

"Oh, Jesus," the manager gasped.

Russell touched his own ear, and Shaw too heard the siren in the distance.

Goddamn it.

"Jimmy, I need you to do two things."

"The fuck're you? You the nephew of that bitch who—"

Shaw put the phone on speaker and glanced at the manager. "Two things, Jimmy, if you want your friend to be okay."

Barney called, "Please, Jimmy. Do whatever he asks."

"Okay, okay," came the voice.

"First, we're going to hang up and you call nine-one-one back and tell them it was a mistake. Somebody was playing a joke on you. Or something. Be credible. Then call me back."

Russell was on his phone. He lifted it toward Shaw.

"And, Jimmy," Shaw said, "we've got a scanner here, police scanner. We'll know if you don't do it. And that means you can say goodbye to Barney, and we'll come visit you too."

"Jesus, no, no, no! I'll do it. I'll do it!"

"Call. The. Police." Shaw disconnected.

What Russell was displaying probably wasn't a scanner app. More likely, Shaw guessed, he'd be speaking with Karin, but **she** would be patched into the city's emergency frequencies.

Fifteen, twenty seconds later the sirens stopped and Russell, listening into his mobile, nodded.

Just after that, Barney's phone hummed.

Shaw glanced at it and answered, punching the speaker button once more. "Okay, Jimmy, good job. The second thing you need to do. Answer some questions. Then we'll leave you and your buddy alone. Are we happy with that?"

"Yes, yes, anything."

"Tell us exactly what happened that day our aunt came to the warehouse."

"The hell **are** you?"

Barney cried, "Jesus, Jimmy! Answer the man's question. He's got a gun. Are you fucking crazy?"

"All right, all right. It was some weekday morning, I was the only one working. You know for the past fifty years the place's just been a repository. Nobody brings stuff in or takes it out. Your aunt comes in and asks for some records. I tell her it's not like a library. Only polite. I was real polite to her. Before I can release anything, I need a form filled out at city hall. She says she doesn't have time. And she's with this guy who's acting weird, twitchy, you know. They both scared me."

"Did he look like a rat?" Shaw asked.

"Yeah, kinda."

Russell: "What did she want?"

"Judicial records, she said. Judges' files. I tell her again I can't do anything without the form from city hall or the state, filled out proper. I tell her to leave and that's when she pulls a gun. The guy with her puts handcuffs on me.

"I tell them I don't know where judicial files'd be. She asks me how they're organized and I tell her by year. She says that's good enough. So, we go in the back and, and I point them to the year she wants, nineteen oh-six. And they both start going through everything, throwing stuff all over the floor. This goes on for an hour, maybe less but it **seemed** like an hour. Then she finds something and is like, 'Goddamn. At last,' or something.

"They look at me like they're deciding to kill me, not to kill me . . . Jesus. I'm begging them. She says, 'We were never here.' I just nod. I can't even speak. Then they leave."

"What was it she found?" Shaw took over the questioning.

"I have no idea. I didn't ask. They were ready to shoot me!"

"Was it a single sheet of paper or a bound document?"

"One page."

"Judicial records. So, a court decision?"

"No, we don't have those. They're published anyway. They could've found those in a law library or online. She wanted correspondence, notes, anything in judges' individual files."

"You call the police?" Russell asked.

"Of course not. They knew where I worked. They might come back."

Shaw said, "Listen, Jimmy. Just forget we talked to you."

"You fucking bet I'll forget."

Shaw disconnected and set Barney's phone on the desk.

Russell held up the peashooter of a gun. He hit a button and pulled the slide off. "This'll be in one trashcan outside, the magazine in another."

Shaw was amused. Maybe this was playbook procedure in some circles. Ebbitt Droon had done the same thing with Shaw's weapons in Silicon Valley not three weeks ago.

As the brothers walked to the door Shaw looked back.

Barney held up his hands, as if he were a surrendering soldier. "I get it. I get it. Just like your aunt—you were never here."

46

The new safe house wasn't bad; it certainly was in a better neighborhood than the one in the Mission.

Located in picturesque Pacific Heights, in the northern part of the city, the two-bedroom suite was in a sandstone apartment building whose front windows offered views of the Bay, Alcatraz, the Golden Gate Bridge and Sausalito, where some of the faint, distant greenery might have been Earnest La Fleur's yard.

The building was three stories high and represented classic 1960s architectural style, no frills, functional, uninspired.

The suite featured three escape routes—front stairs, back stairs and windows overlooking the roof of the one-story bicycle shop next door. Neither Shaw nor his brother had studied parkour—the leaping, sprinting and diving art of urban gymnastics— but they practiced tumbling and how to land safely when jumping from heights. Shaw was inspecting this particular exit now: out the open window he could look down and see tarred roof about eight feet below.

The safe house complied with Ashton's rule: **Never be without an escape plan**. (The accompanying dictum, **Never be without access to a weapon**, was taken care of, given the firepower the brothers carried.)

"Here," Shaw said, handing his brother a box of nine-millimeter ammunition.

Russell glanced down.

They were safety slugs, specially made to penetrate flesh but not exit and continue their path, injuring bystanders. The bullets would go through a piece of Sheetrock, if you missed your human target, but they lost deadly muzzle velocity soon after. In a setting like this new structure, where innocents might be just feet away behind walls and doors, they were a necessity.

Russell, though, looked at the ammo with a frown. Maybe he was thinking he was a good enough shot that he wouldn't miss and endanger anyone else. Maybe he found it helpful to shoot through walls and doors sometimes, in spite of Ashton's proscription:

Never fire a weapon when you don't have clear sight of your target . . .

"We have to," Shaw said.

"Not a firing solution I'm comfortable with. That's not standard procedure."

And his brother did not reload.

"Up to you." Shaw himself ejected the rounds and replaced them with the blue-tipped bullets. He was thinking: The brothers had worked well together on the investigation so far—especially their choreographed performances at the warehouse. Now tension seemed to have returned.

You don't want to be doing this, do you?

Just, we should get it done . . .

Shaw wondered if the resentment about Shaw's tacit accusation regarding Russell's role in Ashton's death was surfacing.

And, if so, where would it lead?

Shaw opened his backpack and emptied the BlackBridge courier bag's contents onto the table. Once again he and Russell divided it up and flipped through the documents, now knowing that the Endgame Sanction was judicial in nature and from 1906.

"Got it," Shaw said. "I saw it before but didn't think anything of it."

He set the aging sheet of paper on the table.

So here it was: the Endgame Sanction.

In the matter of the Voting Tally in the Twelfth Congressional District,

regarding Proposition 06, being a referendum put before the People of the State, I, the Right Honorable Selmer P. Clarke, Superior Court, do find as a matter of fact the following:

The initial ballot results as reported were in error. The correct vote tally was 1,244 in favor of the Proposition, 1,043 against.

Accordingly, I order that the Vote Tally as amended to reflect the yea and nay ballots set forth herein, be entered into the record in the State Assembly and Senate, effective as of this date, April 17, 1906.

An elaborate signature was beneath the text.

Russell picked up the sheet and turned it over. The back was empty. He then held it up to the light to look for hidden, or obscured, messages.

"Nothing." Russell rubbed the back. "It's an original, not a copy." A typewriter had been used to produce the document and you could just feel indentations from the keys.

Shaw read it once more. "I don't see how 'sanction' fits."

"La Fleur said it might be just a code. Maybe Helms and Devereux didn't want anyone to use the words 'tally' or 'ruling' in public. They wanted to keep this secret."

Shaw shook his head. "Devereux is desperate to find it." He recalled that La Fleur said if the Sanction were found the consequences would be disastrous.

Russell asked, "What's Proposition Oh-Six?"

Shaw booted up his computer and logged on through an encrypted server. He Googled the question. There was nothing in Wikipedia but he found a reference in an archive of California State constitutional and legislative measures. "It was a referendum in nineteen oh-six to amend the state constitution." He turned the Dell so both he and Russell could read. They scrolled through paragraph after paragraph of legalese, having to do with taxation, immigration and trade mostly.

Why was Gahl as desperate to destroy this document as Devereux was to get his hands on it?

Then an idea occurred to Shaw. He pulled out his Android and placed a call to her equally shielded burner phone.

Mary Dove answered on the second ring.

"How is it there?"

"We're good. Tom Pepper's men are here. They've set up a perimeter. Electronic warning. And, Colt, they have a machine gun. I mean, a big one, on a bipod. Can you imagine?"

"Good. I don't think it'll come to that."

"Hope not. We don't want to disturb the bears. We're right in the heart of mating season. Are you all right?"

"We're both good, Russell and I."

"Russell?"

"He came back to help me on Ashton's job."

"Well."

"I just have a minute. But I've got a question. And you're the only one who can answer it."

47

After a complicated drive, to make sure no one was following—and a scan for drones in the area by the resourceful Karin—they arrived in Berkeley, across the Bay, north of Oakland.

They were on their way to meet one of Ashton Shaw's academic colleagues, who lived near campus: Steven Field. He was a semi-retired professor of political history. When Shaw had called his mother a half hour ago, he'd asked if she knew of any of Ashton's associates who had this specialty. Mary Dove immediately mentioned Field.

Shaw had a vague recollection of seeing the man several times years back. Field had come to visit at the Compound. Those were the days when Ashton was at his peak. Oh, Shaw could remember a few bouts of bizarre behavior but Mary Dove would put on her psychiatrist's hat and make sure he got the right meds and monitored his behavior and he'd soon return to his animated, witty self.

One of the hardest parts of the move from the Bay Area to the Compound was the severing of social contacts. This was true for Colter and, particularly, his older brother; Dorion was just a toddler. Looking back, Shaw was sure it had been tough on Ashton and his wife too. They had both been professors and she had had the additional job of university principal investigator. Those vocations were callings that came with daily contact with colleagues, administrators, corporate executives and students. All of that vanished abruptly when he took the family to the Sierra Nevadas.

He would, however, encourage a few, select colleagues from the Bay Area to come for visits. Young Colter could recall men and women sitting in the living room in front of the huge fireplace, talking far into the night. Like all children, he paid little attention to the words but from time to time he would note the adults' animation, and feel, rather than hear, the laughter. As a child he didn't grasp all the nuances, but he enjoyed the animated talk about political science, law, government, American history and—Ashton's odd hobby—advanced physics.

Though invariably as the night grew later, the restless boy would become bored and head outside to listen to owls and wolves and gaze at the radiant canopy of stars.

Sometimes he'd take short nighttime hikes.

Often, with Russell.

His brother now asked, "You think Field was part of Ash's circle—to take on BlackBridge?"

Shaw had wondered that himself. Then, considering the matter, he said, "Doubt it. Those people're all gone now. I'd say they were just friends, fellow professors."

Earlier, Shaw had called Field and arranged to meet him in the privacy of his home.

But with a stipulation.

"We'd like to come in through your back door, off the alley."

The man's cheerful voice had said, "You must be a Shaw. You sound just like your father. He was always going on: They're watching me." Then he paused and laughed. "I was going to give you my address but if you know there's an alley—I won't even ask how you found that out—I guess you don't need it."

Shaw was aware of an urgency—the attack on the SP family was now a little more than twenty-four hours away. But they had to be careful and were taking a long route to Field's house, looking out for any sign of Droon or Braxton, as well as the mysterious green Honda.

They registered no threats, and Russell turned onto the street that would take them to the professor's home.

He found they had to divert, though. A protest was underway and the street was blocked.

Ashton had read his children plenty of fiction as bedtime approached in the Compound, but he also read them the news and history too—among those the rich history of demonstrations at the university and in the town itself. Civil rights, the Vietnam War and free speech were the main topics in the mid-sixties protests. Recently there'd been a series of violent clashes, mostly political and often involving free speech.

Shaw caught a glimpse of one of the signs.

CORPORATE SELLOUTS—NO!

That seemed to be the theme of the past few days.

Russell parked the SUV on the street two blocks from Field's house, standard procedure within his group, Shaw guessed. The huge vehicle was a sore thumb at the curb. Most of the modes of transportation here were hybrids, electric or human powered. Shaw even noted a few of the now-discontinued Smart cars.

Berkeley. Say no more.

The men proceeded into the alley. They continued along the pebbly lane for about fifty yards and then slipped through the gate in the picket fence into Field's backyard, where they followed a gently curving, moss-dotted flagstone path to the back door. The house might have been transplanted from a small English Midlands village. Clapboard siding in brown, forest-green windows, trim and doors.

The garden was more lush and meticulously tended than the garden of Eleanor Nadler—Amos Gahl's mother.

Goateed Steven Field invited them into the kitchen, fragrant with the scents of baking. He was thin, balding and of grayish pallor—though he didn't seem unhealthy. He probably didn't get outside very much. He certainly had plenty to occupy him here. There must have been five thousand books neatly arranged on shelves in all the visible rooms—which didn't include the bedrooms. Even the kitchen was filled with reading matter.

Field wore pressed gray wool slacks, a white shirt and tie and a gray cardigan sweater. Shaw had a sense that he dressed this way every day, whether he was teaching or staying home.

He was sorry they couldn't meet his wife. She was teaching a class.

"Gertie's a professor at Cal too." His eyes crinkled. "Last year, I got married. A younger woman . . . One month younger!" He chuckled.

The three men sat in overstuffed chairs in the library, Field, against a dark wood-paneled wall, on which were mounted delft blue plates, pastoral scenes of Dutch farmhouses, windmills and level countryside.

Shaw and Russell opted out of any offered refreshments. Field was drinking tea from a cup that still had the bags—two of them—inside. The aroma was of herbs.

He looked them over. Now came the resemblance comment, how each brother bore some characteristics of his father, and how they differed. "I was so sorry to hear about Ash. An accident of some kind?"

"That's right." There was no time for details. To explain what had happened at Echo Ridge could take hours, and the clock was ticking down on SP and their family.

"Unfortunate. And Mary Dove, and Dorion?"

"They're doing well."

As well as can be expected while hunkering down in survival mode.

"Dorion's married and has two girls."

"Ah, wonderful." He looked them over carefully. "Now what can I do you gentlemen for?"

Shaw explained that they'd found a document, an old one. "A lot of people want to get their hands on it. I remember you and Ashton would spend hours talking political science and law and government. We thought maybe you could help us figure out what it is, why it's so important."

"Ash didn't teach poli sci, I believe, but it was one of his passions. And with your father, that's passion with an uppercase 'P.'"

Shaw took the ruling from his backpack and handed it to the professor.

Before he read, Field turned it over in his hand, held it up to the light. "Original."

"That's right. Nineteen oh-six."

"Typewritten. Most official documents were,

back then. People think typewriters're a modern invention." Field produced glasses and pulled it closer, pushing aside the teacup so there'd be no accidents. He began to read, speaking absently. "Did you know the first electric typewriter was invented by Edison in the eighteen seventies? It became the ticker tape for the stock market and—"

He stopped speaking abruptly and his eyes grew wide as he stared at the words.

"Professor Field?" Shaw asked.

The man didn't seem to hear. He leapt to his feet and pulled down an old leather-bound book from the shelf. He cracked it open and read, his face a knot of concentration. He closed this volume and found another. He flipped pages again and, still standing, traced a passage with his finger.

Then he uttered a gasp of shock and whispered, "Holy Jesus."

48

Field ushered the brothers into the kitchen. "Bigger table. We need a bigger table."

The professor cleared the round piece of furniture of flowers and cookbooks. Then he set about gathering books from the library and stacking them here.

"Can we help?" Shaw asked.

Field didn't answer. He was lost in thought—and clearly dismayed.

Russell ran the back of his hand over the beard and he and his brother eyed the titles of the books the professor had plucked from shelves, all of which seemed to have to do with California history.

The last batch involved law books, California reporters and treatises. A U.S. **Supreme Court Reporter** too.

The professor didn't say a word. He kept skimming passages, marking some with a Post-it note and, in other instances, apparently synopsizing them on a yellow pad. Finally he sat back and muttered to himself. "It's true. It can't be but it is . . ."

"Professor?" Shaw was getting impatient. It was clear that Russell was too.

Staring at the tally certificate as if it were a land mine, Field said, "California's always had direct democracy—where citizens themselves approve or reject a certain law, including constitutional amendments. The governor and legislature approve a measure and then it goes to the people directly for a vote. If the majority approves, it changes the constitution. No further action's required.

"Enter Roland C. T. Briggs. Nineteen oh-six." Field tapped a thin, leather-bound volume with the man's name embossed in gold on the cover and spine. "He commissioned this biography himself. It wasn't exactly a bestseller. The subject was, let's say, unappealing. He should have had a co-author byline: written with his ego. Briggs was a real estate and railroad baron. Typical of the time: stole Native American land, worked his employees to death, drove competitors out of business illegally, monopolized industries. And I won't even get into his personal peccadillos."

Shaw thought immediately of Devereux.

"His team of lawyers drafted Proposition Oh-Six. It was full of obscure changes to trade and taxation.

Briggs and his operatives managed to coerce and cajole—and bribe—the state assembly and the governor into approving the referendum vote. And it went on the ballot.

"His bludgeoning didn't stop there. He and his political machine pressured the people to vote for the referendum and it nearly made it. But it failed by a hairsbreadth. Everyone thought that was the end of the matter. But—according to this—no. It actually passed." He nodded at the tally.

"I guess someone noticed irregularities in voting in the Twelfth Congressional District. That's San Francisco. Maybe new ballots were discovered or there was evidence some were forged or duplicates. Anyway, a complaint must have been lodged and a state court judge reviewed the ballots and certified the new count—which was enough for the measure to pass and amend the constitution. Except that never happened."

"Why?"

"Because of the earthquake. Look at the date on the certified vote tally. April seventeenth. The earthquake was at five in the morning the next day. A number of government buildings and records were destroyed, and dozens of officials were killed. The judge, this Selmer Clarke, was one of the fatalities. In the chaos and destruction after the earthquake, the recount was forgotten—and no one knew the proposition had in fact passed. Briggs probably wanted to put the matter on the ballot again but he died not long after—of syphilis, it seems—and the whole question of the amendment went away."

Shaw asked, "What's the 'Holy Jesus' factor?"

"Proposition Oh-Six was dozens of pages long, but Briggs didn't care about ninety-nine percent of the measure. That was all smoke screen—so no one would focus on the only provision he cared about. Paragraph Fifteen."

Field opened a book and thumbed through musty pages. "Here." He pushed the volume toward the brothers.

Proposition 06

Paragraph 15. That section of the Constitution of the State of California which sets forth the requirements to hold office in the State shall be amended by the following:

To hold any public office in this State, all persons:

1. must have been a resident of California for the five years preceding their election or appointment,

2. **must have attained the age of 21 years, and**

3. **must have been a citizen of these United States for 10 years, if a natural person.**

Shaw and Russell read the passage then both looked toward the professor questioningly.

"Let me explain. Like all business tycoons of the day Briggs hated Marxism, and the growing communist movement, which said basically all the woes of the earth come from the elite owning the means of production and oppressing the working class. Lenin wouldn't start the revolution in Russia for another ten years but there was plenty of evidence that communism as a form of government was coming.

"Briggs—and more than a few of his 'comrades,' if I may use the word—wanted to start an opposing movement. He wanted **capitalism** intertwined with government. And so—this."

Another tap of the book containing the language of Proposition 06.

Field said, in a whisper, "Does anything strike you as odd about those words? Anything bizarre? Anything revolutionary?"

Russell looked his way impatiently.

"Maybe in the **third** qualification," Field prompted.

Shaw suddenly understood. "Can't be," he whispered.

Field replied, "Oh, yes. This amendment gives a corporation the right to run for and hold office in California."

49

mpossible," Russell said.

The professor said, "Not impossible at all. It's one of the smartest political coups of all time. Most subversive too."

His finger traced the tally, then perhaps realizing it was an original, historic document he quickly removed his hand.

Russell said, "It doesn't say anything about corporations."

It was Shaw's legal experience that had given him a rough understanding of the implication. "Yes, it actually does."

Field nodded. "You're right, Colter. Let me explain." Field's eyes shone, both troubled and exhibiting a hint of admiration, as he stared at the paragraph. "Read it again."

The brothers both did.

"One, to hold office a person must have been a California resident for five years. The law is well settled that corporations can be residents of states. For tax purposes, they **must** be. Two, the person must have attained the age of twenty-one. It's an easy argument to make that a corporation begins to age from the date of incorporation.

"Ah, but the third line . . ." Field said this as if the words he was referring to were a magical incantation. "The third line is the key. To hold office a person must have been a U.S. citizen for ten years, but **only** if you're a **natural** person, not a **corporate** one. Corporations are excluded from that requirement. So to hold office in California, a company need only be a resident of the state for five years and incorporated at least twenty-one years ago."

His eyes on the judge's order, Russell said, "But this thing is over a hundred years old. It can't become law."

Field said, "It **is** the law. Now."

Shaw frowned. This was beyond his legal ken.

"In nineteen oh-six, the minute it passed, the constitution was amended. The governor, the state assembly—they don't need to approve anything. This has been the law for a hundred and ten years. It's just that nobody knows it."

Russell's face was still, as he stared out the window.

"And there's more." The man's visage revealed how unnerved he was.

"Go on," Shaw encouraged.

"Now, **any** U.S. citizen can run for office in California, unless you're a convicted felon or disqualified by term limits. The law doesn't require you to have been a citizen for a certain amount of time." A tap near the voting tally. "This, though, requires you to be a citizen for ten years."

Shaw said, "Which has the effect of ousting, what? Hundreds of people holding office now?"

Field nodded. "There'll have to be special elections or appointments for all the seats."

Shaw looked at Russell, who apparently had Shaw's very thought in mind.

To Field, Shaw said, "There's a man who's been looking for this: Jonathan Stuart Devereux."

Field's face filled with understanding. "Devereux, of course—mastermind of multinational conglomerates and corporate acquisitions. What's his company again? I can't recall."

"Banyan Tree."

"That's right, sure. So he's the Roland C. T. Briggs of today. Of course he'd want the tally. Devereux can enter his company in any elections in the state . . . And he can bring all the company's resources to the campaign. You can spend as much money as you want on your own election. Campaign finance limits are on third-party donations. How can anyone win against an opponent who can spend a billion dollars?"

The professor was shaking his head. "And the language of Prop Oh-Six says 'hold' office, not just run in an election. The corporation could be appointed as head of the state environmental board, taxing authorities, immigration board, planning and zoning, financial regulation, sheriff, judges. My God. He could spin off subsidiaries and each one could run for office. Devereux could eventually control the legislature, judgeships, the state supreme court. And even if his companies didn't run for office, he could threaten other candidates, get them to agree to positions he wants in exchange for not crushing them at the polls."

Russell said, "Afraid there's something else."

Field sighed and seemed to prepare himself.

Shaw delivered the news: "Over the last few years, Devereux has been on a buying spree. He's acquired nearly one hundred and fifty subsidiaries in California. I'm sure they were incorporated more than twenty-one years ago—to meet the 'age' requirement."

"My God. He knows that those assemblymen and senators will be out of office. His companies'll run for the seat and bring all of Banyan Tree's money to the game. And of course, because of the new citizenship requirement, the politicians who'll be ousted are minorities. Asian and Latinx. People who fought for equal rights in the state. With them gone and Devereux calling the shots . . . I can't imagine what'll happen. It's like going back to the days before the Civil Rights Act."

It now occurred to Colter Shaw that the phrase **Endgame Sanction** was not a randomly picked code name at all. The first word could describe Devereux's companies coming into political power. And **sanction** ironically could be read in both senses. Banyan Tree would have permission to do what it wanted . . . and the power to punish.

"But how would it work? Who would actually sit in the assembly?"

Field said, "There are some practical issues, yes. But that could be worked out. The CEO or shareholders could appoint a representative."

Shaw said, "There'll be a court challenge."

Russell sat back in the chair. "Has to be struck down."

Field was looking out the window at some striking red flower. The Bay Area was a perpetual greenhouse. "I wish that were the case. But I wouldn't be too sure. At one point in our history, that would have been true. The founding fathers were smart enough to draw a distinction between corporations that ran cities and performed civic duties, on the one hand, and, on the other, those that were purely for profit, which they knew could be predatory. They looked at the British East India Company and called it '**imperium in imperio**,' an empire within an empire. They distrusted that.

"But eventually corporations began to grow in power and the owners and their lawyers found it helpful to, quote, 'impersonate' humans—so they could bring lawsuits in their own names. Eventually the federal government and all of the states enacted legislation that defined 'person' as including corporations for all legal purposes.

"And the expansion continues: A few years ago, we had the 'Citizens United' case. The Supreme Court ruled that corporations had a First Amendment right, just like humans, to make campaign contributions.

"Some think the decision might open the door for corporations to do more than just exercise freedom of speech." Field browsed his shelves and lifted a **Supreme Court Reporter**, a large hardcover bound in yellow, and thumbed through the densely packed pages. "I'm going to read you something. This is from Justice Stevens's dissent in 'Citizen's United.'

"'Corporations have no consciences, no beliefs, no feelings, no thoughts, no desires . . . They are not themselves members of "We the People" by whom and for whom our Constitution was established . . . At bottom, the Court's opinion is thus a rejection of the common sense of the American people, who have recognized a need to prevent corporations from undermining self-government since the founding, and who have fought against the distinctive corrupting potential of corporate electioneering since the days of Theodore Roosevelt.'"

Field closed the book.

Shaw said, "So, some sharp lawyer might claim that holding office is a form of expression and a First Amendment right."

"Oh, I could see that argument being made. There'd be others too." He looked at Russell. "So would it be struck down? Who knows? But I guarantee that Devereux'll throw massive amounts of money into lobbying for his side. I wouldn't put it past him to bribe or threaten to make sure the amendment stands."

That would be just the job for BlackBridge.

"And this is only the start. Devereux has to have plans to move into other states too."

"The man who would be king," Shaw said. Russell caught his eye, nodding.

Before they left the Bay Area for the media-free Compound, the young brothers had watched television. One night they'd seen an old movie, **The Man Who Would Be King**. Based on a Rudyard Kipling novella. It was about a couple of former British soldiers who set off to India and Afghanistan, aspiring to become just what the title suggested.

"That's Devereux," Field muttered.

Russell said, "We know what his agenda is too—his company gets elected."

Shaw recalled the memos in the courier bag: legislation and regulations to eliminate protections on the environment, banking, working conditions, civil rights. They hadn't made much sense at the time. Now the purpose was terribly clear. He explained this to Field, who took the news with an expression of disgust.

"Our country's two hundred and fifty years old. That's a long time by some standards. No country lasts forever, and there have been more governments overturned from within than by invasions." A scornful look at the tally.

Shaw slipped it into an envelope and placed that in his backpack.

"What . . ." Field cleared his throat. "What are you going to do with it?"

Shaw had not yet thought about this. He glanced at his brother, who shrugged.

Field walked them to the rear door. Before he opened it, he eyed Shaw closely, then Russell. His eyes were focused. His brows furrowed. "Does Devereux know you have it?"

"Not for certain."

"Then I see you have two options. One: Convince him that you never unearthed it. Hide it somewhere. Pray he gives up looking and never finds it."

"What's the other option?"

"It's an amendment that passed, yes. But I imagine that the people wouldn't have voted for it if they'd known the truth. So, I say: as Americans and lovers of democracy, you should light a bonfire and throw the damn thing in."

50

North Beach.

This neighborhood, the jewel in the crown above Chinatown, was one of the main Italian American portions of the city. The seashore part of the name came from one end of the district, the Barbary Coast, maybe the most notorious red-light district of any city along the Pacific coastline.

More sustaining was the Bohemian culture that developed in the 1950s and early '60s. North Beach was folk music at the hungry i and pot and **Mad** magazine wit. It was the half-century-old City Lights bookshop, owned and managed by poet Lawrence Ferlin-ghetti, making it the epicenter of the Beat movement. It had a tastefully risqué side too. North Beach was home to the Condor Club, a gentlemen's establishment that morphed through many iterations and was known internationally as the venue were the famed Carol Doda performed.

Shaw paused at the crest and caught his breath. Grant was not the steepest street in hilly San Francisco but it was one of them. He turned to his right and continued several blocks until he came to a storefront, Davis & Sons Rare Books and Antiquities.

Walking inside—his presence announced by an actual bell, mounted to the door—Shaw was greeted with a smell that took him back immediately to the wilderness cabin where he and his siblings had grown up. In the escape from the Bay Area to the Sierra Nevadas, Ashton and Mary Dove had carted with them a ton—quite literally—of books of all sorts. Hardbound mostly. That perfume of paper, cardboard, leather, glue and must was unforgettable and present in abundance here.

He looked around the large, jam-packed store. Every shelf was filled with volumes, organized according to curious categories.

Fiction, Scottish, 1700–1725
Nonfiction, British Literary Criticism,
 1800–1810
Poetry, Caribbean, 1850–1875

On and on.
A young man behind the counter was on the

phone and he smiled at Shaw and held up a just-be-a-sec finger.

Shaw nodded and browsed. In addition to books the store also offered writing and drawing implements and supplies going back hundreds of years. He walked to a case in which were fountain pens, holders and nibs, even quills. Antique notebooks too, early-era versions of the one he'd used in his meeting with Maria Vasquez in the reward job to find Tessy.

The man hung up and joined him.

"Hi."

Shaw nodded. The shop was Dickensian, to be sure, but the clerk wasn't Oliver or Pip. His stylish hair was moussed up, he bore an earring, and if his white shirt, floral tie and black slacks had been purchased with proceeds from the shop, then the antiquarian book business was doing exceedingly well.

"You interested in anything in the case?" He produced a key.

"I might be. But first, I'm interested in framing."

From his backpack he extracted a manila folder. Inside was a sketch he had drawn of Sierra Nevada mountain peaks as seen from Echo Ridge. He'd inherited his father's penmanship and skills at cartography, so he was not a bad artist.

Donning white cloth gloves, the man picked it up. "Not bad."

He turned it over, glancing at the typewritten words on the back.

In the matter of the Voting Tally in the Twelfth Congressional District, regarding Proposition 06, being a referendum put before the People of the State, I, the Right Honorable Selmer P. Clarke, Superior Court, do find as a matter of fact the following:

"Oh, that's nothing. Some scrap paper my father found at work and did the sketch on."

The Maybe-Davis turned it over without finishing the earth-shattering words.

He then took a loupe and examined the sheet. Finally he set it down. "You want it framed but also protected."

"Do I?"

"Of course you do. Now, before the mid–eighteen hundreds, most paper was made from cloth, usually by mechanical means. This meant that the stock was composed of long fibers. It was strong and chemical free. After that, manufacturing shifted to chemical pulping and the use of alum-rosin sizing—that led, of course, to sulfuric acid. Then too you've got your nitrogen oxides, formic, acetic, lactic and oxalic acids. Generated by cellulose itself. And, heavens, we haven't even gotten to pollutants in the air and the water in the factory."

Shaw took this in, nodding, having no idea what the point of the lecture might be.

"In other words, for framing, I can do some things to protect it but your basic plastic won't keep it from disintegrating. That would require a complete acid reduction or removal process."

"How long would I have?"

"I'm sorry?"

"I'm in a hurry, so if you just mounted it in a normal frame, how long until it disintegrated?"

The young man's face screwed up, as he prepared to deliver the bad news. A breath. "Your best-case scenario? I'd give it two hundred years."

Which, Shaw supposed, in the world of antiquarian documents, might be like a doctor looking up from an MRI scan and saying, "You'll be dead by Tuesday."

"I'll go with the plastic."

"Ah. Well. The customer is always right."

Though what he was really saying was: It's your funeral.

51

At 9:15 that evening, Colter Shaw braked the Yamaha to a stop.

He was in the heart of Haight-Ashbury. It was ironic in the extreme that the area, named after two ardent nineteenth-century capitalists, was the birthplace of the Diggers, one of the most successful socialist movements in the history of the country. It was also where hippies first appeared and was ground zero for the Summer of Love in 1967.

A Whole Foods was not far away but the street where Shaw parked didn't reflect such recent aesthetic and economic enlightenment. Metal shutters as thick with layers of paint as a Leonardo da Vinci canvas were ratcheted down, protecting a tattoo parlor, a nail salon, a bodega and, of all things, what seemed to be an old-fashioned cobbler. A sepia painting of a woman's buttonhook boot was above the door.

Shaw parked and chained. Then stood and looked up at a huge red-brick building, which was old, and at the painted metal sign on the front, which was new.

THE STEELWORKS

The club was housed in a three-story former factory, constructed of smudged and soiled red brick, in whose walls were set windows that were painted over. As the name explained, it had in the early twentieth century been a steel-fabricating operation.

The only clues as to what was occurring inside were the line of people outside waiting admittance, and the resonating bass beats that assaulted anyone within fifty feet of the building. Colter Shaw looked the place over clinically and decided: pure hell.

In the days when he might have clubbed he was working out for the wrestling team at the University of Michigan, studying for classes, and engaging in orienteering competitions in the Upper Peninsula or camping with one of several equally outdoor-minded girlfriends.

He zipped his leather jacket up, then walked past the crowd to the front door, where a skinny man, lanky and sporting a mop of unruly red hair, sat on a stool.

Some in the queue of about thirty or forty also

studied him, with glares. They were mostly in their twenties. The dress code was jeans or cargo pants, sweats, tank tops, faded loafers and boots. Impressive beards, though, unlike Russell's, they were overly topiaried. Tattoo artists had made thousands of dollars inking and modifying this crowd. Shaw sensed bathing was not a priority.

He said to the bouncer, "I need to find somebody in there."

"You gotta wait. We're at capacity."

Shaw laughed.

The skinny guy looked at him quizzically.

"No. You're **over** capacity. How many fire doors you have?"

Exits are vital to survivalists, fire exits in particular. The odds of having to escape from murderers, terrorists, kidnappers or black bears were infinitely small. Fleeing a tall wave of speedy, thousand-degree flames, however, was well within the realm of possibility.

"The hell **are** you?"

"I won't be long." Shaw started inside. The man who was next in line for entrance shouted, "There's a line here! No budging!" He lunged and went for Shaw's arm. Shaw stopped and stared. The man froze.

Shaw frowned. "Did you really say 'budging'?" He turned to the man's girlfriend. "Did he really say 'budging'? Are we in the high school lunch line?"

Blushing, the man grimaced and backed off. His

girlfriend muttered to him acerbically, "Told you not to be an asshole."

The bouncer took over the defense of the castle. "You can't come in. I told you." He stood up. He wore an expandable baton on his hip. Shaw had been whipped by one. They really hurt.

He looked over the man. "I'm going inside to get my niece and then we're going to leave. She's sixteen."

The bouncer paused. His eyes swept the sidewalk. "She's **what**?"

The man, trying not to look stricken, glanced inside. Then back to Shaw. "All right. Go in. Get her. Just make it fast."

Shaw strode into the packed, sweaty crowd. He wasn't exactly sure what the point of the place was. There was a disc jockey and some people were dancing, or gyrating, on a large hardwood floor. Many sat on mismatched chairs and couches or were perched on stairways or wooden crates. They were shouting and drinking and vaping and smoking pot. Some were passed out. A few had thrown up; he navigated carefully.

No, this wasn't just hell, Shaw thought. It was Dante's Ninth Level—an appropriate metaphor, considering that a man named Dante Mladic was the owner of the club.

He made a circuit of the mad place, making his way through the sweating bodies, avoiding jostling, avoiding several drunk women and one man who came on to him.

Then, in the back, he noted two doors.

It was the one on the right he wanted because a guard sat on the chair just beside it. He was lean and about thirty, with curly blond hair and razor-sharp features—his nose, cheekbones, his chin. He was hunched over, reading something on his phone.

Shaw staggered up and tried the door. It was open, but instantly the man was on his feet, pushing it closed. "What're you doing?"

"Bathroom." Shaw's speech was slurred. He thought he was doing a pretty good job. The rewards business from time to time required a bit of acting.

"S'over there." The big man gestured with a thumb.

"No, it's broken. Something's broken. A pipe."

"Get the fuck out of here. I'll have you thrown out." The Balkan accent was faint.

"Bathroom," Shaw said again and walked to the second door, and stepped into a business office, which was empty and dark.

"The fuck," the man said and followed him in.

"Bathroom." Shaw kept with his preferred line of dialogue.

When the guard's fist drove forward toward Shaw's solar plexus, he easily sidestepped and dropped his center of gravity. He executed a fair wrestling take-down, his right arm going between the man's legs and around to his spine. In college his coach had said, "Can't be shy in this sport. You queasy about going for the jewels, take up fencing."

Shaw leveraged up and, gripping the man's collar with his left hand, he took him off the floor entirely and dropped him hard on the oak. Factories made very hard floors and his head banged with a sound you could hear over the music.

Still he needed to debilitate the man, so he dropped his fist into his gut. Hard but nothing broke.

He got out of the way in time to avoid the vomiting.

It was one hundred percent certain that Colter Shaw had just committed an unprovoked assault (the fear of an attack) and battery (an unwanted touching and, in this case, head banging and gut punching).

The question remained: Was it justifiable?

He believed it was.

Shaw was here because Mack McKenzie had finally traced the gray van into which Tessy Vasquez had possibly disappeared near Ghirardelli Square. Through several layers of offshore corporations, she'd learned that it was ultimately owned by a company controlled by Mladic, a San Francisco club owner. And suspected drug dealer and sex trafficker.

His base of operations was this club, the Steelworks.

If the man presently gasping for breath in front of him was not involved in crimes, Shaw would have some consequences to face. But he'd seen no option.

So he searched the man.

And discovered two things. One was a Glock 17 semiauto pistol, which he slipped into his waistband. The other was some information. His driver's license indicated he was Gregor Mladic, presumably Dante's son or nephew.

Make that three things.

In his rear pocket was a packet of zip ties.

Two of which Shaw used to bind his wrists and ankles.

Now, for the door on the right.

He opened it.

Colter Shaw drew his gun and started silently down the stairs descending into the old building's massive, pungent basement, redolent of mold and heating oil.

52

The pounding feet on the dance floor above them had stopped. Everyone had evacuated. The roar of the flames was the only sound encircling them.

Shaw turned to the hole they broke open in the Sheetrock and said to Nita, "Up the stairs now, fast. There'll be police."

"But . . . what about you?"

He smiled to her. "Not yet."

And turned back, jogging to the far end of the corridor.

It had been twenty minutes since Shaw had descended the stairs from the door on the right down to the cellar of the Steelworks club, and the blaze was growing by the minute—the blaze set by the men in the TV room, under what was surely Dante

Mladic's order to destroy incriminating evidence in the office.

The TV men were gone, Nita was gone.

But Colter Shaw knew that he was not alone down here.

Choking, his mouth covered with his untucked shirt, he made his way down the main corridor, toward the far end.

Shaw believed he heard sirens, though it was hard to say over the raging fire.

At the end of the main corridor he turned down the hallway to the right. He drew his flashlight and hurried forward. Now that the footsteps above were gone and he was around the corner from the flames, he could hear thuds and the muffled cries of "Help" and "Get me out! Please!"

Shaw couldn't kick the door in—it opened outward—so as quickly as he could, he used the knife trick once more. In thirty seconds it was open.

He lifted his flashlight and played the beam over Tessy Vasquez. She gave a brief scream and huddled away. She was still wearing the outfit that she'd worn in the variety shop security video: the red blouse and gypsy skirt.

"Tessy, it's all right. Your mother sent me."

"Mother?"

"I'm going to get you out."

His knife was still open and with it he cut the restraints around her ankle.

"This way. Come on."

Heads down, coughing, both of them returned to the corridor.

"There are men, they have guns."

"They're gone."

She staggered along behind him, her legs not used to activity during her imprisonment.

They came to the turn and stepped into the main corridor.

Where Shaw saw that the escape route no longer existed.

The fire now spread from wall to wall. The two of them faced a roiling sheet of flame, floor to ceiling, slowly moving their way.

Soon, they'd be unconscious from lack of oxygen.

Shaw glanced at Tessy, who was crying.

He pointed toward the storeroom that had been Nita's cell. "Find some cloth or paper towels, soak them with the bottled water and cover your face. Get low."

Ashton had taught the children that a wet cloth was good protection against smoke, but it was a myth that urine was a better liquid to dampen the cloth. That was only helpful, and marginally, in protecting against chlorine gas.

"We're going to die!"

"Do what I told you. Now."

She shuffled into the room, coughing hard.

Shaw got as close as he could to the flames, until he could hardly bear the searing heat. He drew from his waistband the Glock the guard upstairs had been carrying. It was a larger caliber, with a longer barrel, and the magazine contained more rounds.

He squinted into the fire and fired a shot.

A second, third.

Fourth, fifth, sixth.

It was on the seventh that the bullet found its target: the building's boiler. A stunning explosion rocked the basement accompanied by the banshee cry of escaping steam.

Shaw dove for cover in Nita's cell. They were some distance from the explosion, but still were hit with a blast of the moist heat that shot into the corridor and filled the rooms. Superheated steam, in a closed container, can reach extraordinarily high temperatures—900 degrees Fahrenheit. Had that been the case the steam could have melted the Sheetrock like newsprint and Shaw and Tessy might have been scalded to death. But he was ninety percent sure that a boiler this age was probably heated only to the standard 212.

Shaw rose and looked into the corridor. Some flames still flickered, but the path was clear.

"Let's go," he told Tessy and helped her to her feet. He went in lead, having replaced the guard's gun with his own, in case the traffickers returned, which he doubted would happen. The police and firemen would be there soon if they weren't already present.

Shaw glanced in the office and noted that not

everything was destroyed. Crime Scene should probably find enough evidence to convict Mladic.

As they got to the stairs, they stopped. Footsteps were coming down. Shaw lifted his gun.

His tear-filled eyes peered through the smoke.

The heavy steps came closer.

Shaw got the gun into his pocket just before firemen arrived. The large men, fitted with their bulky equipment, plodded down the stairs.

One pulled his oxygen mask off. "Anyone else down here?"

"No. There's still some fire in the office. First door on your right."

Another fireman surveyed the scene. "What happened?"

"Boiler blew. Put out the flames."

"Lucky you."

As they started past, Shaw said, "Save the files and computers. The district attorney'll want to see them."

Shaw felt a fireman's head turn his way, then he and the young woman were climbing the stairs.

53

They sat on the couch of the Pacific Heights safe house.

Shaw and Tessy were alone. Russell was presently conducting surveillance at the Alvarez Street safe house, trying to spot and identify the blonde in the green Honda. He'd reported seeing nothing. Shaw texted his brother that he'd found and rescued the young woman.

The two had taken respective turns in the bathroom, scrubbing away sweat and soot, though the aroma of smoke was embedded in hair and clothing.

Tessy was sipping tea. Ashton was a big tea drinker, he recalled, and apparently so was his older son. The house had come with a supply of staples, including English breakfast and some herbals. Tessy had picked chamomile. Shaw didn't believe he'd had a cup of tea in five or six years.

The young woman's eyes were hollow as she explained what had happened. As Shaw and Russell had deduced, the men in the gray van had grabbed her.

"Was Roman involved?"

Her face screwed up with disgust. "Yes, he was behind it. He was so angry I told him I wasn't going out with him unless he got sober. I didn't want to be with him, but I thought maybe he'd stop using and become a better person. But he was just a psycho. He likes to hurt people."

"He was involved in the human trafficking himself?"

"I'm sure he was. He and the owner, Dante, hung out together."

There'd be records about Roman, probably, in the Steelworks. But to make sure the authorities learned of him, Shaw would also get his full name and particulars from Tessy and send them to his former FBI agent friend, Tom Pepper. He, in turn, would relay the information to SFPD and the Bureau field office here. That way Tessy would remain anonymous and wouldn't have to worry about Immigration and Customs.

"I . . . thank you for what you did. It was terrible. So terrible. There were some men who came to look at me. Like they were buying cattle or hogs at market. I would have died first."

He nodded. Colter Shaw had never been comfortable with gratitude. He didn't discount his contribution, but in most rewards jobs, he was merely returning life to the status quo.

After a minute, Tessy asked, "You have a girlfriend?"

Do I? he wondered. He nodded. A good way to end whatever she was thinking of.

"Good. I'm happy for you."

The doorbell rang. He went to the intercom, spoke with Maria Vasquez and buzzed her in.

She flung her arms around her daughter.

"**Ay**, all the smoke."

"He saved me, Mama. These men kidnapped me."

"It was that club? On TV?"

Shaw nodded. He asked, "Any casualties? I haven't seen the news."

"Some people were hurt. Nobody got killed. The police arrested people there, the owner. Human trafficking. Drugs." She began to sob. Her daughter held her tightly.

When he'd called 911 he'd mentioned he'd seen somebody in an office in the back of the club. "He seemed to be tied up. I don't know what that's about." He hoped Mladic's son was one of those who'd been collared.

Shaw said, "I got her out of there fast. We didn't talk to the police. They don't know your name."

He didn't tell her that he was no more eager to get the police involved than they were.

"I don't have the money with me now."

Shaw said, "Keep it. You can pay me when times are better for you."

"Bless you, bless you." She hugged him hard. Tessy did as well.

After they left, Shaw took his typical hot-then-cold shower and, when he'd dressed again, he drank down a whole bottle of mineral water, then opened a beer.

He caught a whiff of smoke, arising from the pile of clothes he stripped off. Into the trash. No time for dry cleaning.

He lifted his Android off the table and loaded the browser. At the website he sought, he had to scroll through a dozen numbers until he found one he thought might be helpful. He dialed and, despite the late hour, someone answered, a pleasant woman. He gave the name of the person he wanted to speak to and then his own.

It took no more than ten seconds to be connected.

PART THREE

JUNE 26

THE MAN WHO
WOULD BE KING

Time until the family dies: eight hours.

54

The water was a chameleon.

Back on the Embarcadero, Colter Shaw was looking over the Bay. One thing he recalled from living here ages ago: the hue of the rocking waves would change from day to day. A riveting blue, rich as an empress's sapphire. Then a matte gray. Sometimes tropical green.

Today, under yet another June gloom overcast, the Bay was dun, the color—he couldn't help but think—of a newly turned grave in a cemetery rich with clay.

He kept his eye on the street, the traffic. Russell hadn't seen the green Honda or its blond driver recently but Shaw decided that she was too persistent to have given up.

He also suspected she'd rented a new car, now that he'd made her. It's what he would've done.

But that sedan wasn't the only vehicle he was interested in. There was another one he kept looking for.

And it happened to pull up to the curb now near him.

You didn't see many Rolls-Royces in the Bay Area. Of course, there was plenty of money to buy everything from Teslas to Ferraris to Bugattis, but the Rolls—and sibling Bentley—marque was not the sort that appealed to the Silicon Valley crowd, it seemed. Maybe the recent designs—you could mistake them for a Dodge at a distance—were not showy or distinctive enough. Maybe they signified old money, which Google, Facebook and YouTube decidedly were not.

Slinging his backpack over his shoulder, Shaw stood and walked to the ruddy-colored vehicle.

The driver, who'd exited the car, was the same man he and his brother had seen at the Tenderloin UIP meeting and the safe house. He was armed, a large 1911 Colt automatic on his hip.

Shaw walked around the car to the driver's side. The man said, "Mr. Shaw. I'm wearing a recording device, which will be running throughout this meeting." He spoke in unaccented American English.

"Are you now?"

"So the record will show that there's been no

coercion. I'm inviting you into the car. And you're free to get in or not."

This was curious, since Shaw himself had arranged the get-together. There perhaps was a history of people being "encouraged" to get into Devereux's car when they were not wholly inclined to do so.

"Fair enough. And since we're setting ground rules, I'll tell **you** that I just texted my associate a photo of your car and its license tag. If I don't text her again in thirty minutes, she'll alert the police that there's been a kidnapping."

Shaw heard a high-pitched chuckle from inside. When the driver looked into the back, apparently getting the okay sign, he opened the door.

Sitting in the driver's side backseat was a gorgeous blonde with teased-up and sprayed-down hair. She was beautiful, no doubt, but would have been more so had she lost the heavy makeup, which favored purples and blues. She was not the woman Shaw and Russell had seen accompanying Devereux in the safe house on Alvarez, though in line with the dress code her skirt was just as short and her blouse just as low.

Devereux slipped his hand into a pocket and extracted several hundred dollar bills. "Get yourself some coffee or a glass of wine. Have some lunch. There's a good girl." The condescension dripped.

"Girl." She huffed but took the money. "Can't I come with?"

"Cassie, please."

"It's **Carrie**."

"I do beg forgiveness. I was distracted." His eyes scanned her figure.

Did men really get away with this crap? Shaw wondered.

She offered a forced smile to Shaw and climbed out, walking away on clattering heels.

He called after her, "If you get lunch, no garlic."

Shaw bent down and looked at Jonathan Stuart Devereux. "Droon and Braxton? Anyone from BlackBridge?"

"They don't even know I'm here, do they? I'm adhering to your requirements, Mr. Shaw. You've set the agenda."

Shaw got into the seat Carrie had occupied. He was enveloped in the cloud of her perfume. He dropped his backpack on the spacious floor before him. He glanced around. Bird's-eye maple, luxurious carpet, polished chrome. This really was a marvelous vehicle. There was a control on the door for what seemed to be a back massager.

The Rolls pulled away from the curb and moved silently and smoothly through the streets. It had to be one hell of a suspension system; some roads in the Embarcadero were cobblestoned.

Shaw had seen Devereux from a distance, in the Tenderloin and through Russell's security camera at the safe house. Up close, observing the man clearly, Shaw decided he could be an ambassador. This suit was gray with darker gray stripes. Maybe he felt the vertical lines made him look thinner. Today's explosive handkerchief was pale blue. Shaw caught a glimpse of a Ferragamo label inside his jacket. Did he keep it unbuttoned to show off the name? How much wealthier would he be if his corporation began holding office in the state? He suspected after a certain decimal place, you begin to focus on power, not gold.

"Mr. Shaw. I was, as you can imagine, surprised when I got your message."

Before they got to business, though, Devereux's phone hummed. He looked at the screen. "Yes?" Upon listening to a caller Shaw could not hear, Devereux grew motionless, his face stilled. "That will hardly work, now, will it?" His face was the epitome of calm but the voice was filled with ice. **"Mais, non."** And launched into what Shaw assumed was perfect French. Shaw had known a number of people from the UK who were multilingual. It was only a fifty-dollar BudgetAir ticket from London to any number of exotic locales. Very different in faraway America.

After five minutes he reverted to English once more, apparently addressing the original speaker. He wiped his brow and shiny head with a handkerchief. "You better do."

He disconnected and turned his attention back to Shaw, who suspected that he had not needed to take the call at all but—like with the suit jacket label—it was a show of power. He'd also like to keep people waiting; he had arrived at the Embarcadero fifteen minutes late. "So. The floor is yours."

"I have something you're after. I want to negotiate a deal. That's why I called you, and not Droon or Braxton. I don't trust them. All of their strong-arm crap. It's not helpful."

Devereux was silent for a moment but the pleasure was obvious in his face. "Always good to eliminate the middleman, if possible. Cheaper in the long run." He added, "Safer too in most instances."

Shaw continued, "You and the people from BlackBridge broke into a house of my father's. Alvarez Street."

The driver glanced in the rearview mirror.

Devereux reassured him with a shake of the head.

To Shaw he said, "That's not accurate. They were already there. I have no idea how they got in. They invited me to join them. I didn't know whose house it was." His fingers were flying, twitchy. It wasn't a palsy; he could control it. "Not at that time."

"My family's in danger."

Devereux nodded. "I see. You heard us. You were bugging the house."

"I don't believe it's bugging if it's your house."

"Well taken. Go on."

Shaw said, "My mother and sister are safe. But I want to make sure they stay safe. I'll give you what you want and you call off Droon and Braxton."

"I'm intrigued. So it **was** in Gahl's courier bag."

"That's right."

"And you want a guarantee of your family's safety for it, of course. But there's more in it for you. Do you know, Mr. Shaw, that one could argue that money dates back more than forty thousand years—to the Upper Paleolithic era. It took the form of barter but look at it this way: there were undoubtedly humans back then who did not need the flint arrowhead they traded ears of corn for. That makes the arrowhead a form of currency. A stone tuppence, you could say.

"Then there's the Mesopotamian shekel. I have one from five thousand years ago. That was among the first coins. The first mints were built in the first millennium B.C. They stamped gold and silver coins for the Lydians and Ionians to use to pay for armies."

"Hobby of yours?"

"Bloody well is!" Devereux blustered. He seemed delighted. "Now, back to business. I get what I want and I'll write you a check—well, you'll want a wire transfer, of course—for quite the pretty sum. You can move your family wherever you want. They'll be completely out of harm's way. What proof could you give me that you have it?"

Shaw said, "Why don't I show it to you." He lifted his backpack to his lap.

The fingers stopped moving, the arms stopped waving. Surprise—what seemed like an alien expression—blossomed in his face, followed by greedy anticipation.

Shaw unzipped the backpack and handed Devereux a thick plastic binder.

Devereux took it and emptied the contents onto his lap. He eagerly began flipping through the sheets of paper inside.

Shaw said, "Of course, these are copies. I have the originals."

Devereux frowned when he'd finished. "What's this?"

Shaw was hesitating, a confused look on his face. "It's what you're looking for."

"No, it's not. I don't know what this is."

"It's what Amos Gahl stole from BlackBridge. What was in the courier bag. Proof about the Urban Improvement Plan. It's evidence for the police."

Devereux shook his head. "Where's the voting tally?"

"What's that?"

He eyed Shaw closely. "The legal ruling from nineteen oh-six? A single sheet of paper signed by a judge?"

Shaw looked toward the papers in Devereux's hand. "That's all that was in the bag. I mean, some magazines and newspapers, some memos, but all dated within the past ten years. I went through every single page. Nothing a hundred years old." Shaw's body language skills came into play again, though in reverse. He made certain that now, when he was lying, he kept his mannerisms and expressions un-changed from a moment ago when he'd been telling the truth. "I thought that's what you wanted. To destroy the evidence about the UIP."

Devereux sighed. The hands began to twitch again. "I don't know what the UIP is."

"Really?"

"No," he muttered.

"BlackBridge's Urban Improvement Plan. Seeding drugs into neighborhoods to lower property values. So people like you can buy up the land for cheap."

The man's face grew rosier, and not in a good way. His jaw was tight. "I have no knowledge of that whatsoever. I hire BlackBridge to help me identify properties to buy, yes, but I know nothing about any drugs. What a horrific idea."

"It is. But it's not my issue. I'm not going on a crusade if it puts my family in danger."

Devereux would be wondering if Shaw was right. Maybe the courier bag **didn't** have the tally in it. But if not, then where was it? His eyes grew cold, and under those small fingers the copies of the UIP documents shivered. He read through them again. "I've dealt with enough solicitors and barristers in my day to know this hardly amounts to evidence, Mr. Shaw."

Silence for a moment as the Rolls climbed California Street and swerved around a cable car, bristling with enthusiastic tourists.

"I don't think I believe you, Mr. Shaw. You're playing hard to get. I'm going to assume you found the vote tally certificate. You hid it somewhere. And you're holding out for more."

Shaw appeared exasperated. He tried not to overdo it. "Voting about what? Why's it so important?"

"It just is." Devereux was growing irritated. Finally the man controlled his pique. "I would be willing to pay seven figures to you, in cash, untraceable, for the certificate. You will never want for anything again."

Curious phrase, archaic. And an odd concept; Colter Shaw had not wanted for anything for a long time. Maybe since birth, and money had nothing to do with it.

"This tally, whatever it is, wasn't in the courier bag. What do you want it for?"

The man who would be king . . .

Devereux didn't answer. He looked out the window. Very few people disappointed Jonathan Stuart Devereux, Shaw supposed. And fewer still did not do what he wished them to.

If this were Ebbitt Droon, of course, Shaw would probably be on his way to a warehouse in a deserted part of the city. Maybe across the Bay Bridge to Oakland, a city where there would be far more industrial spaces practically designed for torture and body disposal.

The Tannery . . .

When they had met once earlier in the month, Droon had tried to extract information by threatening him with a .40 pistol—a big, nasty bullet—targeting joints, which would have the effect of altering them forever. Now, apparently he'd returned to the twisting knife—what he'd used on Amos Gahl.

Devereux turned back to him. "All right. Eight figures."

Shaw wondered where on the scale between ten million and ninety-nine the man was thinking. He guessed the payoff would be on a low rung of the ladder.

"A higher number isn't going to miraculously produce something I didn't have two minutes ago. In exchange for leaving my family alone, I'll give you the Urban Improvement Plan evidence, whether or not you say you don't know what it is." He shrugged. "If it's not enough for the prosecutor, then it might at least point the police in a . . . helpful direction."

Sullen, Devereux muttered. "I doubt that will be a very productive endeavor, Mr. Shaw."

They had arrived back at the place where they had picked Shaw up. Carrie was nowhere to be seen.

The CEO looked around for her.

Perhaps it had been one jab too many.

Devereux shrugged. "It happens. Those girls . . ."

Shaw thought: Good for you, Carrie.

Devereux tapped the driver on the shoulder. The man shut the recorder off. The tape was soon to be erased.

A sigh. "I would hate to have to turn this matter back to Ian Helms and Irena Braxton. They're so . . . unsubtle. Let me encourage you to have another look at the contents of the courier bag. Discuss it with your bearded friend. Eight figures is, after all, eight figures."

He handed the copies back and Shaw slipped them into his backpack.

The driver was out of the car and opening the door. Shaw stepped out onto the sidewalk.

Shaw heard Devereux's voice. "I would look very carefully for that tally, Mr. Shaw. It would be good for everyone."

55

How is it there?" Shaw asked.

Victoria Lesston said through the speaker on Shaw's Android, "We're vigilant. Carrying sidearms. Your friend's guys brought a machine gun."

"Mary Dove told me."

"What're you up to?"

Back in the Pacific Heights safe house, sitting beside an open window and letting a pleasant breeze breathe past him. "Just hung out with a lecherous billionaire."

"You have all the fun."

His eyes were on the sketch he'd done of Echo Ridge, in the Davis & Sons frame, hanging on the wall. Even though it was in save-a-few-bucks plastic, the art didn't look at all bad.

"Your mother," she said, "was telling me about Ash. Sorry I never got a chance to meet him."

"He was quite a man. Troubled, complicated, compassionate. Nobody like him in the world. He was a crusader."

"This thing you found? So, you think it's true?"

He said, "It is, yes. A real voting tally from nineteen oh-six. If it got out in public, it'll change . . . well, it'll change everything."

"Is it safe? The tally."

"I hid it in a picture frame."

"In plain sight?"

"Not really. It's facing backward."

"A framed blank page—isn't that a little obvious?"

"There's a sketch I drew on the back. A landscape."

"But it's not what your father was looking for?"

"The tally? No. He didn't even know it existed." His voice grew terse. "He was looking for evidence to bring down BlackBridge and get the president— this guy named Helms—arrested. But there never was any. Only the vote tally. Oh, he had a mixed tape too."

"A what?"

"Another story for when I see you again." He wished they could have a longer conversation, but this wasn't the time or place.

A pause. "Which will be when?"

Shaw nearly said as soon as possible. He missed

her. But chose: "A few days. Just some loose ends here."

The front door opened and Russell walked into the living room.

"My brother's here. I better go."

"Say hi to the mystery man for me."

Shaw liked the lilt in her voice.

They disconnected.

Russell asked, "How did it go with Devereux?"

"He had an idea we'd found the tally. But he wasn't sure. He might think Gahl hid it somewhere else. He offered to pay us a little money for it."

"Little? Six figures?"

Silence.

"Seven?"

"More."

"Hmm." Russell's go-to response. The accompanying facial expression was: easy come, easy go.

"He suggested that Braxton and Droon were going to step up to bat again."

"Used a baseball analogy?"

"No, that was mine. He collects money. Devereux."

"Who doesn't?"

"No. I mean, he's a real collector. Old coins and bills. Ancient. A hobby. Does that make him a numismatist?"

"Couldn't tell you." Russell walked close to the frame and examined his brother's sketch.

It was only then that Shaw realized that it might be titled **View from Echo Ridge**. Which was, of course, the very spot where Colter had believed his brother had murdered Ashton. What had subconsciously motivated him to pick that scene for the drawing?

His brother studied it closely.

Would he remark on Shaw's choice?

"You can't see the typewriting on the other side" was all he offered. He turned away.

"They used thick paper back then."

Shaw was about to say something but then tensed, cocking his head.

"Colt?" Russell asked.

Shaw held up a finger. He rose and stepped to the front door. He peered through the peephole.

He stepped outside, hand on his gun. He noticed a woman in a maid's uniform, sorting towels on a cart, facing away. He returned a moment later and closed the door. "Maid."

It was then that a brilliant white flash from outside filled the room and an instant later the staccato crack of an explosion rattled windows. Car alarms were wailing.

Both brothers drew their guns and looked out.

Two men in tactical black and ski masks had blown open the door of Russell's SUV. Apparently the vehicle had extra reinforcement and the bang had not completely breached the vehicle. One of them was trying to pull the door open all the way.

Russell muttered, "You flank, the alley."

Shaw nodded.

His brother didn't bother with the subtle approach. He went for a frontal assault. He stepped out the window and balanced briefly on a ledge. He then judged angles and leapt onto the roof of the one-story building below.

Hiding his gun under his jacket, so as not to startle residents in the building and earn a 911 report, Shaw closed and locked the window his brother had just climbed through and then walked into the hallway, now empty. He was in a hurry, yes, but took the time to double-lock the door. He jogged to the stairwell that would take him to the exit in the basement.

On the street it was soon obvious that a firefight was not forthcoming.

The two tactical ops were gone.

Shaw joined Russell, standing beside the car and examining the damage, which was considerable. A six-inch hole had been blown in the door near the lock. It seemed like an efficient, if messy, way to enter a vehicle, but they hadn't known about the extra steel plates. The door held.

"What happened?" Shaw asked.

"They saw me and my weapon and decided not to engage. They had a van waiting up the street."

"BlackBridge? Or one of your customers from the

Oakland operation?" Shaw was thinking of the hidden room in the safe house and his brother's maps of the docks across the Bay—which had a decidedly tactical theme about them.

"BlackBridge or Devereux. My other project? No one is a risk anymore."

"How'd they make us?" Shaw asked.

"I've got some thoughts on that."

But he didn't explain just now. He tilted his head, listening.

Sirens wailed in the distance.

"I'll have to talk to the cops." Russell was the epitome of calm.

"You have weapons inside?"

"Won't be a problem."

"Who's it registered to?" The smoke was acrid, Shaw's eyes burned. The breaching charge involved manganese or phosphorus.

"A company. Offshore. Done this before. Go back upstairs."

Shaw nodded.

He turned and left, walking back to the front door of the residence. The back one, through which he'd exited, was self-locking. And while he could jimmy it, there was no reason to. Shaw entered the building and climbed the stairs. Survivalists tended to avoid elevators. For one thing, he recalled his father's rule:

Never miss the opportunity to strengthen limbs in everyday life.

For another, in an elevator you're subject to someone else's control.

On the second floor, he walked to their unit and undid both locks.

He stepped in and closed the door behind him. He was only three or four feet inside when he glanced up to where he'd hung the Davis & Sons frame, containing the halfway decent sketch of the stark view from Echo Ridge.

The wall was now bare.

56

They'd tagged him.

That's how Droon and Braxton had found the new safe house.

Tagging.

"Got the back of your jacket." Russell scanned the garment with a handheld device that looked like a noncontact thermometer. The display lit up with little yellow dots.

"How?"

"Where were you when you met with Devereux?"

"The backseat of the Rolls."

"They coated it. RFID dust."

Radio frequency identification.

In the Compound, where there was no high-tech, the three children were not exposed to the basic internet, much less the universe of other digital esoterica. In the years since he'd been out in the real world, as a reward-seeker, Shaw had embraced much that was electronic and he'd heard of RFID dust. It was a common technique used by security and military forces—those from countries with sophisticated SIGINT—signals intelligence—operations, and sizable budgets. Radio frequency tracking systems were complicated and worked only with state-of-the-art equipment. Satellites and drones were involved.

Once tagged, you could be trailed even when you ducked out of sight and moved via underground passages. Algorithms compared geographic mapping systems to predict where you would emerge. When you did, another sensor would pick you up again, then hand off to others.

Really remarkable.

"There was a passenger in the seat before me, one of Devereux's dates."

"She got tagged too but there was plenty to go around." Russell added, "He maybe brought her along so you wouldn't be suspicious."

"You'll have to dump your jacket and jeans. Dry cleaning doesn't kill them. Your boots'll be okay."

So Devereux had indeed been lying. Braxton and Droon knew about his meeting and had arranged for the dust in anticipation of it.

Well, Shaw himself hadn't been the model of honesty with the billionaire.

Shaw went into the bedroom, stripped and tossed

his clothes into a garbage bag—the second set of clothing he'd lost in the space of twenty-four hours. He changed into new jeans and a black polo shirt, untucked to keep his Glock concealed.

He found his brother on the phone. Russell nodded to a spot by the door and Shaw dropped the bag there. When he disconnected, his brother said, "I'm going to swap out the SUV. There's a place in South San Francisco we use. I'll take care of this." He picked up the bag. "I'll let you know if Karin gets anything on Blond." With that, he was out the door.

He didn't bother to call the management of the Pacific Heights residence. Shaw was sure that there was no maid service in this particular building at this particular time of day. The woman in the hall was no maid, but a BlackBridge employee.

The brothers could now return to the safe house on Alvarez Street. Why not? They weren't at risk any longer, since Devereux, Ian Helms and Braxton had the document in the plastic frame.

And what was happening with the vote tally now?

Shaw guessed it was already en route to Sacramento, probably via private helicopter or jet. The legal department of the state assembly would be gearing up to consider how to handle an issue that none of them had ever had to face in their collective years as legislators: a century-old amendment to the state constitution that allowed corporations to hold public office. There would be the matter of authentication and a flurry of behind-the-scenes meetings. Shaw had no doubt that Devereux was pulling strings and disbursing cash to key players in the legislative and judicial branches of government. Wielding threats too. BlackBridge would be putting its skills at blackmail and extortion to work to gin up support for the amendment.

He sat down at his laptop. A fast search of the internet revealed that Devereux, the governor, and the chief justice of the California supreme court played golf together with some frequency, and Banyan Tree employed one of the largest lobbying firms in the state.

He wondered what the reaction would be—in California, the United States, the world.

The intercom buzzer hummed. Police, canvassing after the shoot-out? Had somebody followed him from the Steelworks club last night?

"Yes?"

"Mr. Shaw?"

"Who's this?"

"Connie . . . Consuela Ramirez. Maria Vasquez's my dear friend. I'm Tessy's godmother. I'm sorry to trouble you. Can I see you for a few minutes? I won't be long."

He hit the entry button, then pulled his jacket on and lifted his shirt hem over the gun's grip. He could draw faster this way, rather than the two-step, which involved lifting a garment with one hand and drawing with the dominant. Sometimes seconds mattered.

He wasn't, however, too concerned. BlackBridge and Devereux had the document. Why draw attention by racking up bodies? Besides, the visitor had dropped Tessy's and her mother's names.

When the doorbell rang, he looked through the peephole and noted a dark-haired, attractive woman in her early thirties. She was in a nicely cut business suit. For some long seconds, Shaw watched her dark eyes through the lens. If she were with anyone, not visible, she would have glanced to the side. This did not happen.

Finally he let her in, tugging his shirt back down over his weapon.

"I'm Colter."

They shook hands.

"Would you like to sit?"

She picked the couch and Shaw a nearby chair. He detected an ambivalent floral scent, not jasmine, not lilac, not rose. Pleasant, though.

"Only a minute of your time."

"Please."

"Maria told me what you did. You saved Tessy's life." Her voice was breathless. "I don't know what we would have done . . . if . . ." She choked back a sob and wiped at her eyes, which were tearing. She looked in her purse.

Shaw asked if she wanted a tissue and she nodded. He got her a napkin from the kitchen.

She dabbed and tried to wipe the damaged mascara, much as Vasquez had done in her Tenderloin apartment. "Maria said you were a kind man. You would not take any money, the reward."

"She told me her situation, being laid off. I don't need the reward. I sometimes do that in my business."

More often than Velma Bruin liked.

"I don't have any more money than she does, but I do have this." She opened her purse and handed him a black velvet bag. "This was a gift from my mother. Diamond and gold."

Shaw looked inside and shook out a necklace. It was a flower petal, a rose, he thought, with a diamond set in the center.

"I can't take this."

A firm smile crossed her face. "In this life, Mr. Shaw, there is not much good. I would say good with a capital 'G,' you know. I think good must be rewarded. I could not sleep if you didn't accept it. You saved my goddaughter's life."

He had received stocks and bonds on his reward jobs, in lieu of cash. Original art too. Never jewelry.

He hesitated. "Then thank you. I will." He put the piece back in the bag and slipped that into his jacket pocket.

And walked her to the door.

She turned. "One favor? Maria's proud. She would be embarrassed if she knew what I did."

"A secret, sure."

She shook his hand with both of hers. "Good, with a capital 'G.'"

57

Colter Shaw had returned to Hunters Point.

He was all too aware that the clock was counting down on the SP family's murders, and could think of nothing else to do. Kevin Miller, the O.G. with the Hudson Kings, had told him that crews from Salinas were making forays into this part of Hunters Point.

For two hours he canvassed people on the shabby streets, flashing Blond's altered picture and asking if anybody knew him.

He wanted to believe that somewhere here was a lead to the identity of the family that BlackBridge had targeted to die.

A belief that was stubbornly, however, not becoming a reality.

As he walked back to the Yamaha, chained to a

light pole in a large, deserted parking lot, he spotted some construction workers, jeans and T-shirts, tan or gray jackets. They'd just finished boarding up a building to the north side of the lot, the direction where the city proper lay. It was impossible to tell from the faded paint on the side of the place what the single-story structure might once have been. It seemed to say FRESH EGGS though that seemed plain odd.

He waved and walked toward the workers along the waterfront. He noted that the bay near the shoreline was coagulated with grease and probably toxic runoff from the old shipyard. He could see, far away, the massive battleship turret crane, an unobstructed view, and even from this distance it was impressive, a monument to ingenuity and muscle and industry.

The Egg building was masterfully sealed. Substantial plywood boards and many Sheetrock screws had been involved. Maybe the place had fallen into the hands of crack or meth users and the owner wanted to secure it permanently.

Shaw walked up, smiled and nodded.

The six men, half of them Anglo, half Latino, glanced his way, then their eyes slipped to the asphalt.

"You work around here mostly?"

One of them said, "The Point, Bayview." The others remained cautious. Was he a cop? Immigration and Customs Enforcement?

"By any chance, you seen this guy? He was a buddy of mine in the Army. He's gone missing."

Offering his phone, Shaw continued to spin his tall tale. "Got into some drug trouble and ended up in Hunters Point somewhere. I want to find him, get him some help."

They seemed to buy his story. All looked at the picture, then at one another, but finally shook their heads. Shaw's sense was that they—unlike him—were being honest.

He thanked them and they piled into the vehicles and drove out of the parking lot, leaving the whole area deserted, except for Shaw.

It had been a long shot. As he walked back to his bike he wondered, Who are you, SP? And who are the children? How many? Were they sons, daughters, both? What was there about the gangs in Hunters Point that was central to your death sentence?

Questions, questions, questions . . .

And Colter Shaw was filled with anger that he couldn't seem to get a single answer.

He pulled on his helmet, started the bike, tapped it into gear and eased forward. He accelerated and was about a hundred feet from the exit when a battered gray pickup truck shot out from between two small, abandoned warehouses and aimed right for him, speeding with a gassy roar.

The Ford bore down on him at thirty, forty, fifty miles an hour. He had no choice but to brake and spin the bars. The pickup passed within two feet of his front fender.

Shaw tried to steer into the skid, but like much of the parking lot the surface here was sand and disintegrated asphalt. The Yamaha went down and he tumbled off with the bike pinning his right leg and arm under its two hundred pounds of metal. Not a huge weight but he could get no leverage to rise or to reach his weapon.

Which he now saw he needed.

The driver and the passenger had climbed from the pickup and were walking toward him.

Shaw recognized them.

The BNG gangbangers he and Russell had relieved of their drugs, money and guns in the TL yesterday.

They reached under their untucked shirts and pulled out their new weapons and approached the bike.

58

Ang malaking tao," Red Shirt muttered.

White Shirt laughed. **"Hindi ganoon kalaki ngayon."**

Which got a smile in return.

They were thirty feet away. Shaw struggled to shift the bike. It moved a bit, an inch.

Two inches.

Then the skinny men were twenty feet away. "Hey, asshole? Where what you stole?" The accent was thick, the words nearly imperceptible.

"Yeah, where?"

Just a little more and he could grab the Glock. A round was chambered, no safety to click. Point and shoot: the proud legacy of this brand of weapon.

Shaw muscled the bike a little farther off himself. Two more inches.

Come on, push it, come on . . .

Fifteen feet away.

He touched the grip of his weapon.

With one finger.

The men stopped. One whispered to the other. They shared another laugh.

Now two fingers.

White Shirt pulled a knife out of his pocket. It was spring operated and he flicked the black blade out.

Shaw thought: **Insert, twist . . .**

"I don't have the drugs here. I can get them," he said, stalling for time.

His fingers closed around the weapon's grip.

"Where?"

"They're back there." Shaw gestured toward the Egg building.

As they looked, he shouldered the bike up and crouched. The two BNGs turned, guns rising. Shaw's did too. He'd take one out at least, but where would the other one shoot him to wound. Maybe just to wound. They would really want their drugs back.

Weapons rose, fingers on the triggers . . .

At that moment a roar filled the parking lot.

It was a car engine. The vehicle was coming from the side, behind the Egg building.

The smiles vanished from the men's faces and they spun around, lifting the guns.

But they were too late.

The white Chevy Impala slammed into them at speed. One flew against the wall and the other caromed off the hood. They lay still, eyes closed, though breathing.

The car skidded to a stop.

Shaw glanced at the driver, getting out, the blond woman in sunglasses and baseball cap. So she **had** swapped out the green Honda.

She pulled the glasses off and looked at Shaw.

He squinted. **"You?"**

59

He knew her name only as Adelle.

Or more formally, Journeyman Adelle.

"Are you all right?"

Shaw ignored the scraped knee. It was bleeding. Not bad.

He nodded, scanning the area for other hostiles. He saw none. He pulled off his helmet. Shaw walked to the BNGs and collected their guns. He put them into one man's shoulder bag and set it by the motorcycle. He looked the men over. Neither was bleeding badly.

She glanced at the two Filipinos. Her gaze was clinical. Emotionless.

The woman, late twenties, had been a member and employee of the cult in Washington State where he had met Victoria Lesston—the cult he was just telling his brother about the charismatic—and dangerously narcissistic—clan leader had brainwashed her, and her fellow followers. She came to believe that if she were to kill herself, she would be reunited in the next life with her young daughter, who had died several years earlier.

There was no one near enough to have seen the incident. But they'd have to clean up quickly. He sent Russell a text telling him he was needed urgently, giving the GPS coordinates. He concluded:

Déjà vu alley two days ago, near library. Two injured this time.

Need Karin/Ty with van.

The reply was nearly instantaneous.

K.

Slipping his phone away, Shaw said to her, "Thank you."

She nodded, still seemingly indifferent to what she'd just done. He wasn't surprised at her reaction, nor with the vehicular assault in the first place. When he'd first seen her, last week, she had observed with no emotion the brutal beating of a reporter by the sadistic head of the cult's security department.

Shaw could still picture the three dots of the man's blood on her blouse.

She walked the fifteen feet to the water's edge and looked down. He joined her. He had plenty of questions, of course, but remained silent for a moment. Then:

"You got rid of the Honda."

She nodded. "You spotted me. I had to."

"So. How'd you get to San Francisco?"

After a moment she said, "At the camp? I talked to Journeyman Frederick and found out who you really were, that you'd been after this reward for Journeyman Adam, some crime they said he'd done. You were with him when he graduated."

The cult's troublingly sanitized term for suicide.

"He told me you had Adam's notebook and that you were going to give it to his father, Mr. Harper. I drove to his shipping business in Gig Harbor and waited for you."

Shaw couldn't help but appreciate her clever, industrious detective work. And as for following him to San Francisco, if you're going to be tailing a vehicle, when your subject is driving a thirty-foot motor home, your job is pretty damn easy.

"I was going to kill you. I didn't have a gun. But I had my car. I was going to drive you off the road. I felt you ruined my life. You destroyed it. Everything he taught about coming back, it seemed so true. I believed it." A sigh. "I remembered her face, her laugh, her little fingers—Jamie's. My daughter's . . . And all I could think was that you took away my chance to see her again. I wanted you to die. I was working up my courage. A couple times I almost hit you."

"Eli did nothing but lie to you, to everybody. He wanted money and he wanted sex and he wanted power. Trying to sell immortality. It was all fake."

"I know that now. Maybe I knew all along." A sad smile. "Eli was pretty sharp. You can't prove what he taught us doesn't work."

This was true. The only way to know for certain if there was an afterlife was to die, and nobody was going to send back social media pix from there, confirming the theory.

"The nails you threw into the street. You learn that from Journeyman Hugh?" The cult's head of security.

"He said we needed to know how to stop enemies coming after us."

"Why the change of heart, Adelle?"

She blinked, maybe at the use of her given name alone. In the cult you always used a prefix: at first "Novice," then "Apprentice" and finally the coveted "Journeyman."

Shaw had no idea what her last name was. Withholding those from members of the cult had been a way for the leader to control his sheep.

"I can't really say. Maybe . . . Eli's spell wore off."

She'd hesitated again before mentioning the cult

leader's name. It was a serious breach of the rules to fail to refer to him as "Master Eli."

She turned her eyes his way. "I kept thinking, you had to die . . . But I couldn't get out of my head that you **helped** people. You saved lives. Hugh and Eli would have poisoned them. And you nearly got killed . . . So I couldn't hurt you. It would just be wrong."

Noise from the highway. A Lincoln Navigator appeared, paused and then drove to where Adelle and Shaw stood. Russell got out.

"This is Adelle. Russell."

They nodded to each other and Russell looked over the BNGs. "How'd they make you?"

"Been here, asking about Blond. Maybe word got back."

Now the same white van Shaw remembered from several days ago pulled up, and Karin and Ty got out. The other group ops weren't present. Ty assessed one of the injured Filipinos and gave him an injection.

Shaw stirred.

Russell said, "Just a painkiller."

The second man too was treated.

"We'll drop them off at a hospital, take a picture of their licenses and tell them to get amnesia."

Shaw said, "She needs to be safe. Out of the area. Where can you go?"

"My sister's in Vegas."

Russell said, "We'll get you on a plane. It has to happen now."

Adelle nodded.

"I'll drive you to SFO." He nodded at her Impala. "Report it stolen to the rental company."

"But—"

"Report it stolen."

"Okay."

The car would be cubed within the day and in a scrapyard by tomorrow.

Russell asked, "You have things somewhere? A hotel?"

"Motel Six. Near the airport."

Karin took a call, listened then disconnected. "Possible facial recognition hit on Blond from the alley. Came up at a joint OC task force in San Leandro. They're cross-referencing. We should know soon."

The brothers shared a glance. If they could get his ID, that might be enough to crack the code of the Hunters Point gang, which would lead to finding out who the SP family was and stopping the hit.

Shaw checked his motorcycle for damage—there was little.

He said to Adelle, "You know you'll meet somebody, you'll have children. You'll never forget Jamie. But you can move on. Not in a cult. In the real world. We're diminished by things that happen to us in life. But we **can** find a separate happiness."

In his rewards business, Colter Shaw had on

occasion had to counsel the grieving. Not all jobs ended happily.

There was a salute that was used in the cult, an open palm touching the opposite shoulder. By reflex Adelle started to do this now. Then stopped herself and gave a small smile and hugged Shaw hard.

60

After stopping along the way to make a purchase, Shaw returned to Pacific Heights to pack up. The brothers could now return to Alvarez Street, as the safe house was indeed safe once again. Mary Dove and Dorie and her family would not be in danger any longer either. There'd be no point in targeting them, though out of prudence Shaw texted them to keep Plans A and B in place for the time being.

Shaw brewed another cup of coffee, this one Guatemalan, and a fine brew it was, deriving from a grower that, in his opinion, had been sadly over-looked for years. He and the farmer knew each other. The man had suggested Shaw come to Central America, where abductions were common, and said,

"You, Mr. Colter, can make a great deal of money, I would think, at rewards."

Shaw had explained that he was familiar with Latin American kidnappings. They occurred for two reasons. One was snatching corporate execs. The bad guys throw a CEO or general manager into the back of a van, submit a demand for a quarter million and release him or her when the money is dropped. The victim's company and family never post a reward offer; they buy kidnap insurance and in ninety-five percent of those cases the victim is returned largely unharmed.

The other reason people are kidnapped down there is because of politics or cartel business, in which case the vics are dead five minutes after they vanish and rescue is not an option.

This put Shaw in mind of SP and his, or her, family once again.

Confirmation from Hunters Point crew. 6/26, 7:00 p.m. SP and family. All ↓

Did SP have some connection with the voting tally? If so, the kill order might have been rescinded, now that the document was in Devereux's possession. But Shaw and Russell couldn't make that assumption. It seemed more likely that since the gangs in Hunters Point were involved, SP was targeted because they knew something about the Urban

Improvement Plan. Maybe they had discovered the source of the opioids and other drugs being strewn around the city by BlackBridge and its subcontracting gangs.

He was lifting the cup to his lips when a knocking on the door resounded.

A man's low, threatening voice shouted, "Police! Warrant. Open the door!"

61

Colter Shaw stood, leaning forward, with his hands against the yellow-painted living room wall of the residence, a pleasant shade. His feet were back and spread. His palms were in roughly the same spot that the Davis & Sons Rare Books frame had rested before it had been stolen. He was looking at the nail, eight inches away from his face, on which it had hung.

"Don't move," the voice instructed. It belonged to a large Black SFPD officer, uniformed.

"I won't."

"Don't turn around."

"I won't."

Shaw knew the drill. He'd been arrested before. Detained too, which was arrest lite. He'd never been convicted, but that didn't mean there wouldn't be a first time.

"I'm armed." It was always a good idea to tell this to law enforcers when they were confronting or arresting/detaining you. In some jurisdictions it was required to so inform them.

"Okay."

Police always said that. Every single cop who'd arrested or detained him had said "Okay" pretty frequently.

He lifted Shaw's untucked shirt and plucked the Glock 42 from the Blackhawk holster. The gun would be tiny in his hand. The man was massive.

The cop wore a Glock 17, the full size, double-stack model, with seventeen rounds to play with. Nine-millimeter. Shaw's was a .380, and had only six in the mag.

It's never the number of rounds you have; it's where you put them.

The gun, Shaw's knife and the black velvet bag went on the coffee table.

Another cop—a short man, Anglo, with similar close-cropped hair, though blond in his case—was going through Shaw's wallet.

"He's got a conceal carry. California. Up to date."

"Okay." The big cop, named Q. Barnes according to the tag, was the one in charge. He un-holstered his cuffs and stepped closer. Shaw knew this was coming.

"I'm going to cuff you now for my safety and for yours."

More or less exactly what he'd told Earnest La Fleur in Sausalito.

"Put your hands behind your back, please."

Polite.

Shaw did and he felt the cuffs ratchet on. The man did a good job. They were tight enough so he couldn't get free but there was no pain.

"You're not under arrest at this point."

Because I haven't done anything that I can be arrested for. Shaw did not verbalize this, however. He said, "Okay."

The man turned Shaw around.

That was when he saw her.

Consuela Ramirez.

The young woman was walking into the safe house suite with a policewoman, an intensely focused redhead, hair in a tight ponytail. Makeup-free, save for a little blue eye shadow. She was petite but stood perfectly erect, even with all the cop accessories she wore: gun, mags, Taser, cuffs, pepper spray. You needed to be in good shape to do public safety. The bulletproof plate alone had to weigh ten pounds.

"Consuela," said Shaw. "What is this?"

She cocked her head with a faint frown. But she said nothing.

"This is the man you told us about?"

"Consuela . . ." Shaw repeated.

"Yessir," she said.

"It's okay, miss. Don't worry. You're okay. He's not going to hurt you."

"Hurt you?" Shaw said, frowning. "What's going on? What did she say?"

"Ms. Ramirez filled out an affidavit saying that she saw you with a significant quantity of narcotics. She had a relative who overdosed and was doing her civic duty to get them off the street. Now, you can help yourself here by cooperating. And I'll tell you, sir, it'll go a long way if you do."

"I don't know what's going on. I've never done drugs, let alone sold them."

"Cooperation?" Barnes reminded, steering back to his theme.

"Of course. Sure."

Barnes's face registered some relaxation. "So," he said. "The drugs?"

Shaw frowned broadly. "I don't know anything about any drugs. I assume you've looked my name up in NCIC. Nothing there, right?" His eyes were fixed on the young woman's, which were cast defiantly toward Shaw. She really was quite beautiful.

Barnes asked, "How do you know each other?"

Shaw beat her to whatever she was going to say, "I don't really know her. We have a mutual friend."

To Shaw, he said, "Tell me about the drugs."

"There are no drugs."

"Ms. Ramirez tells a different story." Barnes sighed, as if autonomically responding to what he'd heard a thousand times before. The officer returned to his favorite subject with: "You should be more cooperative than you're being."

"Doesn't get any more cooperative than this. I'm telling you the truth."

"All right."

A variation on "Okay."

Shaw shrugged. The cuffs jingled.

Barnes asked Connie, "Where?"

She pointed to the end table beside the couch, where she'd sat earlier. "The drawer."

Barnes jerked his head toward another patrolman, an underling, a short, uniformed cop with a shaved head and the complexion of mixed races. He fit the description of Roman, Tessy's stalker former boyfriend. The man opened the drawer. "Got something." After donning blue latex gloves, he removed the bag and set it on the table, near Shaw's accessories.

The woman's look of vindication was smug.

"About eight ounces, Quentin," the woman officer said, eyeing the bag. "Way over felony."

Barnes sized up Shaw, assessing the offense not of drugs but of failure to cooperate. He nodded to the underling who'd discovered the bag. The officer removed a folding-blade knife and cut a small slit in the top of the bag. From one of the many pockets in his service vest he extracted a small bottle. He broke a liquid capsule inside and added a bit of the white powder. He shook it. There was no color change.

"More," Barnes said.

The young officer added powder. It still didn't turn blue or green or red, whatever it was supposed to.

"What?" Connie whispered. Her expression registered a minor Richter number of concern.

Shaw said, "It's not drugs."

Barnes asked, "No? What is it?"

"Chalk. I rock climb. This is just a misunderstanding. I appreciate her concern. Drugs are terrible." He looked into her lovely eyes. "I see why you'd think that, of course, but I'd never have anything to do with narcotics."

Barnes took the knife and sniffed. He handed the blade back to the other officer. He looked from one to the other. "Whole room," Barnes ordered. "Search it."

The others—four cops in total—began searching. They were good. Every place where a four-by-eight-by-two-inch pouch of cocaine could be hidden was examined.

After the dining room came the kitchen then the two bedrooms, the living room. All of the closets, of which there were a fair number, and they were big ones. For a last-minute safe house, it really offered some nice features.

Barnes was frustrated. He snapped, "Dog," to the patrolman who'd searched Shaw's wallet.

A moment later the canine made his appearance with a young Latina handler. He was a lithe and focused Malinois, one of the four Belgian herding breeds, the others being the Tervuren, Laekenois and the Belgian sheepdog. The Malinois was smaller and wirier than the German shepherd and had largely taken over law enforcement duties from the latter around the country.

The dog—whose name was Beau or Bo—zipped up and down the floor twitchily. Nose up, nose down, turning corners fast, sticking the lengthy muzzle into cushions and the gap between cabinets. Everywhere.

But he never once sat. Sitting is the signal that police K9s learn to indicate that they've found what they were searching for: the drugs, the explosives, the body. They don't point or bark and they never bring a treasure back to their handler in their eager and powerful jaws.

They sit.

But Beau or Bo didn't.

Barnes was no longer relaxed. And he definitely wasn't happy.

The handler gave the dog a dried meat treat. His confirmation that the suite was drug free was as much a win for the muscular animal as if he'd found a thousand pounds of smack.

"Officer Barnes?" Shaw asked.

The man continued to scan the residence, then finally looked toward Shaw. His massive, round face displayed no expression whatsoever. "Yes?"

"In your experience how many people who have CCPs are involved in criminal activity?"

To get a concealed carry permit you undergo an extensive background check. If a criminal past shows up, you're disqualified. If you can legally carry a sidearm—especially in California, where the requirements are more rigorous than in any other state in the union—that means you've been vetted about as well as a civilian can be.

Barnes looked at Connie. "Ms. Ramirez?"

"I'm sorry. I saw the package. I just thought . . ."

Barnes stepped away to make a radio call. This left Shaw and Connie in the living room, standing near each other. The woman officer with the taut hair was nearby, keeping an eye on them but she was out of earshot.

Shaw whispered, "Here's the deal, whoever you are. You come back here later. Alone. If you don't, I give the cop the video of you planting the real drugs in the drawer when I was getting you that tissue. I saw you wipe it, so it may not have your fingerprints on it, but it still has your DNA. Roll you up for felony possession."

The tears had been real, but a little Tabasco on the fingertips does the same thing as true sorrow or method acting.

"Do you understand?"

Silence. Her lip trembled. A nod.

Barnes and the others returned. The blond male cop took the cuffs off Shaw.

"Chalk," the big officer muttered. As the men and women in blue left, he added, "You should leave too, Ms. Ramirez."

"I'm sorry," she said. "I was worried. All those drugs . . . I did it for the children."

Which, Shaw reflected, was rather a nice touch.

62

Shaw opted for an Altamont Beer Works IPA and drank long.

Typically, he'd been cautious about the Maria Vasquez reward offer.

From Teddy Bruin's starting the conversation with "coincidence" to Mack McKenzie's assessment—"probably legit"—he had remained wary. There were too many people in the San Francisco area—from a video gaming exec in Silicon Valley to BlackBridge—who were not pleased with his recent visits here.

He was always skeptical of those posting rewards and he generally spent hours, sometimes days, researching the offerors. It was not unheard of, for example, for a murderer to post a reward for the "loved one" they themselves had dispatched, in a numb-headed attempt to appear blameless. Tessy's disappearance, though, had happened fast. He was no less cautious than on any other job but he didn't have the luxury of in-depth research. And, if her mother **was** telling the truth, she could have been in real danger from her abusive ex, Roman.

Of course, the girl's disappearance and the reward offer turned out to be one hundred percent genuine.

The "dear friend," though? He just didn't quite trust that scenario. Why hadn't Maria given him her name as someone whom Tessy might contact?

So he'd simply ignored the keep-it-between-us plea and called Maria, asked her about Tessy's godmother.

Alarmed, Vasquez had said, "**Dios mio!** Did something happen in Guadalajara?"

Answering his question.

Then he'd inquired: Had anybody called and asked her about the reward? Yes, a woman had seen the offer and called her and said that she too had a missing child, a son; did someone answer Maria's ad?

Yes, someone named Colter Shaw, Maria had explained to the woman. She had given her Shaw's number and address. "I'm sorry. I shouldn't have . . . I thought, maybe she has more money to pay you than I do."

"It's all right."

"This person, is she a problem?"

"I'll handle it." Shaw had told her, "It's probably nothing, but I'd recommend you go stay someplace else for a few days."

"Yes, of course. Okay, we'll leave now. And, Mr. Shaw, again, bless you!"

Immediately after disconnecting, he'd called up the security camera recording and watched "Connie" planting the drugs. Using a plastic bag, to avoid transferring his fingerprints, he'd collected the coke and put it, and the necklace, in another bag and hid them some blocks away in a vacant lot. Then on the way back from Hunters Point, he'd stopped at a sporting goods store and bought a bag of hand chalk. He returned to the Pacific Heights safe house and awaited the law. He was sure officers would descend at some point. What he didn't know was what the woman's game was.

Now, sipping more beer, he heard the buzzer.

"Yes?"

"It's me," came the sullen voice through the intercom.

When she arrived at the door upstairs, he checked her eye movement once more, hand on the gun.

She was alone now too.

He let her in and told her to stop. His voice was abrupt. "Hands."

"Come on," she whined.

"Up."

She grudgingly complied and he frisked her. She was clean. "Sit down." Pointing to the couch.

The woman complied. He pulled up a chair across from her.

"Did you really think I wouldn't call Maria?"

"You said you wouldn't." As if he'd cheated at checkers.

"Is this something you **do**? In addition to tricks? Planting drugs and getting people busted?"

He suspected she was a call girl.

She tried to look offended but it didn't work, and that answered his question. Shaw was continually amused at how the guilty can look so indignant when they get caught.

He opened her purse and shook out the contents. He pushed the pepper spray out of reach. There were no other weapons.

He shuffled through three driver's licenses, same picture, different names. One read "Consuela Ramirez."

"Which is real?"

"Sophia Ionescu."

"That's Romanian?"

She nodded.

Shaw asked, "**¿Y si te hubiera preguntado algo en español?**"

"I speak Spanish too."

He took a picture of the Sophia license and sent it to Mack. Less than thirty seconds later:

That's her. Two arrests for prostitution in California. One in Florida.

"You didn't answer my question. Is this something you do? A franchise?"

"A guy wanted to take you down. Get you in the system. He had this idea. He knew what you did for a living so he checked for people around here who'd posted rewards for missing kids or wives. He gave me the numbers and I called them up. Maria Vasquez told me you'd saved her daughter. You were so nice, you didn't even take the reward. This guy told me to pretend to be the girl's godmother. I do some acting too." Sophia said this with a wisp of pride.

"Yeah, you'd get an Oscar. Who hired you?"

"This guy I have dates with."

A phrase he figured meant something different from "This guy I date."

Shaw said, "That's half an answer."

"Ian. Ian Helm. Or Helms. Maybe an 's.' I don't know. He's rich, has some consulting company, he says."

Well. Interesting, but not utterly surprising, news.

"What'd he pay?"

"Ten thousand."

"You get along with him? Helms?"

"We fuck."

"Would you testify against him?"

Sophia laughed at Shaw's naivete.

He considered the issue but decided that this wasn't the way to go. Even if the woman cooperated, what could Helms be busted for? Nothing serious. Shaw didn't want to swipe at the men. He wanted to take the entire BlackBridge operation down permanently and send Helms to prison for decades.

Shaw leaned close, staring. He saw uneasiness cloud her eyes. He was using Russell's approach. "Is there any risk to Maria or Tessy?"

"No, no. We just wanted information."

"Because if there is . . ." He tapped her authentic driver's license.

"No, I swear. I told Ian no way would I help if anybody'd get hurt. I don't get involved in anything like that. I'm a three-G-a-night girl."

Offered, he guessed, as proof of her moral caliber.

"Give me your number. Your real one. And keep the phone alive. I may need to be in touch with you. If it goes out of service, a friend of mine comes to pay a visit at Eight Five Four Sumner Street. Or wherever you've moved. I will find you. You're in our system now."

Which meant nothing but sounded good, and certainly unnerved her.

"Jesus."

Shaw raised an eyebrow.

A tight-lipped nod, still looking victimized. She recited her cell number and Shaw memorized it.

"How much was the necklace?"

A shrug. "Fifty-nine ninety-nine. It's not a real diamond."

She looked at the pepper spray.

Shaw laughed and ushered her out the door.

63

The Alvarez Street safe house once again.

Karin and Ty were handling cleanup. The Filipino BNGs' pickup truck and the weapons were gone. The injured men, now practicing vows of silence, were in the hospital. Adelle was on her way to Vegas. And somewhere in Oakland a perfectly fine Chevrolet Impala, if somewhat bloodstained, was soon to become a two-ton block of scrap.

He wondered if Karin was having any luck finding the identity of Blond, with the task force in San Leandro.

Once they knew who he was, they could deep-background him and, ideally, find out where he'd been recently, whom he associated with, where he lived, what division of BlackBridge he worked for, which gang in Hunters Point he had a connection to.

And who SP was, and why he or she had been targeted for death.

Once those unknowns were brought to light, they would have a chance to save the family.

The time was 1:10 p.m. The kill order would go into effect in less than six hours.

His phone hummed with a text from Professor Steven Field.

It's on the news.

He flipped to a live TV streaming app on his phone and turned the unit horizontal.

The woman newscaster looked calm and in control and did a fine job reading the words that scrolled up on the teleprompter, but Shaw could see that she was having a bit of trouble understanding the concept. Then again, who wouldn't?

"**. . . government document from more than a hundred years ago has been discovered in San Francisco. It's a voting tally of a recount in a statewide referendum in nineteen oh-six where the citizens of the state voted to allow . . .**" A dramatic pause. "**. . . corporations to run for public office. Officials say that the tally was lost among hundreds of thousands of documents that went missing after the earthquake that year, which destroyed three-quarters of the city. It's believed that the judge certifying the recount was killed** in the disaster, which is why no one learned of it at the time."

Well. That didn't take long. Shaw supposed this was no surprise. Devereux had waited years to find his magic document. He'd move as quickly as possible to use his ring of power.

"Joining us now is University of Utah business law professor, C. Edward Hobbs. Welcome, Dr. Hobbs. Explain how this amendment could become law after more than a hundred years."

"Hello. Thank you for having me. There's no time limit on amendments going into effect once they've been approved. No statute of limitations, you might say. A proposition for an amendment doesn't need to be signed by the governor; it's not like a bill. Once a majority of the people have voted in favor, it becomes law."

"So it's true then. This amendment will allow corporations to run for office?"

"Yes. And, we should say, not just run in an election. A corporation could be appointed to a position too. Judges, sheriffs, regulatory board presidents."

"Will it be challenged?"

"No doubt it will. The tally itself will have to be authenticated. I'm sure there are experts doing that right now. But we have to remember there's been a groundswell of support lately to expand the rights of corporations. Look at 'Citizens

United'—the 2010 case that extended the First Amendment right of free speech to corporations.

"The majority of Americans support that. And many professors and politicians I've spoken with consider the movement a good one—good for the country, good for democracy. If a corporation holds office, the authority is decentralized. There'll be an automatic system of checks and balances with the shareholders, the board and the CEO. Remember that the greatest innovations in the past century have come from corporate research. Corporations represent the best brain trusts in the world."

The shill—on Devereux's payroll, of course— gave no mention of the man's troubling policies described in the documents that Shaw and Russell had found in the courier bag, undermining human rights.

"So Facebook or Apple or Amazon could one day be governor of California."

"In theory, yes."

"But a corporation couldn't run for president of the United States?"

"No, the U.S. Constitution is clear on that. The amendment doesn't apply to federal elections or appointments either. Only state and local. But this is an important precedent. In law, we say, as California goes, so goes the nation . . ."

Shaw shut the broadcast off. He glanced around the safe house. In a windowless corner sat a brown

Naugahyde armchair facing the bay window that overlooked the street. This would have been where his father sat—his back was never exposed to door or window. Beside the chair was a scuffed and unsteady side table. Shaw walked to the chair and sat in it. He ran his hand over the arms, torn and scuffed. His father had been in San Francisco, just before he returned to the Compound, and not long after that he'd died. Maybe it was here that he'd sat as he assembled the clues that would lead someone— his son, as it turned out—to continue the quest to bring down BlackBridge Corporate Solutions, if he couldn't finish the job.

Maybe it was in this chair that he'd written the letter and circled the eighteen magic locations on the map that he'd hidden on Echo Ridge.

It was then that his phone hummed with a text from Russell.

Karin: Negative on San Leandro lead to Blond identity. If we don't find something in a few hours, the family's gone.

64

At three that afternoon, Shaw's iPhone trilled. He answered, "Hello?"

"Is this Colter Shaw?" The woman's voice was low, matter-of-fact.

"That's right."

"I was just speaking to your brother, Russell. I'm Julia Callahan. I'm with Systems Support in Bayshore Heights. He called me earlier about an analysis of an old cassette audiotape."

"I was with him then. You work with Russell, right? He never said exactly."

"My company does contract work for his organization. He told me to call you ASAP."

"Russell said you were going to do a deeper analysis. You find something else on the tape?"

"I did. They were smart, whoever made it. The

first run through the analyzer showed only music tracks. But the more I listened to it I decided there was a pattern of sounds within the static between the tracks." Her voice was excited.

"Static?"

"Which wasn't static at all. I isolated it and slowed it down. Way down."

"What was on it?"

"A man's voice, reciting account numbers, routing instructions to offshore corporations and banks, wire transfers to individuals. The man specifically mentioned that the purpose of the transfers was to evade taxes. And some payments were made to outside contractors. And by contractors, It sounded like he meant . . . well . . ."

"Hitmen?"

"That was my impression. I'm just an audio analyst. But we work with companies that do security consulting, so I've got experience in the subject. He also mentioned some names. Braxton, Droon—I think that's a name. And the company they worked for, BlackBridge. And something called UIP was mentioned a half-dozen times. He gave sources for what he called 'product.'"

"Drugs."

"I figured."

Shaw asked, "So you've extracted what was said?"

"Yes, it's a separate recording. An MP3 file."

"Good. I need to get a copy. I can use it as leverage in an operation Russell and I are running."

"Give me an email address and I'll upload it."

Shaw said, "No. We need to keep it off the internet. Can you get me a physical copy? Maybe on a thumb drive?"

"I can."

"We only have a few hours. Bayshore's south of the city?"

"That's right."

"You know San Bruno state park?"

"Sure. I jog there some."

Shaw asked, "Is there a deserted place we can meet?"

"The south entrance, off McGuire Road. Nobody ever uses it."

"A half hour?"

"Okay."

"I'll be on a motorcycle. Black leather jacket."

"I've got a Toyota Camry. Blue."

"I'll bring the original tape."

"Good. I can do some deeper analysis."

Shaw paused. He whispered, "Evidence against them . . . So Ashton was right after all."

"What was that?"

"Oh. Just thinking out loud. I'll see you soon."

65

Many years ago, San Bruno, south of San Francisco, was an Ohlone village.

The Ohlones lived in scores of indigenous settlements from San Francisco down to Big Sur in precolonial America. Numbering in the tens of thousands, they were hunters, fishers and gatherers, and did some farming too. They were the first people in America to learn how to make bitter acorns into food. The Ohlone practiced the Kuksu religion, heavy into rites and rituals, usually practiced in secretive underground chambers.

Life was fine among these people until the conquistadores arrived and, with the Franciscans, set to work "missionizing" the tribes, moving them off their lands and forcing conversion to Christianity. The population was reduced by three-quarters on account of European diseases, against which the Ohlone had no natural immunity. The coup de grâce for the tribes, however, was not the missions, the Spanish or bacteria, but the state of California itself, whose first governor, Peter Burnett, said, in an address to the legislature in 1851, he would wage a war of extermination against the native people "until the Indian race becomes extinct." He pursued that policy to grim effect, though several Ohlone tribes still existed in the Central Coastal region.

Shaw knew this because he had some Ohlone blood in his veins, through Mary Dove, who'd taught him about their distant ancestry. San Bruno park, which had been in the heart of their territory, was a sample of what their home had been like two hundred and fifty years ago, before the gold, silver and silicon rushes: Lush and rich and verdant, covered with undulating hills.

It was into a small parking lot here that Colter Shaw now steered his Yamaha. He traversed the smooth asphalt, stopping in the center. He looked with some envy at nearby hiking trails, which would make for an exhilarating dirt bike ride.

That diversion would, of course, have to wait.

The place was not quite deserted. On one side of the small parking lot was a commercial van—a plumbing company. The driver, in overalls, was eating a sandwich and sipping from a very large soda cup. Also present was a California State Parks service pickup, its driver—in an oversize Smokey-the-Bear hat—making a call and referring to a clipboard. No joggers or hikers or sightseers were present. The gray sky shed mist and teased with the promise of rain.

A blue Toyota sedan pulled into the lot and edged slowly toward him. The car stopped and the door opened.

Shaw nodded to the woman in black leggings and sweater and a navy-blue windbreaker. "Julia?"

"Colter."

He joined her. "You weren't followed?"

"No. I'm sure. You?"

"I have an anti-tailing device."

She frowned. "What's that?"

He nodded to the Yamaha.

"In your motorcycle?" she asked.

"It **is** my motorcycle. You drive on the lane stripes seven miles over the limit and nobody can follow."

"I might try that someday."

"You ride?"

"No. But I always wanted to. I'd need somebody to teach me how. You have to take a test, don't you? To get a license."

"Piece of cake. You'll pass with flying colors."

She pursed her lips. "What **are** flying colors exactly? I'm always curious where expressions come from."

Shaw didn't know and he told her so.

She pulled a hair elastic off her wrist and tied her tangle of dark-blond hair up into a ponytail, centered high on the back of her head. "Where's Russell?"

"He's back at the safe house. Following up on some other leads for our operation." He looked her over, frowning. "You're not armed, are you?"

"Me?" She gave a laugh as if this were an absurd idea. "I work for a tech company. We don't carry guns. Why?"

Shaw nodded at the state park pickup. "Government property. Weapons aren't allowed."

"Are **you** armed?"

Shaw shrugged. "I am but I've had plenty of practice keeping mine out of sight."

The parks department truck's engine fired up and the unsmiling driver touched the brim of his hat as he pulled past them. Shaw nodded in reply. The truck vanished up a dirt trail into the woods.

She said, "I've got a thumb drive but I also ran a transcription program. It printed out everything. I got about a hundred pages." She retrieved a large white envelope from the front seat of her car.

"Excellent."

"I might pick up something more from the original. Second generation there's always some fallout. I was thinking . . ." Her voice faded, then she gasped, looking past Shaw.

The front door of the plumbing van was swinging open and the driver, a pale-faced man, climbed out. Blond as the dead man in the alley. He was huge, dressed in black tactical gear and was holding a pistol.

Then the side panel slid open and two others

stepped to the ground: Ebbitt Droon, armed as well, and—looking every inch the harmless grandmother—Irena Braxton.

When they were out, standing on the ground, another figure emerged and joined them.

The head of BlackBridge, Ian Helms, stared his way. In a voice that was a rich, resonant baritone—as one might expect, coming from such a handsome leading man—he said, "Well, Colter Shaw."

66

Arms crossed, studying Shaw, Helms said, "Would've been in your best interest not to outsmart my friend."

Shaw supposed Helms was referring to Sophia/Connie and his dodging the bust at the Pacific Heights safe house.

I was worried. All those drugs . . . I did it for the children . . .

At least there he wouldn't be facing that fate they now had planned for him here in the park.

Droon took over. "Okay, Shaw, pull your shirt up. Slow, don'tcha know?"

"Just take it easy, Droon."

"What is this? What's going on?"

"Hush, there, Miss Julia," Droon scolded.

"How do you . . ." Her voice faded.

"Sit tight. I'll get to you in a minute, Lovely." He turned to Shaw. "Now, Righty, use that **left** hand of yours and pluck that sissy Glock off your hip and toss it in the bushes there. I want to see fingers out, like you're sipping tea from a dainty little cup."

"If I do that, it might go off and hurt someone."

"Now, now, you know better'n that. Those Austrians're too clever for accidents. Be a good boy and behave. Miss Julia's looking a little queasy. We don't want to upset her. Be a sorrow and shame. Go on, go on."

"What **is** this?" she repeated, her voice quavering.

Droon snapped to Shaw, "**Pistole**, son."

Shaw did as he'd been told, tugging his shirt up, revealing the weapon.

"Look at those abs. You must work out till the cows come home."

Shaw pitched the gun to the ground.

"Pull those jeans cuffs up too, would'ya, boy? You look like an ankle holster kind of guy."

Shaw complied.

"Goody good. Now. You, Miss Julia, you can stay fully clothed, much to my disappointment, don'tcha know? I heard you say you're not packing heat."

"You heard?"

Shaw glanced at the plumbing van. "They were listening. They know about the cassette. The analysis." He looked to Braxton. "After you stole the voting tally I thought you'd forget about us."

"We couldn't afford to do that."

Droon said, "You're our favorite number-one reward-seeker, Mr. Colter Shaw." He chuckled. "It'd hurt too much to say goodbye."

Helms waved his hand to silence the irritating man and stepped forward. "I wanted to see you in person, Shaw." He looked him over, and the man seemed enormously unimpressed. This was mutual. "The Shaw family . . . you've caused me nothing but grief."

"Grief?" Shaw laughed cynically. "My mother's a widow, thanks to you."

He sighed. "That again. It wasn't supposed to happen the way it did. We thought Ashton had found the vote tally certificate. Our man was simply going to pay him a lot of money for it."

"Your representative for those quote 'negotiations' was an armed trespasser on our property at three in the morning, tracking my father in the woods. What you meant to say was torture him until he told you where it was hidden, and **then** kill him. You're tedious, Helms."

"Tedious?" The handsome face darkened. The word had insulted him. Shaw realized whom he resembled: a younger Warren Beatty. His voice honed: "The Endgame Sanction. It's going to change the country fundamentally."

"Stalin changed Russia fundamentally. I don't think that's the kind of standard you want to be touting."

"BlackBridge didn't vote on Proposition Oh-Six.

Mr. Devereux didn't vote on it. We were hired to locate a document that'd been duly passed by the citizens of the state in a legal election. We're just enabling the will of the people."

The words sounded like they came from a spokesperson at a press conference.

Helms continued, "Just think, Shaw. The amendment gives **any** corporation the right to run for office. A do-good nonprofit."

"You're not the shining light of social conscience, Helms. You're destroying neighborhoods with your Urban Improvement Plan."

Helms shrugged. "I never held a gun to anybody's head and said, 'Here. Take these drugs. Or else.'"

The big man with pale skin, the van driver, just watched everything quietly. Maybe he was the hitman who'd been brought in to replace Blond. The man who had his sights on the SP family.

Irena Braxton appeared impatient. "We knew that Gahl had found the voting tally and hid it." She glanced toward the white envelope. "We never knew he was sucking up evidence too."

"The tape recorder was in our safe house when you broke in," Shaw said. "You had a chance to get it then."

Helms muttered, "Well, better late . . ."

A nod toward Droon, who said, "Now, Miss Julia. Here's what's going to happen. You're going to give us that envelope and your purse—or wallet, if 'purse' is too sexist a thing to say. Sorry for the offense. I'm going to get your partic'lars, find out where you live and your family or, if you prefer, **loved ones** live."

"No, please!"

"Yes, please!" he mocked. "Then you're going back to the office and you're overwriting every single bit of that digital copy of that cassette. 'Overwrite' is the key word. 'Member that. Nothing really gets deleted 'less you overwrite it, as you probably know, being in this business."

Braxton said, "No calls to the police. Or my associates'll drive straight to your house."

"No!" Her voice choked. "I have children!" Her hand kneaded the envelope manically.

Droon said, "Settle there, Lovely. You make sure everything's gone and . . . promise never to say a word about this again. And your little ones and hubby'll be fine."

"How could you do this?" she raged.

Droon frowned as if he didn't understand the question. He turned to Shaw. "I want the original cassette too, don'tcha know? Where is it? And don't be playful. We don't have all day here."

Shaw's face darkened. "All right." He held up his right hand—indicating no threat—and reached into his jacket pocket with his left, removed the cassette.

"Lookee. Wasn't that easy and painless? Toss it here."

Shaw did and the man picked it up.

In that giddy, grating tone, Droon said, "All right,

Miss Julia, the sooner you hightail to the office, the sooner—"

"Wait." The urgent word came from Braxton. Her head was angled, eyes squinting. "Wait."

Helms was frowning, and Droon turned toward her.

"You were scanning his safe house when you picked up the call from Julia, right?" Braxton asked.

Droon said, "Well, yup." There was an uneasiness in his voice, as he looked at his boss's powdered, troubled face.

"What phone did he pick up on? What was the number?"

"I . . ." Droon was thinking. "It started with eight-four-five or eight-four-something, I'm pretty sure. I can look up—"

"Jesus Christ!" Braxton's voice raged. "That's his iPhone!"

The woman would know that Shaw had been using his encrypted burner—the Android platform—since he'd been in San Francisco because he knew BlackBridge could listen in on the iPhone, which was unprotected.

If Shaw had picked up the call about the audio-tape on the Apple, it was because he **wanted** them to hear the conversation.

"It's a trap! There's nothing on the tape. The static? That was just bullshit. He's got people here."

The pale man and Droon lowered their stances and scanned around them, weapons extended.

Shaw was disappointed. He had hoped to play the game out a little longer to get more information from Droon and Braxton—and more incriminating admissions.

Braxton whispered to Helms, "Get back in the truck, Ian. Now."

Colter Shaw then gave a nod.

From the woods nearby, the "park ranger," who was, in reality, Ty, Russell's associate from his group, called, "You with BlackBridge, hands where I can see them! Drop the weapons. Lie face-down on the ground! If you present with a weapon or any threat, you will be fired on." He let loose a burst of rounds from his silenced H&K submachine gun. Dirt kicked up ten feet in front of the BlackBridge crew. "Now!"

The pale op did exactly as told, tossing his pistol away as if it were burning his skin. Braxton, grimacing, unhooked her macramé hippie purse from her shoulder and dropped it. She began kneeling. When finally down, she eased face forward to the dirt. Ian Helms followed suit.

Ebbitt Droon began to do the same, making a show of reaching out to set his gun gingerly on the ground. But he suddenly reared backward, putting the plumbing van between himself and Ty. He looked right at Shaw, his eyes both sadistic and amused. "No, sir, no, sir."

He began to lift his gun toward him. Shaw

instinctively crouched, hands forward in a defensive posture.

Which is when the woman beside him— not audio expert Julia but Shaw's friend Victoria Lesston—pulled the trigger of Shaw's Colt Python .357, which was in the white envelope. Because she wasn't able to aim, the big round missed Droon by a few inches and blew apart the side-view mirror of the plumbing van. Droon stumbled backward and fell, his gun flying into the brush. He rose and fled into the woods.

Victoria offered Shaw the Colt, but he said, "No, cover them." Nodding toward the BlackBridge crew. He didn't waste time searching for his Glock. Shaw turned toward the well-trod footpath Droon had disappeared down and sprinted after him.

67

Shaw caught up with the wiry man fifty yards away.

Breathing hard, Droon turned back, drawing the SOG knife from the scabbard on his belt.

"Okay, Reward Man. Pretty much had it with you, don'tcha know?"

Shaw ignored the words and assessed the terrain. A flat grass-covered clearing. Fair ground for both of them.

Never fight from a downhill position.

Droon moved quickly, dancing back and forth, the knife hand—his right—always in motion.

Shaw tried, and he only tried once. "It's over, Droon. You know it. Don't make it harder on yourself."

"Haw, you're a funny man to speak, Shaw." He

lunged and swept the blade back and forth. Shaw easily dodged. "We debated finishing you in the camper in Tacoma. I was for that. But Irena said you might have something else for us. Something helpful." Another swipe. "And damn if you didn't. You found that certificate. That made her day, my oh my."

Shaw was paying no attention to the words. Let him talk, let him use up oxygen. What he was doing was studying Droon's arms and hands. That's what you always watched in a knife fight. He kept his own in front and kept dancing away from Droon, making the small man come to him, then backing off.

Instinctively, Shaw was thinking of the rules of combat with blade.

Rule One: If you're attacked by someone with a knife and you're unarmed, run.

Not an option here.

Droon, laughing, giddy, eyes filled with glittery light, kept jogging forward and back, sweeping the knife between the men. Shaw moved back, but returned immediately, keeping his own hands up and open—to avoid breaking a finger—and slammed them into Droon's right arm, knocking it aside. As soon as the blade was past, Shaw cuffed Droon painfully in the face. Then moved back.

This infuriated the man, and his resulting expression accentuated his rodent features.

At one point Shaw, thinking the ground behind

him was flat, stumbled on a root he hadn't seen. He didn't fall, but lost balance momentarily. Droon sprung and Shaw felt pain as the blade slashed the back of his hand.

Rule Two: You will be stabbed in a knife fight. Accept it and try to present non-vital portions of your body.

Shaw continued to dance away every time Droon lunged. Shaw kept up the palm slugging at his opponent's face, stunning him.

He didn't go for the knife.

Rule Three: Do not try to get the knife away from the attacker. He has a religious connection with it and no martial arts move will cause him to drop it.

Droon was no longer smiling. Shaw was not playing fair, dancing in and out, cuffing ears and eyes. Another slash to the upper arm. The jacket took the brunt.

Droon would pounce and Shaw would leap back, but every time he did so his right palm or left would connect with Droon's face, which was now red in places and bleeding. That was his only target. In fast, out fast.

"How'd you like . . ." Droon took a deep breath. ". . . to be blind, son? That suit your way of life?" Like a fencer he thrust the knife forward. Shaw saw it coming. He stunned Droon with a blow to the ear. Hard enough and such a move can render your opponent unconscious. This strike didn't do that but it disoriented him.

"I'm tired of you, Shaw. Let's finish this."

Rule Four: When the attacker draws back, counterattack to the eyes and throat.

Droon leapt forward, and the blade missed Shaw's chest by inches. The second that the scrawny man turned slightly and drew the blade back, Shaw was on him, gripping the knife wrist in his left hand and clawing at the eyes. The man howled.

Shaw pressed his advantage and, still holding the knife hand, gripped the man under his right knee, lifted him into the air and slammed him onto his back on the hard, rock-strewn ground. His breath went out of his lungs.

The knife tumbled to the ground.

"No, son, no." Droon held up his hands, as if for mercy, but then pressed forward and seized Shaw's throat. Though he wasn't a large man, there was formidable strength in the grip.

As his vision began to fade, Shaw picked up the SOG knife and, holding it firmly in his right hand, plunged it into Droon's neck.

"No, wait, no." He seemed surprised. Maybe he thought that for some odd cosmic reason Colter Shaw didn't have the right, or wasn't able, to stab him with his own blade.

The pressure on Shaw's neck continued.

Colter Shaw thought of his father.

Thinking of one word:

Survival . . .

He twisted the blade, opening the rent in the man's neck wider. Blood propelled.

"Look . . . No . . . I . . ."

The arms dropped.

In no more than ten seconds, the man had gone limp.

Breathing hard, Shaw rolled off him, rose and stepped away ten feet. He kept a firm grip on the knife.

Never assume even a downed enemy is no threat . . .

Droon coughed once. Then his breathing ceased. Shaw watched him, motionless, his unblinking eyes staring upward. They were aimed toward an oak bough, not far overhead, stark in the gray sky, thick with clusters of early-season acorns, which were a pleasant green in color, a deep shade.

Colter Shaw thought: Not a bad image to carry with you in your last moments on earth.

68

Got 'em on the wire," Ty said to Shaw. "Listen."

The operative, no longer in the park ranger hat, was playing the recording he'd made of the conversation among the BlackBridge crew as they'd waited in the plumbing truck.

BRAXTON: **We can't do anything with a damn ranger there.**
DROON: **We'll hope he leaves. If he doesn't, well, accidents happen, don'tcha know?**
BRAXTON: **No. We wait till he's gone. I want it as clean as possible.**
DROON: **We're going to have two bodies 'ventually. Three can't gum up the works any more.**
HELMS: **Not the ranger.**

A third voice was that of the pale man, whose name turned out to be George Stone, a BlackBridge employee. He'd been a mercenary in Africa and the Balkans, Ty had learned.

STONE: **We kill Shaw now?**

DROON: **Does that make sense? Don't you think it might be better to wait till she comes** back **from the office, then take them out together?**

HELMS: **All right, all right . . . Maybe make it look, murder-suicide.**

DROON: **Now there's an idea for you.**

HELMS: **Gahl. That son of a bitch. How did he even know about the money laundering? He was research**.

STONE: **He overheard something. Was in the old building. Nobody was separate then.**

BRAXTON: **Right. Was years ago.**

HELMS: **At least half the finance infrastructure's still in place. Most of the banks're the same. And the contractors? Maybe he knew about taking out the councilman. Maybe there's an email, a note. Jesus, that info could burn us to the ground.**

DROON: **Yeah, the councilman. Todd Zaleski. Forgot all about that. Now that job went smooth as oil.**

HELMS: **Droon. Jesus. This isn't a performance review.**

DROON: **Sure, sir. Sorry. Oh, lookee here. S'that woman. Julia. Get ready to move.**

Ty shut the recorder off.

"That should be enough for the Bureau to get started," Shaw said.

"I'd think. Conspiracy to commit murder, extortion. **Admission** of murder. That's a sweet one. The councilman."

Shaw told him that the death of Zaleski, his father's protégé, was what had started Ashton Shaw on the trail of BlackBridge, all those many years ago.

Helms snapped, "Did you have a warrant for that recording?" His wrists, like those of the others, were zip-tied behind him.

Ty glanced at him briefly, the way you'd regard a fly that buzzed a bit close. "You just executed an illegal wiretap, you extorted Mr. Shaw and Ms. Lesston here under threat of force and your associate tried to kill two people and got killed himself. That means **you're** guilty of felony murder. And I haven't even got near conspiracy yet. Oh, by the way, we didn't trespass in your vehicle to plant a listening device. Your window was open, and my microphone just happens to be very good. So, no warrant needed."

Shaw gazed over at Braxton. He took satisfaction in the fact that the woman who was responsible for his father's death looked truly stricken. Her overly made-up face was taut. She was no longer grand-motherly, but ghostly.

Helms muttered, "I want an attorney."

Ty said in an oddly formal voice, "That will be arranged, I'm sure."

The takedown operation had been improvised and more than a little rushed. But no matter. It had worked. They now had everything they needed to get BlackBridge. Shaw texted Russell then walked up to Victoria, who was rubbing her shoulder—the one she'd injured last week. "You okay?"

"Just sore is all."

Her eyes widened slightly as she saw the slash on his hand, the messy blood.

"It's okay." He walked to his bike, lifted the seat and got a bottle of alcohol. He poured it over the wound, exhaling at the hot pain that radiated up to his jaw. She tore open the bandage he'd taken out, and when the liquid had evaporated off, she pressed on the skin and smoothed the edges.

"Droon?" She nodded toward the woods.

Shaw shook his head.

"I was going to say sorry I missed him. But worked out better this way, right?" she asked, in a soft voice.

Yes, Droon had been his. It couldn't end any differently.

He was about to ask her a question, when he suddenly sensed that the ambient sound had changed.

The parking lot had been filled with the white noise of traffic. San Bruno is bordered by the 101 and 280, both multilane Silicon Valley arteries and as busy as can be at all hours.

He'd been aware of the sticky rush of traffic. Been aware of the guttural whine of aircraft descending toward or departing from San Francisco and San Jose airports. Been aware of the wind in the pine and maples, a distant dog complaining.

Then, rising, rising, was the sound of a vehicle engine, growing louder.

Insistent.

He found his Glock in the brush, and he thought: Helms, Stone and Braxton had had their phones in the chaotic moments after she figured out the trap. She might have a speed-dial button on her mobile: NEED BACKUP or DISTRESS.

Shaw's team had a good defensive position where they were.

But the black Escalade was plowing unexpectedly over a pedestrian trail.

"Ty!" Shaw called. "Hostiles."

The big man nodded and clicked off the safety of his H&K.

He glanced at the Colt in Victoria's grip and, digging into his pocket, handed her ten loose shells. She reloaded and slipped the live shells in her pocket, then crouched, looking toward the approaching SUV.

A smoke grenade spiraled from the window of the SUV and popped, filling the area with dense gray cover. Shaw couldn't see for certain but he believed at least two men were out, firing automatic weapons—loud, unsilenced—in three-shot bursts. Shaw and Victoria rolled to cover behind a fallen tree. Ty was behind a low berm of grassy earth.

But he and Shaw lowered their weapons. It was impossible to acquire a target. Shaw squinted through the raw, pungent smoke, Victoria too. She said, "Flank them?"

A nod. He started left, she right.

But they got only a few feet before the relentless machine-gun fire tore into the air and ground around them, spitting dirt and rocks and branches high into the air. The stream of slugs swept toward her.

"Victoria!" Shaw called, as he saw her go down.

69

Too much incoming fire, too much smoke to acquire targets.

Angry shouts from the attackers. "Move it, move it!"

Both Victoria and Ty were hidden from sight by the smoke.

"Victoria!"

No response. Shaw's heart was slamming.

He tried to find a target. But it was impossible to see anything clearly through the thick, creamy cloud.

He knew they were in the SUV because the machine-gun spray had ceased. Shaw couldn't hear the doors slam—the weapons fire had partially deafened him—but he knew the Escalade was speeding away along another trail, a narrow one.

He stared in that direction but holstered his Glock.

Never discharge your weapon without a clear target . . .

He turned back. "Victoria!"

Still no response.

Jesus . . .

He'd gotten her into this.

Coughing, spitting out the vile fumes, he strode through the cloud to where he'd seen her fall.

"Victoria!"

Still nothing.

Come on, come on . . . Please.

He pushed through the smoke.

No body, no blood trail.

Had she been wounded and then snatched by one of the attackers?

Then . . . Did he hear a voice?

Again: "Here."

"Victoria."

A bout of coughing.

"Here!"

Then he saw her on her knees in a clump of sedge grass. He ran to her and helped her up. She clutched her torso. Then lowered her hands. No blood. No bullet wounds. She'd fallen hard to the ground, it seemed, the breath knocked from her lungs.

Arm around her shoulders, he helped her out of the haze. They were both coughing and wiping tears from the smoke, which wasn't the sort from wood or paper; the grenades spewed corroding, chemical fumes created by burning potassium chlorate or hexachloroethane and zinc. While not intended to debilitate, the thick clouds stung and choked.

"Ty!" Shaw called, looking around.

The broad-chested man was staggering from the berm behind which he'd taken cover, coughing and spitting as well.

Now that the smoke was drifting away on the breeze, they could see, probably a hundred yards away, the SUV was rocking along the pedestrian trail, about to turn out of sight.

Shaw said to Victoria, "You okay to go after them with me?"

She nodded. Shaw looked to Ty, who did the same.

The three of them started out of the dissipating cloud.

Then, suddenly, the Escalade lurched hard to the left, narrowly missing a tree. Something had flown from the right front tire.

A muted boom rolled over the landscape. Shaw knew it would have been much louder had his ears been functioning better. Then the windshield of the SUV blew to pieces. Another boom.

The Escalade stopped entirely. Several more booms, several more lurches.

Shaw said, "Engine's gone. It's dead."

You can't shoot a car motor by hitting the block,

not with ordinary rounds. But all it takes is one well-placed bullet to destroy the delicate electronics under the hood that make today's cars such miracles of modern transportation—and so vulnerable to hackers.

Ty, Victoria and Shaw moved forward slowly, using trees for cover.

Shaw called, "Everyone, out of the vehicle now!"

Ty: "This is your last warning. Weapons on the ground. Step out with your hands raised. Now!"

A moment passed.

A huge ring as another rifle slug hit the driver's side door, low, tearing into the seat just beneath where he sat.

As the echoing report of the shot from the rifle rolled over them, all at once the doors opened and guns flew out. Soon everyone was on the ground.

"Let's get them bundled up."

While Victoria covered them with the Python, Shaw and Ty searched the whole crew: the Latino driver and another BlackBridge op, a redheaded, muscular ex-military sort, as well as Braxton, Helms and George Stone. Zip ties for the newcomers. The other three remained bound.

More vehicle noise, another SUV approaching, coming down the trail. This one was a Lincoln.

Its arrival didn't trouble Shaw in the least. Or surprise him.

The driver climbed out and walked toward Shaw and the others, leaving in the vehicle the McMillan

TAC-338 sniper rifle he'd been using as he covered the takedown. He now had his own pistol in hand. He saw that the hostiles were down and slipped away his gun.

Shaw introduced Victoria to his brother.

70

Two hours earlier, as Shaw had sat in his father's Naugahyde chair, having learned that the San Leandro lead to finding the identity of the SP family had not panned out, he had glanced around the safe house and his eyes rested on the tape recorder.

With little time left until the family died, he'd forged a plan to ensnare Braxton and Droon and force them to abort the attack on the SP family.

He'd needed someone he could trust, a woman, and someone who wasn't afraid of combat. Russell's resourceful Karin was not a tactical op, and his group had none available. So Shaw had called Victoria Lesston and wondered if she'd help him out in an operation he was putting together.

She'd replied, "There're two types of people, Colter."

He'd laughed.

She said, "I'll get the next flight out."

"No time. My brother's organization'll send a chopper for you."

"Organization. What is it?"

"Don't know. He's tight-lipped."

"Have to say, Colter, with you not here, I've been feeling antsy. Not used to staying in one place for very long."

A Restless Woman . . .

He explained what he had in mind. Her role was to pretend to be Julia, the audio analyst Russell had called from the diner in Quigley Square. Victoria would call Shaw on his iPhone, which was compromised. If Braxton didn't tip to the fact he was using this phone, and not the encrypted Android, she would learn that there was incriminating evidence on the cassette and about the furtive meeting between Shaw and "Julia" at the park in San Bruno. She'd learn too that Russell was elsewhere—an assurance that only Shaw and the audio engineer would be present.

And the "evidence"? None of the science, which Victoria had fabricated on the fly, was real. There was no such thing as hiding voices in static.

But Shaw had figured, rightly as it turned out, that Ian Helms, Braxton and Droon were so desperate to make sure that the lurid details of BlackBridge's operations went undiscovered that they couldn't take any chances; they **had** to assume the evidence was real and destroy it, then kill the audio analyst and Shaw.

He had considered bringing in the law but still didn't know the extent of BlackBridge and Devereux's reach. He'd called Tom Pepper once again and told him his concerns. The former agent didn't know anyone in the San Francisco FBI field office, and so he couldn't vouch for them. But he did have some trusted agent friends in Denver. A team was being assembled. But Shaw and Russell needed to move fast to nail Braxton and Droon and stop the assault on the SP family. So he and Russell and Victoria put together their own private takedown.

"Citizen's arrest, you could call it," Shaw had told his brother.

Russell's response: "Hmm." Then: "It's a good plan, Colt."

And for the first time since they'd been in each other's company, the dourness had faded from his brother's face, replaced by what could pass for enthusiasm.

Russell had enlisted Ty to play the part of a state ranger; it wouldn't be suspicious for him to be in the park just making the rounds, spending time on his mobile, which was connected to sophisticated recording equipment that would suck up the conversation of the BlackBridge ops who came to meet Shaw and Victoria—certainly Braxton and Droon, perhaps others. He hadn't hoped for the other fish they caught: Ian Helms himself.

Russell took a high-cover position in the park with the sniper rifle on a bipod and covered them for the takedown. They hadn't expected a backup SUV, which, in any case, arrived via a tree-covered pedestrian trail; he'd had to move fast to get into a new position to sight in on the Cadillac and disable it.

When the FBI arrived from Denver, in about an hour, they could take this crew into custody, along with the tape and statements from Shaw, Russell, Victoria and Ty.

Shaw said to his brother, "Let's do some horse-trading."

Russell looked around and said, "We're black on the perimeter here." He looked to Ty and Victoria. "I'd get on the west and south."

"That's a go," Victoria said. She snagged one of the machine guns, checked it and scouted out a position to the west. Ty took the south.

Shaw and his brother walked to where Braxton and Helms were sitting on the ground, hands in restraints. Legs in front of them. Braxton surprised Shaw by saying in a raw, wounded voice, "You didn't need to kill him. He would have surrendered."

Shaw didn't respond. It would have been a push-pull conversation, since, no, Droon would not have

surrendered and was a second away from shooting Shaw, in the first case, and stabbing him in the
heart, in the second. The strangulation too.

The woman was clearly shaken by Droon's loss.
This seemed out of character for her, a person who'd
ordered the torture or handled the execution of any
number of people. Maybe there'd been more to their
relationship. Shaw had to admit that he found it
bordered on unpleasant to picture romance between
them, but who was he to judge when it came to matters of the heart, thought the Restless Man, whose
track record in love was not stellar.

As Russell remained standing, a guard of sorts,
Shaw crouched in front of Braxton and Helms,
who said, "I'm not saying another word without my
lawyer."

"We're not cops. We're not recording anymore.
This isn't about evidence."

"Then?" Braxton muttered.

"We assume the SP hit is off now. Can you confirm that?"

A pause. "The what?" she asked.

Shaw looked from her to Helms. "If that family
dies, it'll come back on you. We'll make sure of that.
If the motive is to kill a witness, that's capital murder. Death penalty in California."

Helms appeared perplexed.

Russell said, "Give us the name."

Shaw, again in the good-cop role: "We'll tell the

U.S. attorney you cooperated. That'll go a long way in your favor."

"Who the hell is SP?" Helms muttered. He turned to Braxton, who shook her head. She too seemed confused.

Shaw glanced at Russell. "Show them."

Russell took his phone and displayed the picture of the note that Karin had found on Blond's body, the kill order.

Confirmation from Hunters Point crew. 6/26, 7:00 p.m. SP and family. All ↓

Helms muttered, "I have no idea what that is."

Braxton shook her head yet again.

Russell said, "The Stanford library the other day? The man with Droon? This kill order was in his pocket."

Braxton said, "He was just a friend of Ebbitt Droon's. He was meeting him at the library to drop something off. Whatever that's about, the note isn't about one of our projects."

"He didn't work for BlackBridge?"

Helms said, "No."

The words—and the timbre of their voices—had moved Shaw from ten percent alert to ninety percent. He was in set mode.

Shaw asked Braxton, "Who is he?"

"Security. Works for a subsidiary of Banyan Tree."

"Name. Give me his name."

Russell crouched and leaned very close. His brother's chosen method for retrieving information.

"He's . . ." Braxton thought for a moment. "I think it's Richard Hogan."

Russell rose and said to his brother, "We got it wrong. Devereux's the one that wants SP dead, not BlackBridge."

"So the hit's still on." Shaw looked at his phone.

Three hours until the family died.

71

The brothers obtained Richard Hogan's address nearly simultaneously.

Shaw had sent a request to Mack, Russell to Karin.

Shaw's phone dinged first, but only seconds before his brother's.

The place where the hitman had lived was a yellow Victorian-façaded townhome in the shadow of Coit Tower on Telegraph Hill. An upmarket neighborhood. At first Shaw found this surprising, given Hogan's career—muscle work and kill orders—but Shaw supposed that Jonathan Stuart Devereux paid well.

Russell parallel parked on a steep incline and spun the wheel to chock the tire against the curb. Signs warned drivers to do this. Shaw supposed that the odds of a vehicle with an automatic transmission slipping out of park were minimal, but why not go the extra step? The incline had to be twenty degrees.

They climbed out of the SUV and Shaw dipped his head as two red-masked parrots zipped past. He noted several more, twitchily observing the street from the branches of a maple tree. Another pair was perched nearby too. The birds had made this neighborhood their own.

He and Russell crossed the street and approached the front door slowly, in a tactical formation, away from windows and the door itself. Hogan was no more, and Karin's information revealed he was single, but he might have had roommates, who were fellow Devereux employees. Or a lover in the same line of murderous work that he had pursued.

It was just the two of them now. Ty and Victoria had to keep an eye on Helms, Braxton and the other ops until the agents arrived from Denver.

Shaw and his brother looked through the windows, fast and carefully. The living space appeared unoccupied.

"I can't pick these."

Russell too examined the two deadbolts. He tapped his own shoulder and Shaw nodded.

Stepping three feet back, the brothers paused and looked around. The street was deserted.

Russell charged forward and crashed into the

wood. The heavy panel slammed inward as if the hardware were skimpy tin.

The men fanned out, guns drawn, clearing the sparse place. Lacking in furniture, that is, but there were weapons and ammunition aplenty, computers, tactical gear, phones—cellular and satellite, clothing and body armor.

Russell held up an ID badge with Hogan's picture on it. The subsidiary he worked for within the Banyan Tree family was Sequoia Pest Removal.

The computers were passcode protected, as were the phones. Not impossible for an outfit like Russell's group to hack, Shaw supposed, but SP's family had only hours to live. Cracking the electronics would have taken too long.

Shaw said, "The kill order was handwritten. Let's look for paper."

They began rifling through stacks of documents that sat on Hogan's kitchen table and a precarious card table that served as a makeshift desk.

Shaw's pile was mostly receipts, maps, instruction booklets for newly purchased weapons, company memos that had nothing to do with the kill order, checkbooks and ledgers that showed transfers into banks in the Caribbean.

"Got something here," Russell said. Shaw joined him as he spread a sheet of paper flat on the desk.

It has come to my attention that a whistleblower, SP, has discovered

the purpose of our Waste Management program. Following was found on his personal computer through a deep-hack:

"Banyan Tree is enlisting a subsidiary to dredge up toxic waste. Operatives then use unmarked vehicles to transport it to a competitor's facility, where it is dumped, as if the competitor were guilty of the pollution. This has resulted in the competitors being sued and fined, often going out of business, or losing so much money they are no longer players in the market. The plan is smart. Banyan's subsidiary analyzes each competitor's operation and determines what sort of dangerous materials those companies generate. Engineers then extract only those chemicals from the waste they dredge up. That is what is planted on the competitor's property, giving credence to their 'guilt.'"

As of now SP is still compiling information and trying to develop proof of our program. It's anticipated that he will probably have enough facts to go public within the next few weeks.

You'll be receiving further instructions.

"So that's what it's about," Russell said.

Shaw recalled what La Fleur had told them: about the CEO of one of Devereux's competitors committing suicide after going bankrupt—following Devereux's reporting him to the feds. La Fleur hadn't told them what regulations or laws had been broken, but it was now clear that they would have been environmental.

They dug through the rest of the documents and searched Hogan's clothes, looking for anything that might give them more information about SP.

Nothing.

Shaw: "Whistleblower. Means he's got some connection to the subsidiary, maybe he's a contractor, maybe an employee."

Russell went online and searched for Banyan Tree. It had been much in the news over the years and hundreds of employees were mentioned but there was no fast search filter that let him find workers with the potential victim's initials.

And because the company was privately owned, no employee records were available.

"Karin?" Shaw proposed.

"If we had a week or two, we could probably get somebody inside. Not on this time frame."

Shaw was musing, "Dredge. Waste."

The thought struck him almost like a slap on the back. He barked a quick laugh.

Russell looked toward him.

Shaw said, "We got it wrong."

72

Hunters Point yet again.

The vile smells, the trash, the dilapidated buildings, the lots where the skeletons of enterprises were all that remained of capitalist dreams from so many years ago. Seagulls quarreled over the slimmest remnants of garbage. Rats prowled silently but without caution.

The place was as tired as a car abandoned in the woods, not even worth scavenging for parts.

One structure here, though, shone. A white and green one-story building, recently painted. It sat on the water's edge and was surrounded by a parking lot in which a variety of modest vehicles sat.

BAYPOINT ENVIRO-SURE SOLUTIONS, INC.

A BANYAN TREE COMPANY

As the brothers sped into the lot in Russell's SUV, Shaw could see the thirty-foot transport boats they'd seen earlier: the ones leaving the island that had been part of the Hunters Point shipyard, filled with fifty-five-gallon drums, riding low. They would slog their way to the wide pier behind the building, where workers would offload the drums and use forklifts to load them onto long flatbed trucks.

The empty boats, with high drafts, would then return to the dismantled ship works for another load. Shaw wondered where the waste he was looking at was bound for: What competitor did Devereux have in his sights? How many employees and residents living nearby would be poisoned? How many animals? How much land would be tainted for decades to come? He wondered too if the idea of using waste as a weapon had come from the CEO of Banyan Tree himself? Or, like the Urban Improvement Plan, had it been the brainchild of Ian Helms?

Russell braked to a stop near the office and the men climbed out.

They had come back to the waterfront because of Shaw's thought after reading about "dredging" up waste, which is usually performed by a boat. That meant that the word **crew** in the text authorizing the killing of SP probably did not mean crew as in gang, despite the fact that there were plenty of those in Hunters Point. The word was meant in its original sense: those operating vessels.

**Confirmation from Hunters Point crew.
6/26, 7:00 p.m. SP and family. All ↓**

They walked over the parking lot of inky, newly laid asphalt to the office. Shaw noted on the side of one of the trucks was the name of the company, along with the tagline:

MAKING THE WORLD A BETTER
PLACE TO BE . . .

Shaw wondered about the ellipses at the end. That form of punctuation sometimes was meant to suggest forward motion: Now get out there and live that clean life! But ellipses also were used to indicate that something had been omitted from the sentence. Like: "Making the world a better place to be . . . for our company, our shareholders and our illustrious CEO."

They looked through the window into the office, where a woman sat at a desk and several men in gray uniforms and orange vests stood in a cluster, sipping from coffee cups. The pier itself held a dozen workers.

"There," Russell said. He was glancing toward a man in a navy-blue windbreaker, matching slacks with a stripe up the side and headgear you rarely saw: a real captain's hat, the sort sometimes sitting atop lean and fake-tanned women in short blue skirts and tight white blouses, on the arms of rich businessmen.

The man was out of sight of the office and the pier, on the other side of a large rust-scarred fuel tank, where four empty flatbeds sat. He was scanning their license plates with a tablet, then tapping in notes. On his chest was a BayPoint Enviro-Sure Solutions ID badge.

They bypassed the office and, when no one was looking their way, stepped over a gray-painted chain and walked along the stone wall at waterside toward the man. The smell was of white gas—kerosene— and diesel fumes, generic ocean, and some truly foul chemical. The rocking water beside the dock was coated in concentric blue and purple and red circles of oil.

The grizzled man in the captain's hat made a call on his walkie-talkie, then strolled to another truck. He glanced back, seeing the brothers. He looked them up and down. "This's private property." The voice was a growl.

Shaw and Russell continued forward and stopped when they were about fifteen feet away.

His weathered face soured. "I said, case you didn't hear, private property. You get the fuck out of here."

Russell said, "We have some questions."

"Leave! Or you don't know the kind of hurt you'll have. I've whipped Somalian pirates, I've put down mutinies. I whaled on a carjacker so bad he needed his jaw rebuilt. Now!" The head, beneath its jaunty hat, turned toward the exit.

Russell said, "There's an employee—"

"What's with that beard? Are you some kind of Amish person?" His face grew even more fierce. "Or a Muslim?"

Shaw: "An employee at BayPoint Enviro-Sure. His—"

"I'm not telling you again." His cheeks reddened; his temperature must have risen a few degrees. Soon the shade was actually livid.

"—initials are S.P. He has some connection with this facility. We need his name and address. It's important. We'll pay you. A thousand."

"Why would I care what you need and don't need? Fuck-fancy. Get off this property now."

Fuck-fancy. Not a phrase Shaw was familiar with. He kind of liked it.

He continued, "I'm a spit away from calling security."

The expressions got better and better.

"All right. That's it." Up came the radio. Apparently the old salt hadn't whipped those pirates without backup.

But before the call went out, Russell smoothly drew his silenced pistol and blew a nearby rat to eternity.

Not the approach Colter Shaw would have taken.

Then again, as he'd learned very well over the past few days, it wasn't unusual for two siblings to solve a problem in significantly different ways.

73

At 6:45, fifteen minutes before the family was to die, Colter Shaw was sitting, alone, in the front seat of Russell's Lincoln Navigator. He was looking over the house of Samuel Prescott, the BayPoint Enviro-Sure Solutions whistleblower. Shaw watched the garage door rolling down, hiding from view the family's sedan, a red Volvo.

Trevor Little—the belligerent pseudo captain on the Hunters Point dock—had glanced in horror at Russell's gun and quickly told the brothers Prescott's name. It seemed the employee and his family had been out of town at a funeral but were due back today.

This would be the reason for the specific time and date of the hit in the kill order; the murderer would have to wait until the family returned to their home from the airport. Karin had checked passenger manifests and flight schedules. The Prescotts were due back at about 4:30 and would be home about fifty minutes later—the time it would take them to collect luggage and travel from San Francisco International Airport to their home in Forest Hill, a suburb of San Francisco.

Shaw, Russell and Ty had met the family's flight.

A scheduler at BayPoint Enviro-Sure Solutions, Prescott was in his forties, stocky and tanned, with sandy-colored hair. His wife, Bette, was blond and willowy. Their son and daughter were twins and had their mother's pallor and hair, freckled both. They were twelve.

At SFO, Ty had displayed an ID card, which Shaw caught a fast glimpse of. He saw the initials **U.S.** and a round emblem similar to, but not the same as, the Justice Department's. Shaw wondered if it was real. In any case, it took no convincing for Prescott to believe that he and his family were in danger.

Prescott had been surprised Devereux had learned of his espionage. He'd taken care to hide the fruits of his spying on his computer with sophisticated encryption.

He was not, however, surprised that the CEO had issued an order to have him killed. "He's murdering people with toxic waste. Why not kill somebody with a bullet?"

Explaining to the brothers how he'd discovered Devereux's toxic waste scheme, Prescott said, "The numbers, always the numbers. They never lie. I'm a scheduler, right? I keep an eye on transport down to the hour, the **minute**. I noticed that the timing of some of our trucks was off. When they went out and when they came back wasn't right. I knew how far they had to travel to the sites—the legitimate ones— and they were coming back to the dock too soon.

"Not a huge time difference, but it was suspicious. I called in sick one day and followed one of the trucks. It didn't go to the site it was supposed to. It went to a vacant lot in Oakland. The waste was pumped into an unmarked tanker. I followed it to a factory owned by one of Devereux's competitors. These men got out—like special forces, all in black. They dumped the waste into a creek downstream from the factory. I got pictures and samples. I was going to the EPA and the U.S. attorney this week. I just wanted to find a few more target locations."

Shaw looked over the street the family lived on. It was a quiet avenue in Forest Hill, with houses set back behind small front yards of grass or gardens. It was one of the least densely populated parts of the city and, as the name suggested, more arboreal than most. Their house was modest. Prescott made good money at his job and Bette was the senior bookkeeper for a chain of urgent-care clinics. But even with double incomes, this was all they could afford. Home prices in the Bay were crushing.

Though the blinds were drawn, Shaw noted the flickering light from the TV in the living room.

He scanned the street again and saw no threat. He also was watching the rooftops to the east, looking for rifle muzzles or scope flares.

Russell and Ty were in the latter's car, behind the house, scanning Hawk Hill Park, which is where a sniper targeting the Prescott house from the west would be. Those two had already swept the home for IEDs and found no traces of explosives. Drive-bys wouldn't be the order of the day either. To kill the family the team needed to get inside. The two pros in the business, Russell and Ty, believed the attack would be a dynamic entry, two or three ops kicking in the door and charging through the house. They would likely be supported by a sniper.

Why did the kill order include the entire family? he wondered.

Maybe just being meticulous. Maybe Devereux was worried that Prescott had explained what he'd found to his wife, and the children might have overheard.

Maybe to send a message to the rest of the thousands of employees at BayPoint Enviro-Sure Solutions and Banyan Tree, reminding them of where their loyalty should be.

5:56.

He called his brother and asked in a soft voice, "Zero here. Anything in the back?"

"Thought I saw a hostile. Just a jogger. No threat."

"'K." They disconnected.

Would the ops come in an SUV, a couple of jeeps? He doubted a helicopter but supposed with Devereux's money that wasn't impossible.

Shaw was armed with both his Glock and his Colt Python, and, in the backseat, his Enfield .303— the World War One British infantry rifle, old and battered but perfectly accurate. He really hoped he didn't need to fire any weapons; he'd already been present at a fair number of incidents here. At some point the cops would have to get involved and, even if the firefight was justified, he wouldn't want that hassle.

Besides, he needed a shooter alive. He wanted witnesses to testify against Devereux. Sam Prescott had proof that would bring down BayPoint Enviro-Sure Solutions and its executives, but the parent company—and Devereux himself—would be insulated from liability. A hired killer, even working for one of Devereux's subsidiaries, might have evidence leading directly to the arrogant CEO himself.

A motor scooter went by, a young Asian man on the saddle. It vanished around the corner at the end of the block. An SUV, driven by a middle-aged woman, cruised up the hill, and likewise disappeared. A woman bicyclist, in a bold, floral athletic outfit, pedaled past and started up the steep hill, her feet moving rapidly, the gears in low.

At 7:10 his phone hummed.

Shaw answered and told his brother, "They're

late." He said he'd seen a few vehicles. Nobody suspicious and none of the drivers—or the cyclist—had been interested in the Prescott house. "Sniper action? There's nothing in the front."

"No one presenting in the back, and any sniper and his spotter'd need time to set up, adjust for wind, humidity. We would've seen them by now."

"Are they just in good camo?"

"No. Got eyes on every usable nest. Couple of them're perfect . . . Hmm. They would've known the Prescotts landed an hour and a half ago."

Shaw said, "With Hogan disappearing, they're being cautious maybe."

"Think they called it off?"

"Ten percent chance of that. Tops."

"Agree."

They disconnected.

7:15.

Shaw noted the light from the Prescotts' living room change as a commercial came on the TV.

He was checking his phone for the time—it was 7:19—when the gut-punching explosion rocked the SUV. He looked up at the Prescott house to see flame boiling from each shattered window. Shaw climbed from the vehicle and ran toward the structure. He could get no closer than forty or fifty feet. Already the entire home was ablaze.

The device—whatever it was—had been perfectly designed. Not a soul could have gotten out of a trap like that alive.

74

They drove back in silence to the safe house, Colter Shaw and his brother.

Both men were stung by their failure.

"Goddamn it." Shaw's voice was bitter.

What a loss . . .

They had expected an assault. They had expected a C-4 or another nitrate-based bomb.

They weren't prepared for a very different improvised explosive device—and a particularly clever one. Devereux's new kill team had run a gas line disguised as a water pipe into the house and starting about 7:00 or so the timed system had begun filling the place with natural gas—but it was the original substance, before the foul rotten egg smell odorant, to warn of leaks, was added. No one could have detected it.

After a half hour, some type of timed igniter clicked to life. The resulting explosion had destroyed the house.

If no one had known the family was targeted for death, the incident would have been reported as an accident. The intense heat and flames would melt most of the parts of the device. Investigators would assume the real public utility pipe—now destroyed too—had cracked or suffered from a leak. The igniter would be vaporized as well.

Shaw and his brother, though, explained to the fire marshal that the explosion was meant to murder a whistleblower and his family.

"Why the hell didn't you tell anybody?" the marshal had demanded.

Because it never occurred to them that Devereux's men would try something like this.

And also because Shaw and Russell had inherited enough of their father's paranoia to not trust your average civic official—at least not in the case of BlackBridge.

They now arrived at the safe house and Russell parked. He had a good touch behind the wheel of a motor vehicle. All the children did. Homeschooling didn't provide the chance for official driver's ed classes, but Ashton had taught Russell, Colter and Dorion the skills needed to pilot vehicles from cycles to sedans to trucks from age twelve or so. It was curious that Russell drove so conservatively. In his work for the group, he was the blunter of the two brothers; Shaw, whose Yamaha occasionally went airborne vertical and returned to earth horizontal, had an approach to his own profession that was far more cerebral.

The brothers walked to the pale blue safe house on Alvarez and into the entry hall, where the FBI's Denver contingent was standing. Shaw nodded and introduced himself. Russell did too.

Shaw then walked into the living room and up to the four people sitting stiffly on the couch. He said to the four members of the Sam Prescott family, "We were wrong. There weren't any shooters. It was a firebomb. Your house is gone, your car, everything. I'm sorry."

75

Their failure was that they'd missed the chance to apprehend a single member of a dynamic entry team—someone who might be willing to testify against Devereux.

There was, of course, never any question about the family's going home from the airport; Russell, Shaw and Ty had transported them directly to the Alvarez safe house and then sped to Forest Hill to set up the bait and arrange the takedown of the assault team.

Russell had driven the Prescotts' sedan from the airport and had parked it in the garage so spotters would think the family was home. Ty, in his own car, parked behind the property. The men had checked the house for IEDs. When they were finished, they turned the TV and lights on to simulate occupancy, then left via the back door to wait for the attack.

A house destroyed and not a single suspect who might be willing to testify against Jonathan Stuart Devereux.

What a loss . . .

Shaw and Russell had done all they could do and now the case was in the hands of the FBI. The scrubbed, somber agent from the Denver office was named Darrel Gardiner. He and his team would be temporary; the agents would review BlackBridge's records and interrogate suspects to find out if any San Francisco FBI personnel had been compromised. If not, Gardiner would hand over the case to the field office here.

With Victoria Lesston at his side, Shaw sat at the kitchen table in the safe house, as the FBI agent finished his interview with him. The agent had already spoken to Victoria, Russell and Ty.

Karin, it seemed, was the invisible woman. Her name never came up, and Shaw wasn't going to volunteer anything about her.

Looking over his notes, Special Agent Gardiner shook his head, topped with a blond businessman's severe trim. "Extortion, murder, attempted murder and conspiracy, burglary, hacking, eavesdropping . . . Well."

Shaw got the impression there was a stronger word he wished to use but couldn't bring himself to.

Religious maybe. Or just the rigorous standards of the profession.

"Urban Improvement Plan?" A shake of his head. "They must've dumped thousands of kilos of drugs over the years."

Shaw said, "Tip of the iceberg. BlackBridge's got clients all over the world and the UIP was just one of their tactics."

The company was being shut down, and all the facilities were being seized and searched presently. Other warrants would follow. A U.S. congressman and a congresswoman from California were already looking into voting fraud allegations because of the UIP-manipulated congressional districts in the state. The woman legislator issued a statement condemning the gerrymandering and was calling for an investigation of the politicians who had benefited from the redistricting.

One problem remained, however, a serious one. All of the offenses that Gardiner had just recited had been committed by Helms, Braxton and the BlackBridge crew. Not a bit of evidence could be laid at the feet of Jonathan Stuart Devereux or Banyan Tree Holdings.

"The best insulation I've ever seen," Gardiner told Shaw and Victoria. "It's early, I understand, but so far Banyan Tree is driven snow."

Shaw asked the special agent about BayPoint Enviro-Sure Solutions, whose offices were presently being searched too. "Their execs and staff'll go down, but there's no evidence that the parent company or Devereux himself even knew anything about dumping toxic waste on competitors' land. No emails, no memos. We have phone records, but that's just who called who and when. We don't know the content."

"Devereux was the one who ordered it, right?" Victoria asked, her lips tight in anger.

Gardiner answered, "Of course. But the head of Enviro's taking the fall for the whole thing. Claims his boss was in the dark."

Gardiner closed his notebook and shut off the recorder. He slipped them away and handed both Shaw and Victoria his business card.

Other agents—a woman and a man, Latinx—were helping the Prescott family gather their luggage. They would be taken to a federal safe house, where they'd stay during the course of the BayPoint Enviro-Sure Solutions investigation. Shaw wondered if they'd go into witness protection. If Devereux remained free, they would have to.

The family still seemed dazed by what had hit them.

Sam Prescott said, "I don't know what to say, Mr. Shaw. We're alive because of you. And what they did, with that bomb in the house . . . Lord. I can't imagine being in there when the thing went off."

Shaw responded with, "Good luck." The gratitude matter again.

"Thank your brother too."

Russell was in the safe house, but not present

with the family. He was assembling the surveillance gear he'd planted upon his return.

"I'll do that," Shaw said.

Prescott and his family then followed the watchful agents out the door.

Ty stepped inside. "Have to leave, Colter. Got a little bit of paperwork to take care of. Oh, I got a call from SFPD. They responded to a complaint in Hunters Point. Man said an Amish Muslim and his buddy threatened to shoot him and then zip-tied him to a radiator in an old warehouse. He said he's whaled on pirates and if he gets a chance he's going to punch those guys out too. Just a heads-up."

"I'll keep my eye out," Shaw said with a smile.

"You two make a good team. You brothers. You work together in the past?"

"Trained, ages ago. Never worked."

"Looks like it all came back to you. Russ was saying you climb mountains?"

"I do."

"For the fun of it?"

"You should try it some time."

"Jesus." Ty shook his hand.

"Oh. And one thing?" Shaw said, reflecting on meeting Ty for the first time in front of the safe house.

The squat man lifted a gear bag that had to weigh fifty pounds as if it contained pillows, and glanced Shaw's way.

"Be careful with those box cutters."

PART FOUR

JUNE 27

FLAME

76

t's safe."

"You say that. It's easy to **say** it's safe. Anybody can **say** it's safe. It's easy for me to say I can soar like a seagull but I can't."

Colter Shaw stood at the base of the porch and continued speaking to the shadows on the other side of the half-open door of Earnest La Fleur's Sausalito home.

No arrows had been launched, though the man might have gotten a piece of Shaw if he'd been inclined. He'd moved the oil-drum barricades, as Russell had suggested.

Shaw said, "Droon's dead. Braxton and Ian Helms're in jail, and the FBI and state police have locked down all the BlackBridge offices. ATF and SEC're after them too, I heard."

"Okay, okay, given that's true, which I still have to confirm," La Fleur offered by way of meager rebuttal, "what about the chief boilermaker, Devereux?"

Shaw's brow creased. "Nothing to nail him on yet."

"Told you. Man's elusive as a drop of mercury and just as toxic."

"Earnest," Shaw stretched out his unusual name. "Let me in. And could you point the arrow elsewhere?"

"How'd you know I was locked and loaded?"

Shaw exhaled loudly, not bothering to explain that he'd heard the creak of the bow once again—and not troubling either to correct the man, as he had others, by telling him that the "lock and load" phrase applied only to the M1 Garand rifle. And until you **unlocked** the weapon—which slipped a round into the chamber—it was only as dangerous as a baseball bat.

"All right. Come on in."

Shaw stepped into the man's cluttered house, still redolent of ocean and pot.

The scrawny hermit, gripping the bow and a de-notched arrow, pushed past Shaw and strode into the yard. There he stood for a moment and then disappeared into the complicated growth of plants most of whose genus and species Shaw did not know. Beyond them, however, was a landscape of plants featuring rich green leaves pointing outward like splayed fingers. Shaw knew what **this** crop was.

Returning, La Fleur said, "You might've been followed. It looked clear. But, listen to me: never assume you're safe."

Shaw nearly smiled. That was the last line of the letter his father had left in Echo Ridge.

La Fleur re-latched the door. There was a chain—that most insubstantial of protective devices. But it wasn't alone. The other security mechanisms were a knob lock, a massive deadbolt, a crossbar like you'd see in a Middle Ages castle and an iron rod tilting upward at a forty-five-degree angle from floor to door. Shaw wondered if he had a rope ladder somewhere in the place for a fast emergency descent down the cliffside. As a matter of fact, he did: a glance toward the windows revealed a coil of rope, one end of which was tied to a radiator.

"You want coffee, anything?" He was sipping from a chipped mug, as bulletproof as those in the diner where Shaw and his brother dissected the courier bag containing the mixtape and the ancient document that could change the face of American politics forever.

Shaw declined. "Brought you a present." He handed over one of the envelopes he and Russell had taken from the BNG gangbangers at the site of the Urban Improvement Plan meeting in the Tenderloin. "Ten K. Laundered and unmarked. Amos Gahl's mother got one too."

He peered inside and pulled the money out. "Okay, okay. Can't say I can't use it." He walked to a painting of an old-time sailing ship and lifted it down, revealing a wall safe. After turning his back so Shaw couldn't see the combination, he opened the door and slipped the cash inside. Upon closing it, he spun the dial a number of times and reseated the painting.

"Well, thankee." His face grew troubled. "So that son of a bitch Devereux still got what he wanted. Corporations running for office? What does he want more power for, more money? He's got a company worth a couple trillion dollars."

"Just one point two."

"This ain't funny, Shaw. That's bigger than Spain's gross domestic product. Banyan Tree's going to run for office, and then the world goes to shit with his new policies you were telling me about: fucking the environment, civil rights, immigration. Jesus my Lord, just occurred to me: Devereux could start his own schools. They can teach what they want. Indoctrinate the youth. Hitler did that. 'The Future Belongs to Me.'"

"The man who would be king."

La Fleur tilted his head slightly. "That was quite a flick. There was justice in the movie. You remember how it ended? But not here. Devereux? Hell, if he gets enough power he could change the U.S. Constitution and a company could become president of the United States."

"You think it'd come to that?"

A smile, both coy and troubled, spread over

La Fleur's face. "But you don't have to look back too far into U.S. politics to see that pretty damn weird things can happen." He opened one of the metal blinds and looked out. The view of the city was indeed spectacular. And dominating the skyline was the massive office building that housed Banyan Tree. "It's like the missiles have been launched. I'm enjoying the last view of the country before the nukes hit." He gazed back to find Shaw looking at the same scene.

La Fleur was sizing him up. "You seem . . . what'sa word I'm looking for here, Shaw? Detached. Like you don't care about the cataclysm." The man squinted. "Yep, I'm sure of it. De-tached. How come's that? **Don't** you care?"

"Let's put on the TV. Something you might want to see."

La Fleur nodded toward the ancient set. "This one's safe, terrestrial. The only kind I'd ever have. You can't work for BlackBridge and not get this sense of how efficiently electrons can fuck you."

This was a man Ashton Shaw would've counted as a friend.

Shaw clicked the unit on. It had to warm up before the picture crisped into view.

The crawl at the bottom of the screen said BREAKING NEWS . . .

A brunette anchorwoman in a bright red dress was looking out at her invisible audience.

"Repeating this afternoon's top story, three

independent forensic examiners have concluded that a recently discovered California Constitution amendment, to allow corporations to hold office in the state, is a forgery. The tally was dated April seventeenth, nineteen oh-six, but all three examiners found that the paper and ink dated to the nineteen twenties.

"Professor Anthony Rice of the University of California had this to say earlier . . ."

The scene cut to a recorded in-office interview. One shot revealed a large, pale man in a navy suit and a white shirt. His graying hair was thinning and curly.

"Hello, Professor Rice."

He tapped his round glasses higher on a lengthy nose and nodded to the camera.

"Afternoon."

"Tell us about this voting tally."

Rice repeated the story about the implications of Proposition 06 and then added:

"Over the years the voting tally became a kind of Holy Grail for big corporations, which would love nothing more than to hold office in the state."

"But the experts are saying it isn't real."

"I believe what happened is that a businessman in the nineteen twenties hired someone to forge it and hide it in government archives with other documents from around nineteen oh-six. His plan was probably to quote 'miraculously' discover it. Why didn't he? One reason might be the timing. Maybe he went bust in the Depression and his corporation went bankrupt. He faded off into obscurity."

"Do you think there really is a legitimate copy of the voting tally somewhere?"

"No, no. I'm sure there isn't. The tally was just a legal legend. It would be impossible for onc to exist. The recount was a long time ago but it was in the twentieth century. As soon as the judge signed it, word would have spread . . . There were telephones, telegraphs, daily press and as many reporters per capita as we have nowadays. If a re-count meant the proposition passed, that would have been front-page news. No, Prop Oh-Six was defeated by the people."

"Professor, has a corporation ever run for office?"

"A few have tried, as public relations stunts, but they never got very far. All legal scholars and political historians I know think it would be disastrous for democracy."

"Thank you, Professor. In other news—"

Shaw shut the TV off. It crackled to darkness.

"Well," La Fleur said. "That's one kettle of fish . . . You think it's for real? About the thing being forged?"

"It's real."

"You say that like a man who knows."

"I do. Because I was the forger."

77

So, I say: as Americans and lovers of democracy you should light a bonfire and throw the damn thing in . . .

Just after Shaw and Russell had left Professor Steven Field's house in Berkeley, with an understanding of just what Proposition 06 meant, Shaw had made a decision.

He'd considered the academic's advice—either hide or destroy the tally.

But Shaw had concluded that neither of those would work. BlackBridge, on Devereux's orders, would continue to search and would undoubtedly rack up more dead bodies in the scavenger hunt. The businessman had been searching for the tally certificate for years. Why would he stop now? But if it appeared that the tally never existed in the first place—that the rumors were based on a forgery—then he might lick his wounds and forget the matter.

Shaw would create a forgery himself. He would make sure Braxton and Droon stole it from the Pacific Heights safe house. Devereux would then send it to Sacramento to present to the state assembly, where forensic experts would determine it was a fake.

Shaw was confident he could pull it off. He had on occasion in the course of his business needed to track down documents for which people had offered rewards. Usually these were last wills and testaments, corporate purchase documents, adoption papers. Those jobs would occasionally land him square in the esoteric world of document examination and forgery.

He needed help, though, to make sure it was a solid job. And he knew whom to call. An expert skilled at **detecting** forgeries would also have to be an expert on how to create them. He called a friend. Parker Kincaid was a former FBI forensic document examiner. Based outside of Washington, D.C., he was now a consultant.

"Parker."

"Colt. How's it going?"

They caught up with small talk. Kincaid's son, Robby, was now an accomplished martial artist and he'd just won a big competition.

"Congratulations."

"What can I do for you?"

"Let's say I was tracking down some materials someone might use to create a forged document. I'm talking San Francisco."

"Okay."

Ah, the cop word again. Kincaid, after all, had been one.

"I'm speaking hypothetically."

"Hypothetically."

Shaw was amused. Kincaid's repetition suggested suspicion. On the other hand, he knew all about Shaw's rewards business and the number of people he'd rescued and the number of perps he'd collared. If Shaw was being coy, it was for a legitimate reason. Still, Parker had to ask, "I assume my former employer in Washington, D.C., would not have any reason to be concerned by **someone's** document?"

"Absolutely not."

"Good. Are we thinking modern day?"

"No. Nineteen twenties."

"Pen and ink?"

"And typewriter."

Kincaid didn't hesitate. "In the Bay Area, there's only one place a forger would go for supplies. Davis and Sons Rare Books and Antiquities."

"Thanks, Parker. Helpful."

"You ever get reward assignments in Northern Virginia?"

"Haven't yet. My sister lives in Maryland. I've been meaning to visit. I've got your number."

"Tell **someone** good luck."

The men had disconnected and Shaw had headed up to North Beach to the bookstore.

There, he had paid to have the original voting tally, with the sketch on the back, mounted in the cheap plastic frame.

He had bought a few other things too—out of the case he'd studied when he first arrived.

Among his purchases was a ninety-year-old Underwood No. 5 typewriter, the most common of the era. It was a high-standing classic, the work-horse of secretaries and reporters throughout the first half of the twentieth century. He also selected a notebook that dated to the 1920s, containing blank sheets similar in color and weight to the paper of the original tally, and pen-point nibs and holders. Most important, he was able to purchase a bottle of actual ink that was nearly one hundred years old. That had been his biggest concern. Shaw, though, had been surprised to find that there was quite the market among collectors for unopened ink bottles from the past.

No accounting for passions and hobbies . . .

Back in the safe house, he'd saturated the ribbon of the typewriter with the old ink, cranked in a piece of paper he'd cut from the notebook and typed out a voting tally certification identical to the original.

He'd examined it carefully. Nope. Didn't work; the ink wasn't as consistently dark as the original. He prepped the typewriter again. This one was better, but he still wasn't satisfied. Now it was consistent, but too dark for a document that age.

The third one hit the mark. He let it dry then assembled a nib and holder to practice the signature of the Right Honorable Selmer P. Clarke—a wonderful name for a judge. He did what all professional forgers do when faking signatures: not attempt to actually sign the document, mimicking the original signatory, but to turn the page upside down and "draw" the signature, as if he were sketching a landscape or portrait.

After a dozen attempts he was confident, and he inked the man's scrawl onto the phony tally.

He heated the document briefly in the oven to make sure the ink was dry and to give the sheet additional distress and patina of age.

He took apart the frame, extracted the real tally, which went into the lining of his backpack. He drew another sketch on the back of the forgery and mounted that one into the frame, sketch side out. Onto the wall it went.

Shaw had then called Devereux and they met about his proposition to buy his family's safety with the "evidence" against BlackBridge and Banyan Tree. He'd arranged the get-together to give Droon or another op the chance to put a tracker on his bike (not guessing they would take the more sophisticated approach of the RFID dust), which led them back to Pacific Heights. At the safe house he'd purposefully left the window open, knowing that a surveillance outfit from BlackBridge was now eaves-dropping. Shaw had made a pre-arranged call to Victoria Lesston and purposely sat near the open window to explain about the tally being hidden in the frame on the wall. He was pretty sure that the woman in the hall, dressed like a maid, was the op whose job it was to steal the document when her partners created a distraction by trying to blow the door off Russell's SUV.

Shaw knew the document examiners in Sacramento would find his creation to be fake but he wanted some insurance. He had contacted Professor Steven Field and told him of his plan.

The professor had laughed. "Well, aren't **you** your father's sons?"

"When the story breaks that it's fake I want a nail in the coffin—some expert to say that the tally was just a pipe dream. It'd be next to impossible for there really to've been one."

Field knew just whom to call. He got in touch with a colleague, Professor Anthony Rice, who had known Ashton Shaw too. He was more than happy to back up the story. Rice put out a tweet on the topic—that it was almost certain that there was no real voting tally. Media networks picked it up and invited the articulate, airtime-ready professor to be interviewed on the topic.

The entire world would get the word the tally was a myth.

Shaw now said to La Fleur, "You told us that

when Amos found out that the tally was real, he was going to destroy it."

La Fleur nodded. "I know it would've been tough for him. He was a historian. Against his training to destroy an original document."

Never deny history . . .

One of Ashton's rules.

Shaw told La Fleur this.

"Good advice."

Shaw said, "Hitler's and Goebbels's and Himmler's writings were despicable but we don't burn them. That's different, though, from the Nuremberg Laws—nineteen thirty-five. Took away citizenship of Jews in Nazi Germany and became the justification for the death camps. What if there was the same voting tally controversy then? The law was passed but the tally went missing, and you found it. You could submit it and have the law go into effect, or you could burn it. What's your moral duty?"

"No doubt in my mind."

"That's why I'm here."

La Fleur frowned. His fingers drummed.

Shaw dug into his backpack and extracted the original tally. He handed it to La Fleur, who gazed at the document. "Heh. Short, isn't it? Doesn't seem so scary up close." He looked up. "You ever read **Lord of the Rings**?"

Shaw nodded.

La Fleur mused, "This is the ring of power." Then he lit up his bong, took a hit and laughed, as the smoke floated. "I'm an old man. I can be as god-damn melodramatic as I want."

Shaw rose and walked to La Fleur's fireplace. He opened the grate. He took the tally and placed it inside. "You want to do the honors?" Shaw asked, picking up a cigarette lighter and handing it to the man.

"Me?"

"BlackBridge killed your friend for this. Tortured him."

The man thought briefly. "And they killed **your** father. Let's both do it." He produced another lighter.

Shaw debated. It seemed sentimental, contrary to his theory of navigating your way through life by calculation and analysis. But then he recalled the day young Colter had saved the woman in the avalanche and his father had given him and his siblings their respective statuettes.

Never deny the power of ritual . . .

The men crouched before the pungent fireplace. Two clicks of two lighters, and they each touched the blue flame to opposite corners of the tally. They sat back and watched the document ignite and curl under the bright orange blaze, sending embers flitting upward into the flue like bugs curiously repelled by, rather than drawn to, a bright lamp on a gentle summer's dusk.

78

While San Francisco is home to more than forty geographic elevations, the A-list celebrities are the famed Seven Hills, just like in Rome. They are Telegraph Hill, Russian Hill, Rincon Hill, Twin Peaks, Mount Davidson, Lone Mountain, and the most luxurious, Nob Hill.

The name derives from **nabob**, the term referring to a rich and conspicuous businessman, and it was applied to this summit because it was here that the Big Four—the tycoons involved in the creation of the Central Pacific Railroad—had mansions: Leland Stanford, Collis Potter Huntington, Mark Hopkins and Charles Crocker. The men modestly referred to themselves as "the Associates."

Colter Shaw was now enjoying the unstoppable sun and the cool air in this lofty neighborhood, sitting in a rooftop bar and café. The view was fabulous. When the June gloom descends, or the autumn rainy season brings downpours for weeks upon end, San Francisco can be unbearably glum. But on days like this, the sun fully unfurled, the I-left-my-heart town can turn the wordless into Beat-era poets, the tone-deaf into chanteurs.

Shaw was sipping an Anchor Steam, the essential San Francisco beer. In his travels, which took him far afield, he always tended to pick local brews and this was one of his favorites.

Much of his day had been taken up with interviews with the San Francisco FBI agents who were running the BlackBridge case. All of the agents in the Bay Area field offices had been vetted and were clean. Ashton Shaw's concerns had proven to be a bit excessive in that while there was some SFPD corruption, only five patrolmen and brass were in BlackBridge's pocket, out of thousands of officers.

Shaw was sipping the beer and, mostly from curiosity, perusing a menu that was heavy with tourist fare—though of the Nob Hill variety: Manchego cheese, serrano ham, bruschetta, lobster rolls. Also a kids' menu, evidence that trust-fund youngsters enjoyed the same chow as their common counterparts did: cheese sticks, pizza, and potatoes and onion rings that had met their crispy fate in boiling oil.

He was not here for the food, though. He and Victoria would meet later and go to a back alley in Chinatown. He hoped he could find one of the places where, years ago, Ashton Shaw had had meetings over lunch with local Chinese businessmen, art dealers and professors. Occasionally Ash would bring along one or more of the children. Even Dorion too, at the time younger than three years old. His sister had eaten her noodles by hand, one at a time. Young Colter had been mesmerized by the quiet, observant Chinese men who treated Ashton with respect and seemed subtly impressed with the man's ability to discuss Asian philosophy and politics and wield chopsticks as if he'd been weaned from bottle to the lacquered rods at a single-digit age.

The memory faded, and it was on his third sip of Anchor Steam that he noted he was being watched.

A large man, Anglo, in a dark suit and slightly less dark shirt, was standing immobile near the hostess station outside and had been there for more time than seemed normal. Tables were available but he simply stood in one spot, with arms crossed. Through sunglasses he was eyeing the patio, but mostly he was eyeing Colter Shaw.

Shaw's right hand set the bottle down and continued casually to the napkin in his lap and thereafter to the grip of the Glock 42 in the holster, tucked in the waistband of his black jeans and hidden by the shirt, which was roughly the same shade as that of the behemoth man's at the hostess station.

Well, there's the minder.

But where is the mindee?

The answer arrived a moment later like a foraging pigeon.

"No need for that," came the man's voice behind him. It had a delicate English lilt.

Shaw turned.

At a nearby table Jonathan Stuart Devereux lifted a glass of wine Shaw's way. Apparently he'd been observing Shaw observe the admirable scenery—and the substantial bodyguard.

"He's safe." As if talking about a dog. Then: "Join me, join me."

Shaw dropped his own menu on the table. He swiveled his chair, the metal legs gritting unpleasantly on the concrete floor. He easily lifted the heavy piece of furniture and plopped it down across from Devereux. The man was in a garish light blue suit—no stripes today—and pink shirt. The groping octopus of a handkerchief was cream-colored today. The shoes were polished to black mirrors.

"You followed me," Shaw said. "Not easy to miss a Rolls. I wasn't paying attention."

Devereux looked over his guest from behind those large, rectangular TV-screen glasses. Today the frames were baby blue. "Ah, but why here, Mr. Shaw? My word."

"The view. The beer."

"Don't have the soup, whatever you're leaning toward. Fair warning. It's watery and the onions grew from cans."

The man looked around, his hands gesturing before him, fingers bending and straightening, palms up, palms down. The digits adjusted his busy hand-kerchief. Why this look? What impression was he trying to convey? The word **dandy** came to mind.

The melodious voice, with its suave over-the-Pond modulation, offered, "Quite the adventure you've had in this town, haven't you, Shaw? You were born here."

This was not a question.

"Technically Berkeley."

"Cal. That's what the University of California at Berkeley is called. Yes. Berkeley's the town, Cal is the school. Your mother was a professor, a physician, but you were born off campus. **Not** at the medical center where she taught. She did quite the work as a principal investigator too, now, didn't she?"

Again, this was certain information that Devereux had found and kept, like acorns buried by fat-cheeked squirrels in late summer. Meant of course to intimidate.

"Quite the adventure," the man repeated, his voice now an ominous whisper.

"What can I do for you, Devereux?"

His hands became spirited once more and he muttered angrily, "I had such a fine plan. Such a pure design. We'd find the voting certificate, my companies would run for office, we'd win, of course. And then, bang." A palm struck the tabletop and drew attention. "Onward to the new world."

Shaw thought once more of the protests in Berkeley.

CORPORATE SELLOUTS—NO!

Devereux took a sip of yellow wine. "Oaky chardonnay. The sort that makes you shiver. The vintners in California need to work on that. But it's the best they have here."

Devereux would be a man who had to order from the right side of the menu.

"If you hadn't followed me here," Shaw said blandly, "you could've gone someplace with a better list."

Devereux's eyes strayed to a nearby table: two attractive women in business attire—white suit, lime-green dress, both form-fitting. He pushed the lenses higher, the better to study them. Which he did for a moment.

Shaw said, "I saw your political plans once Banyan Tree got into office. It was in Amos Gahl's courier bag. Deregulation was the theme. Environment, banking, healthcare and insurance. Cutting social programs to the bone. Private police. I smelled human rights issues."

Devereux turned away from visually molesting the two women diners.

"Ah, we could argue till the early hours, couldn't we? I could respond that deregulation leads to corporate success, which leads to more employment and a better economy. One could also contend that corporations are far more efficient and ethical than a mere mortal politician: a company would never be caught with its fly open. But you would come up with a counterargument. I would counter-counter. It would become oh-so tedious . . ." Another sip of the wine he was going to finish despite himself. "It would have been a noble experiment . . . But let's not quibble. Do you ride the cable cars?"

"I have."

"You know what the engineer's called."

Shaw answered, "A gripman." He seemed disappointed that Shaw had known. "And they have to be replaced every three days. The grips, not the men." A chuckle.

Shaw had another hit of beer. The leisurely tip of the bottle, accompanied by a glance into Devereux's eyes, was meant also to convey impatience.

The billionaire's face flared with anger. He leaned forward. In a low voice he drew the words out. "Something very wrong went down here, Shaw. I'm not sure what or how. But you were at the epicenter."

This was Devereux's show. There was nothing to do but listen.

"There's no record that we could find of any industrialist or financier in the nineteen twenties interested in a voting tally about Proposition Oh-Six."

"Is that right?" Shaw frowned in confusion.

"Oh, yes it is." Hands zipping here, hands zipping there. "And, from what I heard, the forgery was rather clumsily done. Not clumsy in the sense of technique or penmanship. It got the judge's handwriting down perfectly."

"You checked that too, did you?"

"I mean clumsy in terms of the materials, the supplies. One would think that a millionaire in the nineteen twenties would have hired a forger who'd use inks and paper that dated to nineteen oh-six. Easily come by back then."

"One would think."

Devereux extracted a monogrammed handkerchief. He patted his bald brow. "Of course, we're not here to debate. The people involved, all those many years ago, they know the truth." He couldn't resist adding, with a sardonic grin, "**If** they existed."

Shaw remained silent.

"A forgery it's been declared and that's tainted the whole barrel of apples. The army I had marshalled in Sacramento—quite the array—were enough to stop a court challenge. But now they've got cold feet. All those liberal, human-rights pundits and professors railing against capitalism . . . Yes, if we'd struck fast, we could've pushed it through and made sure it stuck. But t'was not to be." Hands jittering in the air. The waitress thought it was a summons. "No, no, no," he said darkly, and she retreated.

"So, it's fallen out the way it has." Then his fake

thin-lipped smile vanished. "BlackBridge is gone. But I am CEO of one of the wealthiest corporations on the face of the earth, aren't I?"

"I suppose so. Hadn't actually heard of you until a few days ago."

His fingers froze briefly. With a smile on his moonish face, he said, "The voting tally, BayPoint Enviro-Sure Solutions . . . You've crossed me, Shaw. And that means your family has crossed me as well. Bad thing to do."

"I think it's time to say goodbye, Devereux."

"Oh, from your perspective, maybe. Not from mine."

Shaw rose, put a twenty down beside his empty beer bottle.

Devereux's eyes held his for a moment, then swiveled to the menu. He perused. "What to have, what to have . . ."

79

Shaw descended from the rooftop restaurant to the lobby and stepped out into the garish décor, then proceeded outside, putting his phone away, having made two calls.

He waited in front of the hotel, in the shade of an arching, dark red awning, as the intense sunlight made the unshaded portion of the street glow surreally. In ten minutes, a dark-skinned man on a Vespa rolled up and spotted Shaw, braking to a stop. Shaw joined him. "From Mack." Shaw took the slim 4-by-5-inch envelope and instantly the courier was gone.

No more than five minutes later a cab pulled up and the second person he had called after meeting with Devereux climbed out, as the uniformed doorman scuttled forward.

Sophia Ionescu, aka Consuela Ramirez, aka Ksenia Vlanova, was really quite attractive.

Her shades were similar in shape to Devereux's eyeglasses. Hers were pricey too; they bore the Chanel logo. She wore a short white skirt, blue silk blouse, white cotton jacket, and very little else, it seemed. Over her shoulder was a black purse on a chain, also Chanel.

Well, she **was** a three-G-a-night girl.

She appeared glum, an expression that did nothing to diminish her beauty—as she muttered, "You said it was dues time."

Shaw nodded. "Take care of this, and I throw out the drugs you tried to plant. And erase the tape."

"Take care of what?"

"There's a man upstairs on the patio, having lunch." He showed her a picture of Jonathan Stuart Devereux. "You'll go up there, make contact and then take him to the Sherry-Nelson Arms Hotel. It's up the street."

"I know it." A shrug. "He looks like the Wizard of Oz. How do I know he'll come on to me?"

"He will." Shaw wasn't sure his entire plan would work but he had no doubt that Devereux would go for the bait.

After a drink or two, with conversation steeped in flirtation and wine, Devereux would make the offer.

"What if he wants to take me to his house?"

"He's married."

"Pig." But spoken as if identifying a species, not offering an insult.

Shaw opened the paper bag that Mack's delivery man had given him. He took out a plastic bag holding what looked like a credit card, slightly thicker than normal. On the front was printed the name of an airline and below that **Prestige Club** and a meaningless account number. He handed it to her. "Here's what's going to happen. You go up to the room with him. When you're inside, take his jacket off and kiss him."

"Do I have to?"

Shaw said, "Yes. Then tell him to go brush his teeth."

"Oh, that's why."

He'd told her to bring paste and a brush.

"When he's in the bathroom slip this into his wallet. He keeps it in his jacket pocket."

"And?

"You leave. You got cold feet."

"That's it?"

"That's it."

"Okay."

"Once I know you've done that, I'll dump the tape and drugs."

"How do I know you'll do it?"

Shaw shook his head, offering a tight-lipped smile.

A glance at the Prestige Club card. "It's not a bomb or poison or anything?"

"No."

She looked up at the hotel. "What did this guy do to you? I mean, to deserve this?"

Shaw kept to himself that his father, Todd Zaleski, other colleagues and Amos Gahl were dead because of Jonathan Stuart Devereux's quest for the Holy Proposition. He settled for: "A story for another day."

Then the three-G girl stepped toward the entrance of the building and fired a faintly impatient glance at the doorman, who had fallen in love in the past five minutes, and he adoringly pushed open the heavy door for her.

80

Devereux's still a problem."

Shaw had just walked into the safe house on Alvarez.

He continued speaking to Russell. "Mary Dove and Dorie . . . They're still at risk. We are too."

"Didn't figure him for the revenge sort. Thought he'd put his energics elsewhere."

"Yeah, well, we blew up his Grail."

Sitting at the coffee table, Shaw opened his laptop. He typed. "I'm tracing him."

"You got a device on him?"

"Correct."

Russell seemed impressed.

Shaw continued, "He can't operate the Urban Improvement Plan without another group like

BlackBridge. I'm hoping he'll find some other dirty-tricks outfit. I'll let our Bureau contacts here know. Let's hope he stumbles."

"Hmm." On the screen Russell was watching the glowing dot representing the Rolls-Royce, which had left Nob Hill and was making its way south. "How long will it last?"

"Four days, five."

"You know it's a long shot, finding a meeting, identifying principals."

"It is. But I'm hoping to find another UIP drop-off point, and the Bureau can get eyes and ears there in time."

"What system are you using?"

"MicroTrace."

"It's a good one. We use it. Send me the number of that unit. I'll have Karin keep eyes on him too."

Shaw sent the text to Russell's phone.

Both men watched the dot.

Then Shaw noted his brother's duffel bag and backpack sitting near the stairs.

Why the hell the Oakland A's? . . .

"Come back to the Compound. Victoria and I are driving down there. Until I can get some evidence on Devereux, I want to keep an eye on Mary Dove. Maybe have Dorie come too."

"Can't. There's that problem in Alaska. I told you about it."

Shaw said, "You can't be the only one with a beard and a SIG Sauer."

He thought this might, at last, raise a smile. No. His brother shook his head.

"Mary Dove'd love it." He hesitated then added, "Been forever."

Another pause. "Just can't."

"Sure."

You make a good team . . .

Well, after a rocky start, they had. He was thinking of Russell's enthusiastic embrace of his brother's plan to finally nail the BlackBridge crew at San Bruno park.

Which made his brother's abrupt departure now all the more painful.

Shaw was looking down at the floor. There was a black scuff mark in the shape of a crescent moon. Had it been left by Shaw or Russell? Maybe Droon or one of the ops when they'd assaulted the safe house in search of the tally. Maybe by Ashton Shaw himself, if the mark was indelible enough to survive polishings over the years.

"Better go."

When it came to his brother there was no true north, there was not even a constellation to help Colter Shaw navigate through the words he wanted to say. He and Russell had never had serious conversations. They talked about how to cure pike for longest storage or which caliber and load were best for charging mountain lions. And for human intruders, armed and with intent. But never words about themselves.

That wasn't acceptable to Colter Shaw, not after all that had happened over the past few days. "Wait."

His brother turned back.

"Why . . . Why'd you disappear? All these years. We're blood. I've got a right to know."

A long moment passed. "What Ash taught us: survival."

Shaw could only shake his head.

"Survival for you, for everyone in the family. You have an idea of my job. I do bad things. I was afraid I'd put everybody at risk. There're prices on my head—sort of like a reward, if you think about it."

Just last week, in the cult in Washington State, one of the self-help gurus had told Shaw much the same.

I think he didn't want **to leave. He felt he had no choice. If you pursue him now, and find him, he's just going to keep running . . . A protector sometimes protects best by leaving those in his care. The way a bird leads predators away from their young.**

"Russell, we all know how to handle risks. It's what Ashton taught us. From day one in the Compound."

"All right." His brother inhaled twice before continuing: "It was survival for me too." The white noise roared like a deadly wave. "You really believed I'd hurt Ash?"

So we get to it. At last.

"I looked at the facts—the fight you two had

about Dorie, the knife. Then you lied, you said you were in L.A. when he died. You were near the Compound."

"It was one of my first assignments. An op near Fresno. They gave it to me because I knew the territory. Nobody could know about it. Okay, Ashton taught us to look at facts. 'Never make decisions based on emotion.' But who somebody is, that's a fact too, isn't it? What you thought, what you accused me of . . . That was tough. It was easier to go away."

"I was wrong."

Was this a transgression that could be remedied by apology? Colter Shaw simply couldn't tell.

Russell's eyes went to the statue of the soaring eagle.

"Remember that?" Shaw asked, nodding at it. "Do you have the bear?"

"No."

Had he thrown it away because Ashton's ritual gave first prize to Colter? Russell's was for the supporting role.

His brother surprised him by saying, "I'd been meaning to send it back. Never got around to it."

Shaw considered this. "**You** had it, not Ash?"

"I took it, after the funeral."

"Why?"

Russell was silent for a moment. "I couldn't tell you."

"Keep it," Shaw said.

"No, it's yours."

Silence flowed and within it, this thought: the words he'd rehearsed for so long had finally been spoken . . . but had done nothing to bridge the chasm between them.

"Okay. Got to get the team up north. I'm glad this reward thing's working out. It suits you. The Restless Man."

"You were right. This BlackBridge operation, it wasn't what I do. I needed you."

A nod. There was no question of a handshake, much less an embrace. With backpack on his shoulder and duffel bag in hand, his older brother was out the door.

81

At ten that evening, Shaw and Victoria were returning to the Alvarez Street safe house from a fine Italian dinner in the Embarcadero. The day had been rainy and the streets slick, so they had taken her rental, the car that had been at the scene of the takedown in San Bruno park. They both were curious what Avis would make of the bullet hole in the fender. At least she'd bought the loss-damage waiver, so she would not be charged, though Shaw wondered if gunfire invalidated the coverage.

They paused outside.

"Anything?" Victoria asked.

Shaw was looking at the security app on his phone. Russell had left several cameras in the house. With Devereux still a wild card, and with him knowing where the safe house was located, they were being cautious, though Shaw believed the man would play the long game. Nothing would happen to Shaw or the family just yet. That would be too suspicious. The descendant of the beheaded member of English royalty was dangerous, greedy and narcissistic, but not stupid.

"Clear." Shaw put the phone away.

They went inside, set the security system to at-home mode and opened wine and beer. "Think the fireplace works?" she asked.

"I checked. It's sealed. My father and his colleagues? Didn't want any surprise packages dropping in."

"Your mother and I had a conversation about him. He had a reputation for being paranoid," she said.

"That's right."

"But I guess after all this, he was just being cautious."

"Russell said some of his concerns were smoke. That was true. But what he really was? A survivalist before anything else. That's how I think of him now."

Shaw had some beer and called up the tracking program on his laptop. The red dot that was Devereux pulsed, but didn't move. Shaw panned in and saw that he was in a developed area off Highway 1, south of the city. He'd probably stopped off for a meal at one of the many seafood places along that sidewinding road. Perhaps he was on his way to Carmel, the magical kingdom on the Monterey Peninsula—it was the sort of place where he would have one of his mansions. And if so, was he accompanied by a tall, picturesque woman?

It was then that he heard Victoria's alarmed voice, "Well."

He noted her attention was on her phone.

"You have a news feed?"

Shaw asked, "Which one?"

"**Any** of them."

He picked one at random. And read.

BILLIONAIRE BUSINESSMAN JONATHAN STUART DEVEREUX, CEO OF BANYAN TREE HOLDINGS, WAS SHOT AND KILLED TONIGHT IN THE TOWN OF HALF MOON BAY, SOUTH OF SAN FRANCISCO.

MR. DEVEREUX WAS LEAVING AN EXCLUSIVE GOLF RESORT WHEN HE WAS FELLED BY A SINGLE SNIPER SHOT FROM THE HIGHWAY. HE WAS LEAVING THE RESTAURANT IN THE COMPANY OF EXECUTIVES OF ABERNATHY CONSULTING, SANTA CRUZ, AND A BODYGUARD. NO ONE ELSE WAS INJURED.

THE SAN FRANCISCO DAILY HERALD REPORTED THAT AN ANONYMOUS CALLER

TO THE PAPER STATED THAT A LOCAL
GANG WAS BEHIND THE DEATH BECAUSE
OF DEVEREUX'S INVOLVEMENT IN ILLEGAL
DRUG OPERATIONS THROUGHOUT THE
BAY AREA. A SAN MATEO COUNTY
SHERIFF'S OFFICE SPOKESPERSON SAID
THE INVESTIGATION WAS ONGOING.

"God," Victoria said. "The UIP thing."

Shaw was doubtful. "He was insulated. That was BlackBridge's thing. Nobody'd know that he was the ultimate client. He was careful about that."

Dangerous, greedy and narcissistic, but not stupid . . .

It was then that his phone hummed with a text, and he read the brief message from an unknown number.

Delete the tracking app.

He stared at the words for a moment. Then the meaning hit him. Jesus. He did as the message instructed. Shaw replied.

Done.

A moment went by. Shaw debated. He sent another.

Take care . . .

Shaw wondered if he would get a response. Seconds later the phone vibrated again.

The number you are trying to reach is
no longer in service.

PART FIVE

JULY 3

ASH

82

One of those stainless-steel afternoons, when humidity, temperature, clarity of the air and a show-off of a sun conspire to make the setting as perfect as a setting can be.

Colter Shaw parked the Winnebago near the cabin and climbed out, stretching after the seven-plus-hour drive from the north, eyeing the craggy and soaring peaks to the west of the property, the dense pelt of pine and oak to the east and south. Sun danced off the pond where he and Russell had fished for hours upon hours.

There'd been several days of matters to attend to in San Francisco, answering more questions—and there'd been quite a few—about the San Bruno shootout, Droon's death and the explosion of the

Prescott home, the Urban Improvement Plan, BlackBridge. Yes, the various authorities had quite the list. Unfortunately Shaw could offer no insights into the tragic death of Devereux, but he said there was some credibility to the drug claim, since he knew for a fact that the man was one of the chief beneficiaries of the UIP.

Shaw had spent a day closing up the safe house on Alvarez, feeling his brother's absence even more keenly than he had after Russell had departed the first time, following the rescue at the library. He thought back to his surprise and pleasure when the man had returned to explain that he would be helping Shaw identify the victims of the kill order.

It's not a reward job, Colt. You can't do it on your own . . .

Then he'd tucked the feeling away and finished filling his backpack. He had hopped onto the Yamaha for the zipping ride to the RV camp to pick up the Winnebago.

Upon leaving the park, Shaw had not headed south toward the Sierra Nevadas. And the reason for this was that he was not alone in the camper. Beside him in the passenger seat was Victoria Lesston. It turned out that she found the idea of a vacation as alien as he, but they decided to take the plunge and spend some R & R in wine country.

They had found a charming bed-and-breakfast nestled into a verdant quadrant of a vineyard. The place was long on views and complex, tasty meals, and—thank God—short on gingham and plaques of ducks and geese in bonnets.

Those days—in the safe house and then in Napa— were the first time in ages that he had spent several contiguous nights in the company of a woman. Oh, he'd been wary of the trip at first, very wary, but Shaw soon found there was nothing to worry about; all the vineyards they toured offered good beer.

The amount of time in each other's company had been just right. At almost exactly the same moment, silence materialized between them, like a summoned spirit at a seance. It was benign, but it was silence nonetheless and they'd smiled, both understanding simultaneously that it was time to get back to their real worlds.

Now, in the Compound, Victoria climbed out of the camper too and stretched, somewhat more carefully than Shaw, given her hundred-foot high dive from a cliff not long ago—and the tumble to cover in San Bruno park. Together they walked toward the cabin, where they saw Mary Dove approaching from a field. She carried a heavy basket of vegetables.

Smiling, she nodded toward them, then the house, meaning she would off-load the provisions and then join them.

Victoria pulled off her sweater—Napa and Sonoma had been far more damp and chill than the weather here. Beneath she wore a gray silk blouse.

And beneath that was a pale blue, lacey garment, not presently visible, though Shaw was by now quite familiar with its construction and the mechanics of the clasps.

She wore blue jeans, as did Shaw. He was in a black T-shirt and the leather jacket that still bore evidence of damage various skirmishes in the past few days, most notably the cuts from the knife duel with Droon. He had examined the marks and decided to leave the blemishes. He had no clue how to go about mending a garment that had come from a department store. His expertise in leather was limited to hides and skins that he had fleshed, salted and tanned.

They carried their bags to their respective rooms. Shaw stripped and took a scorching hot, then a freezing shower. He toweled off and dressed in clean jeans and a dress shirt. Then digging through his bag, he removed the eagle statue and replaced it on the shelf from which Russell had taken it so many years ago. He'd thought about keeping it in the camper but for some reason it seemed more appropriate here.

He joined Victoria on the front porch. Mary Dove now brought out three cups of coffee, along with the milk and sugar service, which she set on the table.

All three sat, fixed up the beverages to their liking and sipped.

Victoria had dozed for a portion of the trip but

had apparently been aware of several calls Shaw had taken and made on the drive.

She mentioned this now and asked, "Status?"

"Bail denied for everybody."

"I noticed the streaks," Mary Dove said, nodding at his jacket. "And that." Now she looked to his hand, still bandaged following the slash from Droon's knife. "I do hope you wear your body armor when you ought to." Spoken in the same casual way another parent might say, "Wear your raincoat and galoshes; it's going to pour."

Shaw added, "The Bureau rolled up all the Bay-Point Enviro-Sure Solutions executives and some BlackBridge people in L.A., Miami and New York. The company's gone."

The reason for this, of course, was ultimately Ashton Shaw's mission. Had he not started on his quest years ago to bring the outfit down, it would still be going full force, addicting people to drugs, engaging in dirty-tricks operations and leveraging companies like Devereux's into the pilot's seat of political office.

Mary Dove asked, "That wouldn't really have worked, would it? A corporation running for office?"

"I wouldn't have thought so, but who knows?" Shaw told her what Professor Field had said.

Mary Dove said, "That's a question Ash would've loved to think about—and debate until the wee hours." She looked toward Victoria. "He was quite the historical and political scientist, you know."

"Colt told me." Victoria said, "I wish I'd known him."

"He would've liked you," Mary Dove said. "He enjoyed his rappelling buddies."

The woman looked Victoria over. "You're free to stay as long as you like. I'm hosting a women's health retreat next week. Some good people."

"I need to leave in a day or so. I have a job interview on the East Coast."

They'd talked about this on the drive here. The job interview was not exactly that, but, like Russell's, Victoria's line of work required the occasional euphemism.

Her eyes were on his when she added, "But I'd like to come back."

"Always welcome," Mary Dove said and pressed Victoria's arm.

Shaw's glance seconded the motion.

"Tell me about him?" Mary Dove asked.

He knew that she was speaking of Russell.

"Mysterious, doesn't say much, sharp as a whip. Looks exactly the same—well, aside from the beard. It's longer now. His hair too. Still couldn't find out where he's working. Government, deep cover."

Victoria said, "Has or had some Pentagon connection. DoD."

"Why's that?"

"In San Bruno, after the shoot-out, he said we were 'black on backup.' That's Army talk. We used that on operations in Delta."

Shaw thought, Oh, yeah, Ashton Shaw would have loved this woman.

Mary Dove gave a soft smile, and gentle wrinkles folded around her mouth and eyes. "Did Russell say anything about a family?"

"Said he didn't have one."

There was a pause as Mary Dove's eyes fixed on a sunlit peak. "Did you ask him about visiting?"

One never evaded, much less lied, within the Shaw family. "I did. He said he couldn't. An assignment. Important."

"It's his job and his life."

"He's hard to read but I could tell he's content."

Leaving another thought understood, but unstated: both she and Ash had made the right decision in plotting out and executing the most difficult task in the world: their children's upbringing.

His mother said, "I've got to get dinner going. Venison with blackberry glaze. It's been soaking all day."

Her habit was to steep the meat in buttermilk, which eliminated the gamey flavor.

Motion in the corner of Shaw's eye. A nighthawk jotted above the field in his buoyant, erratic path. These particular birds have among the most complicated markings of any avian—their camo makes them virtually invisible during the day, but now, in approaching dusk, they're easily spotted as they hunt for flying insects. They're easily heard too: they issue a repetitive, raspy **creek-creek** when on wing. Colter had once been attacked by one when he had unknowingly trod too close to a nest. Both man and bird disengaged unharmed.

Looking away from the spirited bird, Shaw said, "Have a thought. What do you say about the three of us hiking Echo Ridge tomorrow."

"Lovely idea," said Mary Dove.

"Sounds good to me," Victoria said. Then after a brief pause she turned her head slightly and squinted. "But I think it's going to be four."

Shaw glanced at her and noted she was looking past him. Both he and his mother turned.

A figure stepped from the dirt road onto the driveway. The man was dressed in black and wearing a stocking cap. He carried a duffel bag in one hand, and a backpack was over his right shoulder. He paused, looking at the house and, seeing the trio on the porch, he brushed at his long beard with the back of his left hand and continued in a slow lope toward them.

"My," Mary Dove whispered, a hint of uncharacteristic emotion in her voice. She stepped off the planks, into the grass, to greet her eldest son.

Acknowledgments

Novels are not one-person endeavors. Creating them and getting them into the hands and hearts of readers is a team effort, and I am beyond lucky to have the best team in the world. My thanks to Sophie Baker, Felicity Blunt, Berit Böhm, Dominika Bojanowska, Penelope Burns, Annie Chen, Sophie Churcher, Francesca Cinelli, Isabel Coburn, Luisa Collichio, Jane Davis, Liz Dawson, Julie Reece Deaver, Danielle Dieterich, Jenna Dolan, Mira Droumeva, Jodi Fabbri, Cathy Gleason, Alice Gomer, Iven Held, Ashley Hewlett, Sally Kim, Hamish Macaskill, Cristina Marino, Ashley McClay, Emily Mlynek, Nishtha Patel, Seba Pezzani, Rosie Pierce, Abbie Salter, Roberto Santachiara, Deborah Schneider, Sarah Shea, Mark Tavani, Madelyn Warcholik, Claire Ward, Alexis Welby, Sue and Jackie Yang. You're the best!

ABOUT THE AUTHOR

JEFFERY DEAVER is the #1 international bestselling author of forty-four novels, three collections of short stories and a nonfiction law book. His books are sold in 150 countries and translated into twenty-five languages. His first novel featuring Lincoln Rhyme, **The Bone Collector**, was made into a major motion picture starring Denzel Washington and Angelina Jolie and was the basis for the hit NBC primetime TV series **Lincoln Rhyme: Hunt for the Bone Collector**. He has received or been shortlisted for a number of awards around the world, and has won the Novel of the Year prize from the International Thriller Writers and the Steel Dagger from the Crime Writers' Association in the United Kingdom. In 2014, he was the recipient of three lifetime achievement awards. A Grand Master of Mystery Writers of America, Deaver served two terms as president of that organization and has been nominated for eight Edgar Awards. A former journalist, folksinger and attorney, he was born outside of Chicago and has a bachelor of journalism degree from the University of Missouri and a law degree from Fordham University.

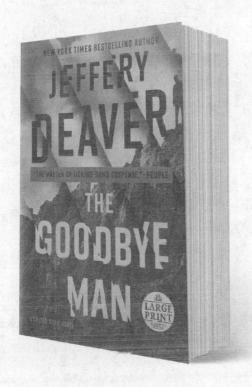 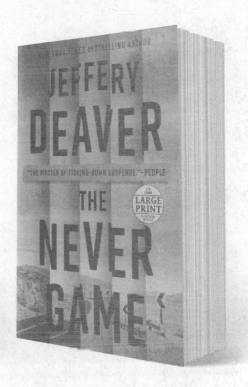